WOLF HOUR

ALSO BY JO NESBO

HARRY HOLE THRILLERS

The Bat

Cockroaches

The Redbreast

Nemesis

The Devil's Star

The Redeemer

The Snowman

The Leopard

Phantom

Police

The Thirst

Knife

Killing Moon

THRILLERS

Headhunters

The Son

Blood on Snow

Midnight Sun

Macbeth

The Kingdom

The Night House

Blood Ties

STORIES

The Jealousy Man

Jo Nesbo

WOLF HOUR

Translated from the Norwegian
by Robert Ferguson

Harvill
Secker

3 5 7 9 10 8 6 4 2

Harvill Secker, an imprint of Vintage, is part of the
Penguin Random House group of companies

Vintage, Penguin Random House UK, One Embassy Gardens,
8 Viaduct Gardens, London SW11 7BW

penguin.co.uk/vintage
global.penguinrandomhouse.com

Penguin Random House UK

First published by Harvill Secker in 2025
First published in Norway by H. Aschehoug & Co. (W. Nygaard),
Oslo, in 2025 with the title *Minnesota*

Typeset in 12/17pt Scala Pro by Jouve (UK), Milton Keynes
Printed and bound in Great Britain by Clays Ltd, Elcograf S.p.A.

The authorised representative in the EEA is Penguin Random House Ireland,
Morrison Chambers, 32 Nassau Street, Dublin D02 YH68

A CIP catalogue record for this book is available from the British Library

HB ISBN 9781787303768
TPB ISBN 9781787303775

Penguin Random House is committed to a sustainable future
for our business, our readers and our planet. This book is made
from Forest Stewardship Council® certified paper.

MIX
Paper | Supporting responsible forestry
FSC® C018179

1

ARRIVAL, SEPTEMBER 2022

'AND WHAT IS THE PURPOSE of your visit, Mr Holger Rudi?'

The CBP officer looks at me without interest as he scratches his upper arm just below the emblem of the US Customs and Border Protection service. His eyes are tired.

'Research,' I answer.

'And what do you intend to research?'

I've just flown from Oslo to Minneapolis via Reykjavik, a seven-hour time difference, and my body is telling me I should have been in bed long ago, so instead of following my instinct to reply 'murder' and end up in an interrogation room I tell him that I'm writing a novel about a policeman with Norwegian heritage.

'So you're a writer?'

I feel like telling him I'm a taxidermist. I stuff things. That I'm here looking to clothe a character, someone in a story I already have clear in my mind. It's an image that has haunted me these past few months, a title I like to give myself. But as I say, I'm tired.

'Yes,' I reply.

'Interesting. As it happens I was baptised in the Norwegian Lutheran Memorial Church.'

'Really?'

'We're all over Minnesota.' The CBP officer chuckles as he hands me my Norwegian passport.

On the taxi ride into the city I can see at once that everything has changed. New roads and buildings that weren't here last time I was in Minneapolis eight years ago. The downtown skyline looms up ahead of us as we turn off the freeway. Between the skyscrapers I see the afternoon sunlight reflecting off the angles of a gigantic structure.

'What's that glass thing?' I ask the driver.

'That? It's the US Bank Stadium. That's where the Vikings play.'

'Wow.'

'You interested in football?'

I shrug. 'I've seen the Vikings play. At the old stadium. Maybe I'll get myself a ticket.'

'Good luck with that.'

'Good luck?'

The driver, a black man who looks to be in his fifties, glances at me in the rear-view mirror through his almond-shaped glasses. 'Very hard to get hold of. I was offered a ticket yesterday, very ordinary ticket, they wanted 350 dollars.'

'Really?'

'Yeah, really. A football game in the old days used to be

something you could take your kids to. Now it's like everything else in this country. For rich folk only.'

I look out of the window. When we used to visit my uncle and aunt we rarely went downtown. Anything we wanted we bought at the corner store or else in the Southdale Mall. Even so, I'm struck by how quiet it seems, how few people there are about. Eight years ago – when my cousin took me to a rooftop restaurant on Hennepin Avenue – the streets were full of bustling life. Especially around the next avenue we cross, Nicollet Mall.

'Where is everybody?' I ask.

'The people, you mean?'

'Yeah.'

'Aw, things haven't been the same since all that stuff happened.'

All that stuff happened. For me, *all that stuff happened* means the murders six years ago; but for him and for everybody else in Minneapolis it means the murder of George Floyd two years back. Just on the drive in from the airport we've passed three murals depicting the black man who was killed by the Minneapolis police.

'That's a long time ago,' I say.

'Don't feel like it,' says the driver. 'Some people thought maybe it would bring the people of this city together. Everyone against the racist police, right? But my view is, it tore this town apart. It came right at the same time as the pandemic, so it was what you might call a perfect storm . . .'

We pull up in front of the Hilton, and I pay cash and give him a good tip. Before he leaves I say I need someone to drive me around the city and ask if he's interested. We agree on an hourly rate, and he gives me his phone number and says I can call him when I'm ready.

There are only a few people in the hotel's large lobby area and the restaurant. Behind the paper face mask the receptionist probably gives me a smile and I hand her my passport. When she notes that I'm booked in for more than a week she informs me that the room will only be cleaned every fifth day. Then she gives me the keycard to room 2406, almost at the top of the hotel, as requested.

'Nosebleed floor?' A man in a cowboy hat smiles at me as I press 24. He says it in that kind of cool and jokey but all the same friendly way that I've only ever noticed in Americans and people from the far north of Norway. I try to think of an equally cool comeback, but I'm from the south of Norway. So instead I work on trying to even out the pressure in my ears.

The bed is big and soft and I fall asleep at once.

When I wake up I need to go to the bathroom. As I don't want to wake myself up too much I don't switch on the light. I can just glimpse the toilet bowl in the dark as I start to sit down and find myself almost falling backward before my rear end lands safely on the ring of the plastic seat. I'd forgotten that toilets in the USA are built lower than in Norway. And at the same instant I recall how, when I was a kid, that made me think of America as a place where they were more fond of children. That, and all those TV channels with cartoons and series for kids, all those endless metres of shelves with sweets in Southdale, the amusement park Valleyfair, where my uncle always had some new attraction to show us when we arrived for our summer holiday. This was a wonderfully childlike country, I thought. In short: I loved America. And even though I gradually came to understand that it wasn't perfect, I understood too that I would love it for the rest of my life.

It's still dark outside when I next wake up. I get up, call the taxi driver's number and ask him to meet me at Nicollet Avenue by South 10th Street, and then leave the hotel. Dawn is already breaking over the twin city of Saint Paul on the other bank of the Mississippi. On the sidewalk I pass a homeless man asleep with his body pressed up against the facade of a skyscraper bearing the logo of one of the USA's biggest banks, as though he thinks there might be some warmth for him there. A police car is parked on Nicollet, but the windows are smoked and I can't see whether anyone is sitting inside. After about fifteen minutes my taxi pulls up next to the sidewalk. I climb into the back seat.

'First let's go to Jordan.'

The driver looks at me in the mirror. 'The town?'

'No. The neighbourhood.'

I can see he's reluctant.

'Something wrong?'

'No, sir. But if you wanna score dope then you best get yourself another car.'

'No, that's not it. I want to see *the projects*.'

'In Jordan? They don't exist no more, sir.'

'No?'

'Pulled down the last one five or six years ago.'

'Then that's where we're going.'

We glide through a city still sleeping. You have to study the details to find out what kind of neighbourhood you're passing through, whether it's affluent or poor. If the lawns in front of the small houses are cut, if there's garbage lying around, what makes of car are parked along the roadside.

We drive by a 24/7 Winner Gas station. Four black youths watch as we go by.

'Is that where people score their dope now?' I ask.

The driver doesn't reply. A few blocks later he stops.

'Here,' he says. 'This is where they stood. The last tower blocks in Jordan.'

I see a sign – NO GUNS PERMITTED BEYOND THIS POINT – and behind it a low, newish-looking building. It's an elementary school. In the half-dark two squirrels dart about in nervous, jerky sprints across the lawns, their big bushy tails following with a strange softness.

And what is the purpose of your visit, Mr Holger Rudi?

The purpose is to try to get inside the head of a killer. To retrace the steps from that time back in 2016. It's for a book. I've already made a start on it. The working title is *The Minneapolis Avenger*. I expect the publisher will have an opinion on that, although they might be less sure exactly how to market it. True crime is the hottest genre in the book market right now. People just can't get enough of stories about bloody and preferably spectacular murders – there's the air of mystery, unexpected turns of events, villains and heroes on both sides of the law, and, if possible, an uncertain denouement that leaves plenty of room for wide-ranging conspiracy theories. My book will have all of these, apart from the last. The answers are all there, there's no question about where the guilt lies. What remains is the business of trying to understand how and why what happened *did* happen. And to achieve this I need to get inside not only the killer's head but the heads of all the players in this story. Use everything I already know plus a bit of my own imagination to see the world, see the sites where it all happened, see it all played out through their eyes. Find the human in among all the inhuman. Force the reader – and myself – to ask the question: could that have been me?

I'm giving these field studies eight days, so I don't have all that much time. I need to make a start. And that means starting with the guy who was where I am now, also at dawn, on that morning six years ago.

I close my eyes and look. I can see the tower blocks rising up from the ground. Blocking out the sky. There, on the sixth floor, is an open window. I fly up there. Right now I'm him. I look out. I can see in all directions. Height means overview.

2

CROSS HAIRS, OCTOBER 2016

THE HEIGHT GAVE PERSPECTIVE. FOR a while I could be a dispassionate observer, or at least pretend I was. Pass what I felt to be an objective judgement on society, human beings and their lives down there. I'd been sitting at that sixth-floor window since seven o'clock looking down on that antheap. At the people emerging from the doors of the apartments of the Jordan projects. It was Tuesday morning. Eleven minutes past eight. I saw cars that pulled away from the kerbside, and the parking lots behind the blocks. The white smoke from the exhausts. Yellow school buses, picking up kids – bars on the windows, like mobile jails, like some kind of prelude to the lives that lay ahead of them. Other buses that ferried people to work. Some to the factories, most to the service industries, at the bottom level. But here at the Jordan projects there were plenty of people who didn't have school or a job to go to, and a lot of them were still in bed. Some lay staring up at the ceiling, having lost any of the hope that came with the country's first black president eight years ago but who, in three months' time, would be leaving the White House, along with everything else in the removal van. So they lay there and tried to come up with an answer to the question that never really went away: Why? Why get up?

One of those who had found a reason emerged from the door now. An interesting feature at Jordan was the way the entrances opened inward, not outward. People said it was because it was harder to break in with the crack protected by the frame, and because in Jordan you were in more danger of being killed during a break-in than you were of being burnt to death inside your apartment, even though Jordan had, statistically, more arson attacks than anywhere else in all Minneapolis.

Thirteen past eight. A pale autumn sun struggled to penetrate the morning haze. I put my eye to the gunsight and adjusted the cross hairs until they focused on the door to Block 3. Yesterday he emerged from that door at exactly 08.16. Yesterday was Monday, today was Tuesday; people are creatures of habit and there was no reason to suppose he wouldn't be heading out to work at about the same time today. And yet, I'd been sitting there since seven o'clock. After all, he was self-employed, so maybe he gave himself a bit of a lie-in on Mondays, but left home earlier on every other weekday.

I rubbed my hands together. There was a frost last night and a cold wind blew in between the drapes. I had taped them to the glass, so they wouldn't blow about and disturb my aim. I had seen the pushers take their places on the street corners, seen the first deals made. Most of the customers were black, a few

Latinos, but a few cars pulled up with white hands sticking out the windows. Quarter past eight. I inhaled the harsh odour of cooking oil, garlic and cigarette smoke. I'd scrubbed this one-room apartment for the last time, but the stink from that old wallpaper was still there. It'll still be there when they pull this block down in a little while.

Sixteen past eight. My thighs had started to ache. I squatted back on my heels again to relieve them. The position was not optimal. I knelt on the couch, which I had pulled over to the window. I leaned the barrel against a chair back. A distance of 330 yards. A little further than ideal, particularly with those gusts of wind. Just one shot to the head and get it over with would be best. But that was too risky, I could miss and spoil the whole thing. So the plan was first a shot to the chest, to bring him down, then reload and give him the kill-shot. The rifle was an M24. I'd bought it six days ago for nineteen hundred dollars. Obviously, I didn't buy it from a gun store, I bought it from a local dealer who used front men, mostly junkies with no criminal record who needed money quick. The dealer sent them into some 'easy' gun store, some place where the owner didn't ask a lot of questions, even though the whole business reeked of a front man, he just checked the application up against the register, and then calmly sold twenty potential murder weapons to some dope fiend who didn't know one end of a gun from the other. The dealer paid the junkie at most twenty dollars for each weapon, then sold them on for one and a half times the price in the store. His name was Dante, a fat peacock of a man, born and raised in the country outside Minneapolis but he dressed like an Italian, ate Italian and talked with a fake Italian accent. And, of course, cheated like an Italian in the business he ran out of a garage just two blocks away from here. His customers were all people with criminal records. Not small-time crooks who sent their girlfriends into the gun store or walked in themselves carrying a fake ID, but people who were willing to pay that little bit extra for a professional service. Pay in the certain knowledge that if they lost the weapon at a crime scene there was no way the police were going to be able to trace the gun back to them.

Dante paid little attention to his weight and his health, but he made up for it with the care he took with his appearance. His hair and beard looked as though they'd been trimmed with nail cutters, and his clothes always matched. And he loved gold. He had gold in his eyebrows, gold in his ears, gold around his neck. And – not least – gold in his teeth.

Those gold teeth of his were the first thing I noticed that day I went to his garage. They blinged wetly at me as he told me he hoped I was going deer hunting and the gun he was selling me wouldn't turn up at some crime scene, because this particular weapon he had bought himself, he hadn't used a front for it.

'I'm just saying, you don't have to tell me, amigo.'

He didn't really have to say that as I hadn't spoken a word since entering the garage. Anyway, what could I have said? That he was the one I was going to be hunting? That he was standing there and selling me the very weapon that was going to be used to kill him? He was alone at the time, but even so I was careful not to remove my sunglasses or pull back the top of the hoodie I was wearing. I just nodded, pointed to the one I wanted – the rifle plus two hand grenades – counted out the money and when he dug out the holster that came with the gun I wrapped it up myself in bubble wrap and put it down beside the telescopic sights and the two hand grenades. He had stared at my hands. Stared and stared at my hands. Maybe he was noting the pentagram on my wrist. Maybe he'd mentioned it to someone. Didn't really matter. No more than that goodbye he had called after me in what he probably thought was a passable Spanish accent – *Hasta la vista.* 'See you later.'

He had no idea how right he would be.

The street door opened.

Dante.

He stepped out and stopped. Just like he did yesterday morning, he looked right and then left. He hit his bunched right fist into the palm of his left hand. As though every day was a fight. As though a man had a choice each day, to head right or left. How naive we are.

His car – a Maserati – was in the parking lot behind the block. It wasn't exactly brand new, but all the same, it was a little miracle a car like that was allowed to stand untouched in a neighbourhood like Jordan. The explanation was pretty straightforward: the car was protected by his gangland customers, and everybody in Jordan knew it.

I focused the cross hairs on his chest. I had worked out the distance and the angle and adjusted the sights down, since he would be so far below me. I held my breath, tried to exert an even pressure on the trigger but knew that my pulse was faster than it ought to be. The trigger moved. Kept moving. But the shot didn't come. My pulse raced. I tried to tell myself not to be impatient, not to think that, in one more second, he would move on and the target would be much harder to hit. Don't jerk. Just a steady, even pressure.

The man down below shivered inside his coat. He blew into his cupped hands. Like a gambler blowing on dice.

He turned right.

In that same instant the rifle jerked. I must have been holding it firmly because he never left my sight. I saw him stiffen, as though he suddenly realised he'd forgotten something. From inside the long coat something or other dropped to the sidewalk. The first association I got was when Monica and I were standing in the bathroom when her waters broke, splashing against the tiles, and the pair of us almost fainted, terrified and happy, terrified and happy.

It was blood. Dante fell. Backward, into the door. It swung open and inward. He lay there in the darkness of the hallway with his feet sticking out in the daylight. There were no screams, no shouts, no running footsteps, no slamming of doors from down there. Only the steady, uninterrupted rumble of the morning rush hour from the highway just beyond. And then, suddenly, hip hop music. Somebody still lying in bed had got up and opened the window to see what was happening.

I felt myself start to tremble, felt nauseous, made myself think of Monica and the children. Think hard about them, as I loaded another shell. Took aim. Eye up against the telescopic sights. Saw him lying there, motionless, and thought how expensive his shoes looked. That it would be a while before the police showed up here in Jordan and that in the meantime maybe someone would steal those shoes. I got something in my eye and had to blink it away. When I looked down again I saw the shoes moving. Someone down in the darkened hallway was dragging him inside to safety. I was about to pull the trigger again but the thought of shooting a neighbour who was only doing what any decent human being ought to do made me pause a moment. And by the time I decided to go ahead and shoot anyway because no one – absolutely no one – is wholly innocent, the door had swung shut.

I stood up and had to steady myself against the kitchen counter because my foot had gone to sleep. Wrapped the gun inside the bubble wrap. Wiped the counter, the arm of the couch, the back of the chair. Then I went into the bathroom and I put on my gear. Plucked an unruly strand of hair from one eyebrow and held it between two fingers before placing it on my tongue and swallowing. It stuck in my throat, like it didn't want to go down. I put on my sunglasses and zipped up the hoodie. Shrugged on the rucksack with all my stuff inside, grabbed the flowerpot with the yucca plant, took a last glance around the apartment then let myself out.

I took the stairs up two floors to Mrs White. Knocked on the door. Heard the shuffling of slippers inside. They stopped, everything went quiet. I guess she was looking at me through the fish-eye lens. Then the door opened. I'd never asked, of course, but Mrs White had to be at least eighty years old. A sweet, grey-haired old black lady who smelled of something that wasn't exactly apricot jelly or honey but something in between.

'Tomás,' she said. 'Well now, it's been a long time since I last saw you. Did you hear that bang too?'

Without a word I handed her the yucca plant.

'For me?' She smiled in slight surprise.

I nodded.

She put her head on one side. 'Is there something wrong, Tomás? You look so . . . dead. Is it the cat? You miss it, don't you? Did he say when he would be finished? You know, you have to be patient.'

I nodded again. Then I turned and walked away. Heard that

she didn't close the door but stood there, watching me walk away. Something on her mind. Maybe she was thinking, maybe she felt it deep in her bones, that it was the last time she would ever see me.

The elevator took me down, down, down.

Outside the air was clear and the morning haze lifting. The sun was going to win through today. I walked at a steady pace, heading downtown.

It took me forty minutes.

Downtown Minneapolis always made me think of cars from Motown in the eighties, trapped in a limbo between the past and the future. Everything clean and neat, conservative and dull, practical and boring. There were skyscrapers and bridges, but no Empire State Building or Golden Gate, and if you asked someone from London, Paris or New York what he thought of when you mentioned Minneapolis, he would probably say lakes and forests. OK, so if he knew a little bit more then maybe he would know that the city has the largest connected network of skyways in the US. On the way to the intersection at Nicollet Mall and 9th Street I passed beneath one of them, a glass-and-metal bridge that linked shopping malls and office complexes, a place where people gathered to seek shelter when the temperature dropped to below zero in the winter or rose into the nineties in the summer.

I entered the little pet store. A customer was being served. Sounded like he wanted a bigger cage for his rabbit. Sometimes you still overhear something that restores your faith in human nature. I stood in front of one of the aquariums and when the assistant came over to me I pointed to one of the little fishes swimming about inside and said, that's the one I want.

'Dwarf pufferfish,' he said as he scooped up the green fish in a little hand net. 'A good aquarium fish, but not for the beginner. The water quality must always be tip-top.'

'I know,' I said.

He slipped it into a plastic bag full of water and tied it closed. 'Mind your cat doesn't eat it. And don't eat it yourself. It's a hundred times more poisonous than –'

'I know. You take cash?'

Then I was back out in the street again.

A black-and-white car came cruising in my direction. On the door was the MPD emblem and motto – *To protect with courage, to serve with compassion.* Maybe they got some kind of feeling about me, the policemen sitting behind those darkened windows. But they wouldn't stop me. After all the criticism in the media for the unmotivated and ethnically biased cases of stop-and-search, MPD police chiefs had announced a change of policy, and from now on, gut feeling was no longer a valid reason for stopping a man like me.

The car passed, but I knew they'd seen me. Same way as I knew I'd been picked up by all the surveillance cameras along Nicollet Mall and 9th Street, more of them around here than anywhere else in town.

And one other thing I knew.

I knew I was dead.

3

DINKYTOWN, SEPTEMBER 2022

I OPEN MY EYES AGAIN. I'm back in the taxi, back inside my own head. Now of course I can't know for certain whether I was really in the killer's head, really thought his thoughts as he made his way down Nicollet Mall six years earlier. If he thought that thought, that he was going to die. What I do know is that he was on Nicollet Mall at the precise moment in time, that's a black-and-white fact, recorded by a surveillance camera and by means of binary code translated into a digital recording which places the matter beyond all doubt.

I tell the driver to take me to Dinkytown.

The sun is rising as we cross the river and glide on into the low-rise settlement. This is a world apart from Jordan. Dinkytown is where the students live. The people with a future. The ones who will occupy the shiny bank buildings, the granite blocks of a city hall, the school staffrooms and the 350-dollar seats at the US Bank Stadium. When my cousin and I were old enough we often came here to drink beer in the dives. For me there was something bohemian and thrilling about Dinkytown. The smell of marijuana and testosterone, the sounds of youth, good music and boy-meets-girl, the sense of some – but not too much – danger. The place to swing through that little arc of freedom that exists between being young and being adult, and not wild enough to stop the straights landing securely on our feet, the way I did. Once my cousin's girlfriend brought a friend along with her, and she and I sneaked out the bar and smoked a joint in one of the alleyways before having what was probably a pretty forgettable bout of sex but which I always remember anyway because of that – to me at least – exotic setting.

Now I hardly recognise the place. It looks like something in an exercise book in which the teacher has corrected all the grammatical mistakes and removed all the obscenities. We pass the place that was once a coffee bar and where the owner swore blind that Bob Dylan had made his very first appearance when he came down from Hibbing to study. Now some vast building is on its way up. I ask the driver if he thinks the purple facade is a tribute to the town's other great musical son, Prince. The driver just chuckles and shakes his head.

'But Al's Breakfast is still here,' I say and point to the door of that little warren of a place where – if the empty seat was down at the front – you had to press your way between the customers crowded at the bar and the sweaty wall.

'The day they try to close Al's there's going to be riots here,' the driver says and roars with laughter.

I tell him to stop at the bridge over the railroad line. I get out of the car and glance down at the tracks. The occasional goods train used to run on that line, and judging by the weeds growing between the rusty tracks traffic hasn't increased much since then. I cross the road and head toward the corner where it still says Bernie's Bar on the wall, try the handle of the locked door, cup my hands against the glass next to the poster advertising that the premises are for rent and peer inside. The bar is still there, but otherwise there isn't a stick of furniture left.

Now I have to get inside the policeman's head.

So I try to imagine how it might have been, what was said and done in here on that morning six years ago.

4

OZ, OCTOBER 2016

BOB OZ HISSED THROUGH HIS teeth and put the empty shot glass back down on the bar. Looked up and saw his own reflection in the mirror between the bottles on the shelves. A new guy at work had asked him yesterday why the others called him One-Night Bob. He told him it must be because he always solved his cases in just one night.

Bob looked at One-Night Bob. He'd turned forty, but wasn't that the same face he'd been staring at for the past twenty years now? He wasn't exactly a good-looking man, but like his father he had the kind of face time didn't seem to sink its teeth into. Well, OK, chewed up a little bit. At least chewed away the puppy fat of youth to reveal the mature man's good or his bad genes, all depending on which way you looked at it. White skin of the type that only got sunburnt, never brown. A thick and unruly thatch of red hair on the kind of head that got Scandinavians nicknamed *squareheads*, back in the day when his ancestors emigrated here from Norway. A relatively healthy-looking set of teeth, a pair of blue eyes that had got more red in the whites since his separation. His eyes bulged slightly, but at least according to one of his one-night-stand ladies that was no bad thing since it gave the impression he was listening closely to whatever they said. Another had said that as soon as they met she had the feeling of being a Little Red Riding Hood and wondering why the wolf had such big eyes. Bob Oz rounded off the stocktaking by sitting up straight on his bar stool. When he was young he wrestled and swam. Though never a champion in either field it had given him a good body that the years had done little to change. Until now, that is. He put his hand on his shirt, beneath his trademark yellow coat. A nasty little pot belly. And this despite the fact he had never eaten less than in the three months that had passed since he and Alice had split up. And it couldn't be the pills, because he wasn't taking those any more. But he was drinking more, no doubt about that. A lot more.

The name One-Night Bob came from a colleague early on in his career, before he met Alice and became One-Woman Bob. It was back in the days when he and his colleagues celebrated every triumph, great and small – and, at a pinch, their defeats too – at the Dinkytown bars, when they were young enough to shake off the hangovers and Bob would more often than not wake up with a woman lying next to him. What especially impressed his male colleagues was the way this pallid, ginger-haired guy could pull women even when he was so drunk he could hardly stand up. Anyone who asked what his secret was always got the same answer: that he tried harder. That he didn't give up. That some of these women *pestered* him to take them to bed. When you haven't the looks, the money or the charm then you have to work harder than the competition. End of story.

'Another?'

Bob nodded and looked up at the female bartender as she poured his whiskey. She reminded him of someone and now he knew who it was. Chrissie Hynde, the singer and guitarist with the Pretenders. Black hair, fringe cut straight. Sassy, self-assured, interesting-looking rather than pretty. High cheekbones, narrow, slightly slanting eyes. A bit too much mascara. Russian genes? Long, thin limbs. Tight jeans she knew she looked good in. A baggy T-shirt, meaning she had nothing there worth promoting. No problem there, Bob had always been more of a *leg-and-ass man*. Sure, the half-closed venetian blinds in the bar blocked out the morning sunlight, but he could make out the lines marking her face. She looked like she'd lived a bit. Mid-thirties going on forty. Good. Gave him more of a chance.

Bob took a sip and hissed through his teeth again. The sign on the sidewalk outside the bar advertised Happy Hour, but just for a handful of whisky brands, and you take what you can get. Bob coughed.

'Liza. It is Liza, right?'

'Whatever,' she said and yawned as she picked up the empty beer glass of a customer who had just left the bar.

'That's what the guy who was just here called you.'

'Well, that's all right then.'

'OK,' said Bob and took another sip. 'I know you've heard this before, Liza, but you know what? My wife doesn't understand me.'

Liza came back at him without missing a beat: 'And there was me hoping you didn't have one.'

Bob smiled stiffly. 'You get tips for that line of yours, honey?'

'You get cunt for yours, honey?'

Bob looked thoughtfully at her expressionless, stony face. 'If you want a ballpark figure, and by cunt you mean the whole way, then we're talking –'

'Forget it,' she interrupted. 'Let's just say never mind about the tip so long as I don't have to be . . .' She mouthed the word *cunt*, then turned her back on him to rinse out a cloth in the sink.

'Fair enough, Liza. But just for the record, my wife really doesn't understand me. For a long time she understood everything, and then it stopped. Suddenly she couldn't make me out at all.'

Liza gazed longingly in the direction of the tables where the only other two customers were sitting, as though hoping they would give her something else to do other than have to stand and listen to this. Bob moved his right hand toward his jacket pocket. The No Smoking law had been in place for the last ten years, but after a drink or two old habits took over and he could still find himself reaching for the cigarette pack that wasn't there. It hadn't been there since that evening twelve years ago when they'd met. He'd been sitting there, minding his own business, listening while a colleague hypothesised about what turned the ladies on; it was Bob's French inhaling, the way he slipped the smoke out of his mouth and at the same time drew it up into his nostrils. That showed muscular coordination at the same time as there was something vulgar about it, he said. Something suggesting an unbridled and dark sexuality. That was the moment another colleague entered the bar with this woman. He'd introduced her, her name was Alice, she was a psychologist, a couple of inches taller than Bob and insanely good-looking. So good-looking Bob immediately crossed her off his list. Another of his pickup rules involved setting realistic goals, and Alice was obviously way out of his league. On top of that – and this was a practical rather than a moral hindrance – she was on a date with a colleague. And anyway, this colleague had already warned her about him, she knew his nickname was One-Night Bob, and even before Alice got the first drink down she'd asked him straight out about it. Not, like the guys, asking him how he did it, but asking him why. Why did he have to have all these women who he didn't really want? Because she was a psychologist, and because anyway he'd already made up his mind she was out of his league, he decided to tell her as honestly and openly as he could, and not give a damn about how bad it would make him look. He said it probably came from having a weak bond with his mother, that he hadn't been loved enough as a child, and that this gave him a compulsion to seek out intimacy and recognition, at the same time as he didn't dare to risk a closer relationship for fear of being rejected. And that, as well as all that, it was exciting and pleasurable to fuck new women. He asked her what she made of this. She said he seemed self-obsessed and radiated a deep loneliness, and that she didn't like men who smoked and had it never occurred to him that the smell would get into the fibres of his cashmere coat? Bob then embarked on an intense lecture on the subject of the difference between the goat hair of his coat and camel hair generally, segueing into an equally intense lecture about how 'Purple Rain' was so much more than the clichéd rock ballad people thought it was, that when the last verse was over the song wasn't even half-way through, after that came five minutes of a brilliant, howling guitar solo, an implosion, followed by two minutes of beautiful, delirious anarchy. He got the bartender to put the record on and sang along with it, doing the guitar parts too, dancing like Axl Rose. Alice looked as though she didn't know whether to laugh or throw up. A month later they were a couple. And from that day on Bob hadn't cast so much as a glance at other women, she'd transformed him, she'd kissed the frog. Until three months ago. Now – twelve years on – the frog was out hopping again.

'If you really want to know, she's left me,' said Bob.

'I don't want to know.'

'No, well, now you know anyway. Isn't that actually part of your job? To listen and pretend to understand?'

'No. But OK, she's dumped you and I can't say I'm surprised.'

'No?' Bob took hold of the lapels of his cashmere coat and parted them, heard how his speech was a little slurred. 'Do I look to you like a guy ladies would dump, Liza?'

'Dunno. But when someone comes in here in the middle of the morning and drinks like an amateur then it's a good guess they've been kicked out either by their lady or by their boss. And from the way you're dressed you look like a guy who has a job to go to.'

'Jesus, you ought to be a detective.'

'You trying to tell me I don't make it as a bartender?'

Bob laughed. 'Tough lady.' He held out his hand. 'The name's Bob.'

'Hello, Bob. No offence, but I don't touch the customers and they don't touch me.'

'Fair enough,' said Bob and withdrew his hand. 'What about you, Liza? You ever had your heart broken?'

'I'm a bartender, that's all you need to know about me.'

'OK, but at least tell me this. A man with a broken heart: in your eyes, does that make him more attractive or less attractive?'

She raised one eyebrow. 'Are you asking me what your chances are of fucking me?'

'What makes you think I want to fuck you?'

'You mean you don't?'

Bob thought about it. 'If what people say is true, that fucking other people is a good remedy for a broken heart, then Christ, yeah, I do.'

Bob couldn't be sure, but he thought he saw the ghost of a smile on that hard, closed face.

She pulled a wine glass from a rack dangling above the bar and began polishing it. 'Helps about as much as pissing in your pants when it's cold, I should think. Does you having a broken heart mean I fancy you? No. For all I know she dumped you because you're no good in bed.'

Bob slumped forward with one hand held to his stomach. 'Ouch, you got me there, Liza. Pour me another drink.'

Liza filled his glass. 'OK. So do you *really* have a broken heart?'

'*Will* you fuck me if I do?'

Bob was sure of himself now; she was smiling.

'Come on, Liza, being here bores you as much as it bores me, so let's just entertain each other a bit. The question is hypothetical and your answer will not be used against you in a court of law.'

'I'd like it better if you entertain me with the story of your broken heart.'

'Her name's Alice.'

'You have kids?'

'No.'

'Hard up?'

'No.'

'Someone else?'

'No.'

'Then what happened?'

'She stopped loving me.'

'But she did love you once, you think?'

'Yes,' said Bob. 'She did.'

'Then why d'you think she stopped?'

'It's . . . complicated.'

She returned the wine glass to the rack and started polishing another, looking at him while she did so.

'I thought you wanted to talk about it.'

'Your turn now,' said Bob, and forced a smile. 'Could I have had a date with you?'

'No.'

'Hypothetically,' he said. 'If you didn't work here.'

She shook her head slightly, and then added, with an exasperated look, like someone humouring a troublesome child: 'It depends.'

'Depends on what?'

'What you have to offer a single mom.'

'Ah, single mom.' Bob smiled broadly. 'I can offer her security. I'm a public servant, it's almost impossible to fire me. And . . .' Bob put his hand into the pocket of his cashmere coat and tossed a small, rectangular plastic package onto the counter.

Liza leaned forward reluctantly for a closer look. Made a face. 'A rubber?'

'Safe sex. This is the best money can buy.'

She raised an eyebrow. 'You're scared you'll have a kid?'

Bob shrugged. 'I'm scared of a premature ejaculation. And with that thing there my prick hardly feels a thing.'

Liza laughed out loud. And from her laughter he could tell

she'd smoked her fair share of cigarettes. 'Dammit, Bob, you really are cute.'

'Cute enough to let me buy you a cup of coffee some place else?' Bob pulled the condom back over to his side of the counter.

She shook her head. 'Is that the way you usually do it?'

'Do what?'

'First the full-frontal assault, then the retreat, then the siege?'

Bob thought about that. 'Yes. Does it work?'

'Sure. Just not on me.'

'Why not?'

Liza rolled her eyes.

'Oh, come on,' said Bob, 'I'm out of training. I need a little constructive feedback here.'

Liza spotted a gesture from one of the other customers, an elderly man still wearing his overcoat. She picked up a glass and unscrewed the top of a vodka bottle. 'Well, OK then. I couldn't be less interested. You come in here, I'm the first woman you see, the first living being you see. You sat there for about five minutes before suggesting a fuck. A fuck to make up for the fact that your lady's dumped you. Let's say – hypothetically – that I'd been up for it and you and me ended up in the same bed tonight. Does that really sound to you like the start of a quality relationship involving two quality people?'

'Ah, but . . .'

'But?'

'Isn't quality in general a bit . . . eh, overrated?'

Liza looked at him and slowly shook her head. She licked her lips a couple of times.

'Then what do you mean by *quality*, Liza?'

Liza screwed the cap back on the vodka bottle. 'Staying power.'

'Staying power? As in . . .?'

'No. As in, a man who sticks around.'

She placed her hands on the counter and Bob Oz met her eyes. Then she picked up the vodka glass, emerged from behind the bar and walked across to the old man sitting at his table. Bob watched her. She put the glass down in front of him and spoke to him as she picked up the crutch that had fallen to the floor and leaned it against the chair.

The phone in the inside pocket of his jacket began to vibrate.

He took it out, saw that the caller was Superintendent Walker. He hesitated before taking the call.

As expected, Walker sounded pretty pissed off. 'Where the hell are you, Oz?'

'Dinkytown, chief.'

'Why aren't you at work?'

'I am. I'm checking the licences at a couple of dodgy premises.'

'You are a homicide detective, Oz.'

'Then let me guess. There's been a murder?'

Pause.

'Have you been drinking, Oz?'

'Any address for that murder, chief?'

Walker sighed heavily before giving the address.

'No surprises there then,' said Bob as he wrote in his notebook. They ended the call and he stood up and buttoned his cashmere coat just as Liza came back round behind the bar again.

'Duty calls?' she asked.

'Yeah,' said Bob as he put some dollar bills down on the bar.

Liza held one up to the light to make sure it was legit. 'Will we be seeing you again, Bob?'

'Do we hope so?'

'If you keep on tipping like this then definitely.'

'When do you close?'

'Nine o'clock. But maybe you need a bit of a break from the drinking. Heart, liver – it all adds up, you know.'

'Thanks for the advice.' Bob smiled. '*Ha det bra.*'

'What did you say?'

'Norwegian. *Be well.*' Bob turned and headed for the exit. Could feel he was a little bit unsteady on his feet. Stopped in the open doorway and walked back to the bar where Liza was standing with her hand out and a grin on her face. Bob Oz grabbed the condom from between her fingers, gave an exaggeratedly gallant bow and then left.

Bob sat behind the steering wheel of the car parked by the sidewalk on the other side of the railroad bridge. Like the majority of the cars in the police service fleet it was a Ford, but it was unmarked and in the state he was in he couldn't give any guarantees about his driving. So he took the Kojak light from the glove compartment, opened the window, pressed the magnetic foot down onto the roof and checked that the blue light was on. This part of Dinkytown was mostly barflies and white farmers' sons come to town to study and to party, but even here the police would never risk stopping a cop car on call-out and ordering a DUI test. Bob took the route through Marshall Street and Broadway Bridge across the river – it shouldn't take more than fifteen minutes anyway. Tucked in behind a car with a blue bumper sticker. GUN OWNERS FOR TRUMP 2016. Donald Trump was entertaining, give him that, but then Hillary Clinton and the Democrats had rejoiced when the Republicans managed to nominate an unelectable lunatic as their candidate. Something the opinion polls now, just before the presidential election, seemed to confirm they had good reason to. Bob pulled out his cell phone, navigated to the last number called and pressed the call button. Listened to the female voice on the answering machine.

'Hello, you've reached Alice's answering machine. Will you please stop calling me, Bob?'

Bob waited for the beep so the recorder would pick up everything he said before he began speaking. 'OK, that was new, Alice, I'll give you that. I'm calling to say I've changed my mind, I'm not going to let you have the house, and definitely not at that price. And to inform you I fucked a girl of twenty-six last week. Says she's an aerobics instructor when she isn't studying law at U of M and that her grandfather was an Ojibwe chieftain. I take that with a pinch of salt, women lie, we all know that, or don't we, Alice? Anyway, I'm not telling you this to make you jealous or anything like that, after all, we are – as you said – adult human beings.' Bob stopped at a red light. He was pleased that he was managing to keep his voice under control. 'I'm only calling to tell you that she called me last night and told me I'd given her a sexually transmitted disease, one I'd never heard of, apparently a new one just arrived from the West Coast. So this is just a bit of friendly, grown-up advice to get yourself checked. Because it's only natural to wonder if the source was Stan the Man, and that you, contrary to what you told me, were actually screwing him before I moved out, and passed it on to me that last time we fucked, on Hidden Beach.'

Bob could hear now that his voice was no longer under control and that he had actually yelled the words *fucked* and *screwing* since they happened to be very well suited to being yelled.

'Because you remember that fuck, right? Yeah, you damn well

bet you do, because I guess you've never been fucked so well since. Or have you? Have you, bitch?'

Bob threw the phone at the windshield and it bounced around the car before disappearing somewhere. Put both hands against the wheel and breathed out heavily. Became aware of the zebra-striped car in the lane to his left, and the man in the passenger seat staring at him through the open window. Glazed eyes and slack mouth. Like he was in the bloody zoological gardens. Bob knew he shouldn't but he couldn't resist it; he lowered the window.

'What the fuck are you staring at? Never seen anyone go berserk before?'

The man's eyes remained glazed, his mouth stayed slack, and Bob wondered if he was a bit simple, but then the guy put his hand out of the window and pointed upward and said in a slow, toneless voice:

'Why stop for a red light when you've got one of those on the roof of your car?'

Bob opened and shut his mouth several times, but his brain came up with nothing. The zebra-striped car next to him pulled away and he heard a horn blaring behind him. Bob cursed under his breath and hit the gas.

5

EXIT WOUND, OCTOBER 2016

BOB TOOK THE KOJAK LIGHT off the roof as he swung into the open space between the apartment blocks of the Jordan projects. The brown-brick buildings around him towered into the sky on all sides, and as he passed into the shadows a breath of damp, cold air entered through the car window. It made him shiver. The whole Jordan project made him shiver. In other places – and that included even down in Phillips – it could be difficult for the untrained eye to see visible signs of the misery, to hear the creaking of bottled-up hate, to smell the testosterone just waiting for the right bad excuse. But not here. It started with a welcome graffiti drawn down the side of the cement stairway leading to the road below. BLOWJOB it said, in gigantic lettering. Next to it was a badly drawn pistol aimed at the side of a head with what was obviously supposed to be brain mass blowing out on the other side. Bob directed his gaze up at the blocks. They made him think of termite mounds. There was something odd about this concentrated assembly of people in a place where there was so much space. He'd seen photographs from the time when his great-great-grandparents came out here from Norway, driven out by hunger and hard times. They'd come to a wide, open landscape with farms and people distant from each other. They built their simple houses and churches here. They never envisaged a city with a skyline, still less entire high-rise settlements with people on welfare, people on the margins of society who sold everyday escape routes to each other, dug graves for each other and directed their hatred and frustration above all against people who suffered as much as themselves. What would Bob's ancestors have said about Jordan and Minneapolis? According to his parents they'd been God-fearing, hard-working and thrifty. As well as conservative racists. Bob's great-great-grandfather had fought in the Civil War, but when the liberated slaves started arriving from the south and settling in the Twin Cities of Minneapolis and Saint Paul, he'd come to regret it, his grandma said. People of Scandinavian and German heritage were still in the majority, but in the towns especially the ethnic mix of the population was much more varied. Latinos started to arrive after the Second World War, mostly Mexicans but some Puerto Ricans too. By the eighties the Vietnamese had arrived, though God knows why people from a coastal land would choose somewhere as far from the sea as this. The Vietnamese who ran Bob's local liquor store explained it by saying that once you'd survived being one of the Boat people you kept well away from salt water for the rest of your life. When refugees from the war in Somalia began arriving in the nineties and settled in Phillips and on the south side of the city, a lot of people began predicting trouble. They'd read about traumatised child soldiers with Kalashnikovs in a war financed by the sale of narcotics, and they could see all this baggage making the journey over with them. But things had gone better than the pessimists feared. Naturally some had ended up in drug gangs, but it wasn't as bad as up on the north side, where for the last six years there had been an average of ten shootings per week. Every time Mayor Kevin Patterson was confronted with a new report on violence he countered by saying that crime *per capita* in Minneapolis was at an all-time low, which was indeed the case for the other parts of the city. But here it had just gone up and up, especially after Patterson had slashed the police budget and forced them to let people go and start to *prioritise*. What priorities and which neighbourhoods the mayor – who lived in wealthy Dellwood – wanted the police to concentrate on wasn't hard to guess.

Bob pulled up beside an MPD police car standing outside the entrance to one of the blocks and climbed out. A bow-legged, slightly overweight policeman in uniform was leaning against the car as his colleague inside spoke on his radio.

'Detective Oz, Homicide Division,' said Bob and flashed his badge.

'That was quick,' said the uniform.

'I was just round the corner. What's the story, Officer . . .?'

'Heinz. Ambulance and technicians are on their way.'

'The body?'

Heinz led the way and opened the door. Oz saw the blood on the sidewalk outside and the trail of blood inside. They walked on till they reached the body, which was lying on its back ten yards inside the hallway, beyond the elevator and the stairs.

'Why no crime scene tape?'

'Because we got witnesses that say he was standing outside and the shot came from a long way off, nobody saw anybody shoot. There's no evidence here to mess up, Detective.'

'Really?' Bob looked at the drag-trail of blood leading from the doorway to where they stood, and at the blood on the victim's shoe. 'Do we know who dragged him in here?'

'No.'

'Right. Get your partner off the radio and get the scene out there and in here taped off and do it now.'

Heinz disappeared. Bob looked down at the body. Noted that he'd been wrong, Bob Oz wasn't the only man in Minneapolis who walked around in a mustard-yellow cashmere coat, just the only mustard-yellow cashmere coat *without* a bullet hole in it. The man had narrow lines of facial hair that framed his mouth and followed the line of his jawbone up to his temples. They were so neatly cut and black, probably dyed, that they looked like they'd been painted on. The corpse had piercings on the eyebrows and ears, the rings looked like gold.

Bob squatted down and carefully unbuttoned the coat. Only now did he realise how fat the man was. The body flopped out of the open coat and seemed held in place by no more than a slim-fit white shirt that was drenched in blood. The discreet emblem on the breast pocket announced that it was an exclusive Italian brand.

Heinz returned. 'My partner's fixing the tape,' he said.

'OK. Help me turn this guy over.'

Heinz bent low with a grunt and took hold of the dead man's hips. 'I heard someone from your division say that the reason there's so many murders here in Jordan is that it's a food desert, that there's only one decent food store here.'

'Is that a fact?' Bob said without interest as he lifted the corpse's shoulders.

'He thought there was a connection between hunger and the level of aggression,' Heinz grunted. 'But I don't buy it. Take the average weight of the people around here and you can see the problem isn't a lack of food.'

'You don't say,' said Bob as he studied the victim's back. No exit wound.

'It's the fat. Fat makes us bad people. Just look at the folks that live around here.'

'Right, now lay him down again,' said Bob.

'They're either skin-and-bone meth heads or fat diabetics who are going to die before they make sixty. No one works and they're all sick. Obamacare means you and me and our children and grandchildren are paying to support these parasites.' Officer Heinz stood up, wheezing. He tucked his stomach back inside his belt.

'Got a pen on you, Heinz?'

Heinz handed him one with MPD's logo on it, hunkered down close by Bob and watched with interest as Bob pushed the pen into the entry wound in the chest, like someone measuring the oil in a car engine. Bob searched his pockets for something square-shaped, rejected the condom and pulled out the appointment card from Guillaume's clinic for anger management and held it more or less level behind the pen. Closed one eye and looked. First across the body and then along it. Drew a line along each side of the card.

'What's that you're doing?' asked Heinz.

'Trying to get some idea of the angle of the shot.' Bob saw Heinz's nostrils dilate and guessed the officer was probably smelling the alcohol on his breath. Just then the body on the floor jerked.

'Jesus!' Heinz yelled.

Bob stared down at what he was no longer quite so sure was a dead body. The chest wasn't moving, but when Bob held three fingers against the neck he could feel the beat of a slight pulse.

'First aid,' said Bob.

'Eh?'

'You take the first-aid course, Heinz?'

'Sure, but –'

'Then on you go.'

'OK, OK. Then help me to –'

'No, no,' said Bob as he stood up. '*He'll* help you.'

Bob nodded in the direction of Heinz's partner who was standing in the doorway with the roll of crime scene tape in his hand.

'Enjoy the mouth-to-mouth resuscitation,' said Bob as he straightened up.

'Where are you going?'

'I'm a homicide detective, so unless this guy dies then my business here is done.'

Bob walked around the bloodstains on the sidewalk. A half-dozen curious onlookers had gathered outside the tape that extended three yards out from each side of the doorway. In the distance he could hear the wailing of the ambulance. He glanced up at the surrounding blocks. Held the appointment card up to his eyes and checked, first along one line, then the other. Let his glance glide down the block on his left. Caught sight of the open window on the sixth floor. The black drapes were slightly parted, and inside that gap was the only place they moved, as though they were attached to the wall. Bob Oz took a few steps back and positioned himself directly behind the pool of blood and once again checked the lines on his card. Then he pulled out his phone and made a call. It was answered before the first ring had died away.

'SWAT.'

'Jesus, anyone would think you were expecting the call.'

'What is it?'

'You cowboys better get saddled up and ride on out here.'

Bob rubbed his hands together and shivered as he stood in front of Block 1 and watched as the Special Weapons and Tactics team jumped out of the armoured truck. There were twelve of them, wearing green uniforms and helmets, black bulletproof vests and automatic weapons that looked so small and neat they always made Bob think of the toy guns he and his childhood friends used to play with. It was their show now, but the few remaining members of the audience had hidden themselves behind the windows of the blocks. The sidewalks and parking lot were deserted, even the onlookers behind the crime scene tape in front of Block 3 had vanished now that the ambulance had been and gone. A solitary boy, hunched over in a hoodie, hurried by.

'Excuse me,' said Bob, 'is there anywhere around here to get something to eat?'

'Fuck you.' The boy neither looked up nor slowed down.

Bob shrugged.

The leader of the SWAT team approached Bob. He was well built, walked like an Iraq vet with landmines on his mind every time his feet hit the ground, and that radar scan of a look that never rested in one place for more than a second. On the name tag above his breast pocket it said 'Sergeant O'Rourke'. He handed Bob a bulletproof vest with the word POLICE on it in yellow lettering.

'What would I want with that?' said Bob, looking blankly at it.

'You not coming in?'

'You need help?'

'No, but –'

'Then go and do your job.' Bob waved O'Rourke toward the entrance. 'Fetch, Bonzo, fetch.'

The SWAT leader stared at Bob in disbelief. Then he turned away, head shaking, and made his way back to his men who had spread out and taken up positions by the front and back entrances to the block. O'Rourke gave a quick command through the microphone in his earpiece. It was as if he'd turned on a vacuum cleaner that sucked his men into the building.

Bob surveyed the area as he stamped his thin brown leather shoes against the asphalt to get the blood circulating through his toes. Tried to understand why he was here. Not just here in Jordan, working for the city police, but here on this earth. Then he thought fuck it. Fuck Alice, for whom he'd sacrificed a life of glorious polyamory just so he could live with her. Fuck the failed attempt to kill someone in this drug- and gang-infested neighbourhood with its murders he'd spent his entire professional career making himself immune to. Because once you've had everything and then lost it all you just don't give a shit. A gravestone with two dates on it, dates too close together – that was all he had left. So yeah, he just said fuck it all.

Bob heard a car stop behind him, turned and saw Kay Myers climb out of a Ford identical to the one he was driving himself. She had her police ID hanging round her neck, identifying her as a detective in the MPD Homicide Unit. Myers was in her late thirties, wore her hair in an afro, which Bob had gathered was back in fashion but which Myers had worn as long as he had known her. She was small and thin and had the best marathon time of anyone in the MPD, male or female. She claimed she never trained, that she must have a runner's genes – she'd traced her roots back to Kenya. She was one of the at most two people in the Homicide Unit whose company Bob could endure. When that sober face of hers occasionally broke into a smile, Bob could see how some might describe her as attractive. But since Kay Myers didn't act like she was interested in anything other than a professional relationship with her male colleagues, and didn't dress that way either, that was how it worked out. It might also have been the case that her tough, self-assured and direct manner scared guys off, at least guys who liked at least a touch of female submissiveness. Which – Bob thought – went for most of them. She wasn't the type to talk about herself much and Bob assumed her tough exterior had something to do with her being raised in Englewood, Chicago.

'Victim's name is Marco Dante,' Kay Myers called out even before she'd shut the car door behind her. 'Arrested three times for illegal sale of weapons but they couldn't hang anything on him, big surprise.'

Bob waited until she came over to him.

'Gun trafficker?'

'Yep. Weapons with probably more lives on their conscience in Minneapolis than all the hunting rifles in this state put together so please excuse me for not shedding a tear. Did . . .?'

'Yeah, they just went in. Sixth floor – that open window up there.'

'We've got witnesses who say they saw that's where the shot came from?'

'Yes, one. Unfortunately they wouldn't give a name and address and did a runner.'

'Really?'

Bob saw that Kay was looking aslant at him.

'So this isn't just Bob Oz's famous gut feeling?'

'Bob Oz's gut feeling tells me that this witness was telling the truth.'

'You remember how much trouble there was last time we went in without a search warrant?'

'No,' said Bob, with a look that suggested honest astonishment. 'I really don't remember that.'

Kay Myers snorted dismissively. 'Where were you this morning, Bob? Or let me put it like this, whose bed did you oversleep in?'

'Unclear. She'd already left.'

'You do realise I can't keep covering up for you much longer?'

'*Longer*? Have I ever asked you to cover up for me at all?'

That was another thing he'd never worked out about Kay Myers, why she backed him the way she did. She was clearly not interested in him as a man; Bob wasn't often tuned in to the rumours circulating at work but he had gathered that word around the unit was that she was gay. And she wasn't interested in having him as a friend either, they had never even had a beer together. Some women like bastards, but Kay Myers didn't seem to belong in that category either. That left only the worst alternative: that she felt sorry for him.

There was a flash between the black drapes in the open window, followed by a dull thud that echoed around the blocks. Stun grenade.

'As usual you're not interested in the fireworks display?' said Kay.

Bob shook his head.

'You know word around the unit is that Bob Oz is chicken?'

'Because I won't play cops and robbers?'

'Because you don't carry a gun, so you always have an excuse not to be part of any life-threatening situations. I've tried telling them they're wrong.'

'Oh, but they aren't wrong, Kay. I *am* chicken.' Bob nodded in the direction of the leader of the SWAT team as he emerged from the entrance, talking and listening on his headset. 'A smart and cowardly homicide detective with an estimated life span eight years longer than that overtrained adrenaline junkie there.'

O'Rourke approached, demonstratively ignoring Bob and addressed himself to Kay Myers. 'It's clear, but I'm afraid our bird has flown.'

'Thanks,' said Myers.

'It's nothing. And if any more bad guys show up . . .' He turned his gaze on Bob and spat on the ground, just missing Bob's brown leather shoes. '. . . just call Bonzo again.'

Myers and Bob watched O'Rourke as he stomped over toward the car and his men emerged from the block.

'Bob, Bob, you make friends wherever you go,' sighed Myers.

They stopped outside the open door of the sixth-floor apartment. Bob saw that the lock had been broken open, probably using a small battering ram.

'I'll go talk to the neighbours,' said Myers.

'OK,' said Bob as he stepped carefully over the threshold. In the first instance he would be looking for things that could be used to put out a BOLO or lead to a quick arrest, but out of habit he kept close to the walls to reduce the risk of contaminating any technical clues. His first thought was that the apartment reminded him of another place that had the same atmosphere of melancholy, maybe the apartment of some lonely woman where one night he and she had tried to make each other feel a little less lonely. This particular apartment was one room with the kitchen area nearest the door, a couch which Bob assumed had originally been over by the window but which had been pulled out further into the room. Of course, it might have been SWAT making sure no one was hiding beneath it, but he doubted that. Water was dripping from the red tablecloth hanging over the table, and that was most definitely SWAT's work. You throw stun grenades into a room containing people you want to neutralise but not actually harm because the flash of light is so bright that for five seconds that person can't see a thing, and the noise is so loud they can't hear either, and that destroys their sense of balance. In the course of those few seconds the perpetrator will probably be immobilised, on the floor and handcuffed. But what sometimes happened – as Bob noted here from the tablecloth – was that the heat developed could easily ignite flammable materials. A few years back an elderly couple had died from smoke inhalation following a narcotics raid in which stun grenades had been used. The whole unit had been disciplined, not least because it turned out the raid had been based on false information. People had lost their jobs.

Bob cursed silently and scanned the room. Myers was right, he didn't have a lot of friends, especially not in the MPD. So why did he do stuff like this? Why call in SWAT? Why act like he had a search warrant? Did he *want* to get fired? Was that it?

Bob crossed to the window. The drapes were taped to the walls on each side. In the opening between them he looked down at the cordoned-off area in front of Block 3. He sniffed at one of the drapes. The acrid smell of gun smoke. There was a chair between the couch and the window, and Bob saw that there were scratch marks on top of the chair back. Bob checked the angle, tried to recreate the shooter's position if he used the chair back as a rest, and concluded he must have been on the couch, possibly on his knees.

He walked to the kitchen cupboard, pulled on the thin latex gloves he always kept in his inside pocket, and opened the cupboard door. The contents didn't tell him much apart from the fact that the tenant had a preference for food from south of the border. Rice, tortillas, empty bottles of Mexican beer. There was a tin of brown beans in the refrigerator, a dried-up pepper and an onion. He lifted up a trash can with a pedal-operated lid, placed it on the counter and quickly sifted through the contents. Kitchen paper, beer bottle caps, a couple of empty food tins, a carton of apple juice, a blackened banana skin, two empty bottles of chilli sauce. Bob picked up something lying in the bottom of the basket and held it up to the light. It was an open box with a label attached: *Insulin. Tomás Gomez. One injection morning and evening. Dr med. Jakob Egeland.* Bob looked inside the box. It had evidently contained several injector pens, but now there was only one left in the box, and that had been used. He opened the refrigerator again, checked all the drawers to make sure he hadn't overlooked anything.

As he was putting the trash can down he noticed, in the spot where it had been standing, something just visible sticking up between the floorboards. He used a knife from the kitchen drawer to flip out what turned out to be a business card from someone called Mike Lunde, Town Taxidermy. For just a moment – as though he'd killed off the last of his brain cells – he couldn't recall what a taxidermist was. Then he recalled an article he'd read in the *Star Tribune*, something about a creative new taxidermist group in Minneapolis. They stuffed dead animals. Bob put the business card in his pocket and walked over to the closet. A few shirts and a hoodie hanging inside. Behind them were several flattened cardboard boxes, the type you use when moving. Bob went through the drawers in the closet. Three pairs of underpants, some T-shirts, socks. As he was closing the door he noticed something black behind the cardboard boxes and he moved them to one side. A long, narrow case leaned up against the rear wall. He lifted it out without touching its handle.

It was a rifle case.

He opened it. Empty.

At that moment Kay Myers appeared in the doorway. She nodded in the direction of the rifle case.

'I hope that means we've raided the right place?'

'I haven't found any weapon nor any ammunition, but people don't make a habit of collecting empty rifle cases,' said Bob.

'I'm asking because if the neighbours are to be believed then our so-called Tomás Gomez is not regarded as the violent type.'

'So-called?' Bob leaned the case against the wall and took a picture of it with his phone.

'That's the name he gave to the landlord here, Mr . . .' She flipped through her notebook. 'Gregory Dupont. But we can't find any reference to any Tomás Gomez with the details he gave Dupont so either it's a false name or he's an illegal immigrant.'

'And, of course, Dupont didn't check?'

'He says Gomez paid his three months' deposit in cash and as far as he was concerned he could be a Martian.'

'Right.' Bob peeled the label off the pack of insulin and put it in his coat pocket. 'Anything else?'

Kay flipped through her notebook. 'The neighbours on both sides say they know practically nothing about him, other than that he's quiet and doesn't say much. No one's had more than the time of day out of him. The neighbours say he's never given any cause for complaint, but one thinks he might have had a cat. Pets aren't allowed.'

Bob gave a short laugh. 'Job?'

'If he had one they don't know what it was. It's not the kind of thing people ask each other around here. But he went out in the mornings and came back in the afternoon, so maybe. Neighbour on the right side thinks he might have had some contact with a Mrs White, two floors up.'

'Shall we have a word with her?'

'Thought we might. But I got a description, so wait while I first give it to the patrol car down there in case he suddenly decides to come back.'

'He won't do that,' said Bob and held up the used insulin pens.

'What's that?'

'Insulin. He's diabetic. He needs these shots daily and you keep them in the refrigerator, but there are none there now. He's taken them with him.'

Mrs White stared at them in alarm from behind the security chain. Based on the little they could see Bob guessed her to be at least seventy, height about five three, black, fond of the colour yellow.

'Tomás? That's not possible!'

'May we come in, Mrs White?' asked Kay.

Mrs White unhooked the security chain and opened the door. Bob and Kay followed the yellow-clad figure into an apartment that was a little larger than Gomez's. It had at least one extra door which Bob assumed was to a bedroom.

'Tomás gave me this,' she said and pointed to the yucca palm standing in a pot in a corner of the room. She shuffled into the kitchen area. 'Tea?'

'No thank you, Mrs White, we'd just like to ask you a few questions.'

'Well, all right. But I can tell you right now you're mistaken. Tomás would never shoot at anybody.'

'What makes you say that?' said Bob as he looked around. It was the apartment of a lonely elderly woman. With old and probably much-loved objects and family photos, to remind her of their existence. Well-looked-after but antiquated furniture. There was a cage with a chirping canary to keep her company.

'Tomás was the very spirit of neighbourliness. If there was some shopping needed doing, or something in the apartment that needed fixing, he was always there to help.'

'One and the same person can be helpful at the same time as capable of shooting someone,' said Bob. He knew he couldn't stay here long, could feel the anger building up inside him already. It wasn't so much Mrs White's naive replies as that yellow bird sitting so stoic and unmoving on its perch and singing that high-pitched monotonous song that was drilling its way inside his head, drilling into an exposed nerve and pretty soon would precipitate an irrational outburst of anger. Damn that Alice!

'Is there anything else you can tell us about Tomás?' Kay asked quickly.

'Anything else?' Mrs White poured tea into two cups. 'Hm. Funny when you ask like that, we talk together so much I ought to be able to tell you a whole lot. But the truth is, Tomás doesn't talk a lot. And never talks about himself.'

'What work does he do?' asked Bob.

'Casual work. Labouring jobs, that's the impression I get. He's a real handyman. And an artist as well.'

'What kind of artist?' asked Kay.

'Some kind of sculptor. He made something, I have it in the cupboard here, would you like –'

'No thanks,' said Bob. 'Did he say anything about where and who he worked for?'

Mrs White stuck out her lower lip, shook her head and handed one teacup to Kay.

'He didn't talk much, you say; it never occurred to you it was because he might have something to hide?' Bob ignored Kay's warning look. She was of the newer school of investigative theory that believed the open question would give a more informative answer. Bob was old school. That meant no theory, just go ahead and ask anything you're curious about.

'No,' said Mrs White. 'I don't think Tomás is selling dope, if that's what you mean. Tomás is silent by nature. I guess you could say I do most of our talking. Don't get me wrong, when Tomás *does* open his mouth he speaks like a schoolteacher. He uses so many words I've never heard before. Did you know this used to be a nice neighbourhood?'

'Did it?' said Kay.

'Oh indeed. Then came the crack epidemic of the eighties.

Because it was an epidemic. A plague, that's what it was. It swept over the whole country, and overnight we were back in the dirt again.'

'I know,' said Kay.

'Do you?'

'I grew up between two crack houses.'

'Yeah, well, then I guess you do know.'

Bob glanced down into the courtyard again. The techs should be here any time now. If not that was just more ammunition for those who claimed the police took their time about things when the neighbourhood involved was black or Latino. A few kids were throwing pebbles at the patrol car down below and the officer stepped out and yelled at them, but the kids just ran off, laughing.

'Now there's more shooting, guns and gang wars here than ever before,' said Mrs White. 'But what does Mayor Patterson do? Right, he pulls the police out of here because he knows that after Minnesota made private prisons illegal it's cheaper for the authorities if the folks down here shoot each other than if they have to be responsible for locking them up. Or am I wrong?'

Bob gave Kay a pleading look which she responded to with an imperceptible nod.

'I don't know how the mayor's office thinks about these things, Mrs White,' said Kay. 'But back to Tomás Gomez. When was the last time you saw him?'

'Oh, that wasn't but a short time ago.'

'A short time ago?'

'Yes, right after that crack out there.'

Bob turned toward them. 'Just now? Did he say anything about –'

'What did you talk about?' Kay interrupted. Open questions.

'As far as I recall he didn't say a word. But I could see something was wrong.'

'Wrong?' asked Kay.

'Yes. He was wearing sunglasses, and he was so pale. Looking back, I think he'd just been crying. Tomás is a very sensitive man, you know. He doesn't show it, but you can tell, that's often the way of it, the sensitive ones protect themselves with silence. But I know for example that he was very upset when his cat died. That's why I told him to have it stuffed. Same as Pippi here.'

Bob turned to the canary in disbelief. It was still sitting there motionless on that perch, but only now did he notice the tiny speaker below the swing, next to the water dish. Mrs White laughed, and Bob realised that the look on his face had betrayed him.

'Mr Lunde's a very skilful taxidermist, though sometimes I think he can be a bit too particular. Anyway, Tomás is still waiting to get his cat back. Have you ever lost anything like a much-loved pet, Miss Myers?'

Kay shook her head.

'What about you, Mr Oz?'

Bob looked at her. Fingered the condom in his pocket. The drilling started up again. He really had to get out of there.

6

GHOSTS, SEPTEMBER 2022

WE'RE BACK IN DOWNTOWN. I tell the taxi driver to wait for me and I get out. The city is awake by now and I hear the whistle blow as the subway train glides out of the station behind me. In front of me is a statue of Mayor Hubert Humphrey. Before he was mayor he was vice president, as well as a presidential candidate. During one of our trips to the USA, Dad brought us here and told us that the man up there on the plinth was half-Norwegian and that his mother, Ragnild Kristine Sannes, came from the same place in Norway as our family. She'd been one of twelve children and had fled from poverty in Norway to a country in which she would give birth to a child who would one day be just a few votes short of becoming the most powerful leader in the world. That's what was so fantastic about this country, our father explained to us. That someone from a humble background – like the man who won that election, Richard Nixon – could end up at the very top. When we got back to Oslo, I bought a map of America and hung it over my bed, along with my posters of Elvis Presley and Marilyn Monroe. It was only later that I realised my father had been lying. In the first place, more or less all presidents except one during the previous hundred years were millionaires, and as for the American dream of social mobility, you had to work your way far down the list before you found my beloved USA, right behind Lithuania, South Korea and Portugal.

But strangely enough it was as though my father's lies only served to further convince me that America is the home of the free and the brave. Because despite all the nice things you can say about my so-called home country of Norway, it's fantastically boring. All you need to do is compare Oslo City Hall with the city hall behind the statue of Humphrey. The city hall in Oslo is just a couple of shoeboxes standing upright. Red brick, small windows, the place could be a factory. But Minneapolis City Hall, with its spires and its ornamentations and huge blocks of stone, radiates something exalted, like a cathedral, or a castle. Or like the Disneyland castle. The original intention was that these costly granite blocks, some weighing up to twenty tons, should be used only for the foundations and the rest be built of less expensive brick. But once the people of Minneapolis saw how mighty those granite blocks were they overruled the penny-pinching bureaucrats and made sure the whole building was made of granite. Which, of course, blew the budget to pieces. Which is the way to do it, if you ask me!

I have come here to get a closer look at this building because it is going to play an important part in my book. Inside, behind the granite blocks, you'll find not just the mayor's office, but courtrooms, police headquarters, even prison cells. And up on the sixth floor, the Homicide Department.

With the Ghost of City Hall.

It was in the Oslo public library that I came across a true-crime pamphlet about John Moshik, and the first and last public execution to take place at the city hall, back in 1898. Moshik was sentenced for killing a man for just fourteen dollars. But the means employed – hanging by the neck until dead – didn't go according to plan. It took eight minutes for Moshik to die. Meaning just a minute less than the amount of time Derek Chauvin held his knee against George Floyd's neck after Floyd had been arrested on suspicion of having paid for a pack of cigarettes with a counterfeit twenty-dollar bill. According to my contact in the MPD, Moshik's ghost still walks the floor up there in the Homicide Department. But my business here is not Moshik's ghost, or George Floyd's either. The ghost I'm looking for was seen passing a CCTV camera six years ago, following a shooting in Jordan. And no one knew back then that this was only the beginning. I don't know if this makes me a bad person, but the thought gives me a pleasurable shiver as I stand there studying the facade of the building. The black windows reveal nothing. My job is to fill in the blank spaces, give lines to the characters and life to the scenes.

7

THE HOMICIDE UNIT, OCTOBER 2016

BOB OZ CROSSED GOVERNMENT PLAZA. Glanced up at the Humphrey statue that always seemed to him to look more like Bob Hope and entered the city hall. His steps echoed as he passed through the venerable hall with its statue of Aquarius, through the security channel and then over to the elevators where three people stood waiting for him.

'Hi, Bob,' said one of them. He turned. It was a woman in a navy-blue skirt and jacket – the battledress of the legal profession. She smiled. Thirty, maybe, though he never found it easy to guess the age of Asian people.

'Hi . . .' He couldn't recall her name. 'The coffee good?'

She looked down in slight surprise at the paper Starbucks cup she was holding. 'Er, it's OK. I never heard back from you.'

Was it Ellen? Or Helen? Or a Chinese name?

'You know what, I lost your number,' said Bob. 'Maybe . . .'

'Maybe?'

He smiled. There was a ping and the elevator doors slid open. 'Maybe you could send it to me.'

Helen. Yes, it was Helen. The enemy. The defence attorney. Lilac underwear.

'How? You didn't give me your number either.' She entered the elevator and turned to face Bob, who was still standing outside. She raised her index finger and pointed upward quizzically.

Bob shook his head. 'Thanks, Helen, but I'm going down.'

She gave him a big smile, flipped her hand round, and as the elevator door slid closed switched fingers and showed him the middle one. Bob brushed his hand over his tie. So, not Helen then. But he was sure he was right about the underwear.

Bob took the next elevator to the fifth floor and stepped out into the Homicide Department's new offices. Until recently the fifth had been used to house prisoners on remand, and despite the complete refurbishment and all the glass and the light furniture, Bob couldn't shake the feeling that the place was a prison. Maybe it was the narrow windows that let in so little daylight, maybe it was the cell-like offices flanking either side of the open-plan office landscape. He walked past the last office, still in the process of being refurbished, said to be the cell occupied by the 'Ghost of City Hall'. The decorator working inside turned toward Bob as he passed. He looked like a ghost himself in there behind the glass wall, in his white overalls and with the white cap, gloves and face mask. All that was visible was a pair of brown eyes, and what Bob interpreted as a smile. He smiled back.

Bob headed for his workspace at the far end of the open office landscape, looking neither to right nor to left of him. He made it over almost every hurdle but of course tripped up at the last one.

'Aaa-ss!' Detective Olav Hanson's pronunciation of Bob's surname had a lot of air in it, and a descending note that made it sound like a cross between an apology and a puncture. Hanson had apparently been just one knee-tackle away from playing in the NFL, and though Bob Oz didn't wish fame and fortune on Hanson he would have preferred that to having the giant blond jerk as part of his life. Hanson was in his fifties and had been with the Homicide squad longer than anyone. There were rumours about why Hanson had never been promoted, but for Bob there was no mystery about it: as an investigator Olav Hanson was useless. Unfortunately that wasn't valid grounds for dismissal in the state. Nor was being an asshole. Fortunately.

'Walker was in here looking for you,' Hanson bellowed, loud enough to be sure everyone in the vicinity heard what he was saying. 'You're to go and see him asap, Aaa-ss.'

'Thanks, Hands-On,' said Bob without breaking his stride.

'Asap, as in as soon . . .' Hanson's voice fell away behind him.

Bob slumped down behind his desk. From the chaos of paper piles, crime scene photographs, torn-out notebook pages, chocolate wrappers and chewed pencils in front of him you might have got the impression Bob Oz had far too much to do. The exact opposite was the truth. Since the break with Alice, Walker had been taking Bob off his involvement in active investigations one by one until now he was down to none. Walker's grounds had been what the personnel report called 'unstable conduct', MPD's psychologist referred to as a failure of anger management, and Walker called giving Bob a break until he pulled himself together again. In the meantime he was handed assignments usually given to newcomers in the unit, such as collating data for other detectives, fact-checking and interviewing witnesses in cases assigned to other investigators.

Bob checked MPD's website to make sure the BOLO for Tomás Gomez had been sent out as he had ordered. No results so far. He pulled the note from his coat pocket and called a number on the red landline telephone. While waiting for it to be picked up he looked at the photograph of Alice that was still pinned to the privacy wall, alongside the Vikings fixture list.

'Hi, Kari, this is Bob. Can you help me trace a doctor? Name is Jakob Egeland. He's an MD. Thanks, Kari, you're a . . . sorry, I can't come up with a euphemism that's sexually neutral enough. What? *Me?* A dinosaur? Come on.'

Bob hung up. Stretched his legs and folded his hands round the back of his head. Looked at the clock. Then the picture of Alice. If he called her using the landline, maybe she would pick up. No, no, fuck it, no! He pulled up the *Star Tribune*'s website and learned that the number of bison in Minnesota was on the increase. Read an article about the National Rifle Association's annual conference which was being held this year in Minneapolis and was due to open in four days. A report on the Vikings' last game, a victory. They were looking good so far, so good Bob figured they would be able to defend their title as the best team in the NFL never to have won the Super Bowl. Nothing else of interest there. His gaze settled once more on the red telephone.

Don't ring Alice. Do *not* ring Alice.

He felt himself itching all over. He glanced at his neighbour's desk, at the handcuffs lying on top of a pile of documents as a paperweight. He felt like he wanted to arrest somebody, anybody at all. Something had to happen, anything at all or else he'd go out of his mind. He regretted now that he'd quit smoking after meeting Alice. The day after she threw him out, he'd bought his first pack in twelve years, but they tasted like shit. She'd even taken that from him. He itched inside, in places he could never reach.

Bob got to his feet so abruptly that the chair was still rolling toward the next desk as he marched out.

Superintendent Brenton Walker stood looking out of the window of his narrow office. The sun blinked from the glass facades of the skyscrapers surrounding them here in downtown that made city hall look like a little sandcastle. He liked this office and this view. He'd miss it.

From behind he heard a knock on the door.

'Boss?' said a voice.

Walker liked Bob Oz. He was a good investigator too. There were others who were smarter, but when Oz was at the top of his game there was no one who worked harder. He was like a wolverine, once he got his teeth into something he didn't let go. Mostly that was a good thing. But over the last twelve months, Oz had brought Walker more trouble than results.

'I didn't send you to Jordan because I want you to take the case,' said Walker. 'I sent you because all my other investigators are tied up. And since the victim turns out not to be dead it's a first-degree assault and not a murder. Now I'm getting calls from the Assaults Unit saying you've sent out a BOLO without informing them.'

He half turned toward Oz, who was standing just inside the door like he wanted the shortest possible route back out of there again. Oz coughed.

'In my view it was more important to get the message out there than have it come from the right unit, chief. Anyway it's quite possible the guy actually will die.'

Walker didn't answer, just swayed silently on his heels. In truth, a small part of him did wish that Marco Dante would die. Not just because he sold weapons to the kids in Jordan and made it more easy for them to kill each other but because the success rate for clearing murder cases in Minneapolis was on its way down toward fifty per cent, and even if the fall in the clear-up rate was part of a national trend, MPD's chief of police would need someone or something to point the finger at when it came to explaining the drop. If Dante died then at least the right man had been killed, and Walker could add that to the right side of the statistics. He tried to ignore the thought. Couldn't. Did it mean that the young man who had joined the police in hopes of making a difference was turning into the kind of egocentric careerist he had sworn he would never be? Walker's family had been part of the black working class who had to move from the Rondo district in Saint Paul when the council decided to run the new freeway through the well-established part of the city. Walker's father had been among the leaders of the protests and there were those who thought Brenton Walker had something of the same type of activist in him, despite his conventional and conflict-free career as a senior police officer. And they were right to suppose he had inherited his father's sense of anger at the inherent injustice of society. Over time it became difficult for him to hide these personality traits, and there were those in the unit who referred to the broad-shouldered, shaven-headed superintendent as 'the socialist'. In the beginning he'd taken it as a badge of distinction. But now?

'OK,' said Walker. 'So then you know this case belongs to Aggravated Assault.'

'It's odd,' said Bob.

'I'm sorry?'

'Attempted murder. You shoot someone from your own apartment and you're asking to be caught.'

'And when was the last time you came across a killer who was rational?'

'But everything else about it seems so professional. It's as though he's giving us some kind of start. As if he feels he has protection.'

'Protection? What kind of protection?'

Bob shrugged. 'There are only two kinds. One of the gangs. Or . . .'

Walker gave Bob a warning look. He was aware that in the past Oz had asked Internal Affairs to investigate the rumour that a serving member of the force was taking drug money in return for steering murder investigations away from certain leading gang members. But everyone knew these rumours about a person they called the Milkman were about as accurate – and about as old – as all those tales about the Ghost of City Hall. When it emerged that it was Bob Oz who had tried to alert Internal Affairs, the only effect was to reinforce his reputation among his colleagues as a paranoid drunk and a potential snitch. On top of that he knew Oz's nickname in the unit: Kentucky Fried. Not exactly original, but the thought behind it was clear enough: Bob Oz was a chicken who refused to carry a gun, and in a crisis he would push armed colleagues ahead of him.

Walker sighed. 'How are the, er . . . anger management sessions going? You are attending?'

'Oh yes.'

Walker assumed Oz was lying. 'And are you improving?'

'Hard to say, chief. Takes time, something like that, they say.'

Walker nodded in the direction of the window. 'We could use you, you know.'

'Mm.'

'The way you used to be,' said Walker as he studied his own reflection.

'Was there anything else, chief?'

Walker sighed. 'No.'

'So then, Aaa-ss,' said Olav Hanson as he rolled out on his chair from behind his desk, 'you get promoted? No? Demoted? In that case I'd like a coffee, three sugars please.'

A snort of laughter from Detective Joe Kjos behind his privacy divider. Kjos was Hanson's number one fan and his personal supplier of canned laughter.

Bob strode on by, unable to come up with a suitable response as the baying laughter followed him back to his desk. No sooner had he sat down than the phone rang. It was Kari.

'There's no Dr Jakob Egeland in Minneapolis. But there is one in Saint Paul. The address is –'

'Thanks, Kari, but call Aggravated Assault, it's their case now.'

'Oh yeah? Who should I talk to there?'

'Good question. Give me the address, Kari, I'll talk to them.'

He wrote it down on his notepad, hung up, picked up the receiver again and called the number for Aggravated Assault. While he was waiting he heard Hanson say something, and then Kjos's hearty and almost happy laughter. Bob took a deep breath. Why the hell didn't they answer? There wasn't exactly a sudden surfeit of aggravated assaults taking place today. More laughter. Fuck. Bob felt like he wanted to break something and realised he had lifted the receiver high above his head. He lowered it and counted in a low voice as he repeated inside his head: *Think before you speak, think before you act. Tell yourself you can control your anger.* That was about as much as he had learned in the two sessions of anger management he had actually attended. He repeated the words. Then, with infinite care, he replaced the receiver in its cradle.

And breathed out.

Smiled.

Sat quite still for several seconds.

Then tore the page from the notepad and hurried toward the door.

8

WOLF, OCTOBER 2016

'I UNDERSTAND YOU HAVE TO consider your oath of confidentiality, Dr Egeland, but what we're dealing with here is a possible murder.'

'You said murder on the telephone, Detective Oz, not *possible* murder.' Egeland repositioned his newly polished spectacles on his nose. The policeman sitting on the chair in front of him, normally occupied by patients, was wearing clothes of a cut and colour that Egeland was inclined to associate with Mafia bosses and pimps rather than police officers: a coat that was almost orange, red silk tie and brown shoes that looked a touch too elegant and delicate for a Minneapolis autumn. But there had been nothing suspicious about the credentials the man had shown him, and it was hard to imagine someone going to all this trouble just to trick a bit of information out of him about a diabetes diagnosis.

'Since you have Gomez's label then you already know he's diabetic,' said Egeland. 'So you really don't need any confirmation from me.'

'No. But there are a couple of things I'm wondering about. The first is, do you have any information at all about where we can contact Gomez?'

'I have his address in Jordan.'

'Phone number?'

'No.'

'OK. My second question is, when will he need to renew his prescription?'

'What do you mean?'

'There was one used injector pen left in the box. The usual thing would be to keep the pens in the box and throw it away when the last needle was used, right?'

'It's perfectly possible.'

'I don't know if this is the last box, but I know that when he runs out he's going to have to contact his regular doctor, which is you. So can you check his journal on your computer and see when he's going to need to renew?'

Egeland looked sullenly at Detective Oz. He disliked the man. He had that air of arrogance you find only in someone who doesn't care if people like him or not.

'The reports from the hospital are pessimistic,' said the police officer. 'Delete *possible* and think of this as a murder.'

Egeland thought about it. Weighed that word up against his own vow of confidentiality. Murder. This was the exception. The place where ethical discussions stopped. He sighed, then worked his keyboard as he studied his computer screen.

'He'll run out in ten days.'

'So before then he'll turn up here?'

'No, most likely he'll phone and I'll email the prescription to a chemist close to where he happens to be calling from.'

Egeland watched Detective Oz as he leaned forward and, placing the notepad on the desk as though it were his own, began to write. 'Now listen, Egeland. When Gomez contacts you I want you to call MPD on the number I'm writing down here. We want to know the name of the chemist where he's going to be picking up his insulin, and we want you to wait until we're in place there before you send the email prescription. Understood?' Oz tore out the sheet of paper and pushed it across the desk.

Jakob Egeland was astonished. 'You want me to cooperate with the police in the arrest of one of my own patients? Don't you understand –'

'Dr Egeland, what I want most of all is for you to cooperate with your own conscience and in doing so prevent Tomás Gomez from killing a number of other people. If the moral algebra of that is too complex for you then I can leave and come back with a judge's order.'

Egeland stared at the number on the sheet of paper as though the figures were an equation that could be solved.

'I'll do it,' he finally conceded. 'But I would like a written judge's order.'

'Fine, but I can't promise we can arrange that before Gomez contacts you. So can I still count on your assistance?'

Jakob Egeland nodded.

Detective Oz pushed the notebook back into his pocket and stood up.

'He's a quiet man,' Egeland said in a faint voice. 'But bright. The first time he came to see me I was surprised at how much of my legal Latin he understood.'

Oz remained standing.

'So I was surprised again when he was due his first biannual check-up and he took off his shirt and his upper body was covered in tattoos. You know . . . gang tattoos.'

Oz sat back down.

'Which gangs?'

'I don't know them all, but on his back he had X-11 tattooed.'

Oz nodded slowly. 'X-11. And the others?'

'He had a tattoo of a wolf which I've seen as graffiti. So I presume that's a gang too.'

The police officer tapped on his phone, raised it and showed Egeland an image of a black wolf tattooed on a naked back. 'Did it look like that?'

'Yes, it could well have done.'

'And now you're worried that if you help us catch him his gang will want to take revenge on you?'

Egeland looked up in alarm. 'No. No, that didn't occur to me until now.' The doctor's Adam's apple bobbed up and down. 'Ought I to . . .?'

'Absolutely not,' said Oz as he stood up again. 'We have a duty of confidentiality too. No one will know that you were my source of information.'

'No one?'

'Absolutely no one.' Oz gave a quick smile. 'I'd better be getting back over to the right side of town. Have a nice day and hope to hear from you soon.'

It was five thirty and already dusk as Bob Oz walked along the corridor of the Regency Hospital. It had been a fairly good day. A day, finally, with a little meaning. He had been able to work undisturbed on the Gomez case since no one else at the Homicide Unit was involved or interested in what he got up to and, so far at least, he'd managed to keep off the Assault Unit's radar. Luckily for him he'd always managed to keep in with Kari at the Fraud Unit. When necessary, she helped out the Homicide Unit and had always been of invaluable assistance. As he reached room 531 Bob showed his ID to the police officer on guard outside. 'Anyone from Aggravated Assault been here?'

'No,' said the police officer. 'He's just come round after the operation.'

'OK,' said Bob and walked in.

The fat man lying in the bed shifted his drugged gaze away from the wall and onto Bob.

'Marco Dante.' Bob pulled a chair up to the bed and looked at the apparatus the fat man was hooked up to. 'I'm from MPD. I want you to take a look at this drawing.'

Bob held his phone up in front of Dante. He'd downloaded the police artist's sketch from the MPD's internal site. The face was Latino, broad, prominent eyebrows. Bob guessed that the people at Assault had used Mrs White to help the police artists. 'I wonder what it is that this man Tomás Gomez has against you.'

Dante's gaze slid over the phone screen and back onto the wall again. 'No idea who it is. Or who you are.' The voice was thick, with an Italian accent straight out of *The Sopranos*.

Bob hadn't spotted any sign of recognition on Dante's face when he saw the drawing. Maybe it was a bad likeness. Or maybe Dante was a good liar. Or maybe Dante and Gomez had never met.

'I'm the man who saved your life,' said Bob.

Dante looked at him, furrowed his brow.

'Mouth-to-mouth,' said Bob.

Dante pulled a face. 'You're lying.'

'Nope. You threw up your breakfast. Some kind of pasta, right?'

Dante blinked.

Bob pulled his chair closer. Someone from Assault could come barging in at any moment.

'I think a gang is after you, Dante. You fallen out with any of them recently?'

'I don't know nothing about any gangs.'

'No? Not supplied X-11 with any weapons?'

'I've no idea what X—'

'Don't bother, Dante. We know you supply them with cheap guns in return for them letting you sell your hardware on their territory.' Bob had called the MPD's Weapons Unit who knew Marco Dante's name but could neither confirm nor rule out any link to X-11.

'I've no idea what you're talking about,' said Dante and yawned loudly. 'I run a car repair business in Jordan. Jordan isn't X-11 territory, it's Black Wolves. Don't you know your gang map, Detective?'

'As far as I know X-11 operate wherever they please. Speaking of weapons, you recognise this?'

Bob held up his phone again, this time displaying a photo he'd taken in Gomez's apartment.

'No.'

'That's funny, because according to Weapons Unit this is a case for an M24. Now I don't know much about weapons, but even I know this is a classic sniper's rifle. One of my colleagues checked the weapons register and it says there that you recently purchased a gun like that.'

'So maybe it also says there that I reported it stolen.'

'Yes. Maybe you should be a little more careful about how

you keep your weapons. In the last twelve months alone you've reported weapons stolen from you six times. Altogether twelve rifles and sixteen revolvers.'

A thin smile appeared between the narrow black strips of hair on the gun dealer's face. 'What can I tell you? I live in a very rough area. So as long as the MPD refuses to patrol there then I'm thinking the break-ins will just keep on happening.'

Bob nodded slowly. 'Yes, I guess they will.'

He heard voices outside in the corridor. Time to get out of there.

'Well, thanks for your help, Dante.'

'It's nothing . . . what you say your name was?'

'And get well soon,' said Bob Oz. He pushed open the door and headed out into the corridor.

'Hey, Bob!' It was Rooble Isack. Bob knew Isack from when he was the new guy in the Homicide Unit. Rooble had come from Mogadishu as a thirteen-year-old, part of a family that clung on tenaciously to Somali traditions. His father dyed his beard orange and his mother worked in a henna store in the Somali shopping mall on 29th and Pillsbury. Rooble was one of these young and ambitious immigrants, so naive in their faith in the promise of a country with equal opportunities for all, and so energetic in their pursuit of a better life for themselves and their families. So it was well deserved when, after two years with Homicide, he was offered a detective posting in Aggravated Assault.

'Hey, Rooble.'

'What are you doing here, Bob?'

'Murder case. We've got a gun we can connect to Dante. I'm guessing you're here in connection with the assault?'

'Yes.' Rooble nodded to his partner, a boy who blushed when

he introduced himself and whose name Bob had forgotten by the next time he breathed in.

'This is Bob Oz, the man who taught me everything I didn't know about being a detective,' said Rooble to the boy, who was trying to look interested. 'A living legend.'

'I think you learned quicker than I could teach.' Bob looked at his watch.

'How's Alice?'

Bob's face stiffened into a smile. 'She's fine.'

Rooble showed no noticeable reaction to the reply. 'It's been a while. Wasn't it that barbecue with Homicide, in your backyard?'

'Could well be,' said Bob as he tried to convey in body language that he didn't have time to engage in the local custom known as the Long Goodbye.

'Holy buckets, all those pork chops we cooked.' Rooble laughed. 'Me and Hani brought our own barbecue, remember?'

'Yes. Listen, I have to go. Say hello to Hani.'

'Sure will. Actually she's pregnant again.'

'Wow, good work. See you.'

'See you.'

But Bob stayed where he was.

'Something?' said Rooble.

'Hey, I just remembered, Hani was pregnant that time too. You went home early and left your barbecue at my place. I put it in the basement.'

'Oh, sorry, I forgot. Want me to come and fetch it?'

'No, no, I'll bring it over. Tomorrow.'

Bob noticed Rooble's look of surprise. 'Thanks, Bob, but that isn't necessary.'

'I insist.'

Rooble frowned. 'It was just one of those cheap ones – we've got a gas barbecue now.'

'You never know when you might need two,' said Bob with a broad smile. He waved and hurried off down the corridor.

9

CRY, OCTOBER 2016

I WAS ON HIGH, I had perspective. But no gun this time, this time I was just an observer.

I was lying in bed and watching TV. Switched between news broadcasts on KSTP, WCCO and KARE and the internet on my phone. I didn't get it. I could see why the murder of a gun dealer in Jordan would get less coverage than the killing of some rich white guy out in Dellwood; what I didn't get is why it didn't even rate a mention. After all, Minneapolis isn't Chicago where they have two or three murders every day. I closed my eyes. They hurt from staring at the screen. My ears were exhausted from all the cackling and the brutal sound effects used by advertisers to attract attention. What I wanted was peace. Rest. I heard a child crying somewhere. I knew there were no children here. I know it was just her.

Then it came. A short item on KARE. And I realised why it hadn't made the headlines. The anchor reported a shooting incident in Jordan in the morning in which the victim had been shot in the stomach outside his own home. Badly injured. Not killed. A person injured in a shooting is everyday stuff in Minneapolis – it hardly rates a mention on the news. The images used to illustrate the ten seconds of the report weren't even from the blocks but from somewhere else in Jordan, on a grey day, and the only connection with the place were the pictures of the police crime scene tape, stock footage from some previous report.

Badly injured.

Not dead.

Not yet.

Bob parked some distance away from the house in the quiet street in Cooper. Retraced familiar steps he'd walked so many times before. Past that row of small houses on a slope, with steps up to the verandas and the front doors. Small but charming middle-class houses. Cooper was regarded as inexpensive, but it still felt like a bold investment back when he and Alice had bought the detached house with its three rooms and kitchen, him with his modest policeman's income and her a young psychologist just starting out in her own practice. But they really did need more space. And they wanted to live somewhere central, not end up in those anaemic suburbs. Maybe Cooper wasn't all that fancy, but it was safe, and it had character. And had its characters too, like Jesse Ventura, a former professional wrestler turned governor who'd grown up round here. Fewer knew that the area was named after James Fenimore Cooper, writer of a whole heap of thrilling stories about Indians. Bob had come across these in his grandparents' bookshelves, and even though the depictions were sympathetic they still reflected contemporary attitudes toward Native Americans. Maybe that was why Cooper's community of liberals preferred not to dwell on the origins of the name. Whatever, Cooper was a place where you could live, there was room to breathe, and you could raise a family there. And since their purchase, house prices in the area had doubled, at least.

Bob stopped in front of the house.

Saw the lights in the windows. Listened out for the sound of laughter. Saw all three of them running around in the garden; it was summer and the shower from the garden hose made their own little rainbow for them. Or on some weekday, after a night shift, with the house all to himself, sitting on the veranda and hearing the playground sounds from the Christian Minnehaha Academy, where nothing bad ever happened, nodding to the FedEx driver as he placed a package outside a neighbour's door on the other side of the road, a package that would not be stolen, not the way it would if you lived just two minutes' drive further west, in Phillips. Sometimes it seemed like their biggest concern was all the squirrels that chewed at the electricity cables around the house. Once, when the lights went while the Super Bowl was on TV, he'd threatened to get his pistol from the bedroom and shoot them down. But Alice didn't laugh at his joke, just stared at him wide-eyed, as though she didn't know what to believe.

Instead of heading for the front door Bob took the steps up to the veranda. Alice had told him not to come around, but when a barbecue has to be returned then it has to be returned. No, he wasn't here to argue, he'd come to sort things out, make sure things were returned to their rightful owner. Who could have an issue with that?

He walked silently to the veranda door but didn't knock. Took a deep breath and peered through the window into the living room. The light was on, so was the TV, but the room was empty. He held his breath. In the silence he heard something, something rhythmical. He looked up. The bedroom window was open. Bob and Alice's bedroom. At first he wasn't sure whether what he was hearing was an echo from back then, or whether it was real, and now. Not until he heard Alice's hoarse voice sighing a name that wasn't his name. A rushing sound spread through his head. He should leave but he couldn't. There was that barbecue that had to be returned. He raised his fist to bang on the door. The rushing sound turned into a howl. Knock hard and call her name out loud, that's what he ought to do.

Think before you speak, think before you act.

Bob bunched his fist so hard it felt as though the skin over the knuckles might split. Silence up there now, as if they were listening out for sounds. He breathed out with a shudder and pressed his forehead against the cool glass. Stayed like that a while. Counted. Heard footsteps on the stairs. Bob pushed away from the glass and silently crept down from the veranda. Back at street level he turned up the collar of his coat and hurried off in the same direction he'd come.

Back in his car he sat and stared through the windshield.

Pulled out his phone and went through his list of contacts.

Anne. Aurora. Beatrice.

'Hello?'

'Hi, Beatrice, it's Bob. It's been a while.'

'Two months.'

'Really? I've often thought I should call you and suggest we meet, but there's been so damn much going on at work. Anyway, I'm out driving and actually not too far away from you, if you feel like a visit?'

Pause.

'Now?'

'Yes?'

'This is not a good time. Some other time, maybe.'

'Of course. Anyway, nice to hear your voice, Beatrice. Later then.'

'Tuesday next week is good.'

'OK. I'll check how that's looking for me and I'll get back to you.'

'OK.'

They ended the connection. Bob closed his eyes and hit the steering wheel. Ants everywhere, under the skin, soap bubbles in the head, prick, prick, shit, shit! The phone rang. That B something, she must have changed her mind. But no, it was from the Homicide Unit.

'Yes?'

'Good evening, Aaa-ss. Your esteemed colleague Hanson here. Are you far from the office?'

'What's this about, Hanson?'

'You've got a visitor. Seems like something important that can't wait.'

'Who is it and what's it about?'

'I guess you best come here and find that out for yourself. What I can tell you is that the information from the person concerned appears to be valid and important.'

Bob checked the time. Seven. His working day was over, he could head home now. Home to an apartment stinking of loneliness, dirty laundry, old masturbation tissues and leftover wedges of pizza.

'There in twenty,' he said and turned on the ignition.

I stood at the reception counter of the Regency Hospital. I didn't yet know whether this was where he was, but there are two hospitals in Minneapolis where they bring people with bullet wounds. My city was not regarded as especially violent in this country, but it has two hospitals with specialists in removing bullets. Of the two, this one was closest to Jordan.

'I'm visiting my cousin,' I said. 'But I don't know which ward he's in.'

I spelled out the name Marco Dante and the woman behind the counter typed it into a computer. Reflected in the lenses of her glasses I could see the screen flickering. Saw her study for a few moments the page that came up before she answered.

'We don't have any record of a patient of that name being admitted,' she said.

But her hesitation and the vagueness of her answer told me all I needed to know. She probably had a note saying no information was to be given to anyone asking about Marco Dante. Which could mean he had some kind of protection. I thanked her, told her I must have got the wrong hospital, and turned away. I headed toward the elevators and stood waiting among people carrying flowers, their shoulders hunched, anxious looks on their faces. There were no checks on visitors, no barriers, maybe because it wasn't a private hospital and they couldn't afford that type of security. No one asked to see my ID, or what I was carrying under my jacket that made it bulge. I entered and exited the elevator on a couple of floors, peered down long corridors but didn't see anything that might have given me a clue. So when a man wearing white with a hospital ID card on his breast pocket got into the elevator I told him I'd been asked to deliver a set of keys to an Officer Smith who was on guard duty here but that someone must have directed me to the wrong floor.

'Ah, that must be the man sitting outside 531,' he replied, and without my asking pushed the button for 5.

I got out on the fifth floor. Read the numbers off the doors as I passed them along the busy corridor. Took a right turn and there, on a chair up against the wall, sat a uniformed policeman. He was staring straight ahead, probably had something on his mind – don't we all? I slowed down. Fewer people here. My plan was to reconnoitre first and work out the best time to act, maybe when the guard had to use the bathroom or went to get himself a coffee. But as a plan I saw now that it was weak, too vague, it called for improvisation and I hadn't reckoned on that. I'd thought of my main plan, my big idea, as being so watertight that Dante ought to be dead by now, so that improvisation wouldn't be necessary.

And in that same instant I realised that this improvised plan was dead too, that I had to get out of there. Because suddenly the police officer turned and was now staring directly at me. Head motionless, neck tensed, like a deer sensing or hearing the presence of danger. The risk involved in going ahead with my plan was too great. I wasn't afraid on my own account, only that the bigger plan would be compromised. So I walked on. I could feel the policeman's gaze following me. As I was about to walk past him the door opened and two men appeared, both wearing suits; one was unusually tall and slender. He made me think of a Maasai warrior. They exchanged a few words with the guard. Police officers.

At the next crossroads in the corridor I took a right and presently found myself close to the elevators again. I could see the backs of the two police officers as they stood waiting. I could've taken the stairs. Of course. Instead I stood behind them and waited too. Listened.

'It doesn't feel right,' one of them whispered.

'What doesn't?'

'All of this, just to find out who shot a man who sells weapons to kids.'

'Guess you're just going to have to get used to it,' said the tall one with a sigh.

'Yeah, well, I hope that hole in his belly is burning like hell.'

The elevator arrived and we stepped inside.

There was a nurse with a girl in a wheelchair. Tears came to my eyes, and as we descended I noticed the tall, slender man looking intently at me. But then he probably remembered that in a hospital it wasn't particularly unusual to see people in tears.

I tried not to look at the girl in the wheelchair, but I'd seen the resemblance already. Looked like my Anna.

10

RUSHING SOUNDS, OCTOBER 2016

WHEN BOB EMERGED FROM THE elevator three men from Homicide were standing by the unit's new coffee machine. Hanson, Joe Kjos and a new guy whose name Bob couldn't remember.

'Here's the wizard,' said Olav Hanson. 'Didn't manage to transport yourself here in twenty minutes after all?'

'Traffic,' said Bob over Joe Kjos's laughter. 'Where is this guy?'

'He's waiting by your desk.'

'Oh yeah? Who let him in?'

'Me,' said Hanson, exchanging looks with the two others. There was an anticipation in their sniggers that made Bob uneasy.

'It's a personal matter so I thought it was best if the two of you dealt with it face-to-face.'

'I see.'

Bob unbuttoned his coat as he headed into the empty office landscape. He heard whispering and knew that the three were following him. He slowed as the person sitting at his desk turned. Even sitting down Bob could see the man was huge. Hanson came up behind Bob.

'He says you screwed his wife,' he whispered.

Bob swallowed. 'Oh yeah? So does that make him your father, Hands-On?'

'Joke all you like, Aaa-ss, but I think you're scared. Maybe you want us to call in a SWAT team?'

Low cackles of laughter from behind. Bob felt that familiar rushing sound start up in his head. He walked on, a little faster now. The man in the chair got up.

'Good evening, I'm Detective Oz,' said Bob. He walked round his desk and sat down in his chair. Looked up at the man. A weak chin and a feminine mouth. Scar on one cheek. It didn't have to mean he got in a lot of fights. But he was big. Very, very big. 'Won't you sit down again, Mr . . .?'

'I'll stay standing. My name is Tony Stärk.' He was shaking. His voice, his lips, his whole body. 'You raped my wife.'

Bob raised his head to meet the man's gaze.

'Raped? Jesus. Have you reported this?'

'More or less raped.' The man was so angry he was tripping over his own words. 'Seduced. Persuaded. I don't know what sort of fucking trick you used but my wife doesn't do something like that of her own free will. Are you listening, you shitbag? You stay away from her, or I'll crush you like a . . . like a . . .'

As Tony searched for a suitable metaphor, Bob glanced over toward his three colleagues who were following things from four yards away. Kjos was sniggering and Hanson's face glowed with pleasure at Bob's uncomfortable predicament. That rushing sound that had started when he was standing on the veranda hadn't completely subsided. Now it sped up again. This had been a long day. Very long.

'Louse,' said Bob Oz.

'What?'

'I think the word you're looking for is "louse". And for what it's worth, the description of me as a "shitbag" is pretty accurate. But "pig" would do even better. Because I am a pig. I have no idea who you're talking about. I don't recognise the name Stärk, and I'm terrible at first names, so maybe you could describe her for me? Is she dark? blonde?'

Tony's heart-shaped mouth stayed open. 'Blonde,' he said.

'Aha. Big breasts?'

'Er, yes.'

By now the rushing sound felt like a large fan going full speed inside Bob's head. He leaned back in his chair, curved his hand and moved it up and down in large gestures in front of his crotch. 'Carry on, Stärk, please. Tell me more.'

He heard the sniggering from Kjos stop and glanced over at the three men watching. They looked shocked, even Hanson, whose face no longer reflected pleasure, just disgust.

Bob looked at Tony. Saw his words sinking in and knew he'd managed to pull the man down with him in his delicious, liberating free fall of rage. Tony took a step toward Bob.

'I'm warning you, Tony,' said Bob, his voice so quiet it sounded as if he was giving advice to a friend. 'It will be a long time before you see your children again. You can get up to three years for assaulting a policeman in the performance of his duty.'

'We have no children,' said Tony.

'Oh, but your wife is pregnant,' said Bob with a smile. 'I promise you. These little swimmers here . . .' He pointed at his crotch.

As Tony leaned across the desk and swung out at him, Bob pushed off with his feet. There was a screeching sound from the wheels of his chair as it spun across the floor. The chair came to a halt against the neighbouring desk, and Tony was coming toward him, teeth bared, right hand ready to swing again. Bob grabbed the handcuffs from the top of the pile of papers so one of the steel brackets covered his knuckles. He stood up, saw the punch coming and dipped his knees so that it struck his forehead instead of full in the face, at the same time reeling backward and lashing out with his right hand. With the difference in height the punch came up from below and there was a crunching sound as the steel crushed the bone in Tony's nose, followed by a second punch from the same fist that hit him full in the mouth. The man stood there, swaying.

'My teeth . . .' he said, before Bob hit him again. And again. A full storm raging in his head by this time. Blood mist. Acid rain.

Bob was still swinging as Hanson and the two others pulled him off the doubled-over body. Bob saw that the man's face was covered in blood, with blood coming from every orifice, but that didn't calm the storm in his head, just the opposite, now was its turn to speak, and it did so in a long, piercing tirade:

'If you can't hold on to your wife that's your own fault, you fucking loser! You pathetic, worthless nothing! Go hang yourself, don't come here blaming other people! It's *your* fault. *Your* fault!'

I was lying in bed again.

I had made a mistake.

Dante was alive. I'd hit him in the stomach, too low down. How could that have happened? I had made allowances for the fact that I was higher than my target. Was there something about the physics, something in the calculations I had got wrong? Because if that was what had happened, I needed to know. It was important. I had to understand these things. If I didn't then I'd get it wrong again, and there was no room for that. OK, easy now, the plan was still holding. But I needed to be sharper.

I closed my eyes. Heard a child crying. Knew it was her, Anna.

Two hand grenades underneath the bed. I don't know why I found the thought so comforting. Maybe it was the certainty that if I couldn't sleep, all I had to do was squeeze the safety catch on one of them, pull the pin and let go, and it would all be over. Anyway, it calmed me and I felt myself falling asleep. But just as I was about to slip away the other thought came back: that lying there in the hospital he was like that Maserati of his, Marco Dante. Protected. Off-limits. I felt the surge of adrenaline again, cursed silently and turned over on my side. Tried to think about something else. Listened out for the sound of crying.

11

LIZA, OCTOBER 2016

LIZA HUMMELS HELD OPEN THE door of Bernie's Bar as one student helped another to make it through.

'Sure you can get him home all right?' she asked.

'We live just round the corner,' the boy snuffled.

Once they'd left, she closed the door and locked it.

'Why didn't you let me throw him out?' asked Eddie, the other bartender at Bernie's. They took turns at covering the day shift, with the older, more alcoholic clientele; but evenings, when the students drank there, they were both on duty.

'It was his birthday,' said Liza.

'Everyone has a birthday,' said Eddie.

'Yes, but this guy found out today that he failed the same exam for the third time.'

Eddie shook his head and buttoned up his jacket. 'OK if you . . .?'

'I'll do the till,' said Liza. They both knew she did the till. On the odd occasion Liza had to stay at home because her boy was sick the whole thing ended up such a mess it left her with twice as much work to sort it all out when she came back the next day. So the routine was that Eddie always asked before he left.

She switched the usual playlist with its permanent hit parade for the Delines' 'Calling In'. She always played it after she closed up. Once somebody asked if that was her singing, some guy who obviously thought she and Amy Boone sounded the same. Liza swayed about behind the counter as she did the takings. Bernie's – which wasn't Bernie's, there was no Bernie, just three sisters who'd inherited the bar – wasn't doing all that well, that was pretty obvious. While the other bars in the neighbourhood decorated and worked hard to attract the students, Bernie's banked everything on minimalist maintenance, low outgoings and lower prices. But the combination of shabby location and shabby clientele had given the place a rock-bottom image, which deterred everyone except those with the least money. That didn't make it a customer profile impossible to make money from, and Liza had her own ideas on how to make Bernie's a bar that was both cheap *and* cool and could attract the alternative section of the student population. These would in turn attract the straight, monied crowd who liked to hang out with the cool artist types in the belief that this made them that bit cooler themselves. It was the same pattern as in uptown; first came the bohemians, attracted by low property prices, and the straights followed them. The sisters had listened when Liza voiced her thoughts, but when it came to funding the small investments such a change would have necessitated they backed off. It was frustrating, and every once in a while it occurred to Liza to make them an outrageously low offer and take over the bar herself. Put her ideas into action. Make some money for once. Buy Bernie's cheap and sell it at a profit. Because once the straights started arriving it would need to be sold pretty quickly. When the straights moved into uptown and drove up standards and prices, they also drove the bohemian element out. The same thing would happen with Bernie's, it was just a question of selling before the buyer understood that within another year or two Bernie's would once again stop being the cool place to hang out.

Yes, yes, a fun way to pass the time, thinking thoughts like these when the days – like today – dragged by.

Liza called her sister's number.

'Hi, Jennifer. Soon finished here. Is he sleeping?'

'Like an angel.'

'Any dinner left?'

'It's in the refrigerator. But hurry up, they've changed the timetable again and my last bus goes just before midnight.'

'Oops, then I better catch an earlier bus myself. See you.'

Liza hurriedly put the evening's takings away in the safe and turned off all the lights, the clearing up could wait until tomorrow. She put her jacket on, turned on the alarm, knew it would hurt her hip but ran for the bus anyway. Got there just in time to see it pull away from the stop and disappear into the night.

'Shit!' she said loudly and pulled out her phone.

'Second that,' said a voice.

She looked up.

A man stood leaning against a Ford parked by the sidewalk. She recognised the coat before she recognised the rest of him.

'Second what?' she said.

'It's shit. I second that opinion.'

'What is?' she said without interest as she scrolled back to her sister's name.

'Most of it, I'm guessing.'

'Like just missing a bus?'

'No, right there we're lucky.'

'We are?'

'I can drive you to wherever you want to go.'

She looked up from the phone. He had a bump on his forehead but seemed to have sobered up from earlier in the day.

'Thanks but no thanks,' she said. 'What are you doing here?'

'I'm waiting for you.'

She felt something stir inside her, a memory, an old fear that had never quite died away. 'Because?'

'Because I want to apologise.'

'Apologise for what?'

'For being an asshole.'

'You weren't an asshole.'

'No?'

'You paid up and you didn't start a fight with anyone. So in my book that's not being an asshole.'

He smiled. 'OK, maybe I *wasn't* an asshole, but I still *am* an asshole. It's more or less a constant. So I'm apologising for that, at least.'

To her surprise, Liza noticed that both his words and his smile of resignation made her feel calmer. Maybe he wasn't what you would call handsome, but he wasn't bad-looking either when he smiled. Charm. Yes, a certain charm. Maybe it had been there earlier too, but her radar for things like that was turned off when she was working behind the bar.

'Anyway,' he said as he straightened up from the car. 'Can an asshole make amends today by offering to drive you somewhere, Liza?'

He must have noticed that she hesitated slightly, because the next moment he opened the passenger door for her with an exaggeratedly gallant gesture.

She laughed drily. 'After the conversation we had what makes you think I'd dare take you up on your offer?'

'Your gut feeling when it comes to people,' said the man. Bob. She didn't know why she remembered the name. Probably because it was short. She glanced up and down the street. Not a taxi in sight, and if she waited for the next bus her sister wouldn't make it for hers. She felt the old fear. It was speaking to her, but in a low voice. And she had gathered from the phone call she overheard at the bar that he was a policeman.

'OK,' she said. 'But no funny business.'

He showed her his open palms and backed away smiling round the car.

'Well?' he said, after she'd given him the address and they had passed the first set of traffic lights on the road south in a strange but not actually embarrassing silence.

'Well what?'

'What's on your mind?'

'I thought you were the one who had something on your mind.'

'Shoe is on the other foot now. I'm your driver and your *confidant*.'

She smiled. 'What if I don't have any issues?'

'Oh but you have some, my lady.'

'Oh yeah? Such as what?'

'You're tough, but you were afraid when I said I'd been waiting for you. You work behind that bar and it hides your limp, but you can't hide it when you run. You probably have trouble making a commitment because you're afraid of being let down again.'

She sighed.

'Am I wrong?' said Bob.

'I guess not, I'm just so tired of men who think a superficial psychoanalysis is the way to a woman's heart. And the zip on her pants.'

They drove on in a silence that was now slightly more oppressive. Liza noticed the plaster on the knuckles of his hand on the steering wheel.

'Do you always give your suitors such a hard time?' he asked.

Liza sighed again. 'Is that what this is? You're paying court to me? And if so, then do you always stalk your victims?'

She saw that she had hurt him and regretted what she'd just said. Why could she never just leave it? The guy was driving her home, his woman had just dumped him, and he was looking for some comfort. How difficult could it be for her – *especially* for her – to understand that?

The radio was playing low. Emmylou Harris's version of Springsteen's 'Tougher Than the Rest'. A playlist from his own phone maybe. OK, so he got bonus points for that.

'All right then,' she said. 'My son's father up and left me. I developed a rare illness, one that eats up the bones. It took parts of my hip and no one believed I would ever walk again. He just couldn't handle looking after a newborn baby and a disabled wife and away he ran. Not hard to understand.'

'But not to forgive and forget, maybe?'

Liza looked out the window. She hoped it would rain soon. She'd always liked the rain, didn't know why. Maybe it was the country blood in her. Maybe it had something to do with purification. And maybe it was just because she liked the rain.

'You're right, a stalker tried to rape me when I was thirteen years old.' She took a deep breath. 'So three out of three. Congratulations.'

Silence. Just Emmylou.

'D'you want to talk about –'

'No,' she interrupted.

'– something more pleasant?'

They drove.

She started to laugh. He glanced over at her and then he began to laugh too.

'Screwed-up people,' she murmured, and he turned up the music, another woman, singing about could you please stop your whining and laugh instead. And Liza began her story. Not much of it, not the whole story, just stuff about her childhood and her parents. A typical white middle-class family facing the future and optimistic about the eighties, and then the shit hits the fan.

'My father lost his job. We had to move to somewhere cheaper, a place where the neighbours didn't go out to work but got as much in social security cheques as my father did for breaking his back in all those casual jobs he took. He told me he had to use all the money they'd been saving to send me to college, because I was bright, you know. Instead we lost everything, while the rich got richer. And no one seems to know just exactly how it happened.'

'Then other people began making cars that weren't just cheaper than ours, they were better than ours too.'

'Could be. My father says that people like us were once the backbone of this country but now we're the crap in the middle, not lucky enough to get rich but still too proud to live off welfare. He's voting for Donald Trump, he says.'

'And you?'

She shrugged. 'I suppose I could vote for Trump, but he just makes me puke. I'm not too crazy about Hillary Clinton either, but maybe it is time for a woman to take over.'

Then they were there. He parked outside her house, and to Liza it seemed the journey hadn't really been all that long.

The police officer leaned forward and looked up at the house. 'Looks cosy.'

'I dated this guy from Tennessee who said that back where he comes from it's what they call a *shotgun shack.*'

'Oh yeah?'

'A house so small you could stand in the doorway and empty both barrels through the window at the other end.'

'That I would like to see.'

'I'm not inviting you in if that's what you think.'

'No, I didn't mean it like that.'

'OK.'

'So he had no staying power?'

'Who? The Tennessee guy?' She grinned. 'I was the one that jumped ship there. He believed in UFOs, and that it was fake news about the world being round. Those two things together were just a little bit too bizarre for me.'

They laughed.

'Some people are just screwed up,' he said, again with that sad smile she suspected was something he deliberately used on women.

'How'd you get the bump on your forehead?' she asked.

He raised his hand as though to hide it, the same way her sister automatically did whenever Liza asked about her most recent bruise or black eye.

'I let a guy hit me so I could beat him up,' said Bob. He sneaked a glance at her, as though checking to see how she took this.

'I see. And what happened to him?'

'I think they took him to hospital. If my colleagues hadn't stopped me, I believe I might even have killed him.'

'Jesus. What had he done?'

'He complained that I'd fucked his wife.'

Liza didn't respond.

'I have an anger management problem,' said Bob. 'And I have . . . other problems too.'

'O . . . K . . .' she said, drawing out the syllables.

'Here is when I ask if you'd like to meet for a coffee one day,' he said. 'And you should answer no.'

'Then I say no.'

He nodded. 'Smart girl. Sleep tight.'

'You too.' She opened the car door. Was about to step out. Stopped. 'Hey.'

'Yeah?'

'You shouldn't try to just fuck her out of your head. Your ex, I mean.'

He licked his lips, as though tasting the thought. 'You sure about that?'

'Yes. You shouldn't drag other people down with you when you're sinking.'

She could see he was about to say something, try to be funny. But then it was as though he felt a sudden jolt and his face twisted in pain. That was definitely not something he used on women, and she felt an urge to reach out and stroke the bruise on his forehead. Instead she climbed out of the car. Then turned back to look inside.

'Thanks for the ride, Bob.'

'Well, thank *you*. See you soon.'

'OK. But not . . .'

'Not?'

'I meant what I said about not meeting for a coffee. All right? I don't want any campaign.'

He gave a big smile. 'I hear you, Liza.'

She shut the door and headed up toward the house. Knew he was watching her. Then she heard the car drive off.

12

HANSON, OCTOBER 2016

AFTER SAYING GOODNIGHT TO KJOS, Olav Hanson crossed the parking lot. Looked at his watch, a present from a time long gone. Already he regretted drinking those three beers. Or had it been four? In the first place there was the risk of being stopped, and he knew that one day he would meet some keen young policeman who would not be influenced by the fact that the man in the car he stopped was a fellow officer. There was a new generation coming up now, one that didn't respect the old rules. In the second place, Violet would moan. Women were like dogs, the smaller they were, the more noise they made. But then Violet was one of the reasons he needed these few hours to himself after work, either in a bar or down by the river with his fishing rod. How come he'd ended up with her? Shouldn't he have seen the warning signs when she said straight out she wouldn't have

Sean – Olav's adult son from his first marriage – in the house? She hadn't been willing to listen to Olav's explanation that Sean had certain difficulties, she made him choose, her or his son, no discussion. So he'd made his choice. The wrong one. The way he'd got it wrong twice, with two different women. As he walked along Olav had to laugh. Bad choices, wasn't that the story of his life? With the start in life he had he should have owned the world by now. If not for a bad knee and a wrong choice made over thirty years ago now. He'd never been caught, but there had been rumours back then. Enough that it was convenient to hop over him the next time a pawn was due for promotion.

Then, of course, it was more opportune to give a hand up to someone like Kay Myers. Female, black, probably lesbian too – the bosses could tick all the diversity boxes there. Diversity, *my ass*, meaning that now white, heterosexual men had to work twice as hard to achieve the same results. But that wasn't what had tripped up Olav Hanson, he'd done that himself. And everything was down to a single moment of weakness, one single bad decision taken thirty years earlier. Did he regret it? Of course he did, but once you've let the genie out of the bottle . . . Sure, he'd got out before the train really left the tracks. And in days to come there would be times when he regretted that too. Regretted not going down in style. Instead, the daily regret and the humiliation of suspicion and the bitterness consumed him, reducing the giant he'd once been to a man whom even a hag like his wife thought she could talk down to.

Olav pulled out the keys to the Ford Mustang. Not that they would help him find a car that was so old you still had to use a key to lock it and start it. Back when he'd bought it and paid in cash it had been a beauty. Back in the days when he could pay for dinners and holidays, and Violet thought he was a helluva guy.

A figure ghosted out from between two cars.

Die Man.

That was Olav's immediate response when he saw the hoodie. In the days when he was on patrol, a hood was always reason enough to stop someone, and surprisingly often it resulted in illegal weapons, narcotics or someone they were looking for. Only when he saw the glint of a knife did Olav start to doubt that he was seeing Die Man. And his mistake was confirmed – fortunately for him – when he heard the trembling voice:

'Give me your money!'

The voice was that of a boy, and he was standing so far away he would have had to take at least two steps before he could use the knife. Die Man would never have sent a frightened amateur out without a gun.

'Easy now, got my wallet here,' said Olav as he dug his hand in under his jacket. The boy didn't protest. Olav pulled the SIG Sauer P320 out of its shoulder holster and levelled it at him.

'Don't move or I'll kill you,' he said calmly but very clearly. In his experience, use of the simple, precise word 'kill' had a more powerful effect than any macho stuff about 'blowing your brains out' and other such euphemisms.

The figure twitched. Flight mechanism – the fight reflex had already disappeared.

He stayed where he was. The freeze alternative had triumphed.

Definitely an amateur. A pro would know the chances of someone bothering to shoot a fleeing would-be robber in the back, someone armed only with a knife, were minimal.

'I'm a police officer,' said Olav. He pulled his jacket aside with his free hand to let the boy see the badge on his belt. 'Drop the knife and raise your arms up in the air. Do it quickly, because I still feel like killing you.'

The boy did as Olav said, and Olav felt something he hadn't felt for years. A combination of excitement and calm. Of control in a critical situation. Of mastery. That was what he had been so good at, on the football field, on patrol, and in his first years as a homicide detective. Too good, perhaps. He had started to believe he could control everything.

The knife clinked against the asphalt and when the boy raised his arms above his head his hood slid down. Olav nearly jumped. Not just because the kid was so young, but because for a fraction of a second he reminded him of Sean. Sure, the kid was younger, and he was black, but the next thought came along just the same. That it could have been Sean standing in this kid's shoes. That he could only hope Sean hadn't already made the wrong choice, like the one the kid standing in front of him had made this evening. The boy's lower lip was quivering, as though this was a result, a defeat, that didn't come as any surprise. How old could he be? Sixteen? Seventeen? Alone, in a world of gangs, armed with a knife in a world of guns, still an amateur when kids of fourteen already had three or four shootings behind them. It was probably not the first criminal act the boy had committed, but perhaps the first robbery, it almost looked that way. And in doing so he had taken that decisive step into a world in which he did not belong, but one in which the door would slam shut behind him. The one wrong choice he would have to look back on for the rest of his life. Unlikely maybe, but not unthinkable either.

'What's your name?' asked Olav.

The boy stopped staring at the gun and looked up at him and said nothing.

'Your first name'll do,' said Olav.

The boy swallowed. 'Elliot,' he said, a sob in his throat.

'OK, now listen here, Elliot. What do you need money for?'

'Need?'

'Is it for dope? Or for your sick mother?'

'For shoes,' said the boy.

'Shoes?'

'New Nike shoes.'

Olav wasn't shocked. He gave an exasperated sigh. 'How much do they cost?'

'Cost?'

'Roughly?'

'Two hundred and forty-one dollars.'

'OK,' said Olav. He pulled out his wallet, wondering whether he was about to make yet another wrong choice. He lowered the gun and counted out the notes. 'Here's two hundred, it's all I have. Is that enough to . . .?'

The boy nodded hesitantly. He looked as though he was wondering what kind of trap he was being lured into.

'All I ask is that you promise me . . . or no, that you promise yourself one thing. That this is the one mistake you get away with. Like a mulligan in golf, get me?'

Olav saw that the boy didn't understand. He held out the money to him.

'Go buy yourself those shoes, Elliot. But every time you lace them up I want you to think that you got them so you could run from the life that's chasing behind you. And I hope you win, boy.'

Elliot grabbed the notes and the next moment was gone in the darkness.

Olav stayed where he was. He could hear himself panting

and guessed that his pulse was racing faster than he realised. He knew he could never tell Violet what had just happened. She wouldn't understand, she'd say he threw his money away, even rewarded a criminal for being just that. Nor could Olav explain to her that he'd been thinking of Sean, and that maybe the world would reward his action by giving his own son another chance. She would have laughed herself sick, and Olav hated, *hated* that laughter.

13

RADICA 20Q, OCTOBER 2016

BOB DROVE AIMLESSLY. TURNED OFF his playlist. He was sick to death of it. It had been on repeat for too long, just the same way he had. The radio was tuned to a heavy rock station and the singer was reeling off the usual brain-dead, aggressive clichés. This time about a guy whose woman had left him. He cruises the highway, horny as a dog, he'll burn a house down if it gets in his way, got his woman by the throat, smashed up her face.

'That was Ted Nugent with "Stranglehold",' the DJ said, with the obligatory heavy rocker's crunch in his voice. 'And rejoice, people – in just four days the NRA's annual conference gets under way right here in our very own Minneapolis, and Nugent is gonna be there!'

'Along with sixty thousand others,' said his sidekick. 'I think it's very generous of the NRA to hold their conference here with the strict gun control legislation we have in this state. In other states you can at least buy yourself a machine gun!'

Laughter.

'I'm reading the programme here and there's going to be seminars, meetings, displays of marksmanship and exhibitions of handguns. What d'you think, Phil, think Kevin Patterson will be handling the display of marksmanship?'

'I hope not, Otis. But on Saturday our esteemed mayor Kevin Patterson himself will be opening the conference at the US Bank Stadium. If you want to get tickets, may we recommend that you . . .'

Bob switched off the radio. Took a deep breath. And had an idea: that if he put his foot down now and waited till the speedometer showed a hundred before closing his eyes then he wouldn't have to face another day. He pushed the thought away, but he was shaken. It wasn't the first time he had thought about taking his own life, but it was the first time the thought hadn't immediately frightened him instead of seeming almost tempting. Well, OK, now he was scared by the fact that he hadn't been scared. He sat up straight in his car. He had to do something. The bar lady had been right. He had to change tack.

Bob reached out and turned on the radio again.

Tried to focus his thoughts. Tomás Gomez. The apartment. Why did he keep returning to the apartment? Was there something he'd seen there, something his subconscious had noticed but which hadn't managed to make it to the surface? He went over the details one by one. The couch. The cupboards. The syringe. The bathroom. The cat. The neighbours. No, that wasn't it. Was it the smell? The decor? No, not that either. It was something about . . . the whole thing. Or the emptiness. It reminded him of something. What was it?

It was past one as Bob slowly cruised the nocturnal silence of the Phillips streets. Passed the tiny, one-storey houses. Some shacks, some with boarded-up windows, but also well-maintained houses behind newly painted white fences and notices with 'We care' on them. Realtors trying to tempt buyers from out of town liked to stress how central Phillips was, how many parks it had, how it was one of the most ethnically diverse neighbourhoods in the city, housing immigrants from all over the world. They never wrote about how poor Phillips was, how many criminal gangs there were, and that after sunset the parks turned into no-go areas and that on Bloomington Avenue, with drug dealers standing in front of every second house, the inhabitants had to clear their lawns of hypo needles before they could mow them. Bob cruised past a dealer's team now, on Bloomington and 29th Street. An ethnic trinity, like a Benetton advert, one black, one white and one brown, those realtors were as good as their word. The three watched him as he cruised by. Two were just teenagers, but the third, a Latino with a porkpie hat, looked nearer thirty. On the house wall above them was some graffiti, the symbol for X-11.

Bob pulled up at the kerb and got out. Breathed in the good, sharp night air. Passed through the gate to a two-storey brick-built house that was squeezed in between all the other single-storey buildings, let himself in to the two-room apartment he rented and tried to ignore the rancid smell that had been there since before he moved in. He hung up his coat and jacket behind the door without turning on the light. He hadn't been living here long enough to be able to filter out the regular noises, and tonight they came from both the flat above and the one on the adjoining wall. Quarrelling from above, hip hop with a juddering bass from the left. In the bathroom he could hear his neighbours even better, the pipes carrying the sounds. He splashed his face with cold water and studied the bump on his forehead while brushing his teeth. The bruise was already turning blue, and in the course of the night the colour would hopefully become even more pronounced. He opened the mirrored door to the bathroom cabinet. Took down a pink tray of pills. It was unopened and he noticed from the date that he hadn't taken one since July. He weighed it in his hand. Hesitated. Then put the tray back, went into the bedroom, lay down on the bed in the dark. Took down a plastic ball the size of a baseball from the shelf behind the bed. It was an electric toy, a Radica 20Q. You ask it something specific and then tap in Yes or No answers to the twenty questions that appear in the small display window. Nine times out of ten it would know whether you were lying. In Bob's case ten times out of ten, because the answer was always 'ex-girlfriend'. He made up his mind to think of something else and chose 'suicide'. Radica 20Q gave up after twenty questions. Bob suspected that the word had been omitted at the programming stage.

He listened to the sound of Phillips. Laughter out in the streets, an angry cry, glass breaking, a car engine revving. Neighbours you never heard during the daytime. Behind the quarrelling of the adults he heard a young girl crying. The sound was faint, at the same time so distinct as to drown out all the others. Yes, he wanted out, to get away from this life, from Bob Oz. But would he give them that satisfaction? No, not yet. He would change tack. Change channels. Change focus, name, the date, himself, life. But more than the future he wanted to change the past. Not all of it, just his. Because the past is everything. Didn't someone once say that?

He unbuttoned his shirt and as he was pulling off his pants felt something in the pocket and took it out. A business card. Mike Lunde – Taxidermist. He thought of that canary. What kind of people have their pets stuffed?

Bob Oz closed his eyes, took a deep breath and steeled himself for another sleepless night. And as he lay there it finally floated up to the surface. What it was that Tomás Gomez's apartment reminded him of. It was this. His own apartment. The emptiness was the same.

14

DOWNTOWN, SEPTEMBER 2022

I STAND WITH MY FACE pressed against the display window and peer into Town Taxidermy. In the darkened interior of the store I can just make out a bear standing up on two legs and a deer with a massive set of antlers. The store doesn't open for another hour, but the arrangement I have with the owner isn't even for today, I just wanted to have a look since I was driving past.

It strikes me that it's such an odd profession, to recreate something that once was. Although actually, a few months ago, when I spoke to the taxidermist who runs the place, he insisted that what he did was not recreate but *create* something. That it isn't an actual recreation but a fiction. Something that tells a story by putting it in a certain context in which it can be *felt*, and for that reason can sometimes feel truer than the cold, isolated facts do.

And that was when it struck me that this is precisely what I'm doing in this book I'm writing. I'm a taxidermist.

15

TAXIDERMY, OCTOBER 2016

THE TIME WAS 9 A.M. and Bob was standing in a narrow street in downtown. He looked at the sign above the store doorway.

Town Taxidermy.

In the display window a black bear stood upright on two legs, and around it, like courtiers, a gathering of birds and various rodents, which, Bob assumed, formed part of the local fauna.

As he entered a bell over the door jingled feebly. But once it stopped, and the door had closed behind him, he noticed how quiet it was. Quieter than simply soundless. Quiet as the grave, he thought, as he looked around at the bodies of the silent animals. A hart, a lynx. A wolverine with bared teeth. Several birds. As far as he could tell they were perfect copies of the original living beings they once had been. He stopped before each one in turn. How lifelike they were. As though they all had a story to tell. So unlike the corpses he was used to seeing. Murder victims with expressions of fear, perhaps, or pain, but who otherwise hid more than they revealed, holding on to secrets it was his job to wrest from them. Bob stood contemplating an owl that returned his gaze. And it occurred to him that the silence in here wasn't oppressive at all, it was . . . restful. Liberating. Balm for the ears and the soul.

'Good morning.' A smiling man with a laurel wreath of hair surrounding a bare dome emerged from a doorway, in the act of removing a pair of latex gloves. 'Sorry to keep you waiting, I was in the middle of something rather complicated in the workshop.'

'Quite all right,' said Bob. 'Mike Lunde?'

'That's right.'

Bob showed him his ID.

'That was quick, I must say, Detective . . .' He leaned closer and read the name aloud: '. . . Oz?'

'My great-grandfather's adaptation of his Norwegian name. A-a-s-s. The pronunciation is the same. At least it is according to our Norwegian relatives.'

'That's correct. Two A's in Norwegian are pronounced like an A with a hoop on top of it. *Å*.'

'You speak Norwegian?'

'No, no.' Mike Lunde laughed and shook his head. 'I learned that about the *Å* from my grandfather.'

'I see. Well, of course, my great-grandfather couldn't have known that Frank Baum would one day write a kids' book about a wizard.'

'Precisely. But I don't suppose that was the worst name you could be called as a child?'

'The wizard of Oz? Better than the alternative, I guess. The wizard of ass would have been harder to shake off.'

Mike Lunde laughed heartily. There was something melodic and disarming in the sound. Perhaps because of the silence of all the animals, it made Bob think of birdsong in a vast forest.

'I'm here about a customer of yours, Tomás Gomez,' said Bob. 'I found your card in his apartment yesterday. A neighbour of his, a Mrs White, said she had recommended you to Gomez.'

'Ah, I see,' said the taxidermist. 'I thought you were here because of my phone call.'

'Your phone call?'

'I saw in the morning newspaper that you were looking for Tomás Gomez. So I rang the police and left a message. A . . . eh, a tip-off, isn't that what it's called? That was just . . .' He looked at his watch. 'Two hours ago. That was what I meant about being quick.'

'If it was about Gomez then it probably didn't get through to us at Homicide, it probably went to Aggravated Assault, because the victim didn't actually die. What did you say in your message?'

'That Tomás Gomez has an order here waiting to be picked up. A cat.'

'I see. Anything else?'

'Anything else?'

'Anything else you can tell us about Tomás Gomez?'

'What might that be?'

Bob didn't respond but just looked at Lunde. He had taken a spontaneous liking to the man. There was something straightforward and natural about him. The type who calls the police because it's the right thing to do. But it was also evident that he wasn't telling Bob everything. He continued to hold Lunde's blue eyes and let the silence work for him. Watching for signs of stress. But Lunde seemed unaffected by the silence. And when he finally did speak, he did so in a calm, assured voice:

'I had no idea he was going to shoot someone, if that's what you mean. If, that is, Tomás really is the one who shot this other person.'

Bob nodded. He studied the owl. The feathers looked so vivid and the eyes so lifelike he wouldn't have been all that surprised if the bird had suddenly taken off from the pedestal on which it stood. 'So you know Tomás Gomez? As more than a customer, I mean?'

'What makes you say that?'

'Tomás Gomez is a very common name. There was no photograph or drawing in the newspaper, and yet you knew that the man in question must be your Tomás Gomez. You call in with information, but now you express doubt about whether it really was Gomez who did the shooting. And you referred to him by his first name just now.'

The taxidermist rubbed his chin. 'My wife always tells me I'm a terrible liar. She says I should practise more.' He gave a resigned smile. 'So yes, I do know Tomás as rather more than just an ordinary customer.'

'Why didn't you say so straight away?'

Mike Lunde sighed. 'I thought it would be enough if I did my civic duty and reported something I supposed would be relevant to the case.'

'So he's a friend?'

'Not a friend. I . . .'

'Yes?'

'I like to get to know a bit about my customers. See what it is they want when they come here. What it is they're really looking for. Even when they're not entirely clear about it themselves.'

'And what is Tomás Gomez really looking for?'

Lunde moved his hand and started rubbing his neck. 'It's rather a long story, Detective Oz.' He gave the name its correct Norwegian pronunciation. 'One that he told me in all confidence. And one which I doubt would bring you any closer to your goal.'

'Let me be the judge of that, Lunde.'

'Of course, but should I not make my own judgement too? I accept that one has a civic duty to provide the police with information that can help them catch dangerous criminals, but I have to weigh that up against the fact that what Tomás Gomez told me about himself he told me on the understanding that it would remain between us.'

'To the best of my knowledge taxidermists are not bound by any oath of confidentiality, Mr Lunde. And we have an innocent man fighting for his life in a hospital bed.' Bob saw no indication that Lunde saw through the untruth. 'Have you any idea where Tomás Gomez might be?'

'I have his address in Jordan. That was how I knew it had to be the Tomás Gomez referred to in the newspaper. But I presume he isn't there now.'

'No.'

'Then beyond that I haven't a clue as to where he might be, alas. Or fortunately.'

'Fortunately?'

Mike Lunde sighed again, raised a glove to dust off the owl's beak. 'I'm in a dilemma here. I must confess I did consider not calling the police.'

'Why?'

'Because I like to think he's a good man.'

'A good man doesn't try to kill people.'

'That's a valid objection.'

'And yet you did call us, Mr Lunde. So that must mean that you understand Gomez *has* to be arrested.'

'Oh indeed yes. The trouble is, one's intellect and one's feelings aren't always in agreement with each other.'

'Well, we certainly can't let our feelings decide.' Bob took out his notebook. 'What can you tell us?'

'Hm. Are you so sure about that, Oz?'

Bob looked up. 'That we can't let our feelings decide?'

'Yes. Can you be sure it isn't the feelings that decide, and that we afterward employ our intellect to rationalise the choice to the point at which we believe it was actually the intellect that made the decision?'

'I'm pretty sure about that, yeah.'

'Yes, you do look pretty sure of yourself.' Lunde smiled. 'The first time Tomás Gomez came here was three months ago. He wanted to have his cat stuffed.'

'It was . . . eh, dead?'

Lunde gave a short laugh. 'Yes. It's in the freezer in the basement if you want to look. Sickness, so natural causes.'

'And?'

'He could not afford to pay what I charge for such a job.'

'Are you very expensive?'

'That depends.'

'On the animal? A canary can't cost all that much.'

'On the customer. If it concerns a pet that was very dear to them then I have to lower my price.'

'So you dropped your price. Feelings took priority over common sense?'

'Perhaps, but I still have to make a living. Six months ago I received a large, lucrative commission which has led to me putting everything else aside while I finish it, so hopefully I'm not too naive. Anyway, the result is that Mr Gomez has had to wait.'

'When was the last time you were in contact with him?'

'I'll need to check in my diary.'

'What about the call log on your phone?'

'We've never spoken on the phone – I don't know whether he has one. Just a moment.'

Lunde disappeared, and again Bob Oz was struck by the silence. Why did he like it so much? Was it the feeling of time standing still, of discovering a moment in which it moved neither forward nor backward, in which nothing happens? In which everything feels safe?

Lunde returned. He was now wearing a small pair of glasses perched on the tip of his nose as he peered down into a book bound in brown leather. 'Now let's see . . .'

'Mind if I tape this, for the record?'

'Of course. The taxidermy of the word.'

'Sorry?'

'I visited Tomás Gomez on October 7.'

'You *visited* him?'

'He invited me for some of his home-made chilli con carne. It was extremely tasty.'

'Do you usually visit your customers' homes?'

'Not always, but if possible I like to see where my work will be displayed. To see what sites are available and find out which spots the pet frequented, how my customers were used to seeing the animal. It can be useful in deciding the ultimate pose of the finished piece. And the lighting is important. Enough to highlight the details, not so much that the work fades.'

'You take this extremely seriously?'

Lunde looked at Bob over the top of his glasses. 'I try to take it every bit as seriously as my customers do. I feel it's something I owe them. But of course –' he smiled wryly – 'it has happened that sometimes I take things a little *more* seriously than my customers. So I need to listen.' He flipped on through his diary. 'By that time we had had three . . . no, four meetings in the store, I see here.'

'And you did what? The cat still being in the freezer, I mean.'

'What I said.'

'What you said?'

'I listened.'

Bob Oz nodded slowly. 'To what he had to say about the cat?'

'To what he had to say.'

Bob put down his pen. 'And what did he say? People I've spoken to already have told me Tomás Gomez was the taciturn type.'

Lunde shrugged. 'It took a while. But in the end, everybody talks.'

'Oh really? Why don't they do that with me?'

Lunde smiled. 'Perhaps because they know you only want to hear one thing: the confession. Gomez told me that he and his family came here to Minneapolis as illegal immigrants from the south.'

Bob picked up his pen again. 'So he has family? Do you have names and addresses?'

'He *had* a family. Even though both Gomez and his wife were university-educated they didn't have much money. They lived in a tiny house in Phillips West and were eating out when two gangs began shooting at each other inside the restaurant. Teenagers with guns. His wife tried to cover the little boy on the floor while Tomás headed for the exit with his daughter, she was in a wheelchair. He got her outside and almost to shelter behind a car when two of the boys came out and shot Tomás in the foot. He fell, and the next bullet, meant for him, instead hit the back of the wheelchair. By that time his son and wife had already been executed. The boys were on their way to deal with Tomás, who was trying to drag himself over to his daughter, when the first police car arrived, and they ran off. The daughter died in her father's arms.'

Bob felt a sudden pain in his jaw and realised that he had clenched his teeth.

'The police later told Tomás that gangs usually only shoot at each other.'

Bob put a finger on his cheek next to his jaw and pressed hard. 'That's correct. As a rule they aren't bothered about witnesses either.'

'Tomás asked what did I think, why had they shot his family.'

'And what did you say?'

'I told him the truth, that I didn't know. What do *you* think, Detective Oz?'

Bob watched through the window as a couple passed arm in arm, her with her head on his shoulder, and it took a moment for him to shake off a memory.

'It's a question of numbers,' said Bob. 'They have shit jobs as foot soldiers for the Black Wolves, X-11 or another of these gangs where they get paid three dollars an hour for standing on street corners getting their balls frozen off selling crack and meth. One in four of them is going to get killed on the job. So it's about moving up the system, becoming a runner, a security chief or a banker for the outfit, straight away you're earning ten times as much and you've got a much better chance of surviving. But to get there you have to be noticed. And the quickest way to be noticed is to show you're willing to kill.'

'Interesting. And this you know from your own experience?'

'I know because I read it in an article about the economics of the narcotics trade.'

'I see. So it was simply a matter of economics?'

'Economics and incentives. Morality is about how we want the world to function, economics is about how it actually does function.'

Lunde nodded.

'You look as though you don't agree,' said Bob and glanced down at his notes.

'You probably want to hear more about Gomez?'

'There's no hurry as long as we have no idea where he is. Go ahead.'

'Right. Well, I think they shoot because they can. Because they recognise no limits. And they have these incredible weapons. Because it feels *good* to shoot, doesn't it?'

Bob Oz coughed. 'Dunno. I don't shoot. Did he mention any other family or friends, here or elsewhere?'

Lunde shook his head. 'Only that his parents live south of the border.'

'What does he live off?'

'Casual work. An education from his own country is no use to him when he doesn't have the necessary residence permit.'

'Can you recall the names of any employers?'

'I'm sorry, we didn't talk about things like that, about . . . about our everyday lives. I remember only that he said the longest he had worked at the same place was two months.'

'Maybe the reason he didn't want to talk about his everyday life was that he made his money working for X-11,' said Bob Oz.

The man in front of him wrinkled his brow in disbelief.

'I spoke to the doctor who writes his insulin prescriptions and he told me that Gomez had an X-11 gang tattoo on his back.'

'But that's . . . ridiculous,' said Lunde.

'Why so?'

'Because he told me that the boys who shot him and his daughter were wearing X-11 jackets.'

A sound cut through the silence. A solitary police siren that rose and fell somewhere out there. Bob checked his watch. 'Do you think he'll be coming back here, Lunde?'

'Maybe. I can't read people, but as long as his cat's here there's a chance. People who have lost loved ones often end up feeling closer to their pets.'

'Will you let me know if and when he does turn up?' Bob offered him his card. Lunde hesitated a moment, then took it.

'I do things slowly,' he said as he placed the card inside his diary. 'As you'll have noticed, I think slowly, and I talk slowly. So if he does show up, I might be a bit slow about calling you too.'

'But you will call?'

Mike Lunde nodded slowly. 'I guess I probably will, yes. This innocent man he shot . . .?'

'The name is Dante and he's a gun dealer in Jordan. Probably works with several gangs, but mostly the Black Wolves.'

'So he . . .'

'Yes, I lied, he probably has a few lives on his conscience.

Always assuming he has a conscience.' Bob pushed the notebook back into his pocket.

The bell above the door tinkled as Bob left. And jingled again when he came back in moments later.

'Yes?' said Mike Lunde, who was squatting in front of the wolverine with a spray.

'So then what did you talk about?'

'What did we talk about?'

'If you didn't talk about jobs, friends, family.'

Mike Lunde stopped spraying and looked up with a sad smile. 'We talked about loneliness.'

Bob Oz nodded.

As he emerged into the main road the sun was shining over the whole city.

16

ALICE, OCTOBER 2016

KAY MYERS STOOD IN THE doorway of an office that was being decorated. In her hand she was holding a coffee mug with I LOVE CHICAGO written on it. She watched the man painting the ceiling. He reminded her of a crime scene technician, masked and dressed in white. Maybe that was why she had decided she liked him even though they had only said 'Hi' to each other when she passed the office. He climbed down from his ladder and turned to her.

'It's going to be nice,' she said. 'You're good.'

The dark eyes behind the mask twinkled as though he was laughing. 'This is just a job. You should come see my art.'

She liked his deep, calm voice too.

'You paint . . . er, paintings?'

He shook his head. 'Not quite. I can show you.' He spoke with a very slight accent. She wondered how old he might be.

'OK,' she said and took a sip of her coffee. 'So you've got an exhibition?'

He laughed. 'Yes. Soon. Very soon.'

'Whereabouts?'

'Can't tell you yet. I'll let you know.'

Kay saw Bob enter the reception area and instead of taking the shortest route to his place he walked in her direction. He didn't look happy, and she figured it had something to do with what she'd heard about the previous evening.

'Hi, Bob. How're things?'

'I'll find out soon enough,' he said. 'Walker wants to see me.'

He carried on walking. She turned to the painter, but he was busy painting again. Kay sighed and went back to her desk.

'Tony Stärk has reported you for attacking him,' said Walker as he stood by the window with his back to Bob. Bob had worked out that this habit must have developed because the chief felt more comfortable talking to the view, or maybe his own reflection, than he did face-to-face with his own subordinates.

'Bullshit,' said Bob. 'It was self-defence. He was the one who attacked me. Take a look at me, chief.'

Walker turned reluctantly. He looked on indifferently as Bob pointed to the lump on his forehead which had now assumed the familiar blue colouring.

'Tony Stärk should be relieved I'm not fucking reporting him for violence against an officer in the performance of his duty. But if he doesn't withdraw his complaint then obviously that's what I'll do. If you tell him that then I think this case will just fade away.'

'Tell his lawyer, you mean? He is of the opinion that your professional status is irrelevant since his client came to see you as a private individual.'

'Tony Stärk came here to the Homicide Unit, chief.'

'Because you are no longer living at your registered address. The lawyer is claiming that you provoked his client to strike the first blow specifically so that you could then attack him without the risk of legal action. Tony Stärk hasn't any martial arts training or anything suggesting he's skilled in unarmed combat.'

'He weighs twice as much as me, chief.'

'The lawyer claims that the fact that it took three of your colleagues to pull you off him is proof enough of your use of excessive force. I've got statements from Olav Hanson and the others, and they confirm the lawyer's account of what happened. I'm sorry, Bob, but I'm going to have to suspend you while this matter is thoroughly investigated.'

'But –'

'No buts, Bob, my decision is made.'

Bob stared at Walker. The superintendent looked like a man who at that particular moment hated his job but had absolutely no intention of not doing it.

'You'll hear from me when we know more. In the meantime you'll have to hand over your ID and your service weapon. Plus the keys to your service car.' Walker coughed. 'I'm sorry.'

Bob opened his mouth and then closed it again. Wondered how things could have worked out any differently. *If* things could have worked out any differently. And even if he actually would have wanted them to. When you start falling into the abyss you might as well enjoy the free fall as best you can. He stuck his hand into the inside pocket of his cashmere coat and placed his ID card on the chief's desk. Followed by the car keys.

'You have a car of your own, right?' Walker sounded troubled. 'A Volvo?'

'Correct,' said Bob. 'But I don't have a gun, it's –'

'I know that.' Walker's voice was a little shaky. 'I know that when something like that happens it can make a father hate his own service weapon.'

Bob looked at his boss. Was the bastard standing there *empathising* with him? He felt the rushing sound start up in his head.

'That business with the gun,' said Walker, and had to clear his throat again. 'A thing like that can destroy a relationship. It happens time after time. It isn't anyone's fault, it's just the way we are as human beings. But you just have to accept it and move on.'

'What are we talking about now, chief?' Walker's features and his body, the features and body of a man Bob respected, some days you would even say liked, seemed to be changing before Bob's eyes into something reptilian and repulsive, the kind of thing that should be beaten to death with a stick.

'Alice,' said the reptile. 'It wasn't easy for her either. Forgive her, Bob. Let it go. If you don't you won't be able to move on. Perhaps you should look on this as a kind of holiday. Take the chance to think about what you want to do with your life.'

'Jesus,' said Bob. 'You're not only the superintendent, you're a psychologist too. Or is that just stuff they teach you on leadership courses?'

Bob saw Walker's jaw muscles tighten. 'I mean it, Oz. Take it easy. Free yourself. Move on.'

'On where?' Bob said loudly as he blinked away tears of rage. If there was an answer he never heard it, he'd already left the office without closing the door behind him. He didn't look either right or left but headed straight for the elevators, punched the button and waited. Turned, walked back through the office, registered that Hanson and Kjos weren't at their desks. He opened the bottom drawer of his desk and took out an old ID card he had reported as lost to the MDP, only to get a phone call two weeks later from a brunette in Near North who told him he'd left it behind in her apartment after using it to cut cocaine. She'd returned it to him in the post, and he'd hung on to it without telling anyone, on the principle that you never know.

Bob took a last look at his place of work.

Was there anything else here he might be needing?

His gaze took in the notes pinned to his desk divider.

Nothing. Absolutely nothing.

He hurried back to the elevators, changed his mind, retraced his steps and pulled out the pin holding the fixture list for the Vikings.

He reached the elevators just in time to see the doors sliding shut.

He felt a strange impulse to laugh as he slowly trudged down the stairs.

Exiting into the square in front of city hall he stopped, breathed in deeply, closed his eyes and summed things up. He was a man with no woman, no job and no car. In other words, he was finished. He tried to think. Then he headed off in the direction of the bank.

The Minneapolis communal impound yard was located at the roughest end of Colfax Avenue, with scrap-metal dealers and used-car sellers as its neighbours. Stella Cibulkova sat in the booth and checked the ID the man in the orange coat had just shown her.

She looked back at the computer screen where she'd typed in the number he'd given her.

'You are aware that there is 2,300 dollars owing on this vehicle, Mr Oz?'

'I confess I didn't realise it was quite so much.'

'That's not just the unpaid parking fines. It also includes reminder fees and the cost of keeping the car here for the past four weeks. This isn't a parking lot.'

'I know, but it's expensive, isn't it? Love your earrings, by the way.'

Stella looked up. The man smiled. She didn't smile. She rarely did at work. It didn't pay.

'If you want to take the car you have to settle up first.'

'Wouldn't have it any other way, Stella.'

Nor did she like the fact that they had to wear these name tags, as if she was a waitress in some restaurant.

'You can transfer –'

'You take cash, Stella?'

'Er, yes. In principle.'

The man produced a bundle of notes and began to lay them on the counter in front of her.

'I swear by paper, see. The paperless society, that isn't for me. The paperless marriage, for example. No, there's no obligation there, Stella. Too easy to just run from it all.'

The notes looked smooth and as if freshly ironed, as if they came straight from the bank. As he peeled off the fifty-dollar bills and laid them down he counted them off in a loud, steady voice. There was something about his voice, a wounded sensitivity that made her feel as though it was the last of his money he was laying down in front of her.

'Two thousand three hundred,' he announced finally as he looked down at the few notes that were left in his hand. Peeled off one last one and held it out to her with a broad smile.

'And this one is for you, Stella.'

Stella Cibulkova didn't smile at work. Not usually. But today she laughed.

Bob left the *Star Tribune* building carrying a paper mug of coffee and with today's newspaper under his arm. Got into the Volvo that was so illegally parked he'd left his ID card easily visible on the dashboard. Opened the paper. He'd read somewhere that the Situations Vacant column would soon be gone completely from the paper. It was bound to be true, he just didn't know if he believed it. The only police job vacancies he found were in neighbouring states, none of them detective level, naturally. He carried on looking, but after a while realised he wasn't taking in the words, that his thoughts were somewhere else completely. He was a cop. Had been all his life, never wanted to do anything else. He'd fulfilled that dream, even managed to join the Homicide Unit. He'd managed it, though it hadn't been easy. He was a good detective. Not brilliant, not the type with supernatural intuition or intelligence, not FBI material. But solid. Someone who made up for everything he lacked by never giving up. Now and then there had been friction with his bosses, of course, as when he couldn't let go of certain cases once other priorities had been announced. He didn't have the highest number of cases solved or even the highest-percentage success rate. But that was because he always angled to get himself the most difficult cases, the most time-consuming ones that often ended up being shelved. He had a few feathers in his cap, but a case being difficult didn't necessarily make it high-profile, and those were the ones his colleagues snapped up.

Bob took a sip of coffee. He had a car and a roof over his head, what more could a man need? Why does a man need a job when he doesn't have a family to look after? He folded the newspaper and put it down on the passenger seat. He could easily have picked up a *Star Tribune* somewhere else besides the paper's headquarters, but it was here he had come. He looked across to the far side of the little central park. The sun sparkled on the glass facade of the building housing Alice's psychology collective. How often had he stood in front of that entrance, waiting to pick her up on those bitterly cold winter days when you didn't want to use your bike or even wait for the bus? Or when it was dark. Not that Alice had a phobia about the dark – that would be him. That, and horror movies. She never tired of reminding him of the time he borrowed *Psycho* from a video store. It was soon after they'd met, and she'd told him she liked horror movies. They'd reached the scene where Lila Crane, to the accompaniment of hysterical violins, walks toward the back of the old woman in the rocking chair. Alice knew that Bob knew it was a mummified corpse sitting there because they had told each other they had both seen the movie before. But in the dark Alice saw Bob with his eyes tight shut. Later, when some friends were visiting, Alice told that story, and said that was the moment she knew she was in love with him.

Bob checked the time. How fucking slowly it crawled along. Maybe look for a bar?

Easy, easy, easy.

We talked about loneliness.

He looked at his phone. Made up his mind. Found the name and made the call.

'Hi, Rooble, Bob here.'

'Hi.'

'Listen, I'm really sorry I haven't managed to drop off that barbecue.'

'Forget it, Bob. Really. You're doing me a favour by hanging on to it.'

'You've got something there, I really ought to be charging. Our place isn't exactly a parking garage.'

Rooble laughed.

'Hey, just to satisfy my curiosity, how is the Gomez investigation coming along?'

'Not good,' said Rooble. 'It's like he's vanished into thin air, no trace at all.'

'Have you done anything else besides send out a BOLO?'

'We've spoken to everyone we know of who had some connection with him, but there aren't many. The janitor, landlord, neighbours. But they don't know much. Nothing, really.'

'Did you get Myers's report from the neighbour we spoke to?'

'Sure we did. But that didn't give us much either. It's never easy with people like Gomez who aren't registered anywhere. You don't find employers, relatives, school friends. Perfect situation for somebody working as a hit man, of course.'

'Good job he isn't then,' said Bob.

'You sure about that?'

'A hit man doesn't shoot his own neighbour. He doesn't miss. He doesn't leave the gun bag behind in the apartment along with a lot of technical traces.'

'You're right there, Bob. But vanishing completely the way he's done, that's pretty good.'

'To go missing for two days isn't difficult. Day three is when the planning has to start.'

'Just like you say, Bob.'

Rooble. Always diplomatic, always listening. Humble when it paid to be, firm when necessary. The boy would go far.

'I gotta go, Rooble. But can you keep me in the loop, d'you think?'

'On the Gomez case?'

'Yes. I've got a homicide that's similar, so I'm wondering if there might be a connection. Just call this number, I'm working mostly from home at the moment.'

'OK. Which homicide would that be?'

Bob hesitated.

'Good to know in case there's information there I can use,' Rooble added.

Bob hoped Rooble didn't notice the amount of time he needed before answering. 'It's on the Saint Paul border so there's some uncertainty about the jurisdiction. I'll let you know if I get the case.'

'OK,' said Rooble. 'Nice to talk to you, Bob. Say hello to Alice.'

They ended the call.

Bob glanced down at the newspaper, which was still open at the Situations Vacant column. He tore out the page, took a Swiss Army knife from the glove compartment, flipped open the little pair of scissors and started cutting the page into strips.

Alice stood by the window in the kitchen of the psychology collective. She'd made herself a cup of green tea and was looking down at the park. Her thoughts were still preoccupied with her last patient, a teenage girl with an eating disorder. The girl had made progress over the four years she'd been coming. And Alice had too; she no longer saw Frankie in every patient under twenty who entered her office and wondered what her daughter would have looked like now. Alice's gaze fell on a Volvo parked on the far side of the park. It was the colour, not the make, that awakened the memories. Mustard yellow. Bob loved that colour, that was why they had agreed that she would choose the make – a family car, strong on safety features – and he – the dandy – would choose the colour. She noticed that unconsciously she had begun to smile. But then she recalled the message he had left on her machine yesterday, about how he was reneging on their agreement about the house, and she stopped smiling. The estimate they'd been given on the house was so high that they both knew Bob couldn't afford to buy her out, so they'd agreed that she was to get the house at market price while he got the car free of all debt. All that remained were the signatures on the transfer of ownership papers. That would be the last practical link between them. Would she miss him? No, she didn't think she would. But she could be wrong about that, some days she could be overcome by a feeling of missing him. Missing those times when she left here in winter and got into the warm car waiting outside, where Bob had put on a song he wanted her to listen to, and him looking like she was the one doing him a favour by letting him pick her up and transport her back home like a princess. And now this was all that remained after twelve years together, a signature. Could things have been different? If what happened that day had never happened, would they still be a couple?

The car on the far side of the park glided out into the traffic. Alice looked at her watch. Next patient in five minutes. She sighed, took a last sip from her cup and went back to the office.

17

AMIGO, OCTOBER 2016

THE TIME WAS SIX IN the evening and the sun hung low over the rooftops of Phillips.

Bob had parked by the playground at Bloomington. He sat eating a hamburger in the Volvo and watched the deal going down outside a nearby house. The same three as before. The Latino in the porkpie hat was clearly running the operation. Rich people from the suburbs in the west often drove to these northern neighbourhoods, like Jordan, to buy grass, or coke or meth. Here in Phillips customers tended to be local. And the goods harder. Heroin. Crack. It looked like that was what was going down here. The same *pas de trois* each time a customer showed up. A few words exchanged, banknotes, small deals changing hands, fists closed to hide as much as possible and always orchestrated in such a way that the notes and the dope were never held by one person at the same time, since the penalty for selling dope was higher than for giving it away, so the one dealing the dope could always claim he'd given it away if no one ever actually saw him taking the money.

Bob chewed down the last morsel, dried his fingers on the paper towel and started the car.

He drove up to the corner and climbed out.

'Police,' he said loudly, holding up the ID card and a pair of handcuffs he'd rescued from one of the packing cases in his apartment. 'Face the wall. Anyone makes a run for it gets shot.'

The three stared, first at Bob, then to left and right, clearly astonished to see that he was alone.

'Now!' Bob shouted.

Reluctantly they turned, put their hands against the wall and spread their legs. Bob approached the oldest of them, knocked the porkpie hat off his head and jerked his left arm, forcing him up against the wall. Then the right arm, and then holding both wrists behind his back handcuffed him.

'Jamar Clark.'

The words were spoken quietly, but Bob turned toward the young black kid who had spoken.

'What did you say?'

The boy gave Bob a hate-filled stare but didn't reply. A couple of years ago Jamar Clark, a black man, had been shot and killed by the MPD during an arrest, and the people who wanted to start a riot spread the word that it had happened while Clark was handcuffed. Bob didn't doubt for a moment that MPD's reputation for brutality and racism was well deserved, you just had to listen to Hanson and Kjos when they enthusiastically quoted Donald Trump's expressed view that the police ought to be tougher with people they arrested; but not even the MPD would kill defenceless people.

'Here.'

Bob led Porkpie Hat over to the passenger side of the car and helped him into the front seat and – without irony – made sure he didn't bang his head on the roof as he got in. He fastened the seat belt over him, then got into the driver's side and drove off.

'What the fuck is this?' said the man. His accent suggested Mexico, just as Bob had been hoping. Bob pressed a finger to his lips.

'Fuck this, man!' Porkpie screamed.

Three blocks later Bob turned into a quiet street and stopped.

'I need a little information, amigo.'

'Amigo my ass!'

'OK, but I still need information.'

'I thought you had snitches for that. Or did we kill them all?' Three front teeth were missing from the man's wide grin.

'Now listen good,' said Bob. 'I don't have a lot of time, so here is my offer, probably the best one you'll get in the course of your probably short life.'

'I ain't saying a word to you, fucking asshole cop!'

'Oh but you will. Because I'm offering you the perfect incentive, which is a fancy word for carrot. *Comprende?*'

The man's eyes flashed.

'I'm not threatening you with prison, I'm not threatening to beat you, I'm not threatening you with what will happen to your kid brother who's doing time in MCF.'

'I don't have no kid brother, you prick!'

'All I'm doing is offering you this.'

Bob tossed a bundle of something with an elastic band around it onto the dashboard. The man in the passenger seat stared at the long-dead general and president whose portrait adorned the fifty-dollar banknote.

'There's two thousand dollars there,' said Bob. 'Go ahead and count it.'

The man looked at him with a well-ain't-you-a-funny-guy look on his face, his jaws working furiously.

'Oh, sorry, I forgot, you're in handcuffs,' said Bob.

The man worked his jaw a little more and then spat. A yellowish globule that coated the general's serious face.

'If that's a rejection then I'm going to ask you to think again,' said Bob. 'You make three dollars an hour for getting shot at by gangs, robbed by customers, arrested by guys like me, and now I'm offering you this for what they're gonna guess I got from you anyway. Because in five minutes' time I'm going to drive you back there and drop you off without a mark on you, and I'll be calling out a cheery "thank you" as I drive away. I leave it up to you to work out what your buddies will think I've got out of you. And what the consequences will be. So it's up to you if you want paying for them or not.'

The man looked at Bob. He blinked as his brain tried to process what this asshole cop had just said to him. Bob waited.

'What d'you wanna know?' the man grunted.

'Tell me about Tomás Gomez.'

'Who?'

Bob sighed. 'I didn't exactly pick you because you're the best-looking or the smartest, I picked you because you're obviously the oldest. And maybe from south of the border. So dig around, go back a few years in your mind and recall Tomás Gomez. It's not like you're snitching on one of your own.'

'What would you know about that?'

'Gomez isn't X-11 any more. He bailed out, right?'

'There's lots of people bail out, that don't mean we snitch on them.'

'That brings us back to the two thousand, amigo.'

The man looked at the money on the dashboard. Bob waited. Let the gravitational pull of logic do its work. Finally the man gave a heavy sigh. 'He came over from south of the border some years back. Called himself Lobo.'

'Wolf?'

'As in lone wolf. Kept himself to himself, a real loner. But he might just as well have called himself Loco. He didn't say much, but according to rumour he'd worked for one of the cartels down there, killed a lot of people, the police put a price on his head. Gang boss didn't believe none of it, I mean, Lobo was just a kid, so he gave him an Uzi and told him to go shoot some of the competition. Lobo went straight to a Black Wolves party, shot the whole thing up.'

'Hang on. You mean *the* Lobo?'

'Well, I dunno, I only know one Lobo.'

Bob stared at the other man. Lobo. The Uzi man. Bob recalled the tales he had heard about the guy when he was starting out in the police, a ghost that showed up and vanished again in the mid-nineties and left nothing behind but a trail of blood. Since the blood in question was gang blood, MPD's hunt for him had been a half-hearted affair. And when Lobo dropped off the radar MPD concluded that he'd probably been killed and most probably by one of his own and they dropped the whole thing.

'Go on,' said Bob.

'After that Lobo was the security boss's right hand. But he was too crazy, he had no discipline, he went ahead and mowed down people from other gangs, even when they weren't even threatening our territory. So they had to take revenge, and that meant gang wars, people going down on both sides, bad for business for everybody. So the bosses took Lobo off the barricades and put him in charge of internal security.'

'Entailing what?'

'Checking that no one's taking money from the counting room or dope from the cutting room, stuff like that. Lobo did a good job. He uncovered not just thieving but snitching too. We had to terminate a lot of guys we'd been trusting blind. Then some of our own people started getting it, Lobo said they'd drawn on him once they knew he was on to them. It happened a few too many times, so the bosses decided they couldn't have Lobo in the gang no more. They threw him out.'

'So they didn't kill him?'

The man shrugged. 'Lobo always said he was still on the payroll of that cartel he was working for back where he came from. Our bosses were scared to have them breathing down our necks. You said five minutes, pig. If I'm gone much longer the boss is going to think I've been giving you fucking state secrets.'

'OK. So what happened to Gomez?'

'How the hell should I know? Try south of the border.'

'You know who Marco Dante is?'

'No.'

'Stupid question. You know who he is, and you know he got shot yesterday. Did you hear the news that it was Gomez that shot him?'

'Like I told you, all I know is that Lobo was plumb crazy. Drive me back.'

'Last question. Did Dante sell guns to X-11?'

'I guess he must have sold to every gang that some time or other had the territory where his garage is. So yeah, sure.'

'Well then, thank you. Lean forward.' Bob unlocked the handcuffs. 'You can walk.'

'*Walk*?'

'Do I look like a taxi driver?'

The pusher reached for the bundle of notes but Bob was quicker and grabbed it.

'Hey!'

'Just the top one,' said Bob, pulling out the fifty and handing the bundle to the man, who sat staring down at the pile of newspaper strips in his hand.

'What the fuck?'

'You don't think we'd pay two thousand for a little general information I could've got for a packet of cigarettes down at the MCF, or free from a snitch? You'd be better off reading these Situations Vacant.' Bob pressed the bundle down into the man's hand. 'At least they pay minimum wage, unlike X—'

'I'll be coming after you and I'll shoot you down, you fucking pig.'

Bob nodded slowly as he looked out of the windshield. 'You know what? I have actually considered that possibility. But I decided you won't be looking for revenge. Know why? It's a question of economic behavioural psychology. Want to hear?'

Bob turned to the pusher, who now looked more surprised than angry.

'Because your disappointment has its limits. Behavioural research shows that our reaction to not getting the dollar we've just been promised is less negative than losing the dollar we already have in our pocket. I haven't stolen from you, so you have no economic or moral incentive to kill me. And you have no social motive, since I haven't publicly humiliated you either, just here, between you and me. See, so you learned something new today as well! Have a profitable evening, amigo.'

He leaned across the man and pushed open the car door.

As Bob drove off he saw the man diminishing in his rear-view mirror. He stood there, arms dangling by his side, and seemed to be shouting something after the Volvo.

18

MILKMAN, OCTOBER 2016

OLAV HANSON PULLED HIS FISHING rod sideways, against the current. Stared out into the night-time darkness that descended over the Mississippi before it took the rest of the city. Sometimes it even felt as though the darkness rose up from the Mississippi and not the other way round. Because it was a river with a lot of darkness in it. A lot of dirt and devilment people dumped there in hopes the river would take it all away, far from where they were. And if it surfaced again it would be someone else's problem. Hanson shifted the weight from his bad knee. Listened to the reassuring hiss from the cars on the freeway on the other side of the river. He came down here more and more often in the evenings now, went on fishing long after the others had gone. The bass bit well after dark, and of course he did sometimes come home with a couple of small fish; but that was mostly to show Violet he really had been fishing and not in some bar with Joe Kjos. He could think while he stood here. Get some respite from all her moaning about how 'the kid', the twenty-seven-year-old son from his previous marriage, still had the keys to the house, and came and went as he pleased, often in the middle of the night, usually high on something or other. She complained that the Ford Mustang was almost as old as she was, that the kitchen and bathroom needed decorating, that she had hoped to see things in general improving a bit, not sliding backward. Either he'd got miserly with age, or else he was worse off now than when she'd met him in the nineties. And it was true, she just didn't know the reason.

Olav Hanson thought about a lot of things as he stood there by the river. There were just a few thoughts it was important to avoid. Things from the past. So he thought about the future. About how he would be able to retire in a couple of years. Be a free man again. Go fishing. Get Sean back on track. He would –

He heard a scraping sound from the fine river-sand behind and instinctively whirled round. Stood there staring into the trees on the steep incline.

'Who's there?' he shouted.

He'd been on the alert for something like half his life and could never completely let it go. All that wasted energy, and still his hand instinctively went for the shoulder holster with the SIG Sauer which he always carried. Just then the moon slipped free of the clouds, illuminating the riverbank, and he caught sight of a black dog standing there. Olav picked up a stone and threw it in the dog's direction. It disappeared soundlessly between the trees. Hanson cursed quietly.

He reeled in.

His phone rang.

He'd told Violet not to call him when he was out, but she was as unpredictable as Sean. This, however, was a caller unknown.

'Yes?'

The voice at the other end breathed in before speaking in a low voice: 'Milkman?'

Olav Hanson felt his heart stop beating in his chest.

Thirty years.

And it took him only a second and two syllables to recognise the voice.

He had to moisten his mouth before he could answer:

'Who is this?'

'I can hear that you know who this is, Milkman. And that you're afraid. That's good. It means you'll listen extra close. One of my guys tells me you're looking for Lobo.'

Wha? It came out as an *a?* as Hanson tried to speak at the same time as swallowing. 'Lobo? But Lobo is . . . gone.'

'Evidently not,' said the voice. 'MPD are looking for him. Suspicion of attempted murder. Which can only mean he's got a bit rusty. Anyway, if Lobo really has shown up again then neither you nor I want the MPD to find him. We don't want him sitting in some interrogation where they suggest a deal that involves him telling them everything he knows. About me. And about you, Milkman. Do you get my drift?'

Olav got it. He understood the nightmare was back. The man at the top, the one they called Die Man, and not just because of the diamonds in his teeth. 'You want me to . . .?'

'Yes, Milkman, I want you to make sure Lobo never gets as far as that interrogation.'

Olav Hanson closed his eyes. He heard something in the

background. A woman, no, several women, groaning with exaggerated ecstasy and gasping 'Oh, fuck, yeah!' He had never asked Die why he called him Milkman. It could of course be because Olav was pale and blond or because people like him were typical of the Scandinavian farmer class. Or because he milked the gang for money. But it might also have been ironically meant, giving a milk-white name to a dirty cop who had done what was necessary each time investigations of some gangland killing made things hot for Die Man and his people. It hadn't taken much. He might neglect to pass on information a witness had given him. Or invent something that suggested other perpetrators. Maybe technical evidence was destroyed by something that looked like an unlucky accident. So no, it hadn't taken much. And they'd paid him well. Very well. All the same he'd quit. Why? It started with the triple homicide that evening thirty years ago. The girl in the wheelchair, the little boy and the mother. It hadn't been one of Olav's cases, but he'd managed to send it off in the wrong direction, and yes, he'd had trouble sleeping after that. But not so much that he hadn't carried on helping Die Man for a while after. But then he'd become a father himself. And Die Man's security boss Lobo had started massacring gangbangers, and Olav started getting scared of being pulled under himself. He had to get out, wake up from his nightmare. And he'd done it, managed to put it behind him.

Until now.

Because when Olav opened his eyes again the nightmare hadn't ended.

'You still there, Milkman?'

'Yeah yeah,' said Olav.

'You know what you have to do?'

Olav thought. Pulled back thirty years in time he began thinking the way he used to think back then, and when he opened his mouth again it was like some familiar and fond old refrain: 'Sure, but we have to talk about the price.'

For a moment the only sound was the monotonous groaning of those women. Then he heard Die burst out laughing. He laughed long and loud.

'Nice try, Milkman. But this time let's say you're doing it for yourself. Because you don't want to end up in jail. Especially not somewhere with my boys on the inside.'

'Listen –' Hanson began, but the connection went dead.

He stared out across the Mississippi. The river rose here in Minnesota, and the shit floated downriver. With every state it ran through the body count rose, until the bloodwater reached the sea and the chance of ending your life with a bullet was three times what it was here. That must have been why the chance of getting away with murder was higher down there. A cloud passed in front of the moon, the blackness returned and for an instant he felt an almost irresistible urge to throw himself into the water and just drift away. But he didn't want that. He wanted to survive. That damned survival instinct would be the death of him one day – but not yet. He straightened out his bad knee. He'd worked, and he'd worn himself out, and mostly it had been honest work. He'd been robbed of opportunities before, been overlooked before, life wasn't fair, death wasn't either.

Sure, but we have to talk about the price.

Word for word that was what he had said the first time, when he made his choice and let the genie out of the bottle. He spat in the direction of the river and saw the foamy white ball carried off into the darkness. All right then. But this time, he wouldn't be the one going under.

19

FOUR HUNDRED YARDS, OCTOBER 2016

THERE WAS A DONALD DUCK in the store. The noonday sun had cast a strip of shadow across its bill. A target had been drawn on the forehead and he was holding a pistol that was pointing at me. I walked to the counter. The wall behind it was hung with rifles for sale. They stocked magazines and pistol butts and put you in mind of Iraq and Afghanistan rather than deer hunting. An advertising poster hanging on a pillar had a picture of a machine gun and the text: *Because sometimes the only thing that is going to make you feel better is shooting a machine gun.*

A man wearing a camouflage cap and a T-shirt with TOTAL DEFENSE on it appeared.

'Welcome to Mitro,' he said. 'What can I help you with today, sir?'

'I have an hour with an instructor booked.'

The man looked down at something on the counter in front of him. 'Mr . . . Jones?'

'That's right. I have problems with targets that are low down in the terrain.'

'Yes, that's what's noted down here. Is that a rifle you've got there?'

I nodded and held up the bubble-wrap package.

'Then just let me get a little ammo here. Follow me. The name's Jim.'

'Tomás.' It just slipped out. No big deal but I would have to watch out, be on guard for any signs my concentration was slipping. Think. Think. All the time.

Jim took me outside. We passed two standard shooting ranges, one where you shot at clay pigeons and one with targets in the shape of human beings. Three-hundred-yard ranges for standard rifles, Jim told me. Two normal, nice-looking armed teenagers standing on a rise greeted us politely, him wearing a jacket with a Stars and Stripes logo, her in a sweater with PRO-GUN written on it.

'Hi, Ola. Can you and Sigrid take a coffee break?'

The two nodded and disappeared. Behind the rise, down on the flat, was a wooden wall with ordinary round targets mounted on it.

'Can you tell me what your specific problem is, Tomás?'

I said again that I couldn't seem to adjust my sights to correct for the difference in height between myself and my target.

'I see.' Jim nodded, serious as a priest who'd just heard my confession. 'But don't worry, Tomás, you and me are gonna fix that here today.'

'Thanks,' I answered, couldn't think of any other response.

'Can I see your shooting position, Tomás?'

I unpacked my rifle and lay flat on one of the two rubber mats.

'Aim and breathe,' said Jim. I did as he said. He walked around and behind me, grunting as he used his foot to adjust my position here and there. Then he lay down next to me on the other mat.

'Right,' he began, clearing his throat. 'It's three hundred yards to those targets and they're quite a bit lower as you can see. A lot of people protest when I say that even though the target is below you or above you, you've got to aim *lower* than you normally would. They can accept it when as is the case here the target *is* lower. But not that you have to aim lower even when your target is *higher*. Their logic protests –'

'I'm not protesting, Jim, I just want to –'

'– because they don't understand that the line of a horizontal shot is affected more by gravity than a shot straight up in the air or right down in the ground. Now just imagine that –'

'I know all this, Jim. I just have one concrete question.'

'Now just imagine that you're lying on a hillside three hundred yards from a deer down on a plain that –'

'Four hundred yards.'

'Sorry?'

'The deer is four hundred yards away from me. And from where I'm standing there's a fifteen-degree angle.'

'Sure, but let's take the example with three hundred.'

'No,' I said.

Jim looked a little confused now; he'd lost his place. But I could see his brain looking for a way to continue playing a game he knew to perfection.

'I don't recommend that a beginner start by shooting at

something that's over three hundred yards away,' said Jim. 'At three hundred you're already flirting with what we call maximum point-blank range, doesn't matter what ammunition you're using. Further than that and the bullet will be affected so much by wind and weather that the beginner will just wound the deer or frighten it off, and you don't want that, Tomás.'

I took off my sunglasses. Our eyes met.

'Four hundred yards,' I repeated. 'All I need to know is whether my calculations are correct or is there something I haven't been taking into consideration.'

He took a breath. Blinked. 'Suit yourself,' he muttered, pushed his cap back and concentrated, his jaws moving around like he was chewing grass.

I waited. I was in no hurry.

He rolled over on his side and pulled out his phone. Tapped the calculator.

'OK, four hundred yards,' he said. 'You have to aim as though the distance was four hundred yards.'

'That's what I thought.'

'Good. What d'you say, Tomás, shall we try a few shots at the target on the left down there?'

I shrugged. 'What are the numbers?'

He gave me the distance and the angle, and I told him I didn't need the cosine, I already knew it for every angle. And I didn't need any calculator to work out how much to adjust the sight. I looked at the flags on the front of the store behind me. Lay out on the mat, loaded, adjusted the sight.

'Shoot when you're ready,' said Jim.

I took a breath, held it. Saw Cody Karlstad's face in front of me the way it looked in the picture. A target on his forehead like that Donald Duck. Pointing a gun at me, my wife, my children. I fired. Loaded. Fired. Loaded. She was so pretty when she laughed, and when her heart broke, my heart would break too. And my heart broke often, because hers could break over the slightest little thing, it could be some stranger she felt pity for, or the way light fell, reminding her of a time she would never get back again.

'It's empty,' said Jim.

'What?'

'The magazine. It's empty. You can quit squeezing the trigger.'

'Sure.' I put the rifle down and stood up.

We walked down the incline to the target.

'Not bad,' said Jim.

All five shots had hit within a radius of five to six inches.

'Could be better,' I said, noting that the spread was more horizontal than vertical. 'Any advice?'

'You could work on your shooting position and your breathing, but you have a fine natural trigger action. Hang this up at home, Tomás.' He took down the paper target, rolled it up and handed it to me. I guessed that was something he did with all his customers, gave them a trophy, something to take home from the hunt.

We headed back up the slope. Jim watched as I packed my rifle back in its bubble wrap.

'What exactly are you going to be hunting?' he finally asked.

I carried on wrapping. 'Why d'you ask?'

'An M24. Not that you can't use it for hunting, I mean, that's what it was originally for. With a few modifications.'

'Beasts of prey,' I said without looking up.

'I never heard that,' Jim said and laughed.

I didn't laugh.

'Not that it's any of my business, Tomás, but you do know that the wolf is protected now, right?'

'Is it?'

'Yup. But relax, I ain't planning to sneak. Wolves have been seen in Cedar Creek, dammit, that's just a half-hour from downtown, and this is a free country, people have the right to protect themselves, if you ask me. Or am I wrong, Tomás?'

'Damn right they do,' I said.

Back inside the store I paid in cash.

'Don't see that too often,' said Jim.

I heard someone enter behind me. Don't know why I turned, maybe it was something about the footsteps, the coughing, the gravelly voice speaking. Two uniformed cops, a man and a woman. I felt my heart beat faster. I picked up my change, wedged the rifle under my arm, looked downward and marched out. I saw the empty cop car in the parking lot. Nothing strange about police coming to a shooting range, I told myself, they probably come here to practise. All the same I walked faster than I normally would. And when I heard that gravelly voice calling 'Sir! Wait!' then I knew that no matter how well you've planned things – whether it's for a family's future, or for how to handle losing one – you haven't a hope against the play of chance.

Should I stop? Run? Tear the bubble wrap off the rifle and attack?

I stopped. Turned slowly.

The cop was running toward me. He hadn't taken the gun out of his holster yet but he was holding something in his hand. I tensed, not quite sure yet what for.

'Jim says you forgot this, sir,' he said as he caught up with me.

I saw now what he was holding. The target. I must have left it on the counter.

'Thank you so much,' I said. I tried to smile as I wedged the target inside the bubble wrap.

'Courtesy of the MPD.' The cop laughed. And I could see then he was a man it would have been easy to like. I laughed too. Because he had no idea he was face-to-face with the man who'd shot a Jordan gun dealer two days before, and in just a few more hours was going to be at work again.

20

THE EYES, OCTOBER 2016

IT WAS THREE THIRTY AND the bell over the door of Town Taxidermy rang.

Mike Lunde emerged from a door behind the counter with a pair of reading glasses pushed up on his forehead.

'Detective Oz,' he said, wiping his hands dry on his rough blue apron.

'Lunde.' Bob looked around. Apart from the animals the place was as deserted as it had been the previous time.

'What can I do for you?'

Bob smiled and patted a white-tailed deer. 'I was wondering if I could hang around here for a while this afternoon.'

Lunde gave Bob a look of mild astonishment.

'We don't have any other leads on Gomez,' Bob explained. 'This is the only place where we can expect him to show up.'

'You're welcome to stay,' said Lunde. 'But I wouldn't hold your breath. I don't have a definite appointment with Tomás.'

'I know that.'

'OK then. Coffee?'

Bob followed Lunde through the door behind the counter and into what was evidently a workshop. It was a large room with several workbenches, tools hanging on the walls. The smell, probably glue, reminded him of something from his childhood, recalling Christmas and sweets, only a little more pungent. Lunde moved four yellowish-white figures that looked like they were carved in polystyrene so Bob could sit down. One resembled a deer, the others were smaller mammals, maybe lynxes or wolves.

'What are these?'

'We call them mannequins,' said Lunde as he poured coffee from a stained pot. 'We order them and they come ready-cut like that.'

'But that's cheating.'

Lunde laughed and handed Bob a mug with NATIONAL TAXIDERMIST ASSOCIATION written on it. 'I still need to file them down a bit, where you can see the crosses I've made. But yes, the days when we used formalin and the soft parts of the animal are over. Now it's just the hide and the horns. And the teeth, if the customer requests it.'

Lunde walked over to the head and neck of a deer mounted on a stand. The hide around the nose and eyeholes was dotted with what looked like needle pricks. He pressed a small ball of clay into one of the eyeholes, opened a drawer in a plastic box and took out two eyes.

'Plastic?'

'Glass. These are special orders. I'm very particular about the eyes. *Too* particular, according to some of my suppliers.' Lunde pushed an eye into the clay. Studied it, turned it a little. 'The hart has oblong pupils that have to be positioned horizontally,' he explained.

'Why?'

'So that they can take in the horizon in one look. They're prey.'

'They're on the lookout for predators?'

'Precisely.'

After he had inserted both eyes and added more clay around them and sculpted to shape, Lunde sat on one of the workbenches, picked up a hide and showed Bob a hole.

'Bullet hole.'

Working from the inside, he cut the hole a little larger before starting to sew it closed. Burned off the end of the thread with a lighter.

'It's quiet here,' said Bob.

'Yes it is,' said Lunde. He walked over to the deer mannequin, applied glue to the clay surrounding the eyes and fitted the hide over the head, pulling it forward over the head like a pullover.

'Right now it looks more like an ass,' he said as he lifted up the floppy ears. 'But we'll deal with that later.'

'How long does it take you to, er . . . make an animal?'

'That depends. Anything from a week to six months. A head like this is a lot less work than if you want the whole animal. A lot of the procedures take time. Flaying, salting, drying the skin. Then you have to find the right expression.'

He picked up a scalpel from the table and started cutting and pushing in the white skin around the eyes. 'This one, for example, I need to give a look of ease and power. A so-called alpha male.'

'Oh?'

'That's the way the client recalled the animal when he shot it, so that's what he's ordered.'

'A hunter who wants to capture his moment of triumph over an animal that thought it was in control,' said Bob.

'Very poetic. And in this particular case, very accurate.'

'And you can do it? Give the animal this type of authentic expression?'

'Well,' said Lunde, 'of course, I don't know if it's authentic. What does an animal feel? I just have to use my imagination and end up, I'm sure, giving it a more or less human look. The thing is, anyway, to see it through the client's eye. To show what the client wants to see.'

'What if you don't like what the client wants to see?'

Lunde shrugged. 'I'm a barber. The customer decides the style. But, within limits, I have a certain degree of freedom to produce something that exceeds the customer's expectations. Their pleasure is mine too.' Lunde looked up. The bell above the door had sounded again. He went out, with Bob following three paces behind.

A woman was standing in the store. She and Lunde had obviously met before and they at once began talking about a job involving a dog. Lunde explained that he was waiting for new eyes, that he wasn't satisfied with the ones that had been sent.

Bob returned to the workshop and to his coffee.

After a while Lunde returned and resumed work.

Bob closed his eyes for a moment and listened to the silence and the small sounds produced by Lunde's work. It relaxed him, watching Lunde at work, seeing the result slowly taking shape. It was like medication. More calming than any pills.

'So you like to watch too,' said Lunde, as if he could read Bob's thoughts.

'Maybe I do. Why do you say *too*?'

'Tomás. He used to sit there, like you. Not saying much, now and then asking a question about some technical aspect of what I was doing. Judging by his questions you would almost think he knew enough about taxidermy to do the cat himself. I told him that once. He said he didn't know anything about the subject but that he was good with his hands.' Lunde smiled. 'But maybe he had hidden reasons, maybe he brought the cat along to steal some of my tricks.'

'Hidden reasons,' Bob echoed. 'Like X-11.'

'X-11?' Lunde switched to a smaller scalpel.

'Yes. I think he infiltrated X-11 in order to avenge the death of his family.'

'Really?'

'He spun them some tale about how he'd worked for a drug cartel south of the border and been sent over here because the police were after him. Because there was nothing that exposed Gomez's story, X-11 believed it. He arranged for the killings of drug dealers in and outside X-11 by starting gang wars. When his bosses pulled him back from the front line he continued the vendetta against his own people.'

'Without being exposed?' Lunde stepped back to study his work.

'One in four drug dealers die within four years. Think about it. In this country a prisoner under sentence of death has less chance of being executed than a crack dealer has of being shot dead in the street. Like the head of X-11 it means you're used to natural shrinkage. They probably didn't respond immediately, but once they made the connection they threw Gomez out. Looks like he stopped after that.'

'Hm. Is this something you know, Oz, or what you might call speculation?'

'Let's call it an educated guess. If he stopped then I have to wonder why he started up again. Did he feel he hadn't avenged his family's deaths enough? Some kind of bottled-up anger that was somehow triggered? Like, for example, his cat dying. A lot of people just lose it when someone or something dies . . . you know, something close, much loved.'

'I'm sure you're right there.' Lunde stepped back to the workbench and wiped off his scalpels.

'What I find a little strange is that he messed it up so badly in Dante's case,' Bob continued. 'The distance was no more than three hundred yards and the rifle case was for an M24 with telescopic sights, same as the snipers in Afghanistan used, same as the police.'

'Maybe he hasn't had much practice with that particular rifle?'

'When you prepare something as carefully as Gomez did then you're pretty certain you're going to get it right. There was no wind to speak of, and the distance was too short for the temperature to make any difference. If he made the beginner's mistake of failing to adjust for the difference in elevation then he would have shot too high, not too low.'

'Maybe he was nervous and his hand shook. A lot of the hunters I get in here talk about what they call "buck fever". Speaking of which, buck, I think we're done with this for today.' Lunde pulled off his gloves. 'Which means it's time for a little *con amore* work.'

'*Con amore*?'

'A labour of love. Come.'

Bob followed Lunde into a smaller workshop. There was just one workbench there, and the mannequin standing on it was quite different from the others in the larger workshop. 'Taxidermy the way it used to be done,' said Lunde as he stroked his hand over the hollow, wolf-like figure. 'Wood, cotton and steel wire. I'll dress this with treated skin the same as those back there, but here I'll use the animal's skull as well.' He indicated a cranium resting on sawdust inside a glass case.

'Why?'

'At the customer's request.'

Bob made a face. 'I know something about corpses, Lunde. If there's so much as a thread of organic material inside that head it'll rot and start to stink.'

'That's right. And that's why the cranium is in that glass case.'

'Oh?'

'There's a colony of carnivorous leather beetles inside that skull and they'll eat it clean before I begin work.'

Bob stared at the cranium. He listened.

'Oh no,' Lunde said with a laugh, 'you can't hear them.'

'OK. But isn't there a simpler way?'

'Oh sure, I could have freeze-dried the whole animal so the customer would get the complete thing.'

'Then why not do that?'

Lunde lifted the lid of the glass case and held an eye up against an eyehole. 'In the first place it's expensive. Secondly, the animal has to be stored in a special freeze-dryer for months. And thirdly, as a rule the corpse will get eaten up by carpet beetles. And anyway, there's something about making these shapes, something to do with *feeling*.' Lunde held up his long, slender hands.

'It's as though the vision lies in the eyes and the fingertips, and without your even noticing it gets transferred to the work in question.'

Bob noticed a row of trophies on a shelf and, above them, a photograph.

'Family?' Bob asked.

'Yes. Grandfather, father, me and my sister Emily. All taxidermists. My grandfather and father are dead, but my sister and I are still at it.'

'Using the original techniques?'

Lunde shrugged. 'When we get the chance. There aren't many of us left who still do it.' He chuckled. 'Emily and I always say we should be stuffed ourselves, as examples of an endangered species.'

'You never . . . feel like you just want to give up?'

'Give up?' Lunde gave Bob a long, thoughtful stare. 'No. There's always a reason to go on.' He gestured toward the mannequin. 'This here, for example. I have a feeling that this is going to be the best thing I've ever done. My masterpiece.'

Bob studied it. 'Looks like a very fine wolf, Lunde.'

'Wolf?' An expression of pained sorrow crossed Lunde's face. 'Ah, I see I've failed already. This is supposed to be a Labrador retriever.'

'Your masterpiece is, eh . . . a dog?'

Lunde smiled. 'Oh yes, I know what you're thinking. Why not a bear? Or a deer? But consider this: the demands posed by a Labrador are sky-high. Everyone's seen one, everyone has a clear idea of what a Labrador should look like. The problem is, as usual, the eyes. These are samples from a manufacturer in Madrid.' Lunde held up the glass eyes. 'They aren't bad. Just not very . . . lifelike.'

'Those owl eyes in the store are lifelike.'

'Yes, aren't they?' Lunde was in the grip of an almost childlike enthusiasm. 'I made them myself. They're ceramic. You get the feeling they're *watching* you, don't you?'

Bob bent forward and studied two photographs lying next to the dog mannequin on the workbench. 'Is this it?'

'Yes.'

'Isn't it a little, er . . . fatter than the mannequin?'

'Oh definitely. The customer is a very wealthy family and I intend to give them the animal as they would remember it when it was young and slender. It's called idealisation. We beautify the portraits, in just the way Van Dyck, Rubens and da Vinci did. The art isn't in the resemblance.'

'Then where does it lie?'

'In the creation of the story.' Lunde placed the eyes back into an envelope. 'Ever heard of John Hancock? I don't mean the one who signed the Declaration of Independence.'

'Can't say I have.'

'No, he's pretty much a forgotten figure. Let's call him the father of modern taxidermy. He exhibited some birds at the Great Exhibition in London in 1851 and, of course, people were impressed by their anatomical accuracy. But as one of the judges remarked, the surprising thing was that one felt *moved* by the exhibits. Do you see? Hancock raised taxidermy to the level of art.'

'You think a stuffed animal is a work of art?'

'Let me show you.'

Bob followed Mike Lunde back into the store, where he took down two large books from a shelf on which two hares acted as bookends.

'In Victorian England it was as common to have stuffed animals in the averagely affluent household as it was to have paintings,' said Lunde, opening one of the books. 'Things moved forward, and in the latter part of the nineteenth century Walter Potter developed so-called anthropomorphic taxidermy. He dressed the animals in clothes and posed them in comic situations, like humans.'

As Lunde turned the pages Bob studied the whole-page photographs in the book. One of rats in human clothing brawling round a poker table as another rat dressed in a policeman's uniform comes storming in. Another showed a classroom full of rabbits sitting neatly at their desks. These montages had a certain cuteness, and at the same time a subtext Bob wasn't immediately able to decode.

'Exhibitions by Potter and by other taxidermists attracted larger audiences than popular theatre performances or athletics meetings. And then taxidermists began including bizarre details, such as a two-headed lamb, or a chicken with four legs. From which there is a direct line to this . . .' Lunde indicated the second book. 'The contribution of our own city, Minneapolis.'

The title on the cover was *Rogue Taxidermy*. He thumbed through it. A stuffed polar bear atop a sinking refrigerator. A squirrel holding up something that looked like a small heart.

'I'm sorry,' said Bob, 'but isn't this just . . . creepy?'

Lunde chuckled. 'I agree, it is creepy. But not *just* creepy. These are artistic expressions. They're stories.'

'But . . . doesn't it do something to you, spending so much time in the company of dead animals?'

Lunde thought about it. 'I don't know. I mean, chefs do the same thing. The difference is that we try to bring the dead back to life. It's what you might call an existential challenge, and it probably does have some effect on you. All those hours, sitting alone, trying to put a mask on death.'

'Who did this?' asked Bob, pointing to one picture. It showed an eagle sitting on a branch. One wing was holding a revolver pointed at its own head.

'Ah, that's by Anonymous,' said Lunde. 'That's to say, that's what they're known as in taxidermy circles. He or she exhibits the work in some public space, most often at night, unsigned, and that's all we know. That eagle was exhibited in a tree right outside the picnic area in the Minnehaha Park. Caused quite a stir, of course, because the bald eagle is a protected species.'

Outside rain started falling. They both looked out into the street. The sounds changed. Car tyres hissed against the wet asphalt. Footsteps along the sidewalk sounded quicker. An animated conversation fell silent.

'When you and Gomez were talking about loneliness,' said Bob, 'what did you discuss in particular?'

'Well, all sorts of things,' said Lunde as he replaced the books on the shelf. 'Why it is that loneliness is so troubling. None of our most basic physical needs require the presence of several or even one other human being. Breathe, eat, work, get food, get dressed, fall ill and recover, shit, piss, sleep. From nature's point of view, we are fully capable of living long, full and wholly satisfactory lives entirely on our own. In many cases better lives than the ones we get when we enter into a union and voluntarily or involuntarily allow our lives to be guided by the needs of others. And yet no one asks themselves whether the ending of *Robinson Crusoe*, when he gets rescued, is a happy ending or not. Think about it. I mean, he's managed to organise things pretty well on that island – what guarantee does he have that the life he gets when he goes back to living with other people will be as good? He's losing his freedom, his daily swims, a territory that's all his own with limitless access to food, no working hours, no boss. And for what? But we don't even wonder about it, we just take it for granted that we're willing to give up all this for just one thing: the company of other people.'

'But if we don't need others, then why is loneliness so intolerable?'

'What do you think?'

'Biology. If we all thought it was fine to be alone, we wouldn't want to reproduce ourselves.'

Lunde raised a finger to point to a glass case full of butterflies hanging on the wall behind him. 'Some species meet up for the purpose of reproduction only.'

'Economics, then. Cooperating with others gives everyone a better chance of survival.'

'You and your economics. Economics doesn't drive people insane. But loneliness does. Am I right?'

'I'm sorry?'

'Loneliness is a fairly novel experience for you, Bob, isn't it?'

Bob didn't reply. Again Mike Lunde smiled that smile that Bob seemed to recognise from somewhere, some faint childhood memory he couldn't quite pull to the surface. The store bell jangled.

A man walked in. He was wearing a suit that looked straight out of one of the Downtown West skyscrapers. Bob waited as the customer explained that he wanted a hunting trophy stuffed – a black rhinoceros. He'd heard that Lunde was the best in the business. Lunde declined politely, explaining that he didn't do rhinoceros. When the man insisted, and demanded an explanation,

Mike Lunde said that he just didn't work with threatened species. The customer got a little heated. He pointed out that he'd had permission from the Namibian authorities, it was one of the five animals a year they allowed. He added that he had an import licence for the animal. Lunde offered his congratulations, and it wasn't easy for Bob to know if he was being ironic. He said the black rhinoceros was on the taxidermists' blacklist, *no pun intended*. The man protested that it wasn't illegal, he'd spent a quarter of a million dollars for the hunting rights at an auction in Dallas, that the money went toward the *preservation* of the black rhinoceros, and that he was prepared to pay well for a good taxidermist to do the job.

'I'm sorry,' said Lunde, gently but firmly. 'But by all means, bring in another animal.'

The bell jingled angrily as the man left.

Mike Lunde sighed.

'Couldn't you have taken that job?' asked Bob.

'Maybe,' said Lunde. 'Ethical dilemmas always give me a headache. While I've got you here, would you mind helping me with the mother lynx?'

Together they manoeuvred down a lynx mounted on a branch that was attached to the wall. Lunde sprayed the lynx's coat with something from a bottle. Bob went over to the glass case with the butterflies.

'How old are these?'

'My father's butterflies? Forty, forty-five.'

'It's wonderful, the way the colour is preserved.'

'My grandfather said that butterfly wings don't fade like other dead bodies, that they're like mementos of the dead. With each passing year the colour gets stronger.'

Bob nodded. Continued to study the butterflies while Lunde dried off the lynx with a tissue. Hesitated a moment. Then asked: 'What makes you think I'm lonely?'

Lunde carried on drying for a few moments before replying. 'It's in the eyes. Always the eyes. I saw it the moment you entered the store. Your eyes expressed the same thing as Tomás. Loss. Anger. Desperation. Loneliness.'

'Did you tell him that too? That you knew he was lonely?'

'Tomás? He said so himself.'

'What did he say *about* being lonely?'

'Lots. That it was slowly driving him mad.'

'And is he mad, do you think?'

Lunde shrugged. 'It looks that way, don't you think? Normal people don't kill other people. Although, the same could be said of those that killed his family. I don't think your guy is any better or any worse than anyone else, he's just been unlucky. His world was shattered. He said that what tormented him most was that those idiots hadn't killed *him*, the only one who could pose any threat to them.'

'Yes,' said Bob. 'I know what he means.'

'Give me a hand again here?'

After returning the lynx to its place they went back into the workshop and Lunde continued working. Bob fell asleep with his head against the wall. He dreamed. It was the same dream. He was holding a pistol and firing at a tiny head with a candyfloss halo of fair hair. And was woken by the sound of Lunde talking on his cell phone:

'Yes, I'm just leaving now.' Bob heard the twittering of a female voice at the other end and saw the broad smile on Mike Lunde's face. 'Meatballs? Mm, that sounds good.'

He hung up.

'Sorry,' said Bob as he sat up in the chair and wiped the dribble from the corner of his mouth. 'I had a bad night.'

'You were sound asleep. That's good.'

'I heard meatballs. With brown sauce, potatoes and mushy peas?'

Lunde smiled. 'Yes, as it happens. How about you?'

'Guess.'

Lunde leaned his head to one side and looked at Bob. 'I'm guessing you're going to eat alone, and you don't care a damn where or what.'

'Bullseye.'

Bob then noticed Lunde's hesitancy. It was as though he was wondering whether to invite Bob home with him. Then perhaps he saw the warning signs in Bob's eyes and let it drop.

'One more thing,' said Bob. 'You said you didn't know if Gomez has a phone, but he has your cell number, it's printed on your business card. Given that he knows we're looking for him, it could be he won't take the chance of turning up here in person but he'll ring you instead.'

Lunde nodded. 'You could be right there.'

'Can I borrow your phone for a few seconds?'

Lunde tapped in a code that opened it and handed it to Bob. Bob went online and downloaded an app.

'Using this app, with just one tap on the keyboard you can record conversations on your phone without the other person knowing about it. It's unbelievable what sound technicians are able to get out of the voice and the background sounds on such a recording.'

'You don't say?' said Lunde. He looked down sceptically at his phone.

'Anyway, the option is there, if you want it,' said Bob. 'And thanks, thanks for letting me hang out here.'

It had stopped raining by the time Lunde locked the store door behind him, but heavy clouds the colour of exhaust fumes still coated the sky. The sidewalks were beginning to dry. Bob breathed in the air. Remembered childhood, and how sharp every sensory impression was, how even the most insignificant of them could seem almost overwhelming, like the special smell, the humid taste of rain-wet asphalt. Now it smelled and tasted of nothing. He thought about eyes. How it's the eyes that are the problem.

21

SOUTHDALE MALL, SEPTEMBER 2022

WE'RE WAITING FOR A RED light in Edina, which is technically speaking another town. The cab driver, whose name I have discovered is Gabriel, tells me that he thinks the mayor of Edina is of Norwegian descent. I'm more preoccupied by the fact that I don't recognise my surroundings. What's happened to my Southdale Mall? Gabriel explains that my shopping mall is hidden from view now behind all the new buildings, that it is actually still there, just behind them. He looks at me in the mirror.

'What made you choose this particular story?' he asks.

'I'm a crime writer,' I answer.

'Well, I'm a cab driver,' he says, 'but I don't go to New York and drive around a lot of streets I don't know.'

I nod. Hesitate. But why not? I cough.

'The hero of the story – if you can call him that – was my cousin. I guess I just want somebody to tell his story.'

'*Was*? You mean he passed away?'

I don't answer.

'You get rich writing books?'

I shake my head. 'But enough to get by.'

'Good for you. That something you always wanted to do, be a crime writer?'

'No. I trained as a priest.'

'Really? Isn't that pretty unusual? For a priest to be writing about gruesome murders?'

'Not as unusual as you might think. Maybe you've heard of Ronald Knox? He was a Catholic priest. He's the one who laid down the ten commandments of crime fiction.'

Gabriel shakes his head. 'As in, "thou shalt not kill"?'

I have to laugh. 'As in, the killer has to be introduced early on in the story, but we're not allowed access to his thoughts.'

'And you follow that commandment?'

'No, not at all. I let the reader follow the murderer's thoughts as I think he must have thought them at the time. But then, I'm writing true crime, not a detective novel. And Knox's commandments aren't meant to be taken seriously. The fifth commandment states that there shouldn't be a Chinaman in the story.'

'And you've got a Chinaman in your story?'

I have to think about it. 'No, not exactly.'

The light changes to green and Gabriel has to concentrate on his driving.

And it turns out he's right, suddenly we're there.

I recognise those low buildings, and the huge surrounding parking lots. When I came here as a boy, Southdale Mall seemed like a complete universe. Only when I was a little older did I realise that Southdale wasn't a particularly big shopping mall, not for example when compared to West Edmonton Mall, which is bigger than the smallest country in the world. But when Southdale opened in 1956 it turned out to be the start of an urban development that would soon characterise the whole country and, in due course, the whole Western world. Victor Gruen, the architect who designed Southdale and fifty other shopping malls, fled Austria when Hitler annexed it in 1938. He arrived in New York with eight dollars, no English, a training in architecture and the idea of building small urban centres where people would live with every facility a country town could need right next to them: post offices, bakeries, police stations, schools. But as the old saying goes, the road to hell is paved with good intentions, and there's an obvious irony in the fact that a dedicated socialist and urbanist like Gruen should be the architect responsible – in my uncle's view – for the gradual destruction of the Minneapolis he had grown up in, a vibrant and living centre with a thriving business, cultural and social life. To him Gruen's shopping malls were parasites that sucked the life out of the towns and left nothing behind but a dying organism choked by exhaust fumes and crime, a lack of public transport and ordinary, everyday humanity, an accretion of cold stone-and-glass castles containing offices where people worked but from which they fled as soon as the working day was over. I remember my uncle once saying to my father that shopping malls like Southdale created psychopaths, whatever that was supposed to mean. Anyway, my uncle must have been mollified to learn that Gruen repented of his sins and atoned for them by returning to Austria to live and to work on the pedestrian precincts in the centre of Vienna, and that two years before his death he publicly expressed his regret for what his shopping malls had turned into.

Me, I love shopping malls.

I don't tell anyone, but I can still feel some of the elation of my childhood as I enter those riotously coloured jungles where everything screeches at you, everyone hunts you, and the ant-like columns of humans move up the escalators as they head for new worlds. It's like something out of a computer game. Where my uncle and my father saw vulgar commercialism I feel the joy of sinking into a warm cacophony of sight and sound, walking through an Eden of temptations and sinful invitations, feeling how your life *might* have been had you owned this thing or that, the sensation and excitement of a possible Fall of biblical dimensions, even if you don't have a krone or a dollar to spend.

We stop in the parking lot and I get out. Six women in red T-shirts carrying placards are standing under some trees at the end of the lot. I walk toward them. They're on strike, nurses from the women's hospital on the other side of the road, they explain. I point to the parking garage next to the hospital and ask if they can tell me anything about what happened there.

'What did happen?' they ask.

I explain, but they've never heard of the incident. Six years is a long time, they say. Before the pandemic, before Floyd, it was another time.

I say thanks and walk away. Close my eyes behind the sunglasses and breathe in deeply, maybe hoping to breathe in the air of my childhood. Open car windows with the smell of Minnesota's sun-scorched fields and the smoke from Dad's cigar in the driving seat. But above all, the smell of freshly baked doughnuts from Southdale Mall.

22

THE DESERT, OCTOBER 2016

A FLAT LIGHT LAY ACROSS the desert. A huge desert that I crossed alone. I saw no other people, there in that monotonous, desolate landscape, no sign of life at all. But of course, cars count as signs of life. And this parking lot. What if every person on earth apart from me had been whirled up into heaven just a moment ago by some generous-spirited Jehovah? That would have been fine actually, it wouldn't have left me any more alone than I already am. That was my first thought as I woke up, and my last as I fell asleep. That I was lonely. Some days it was just fine, but at other times the loneliness and the burden of the emptiness were so great I felt they were going to crush me. But I couldn't let it, not yet. First I had to do what I had to do. That was the only thing that kept me going now, the only thing that made it worth getting up in the morning. Worth going out. Worth eating the food on the plate in front of me. But afterward, when that was out of the way, what then? Then this eternity would end. Then we would be together again, my beloved. And rest. Eternal rest. So I carried on walking.

It was cloudy and at this time of the autumn the daylight was already noticeably less by six o'clock, which was the time he usually left work.

Suddenly I saw someone. She was standing by her car with the trunk open. She was overweight and out of breath and I could tell she'd been using that overfilled shopping cart as a walker on her way through the desert.

'Hi,' I said.

The big body jerked in surprise and she turned toward me. I could see the panic in her eyes. Then the relief.

'Oh, thank God,' she groaned.

She didn't say it, but I knew anyway. That her first thought was that I was black. I guess Latino was a bit less threatening. Just a bit. I smiled. 'I was wondering if you needed any help?'

'Thanks, but that's OK,' she said, with a look that said help is exactly what she needed. She stared at my face, then at my hands. I walked on.

It took me a while to spot that big blue car, even though I knew where it usually stood and navigated there using the floodlight pylon in the centre of the parking lot. It was a Chevrolet Silverado High Country crew cab. I peered in at the driver's seat. Noted that the neck support was at normal height. The seat pushed not too far forward nor too far back. I used the sleeve of my jacket to wipe away the raindrops from the windshield, took out the roll of wide white tape and tore off three strips. Taped them to the windshield on the driver's side, directly under the roof. It formed a white square approximately three by three inches. I looked at my watch. Five thirty. That gave me half an hour.

23

WHEEL OF FORTUNE, OCTOBER 2016

BOB STOPPED THE VOLVO BY the kerb outside Bernie's Bar. The Happy Hour sign wasn't up. He drummed on the steering wheel as he looked toward the yellow light behind the blinds. So what would that make it in there now? Unhappy Hour? And how unhappy would Chrissie Hynde be if he showed up again so quickly? Only one way to find out.

The man tending the bar looked more like a bouncer than a bartender.

'Where's Liza?' asked Bob.

'She's not in today.'

'I can see she's not in, I asked –'

'I heard what you asked, mister. Can I get you something?'

Bob breathed through his open mouth. He could feel the

rushing start up. He laid his police ID on the bar. 'You want to answer my questions here or down at the station?'

The bartender studied the ID as he poured a glass of beer.

'The kid's sick, so she's at home,' he said. 'Is she in trouble?'

No, thought Bob. He grabbed up his ID and walked out again.

Back in the Volvo he beat his head against the steering wheel.

I'm the one who's in trouble.

He tapped in an A. Then an L. Looked at the I and the C in surprise, and then remembered he had deleted her from his Contacts last night. Alas, he could still remember the number.

'Stan.'

The voice was deep and calm.

The fact that Stan answered Alice's phone without saying anything other than his name told him at least two things. That Alice trusted Stan with her phone, which was something she'd never done with him. And that Stan knew it was Bob ringing and he was ready for a confrontation. Bob could scrape the phone against his thigh and pretend it was a pocket dialling. But the rushing in his head had taken over now and it was the rushing that made the decisions.

'Good evening, meathead. Is Alice there?'

'She asked you not to call her, Bob.'

Bob howled into the phone. He didn't know what had happened, for a moment he was lost, and when he came back his phone was gone. He located it and saw a rose-shaped shatter in a corner of the screen. He typed, Couldn't do it, couldn't be alone now. Had to . . . They only had first names, their surnames were the places he had met them for the first time, usually in a bar. For example, it looked like he knew two sisters with the surname 'Riverfront'.

'Carol.'

'Hi, Carol. Bob here.'

Silence.

'Bob Oz.'

'I can see that. I'm wondering what to say to you.'

'Oh?'

'I know you screwed my friend the day after me.'

'Really? Is –' Bob looked at the phone – 'Tonya Riv— Tonya your friend?'

'Tonya? Have you screwed Tonya as well?'

Bob pressed a hand to his forehead. 'OK, Carol, I'm in the doghouse and I deserve it. But I'm not looking to get laid, I just need someone to talk to. As in, a cup of coffee somewhere.'

Bob heard the rough, bitter laughter. Interrupted by a furious: 'Are you sick?'

'You mean venereal, or some other way?'

He never found out whether she enjoyed the joke or not, she'd already hung up.

He scrolled down. Spun through the names with his index finger the way you spin a wheel of fortune. The list stopped and his eye fell on a name. Dory Anvil. Anvil was a bar, he remembered it, but not Dory. So it probably hadn't been that memorable. But that was exactly what he needed tonight, someone he didn't feel he had to screw. He pressed Call.

'Hi, Bob! At last!'

Bob hesitated. It sounded like it might have been more memorable for her than for him. Could mean she wanted seconds. On the other hand it didn't sound like she would say no to a meeting.

'Hi, Dory.'

'Have you missed me?' Her voice had a false, trilling quality, like a grown woman pretending to be a child.

'Hugely,' said Bob, noting as he did so the way he had unconsciously imitated Mike Lunde's cautious irony.

'Then why didn't you call?'

'Well, let me explain, I lost your number, and –'

'Hilarious, just what I thought!' Her laugh was so high up the register that Bob felt as though his brain was being sliced into by a circular saw. 'That's why I sent you a text with my number, Bob.'

'You did?'

'Yes!' Her laughter died out. 'So why are you lying?'

Bob took a breath. He was so tired. Tired and weary. Weary of Bob Oz.

'To be honest, Dory, and that's not something I usually am, I'm lying because it's so much more fucking pleasant. And I think you should regard the obvious lie as a kind of lifebelt. Grab hold of it, and you'll avoid the humiliation of having me tell you that it's because you just weren't interesting enough.'

A long pause. Then that circular saw of a laugh cut another slice through his brain.

'Hilarious, Bob!'

'Thanks. How are things, Dory?'

'Not bad. I'm at home alone. Want to come over?'

Bob was about to say yes, but something held him back. Dory-Dory-Dory. What was the thing he couldn't quite remember? Had she been crazy? Bit of a prude? Needy? Did she have the clap? A husband? Anyway, none of that mattered now.

'Come on, Bob.'

'Er . . .'

'Hey, I feel horny when you play hard to get, Bob. But I know you want me. And I'll do exactly what you want. Just tell me what it is.'

'Can you make meatballs in brown sauce?'

'Eh?'

'Nothing.' Dory, Dory . . . 'Why are you telling me that you're at home and you're alone?'

'Well, you should know the answer to that.'

'I should?'

'You're the one who put Tony in hospital.'

That Dory. Bob swallowed.

'How . . . how's he doing?'

'Tony? Not too good. You broke his nose and his jaw.'

He heard her sigh. Heard the clink of ice cubes against glass.

'Of course I feel sorry for Tony, but I love the way you fought for me, Bob. You fought for me, you did. Even though he's much bigger!'

Bob heard the slur in her voice now. And the tears.

'Dory, I've just remembered, I'm going bowling tonight.'

'After the bowling then.'

'It's a tournament, be a long night.'

Silence at the other end. He heard a couple of snuffles. 'How about tomorrow then?'

'Would love to, but I think *you've* got something on tomorrow, Dory.'

'I do?'

'You're visiting Tony in hospital and telling him you're never going to hurt him again.'

Dory gave a bitter laugh. 'Hilarious, Bob.'

'Maybe, maybe not. But he was the one who was going to fight for you, Dory. Not me.'

In the silence that followed he could hear her sobbing. He waited until the sobbing stopped. The clink of ice cubes on glass. She cleared her throat and then spoke in a slightly deeper, natural register.

'Enjoy your bowling, Bob.'

Bob Oz drove.

He didn't know where he was going, only that it wasn't home to Phillips. And not to Alice in Cooper. He was tired of the music and turned it off. The radio took over. Bob gathered it was a debate programme when he heard the sonorous tones of the mayor of Minneapolis, Kevin Patterson, declaring that the right to own a gun was about the right to defend one's family, one's children, in the same way as his position on abortion was about the right to defend the foetus.

'But, Mayor,' said the chairperson, 'are you aware that in this country, where there are more weapons than adult human beings, figures from 2010 show that a child or young person is getting shot at the rate of one an hour? That more children's lives are lost from shooting accidents in the home – as many as one every two days – than are saved by all the guns in this country put together?'

'Yes, sure, I know the statistics, Simon. But in the first place, they are produced by freedom haters –'

'The figures are from Congress's own survey –'

'– and in the second place, that's not the point. More people die in traffic, but I haven't yet heard anyone suggest we ban cars.'

'But theoretically perhaps one ought to consider it, if the deaths from traffic accidents get high enough?'

The mayor laughed. 'I guess "theoretically" is the key word there, Simon. And as you know, I'm a practical mayor, I think and act on practical grounds. And I think the principle through.

If banning guns means only the criminal element will use them, doesn't that mean we're depriving our citizens of the right to defend themselves? Then what's next? The right to vote?'

'Is that why you've accepted the invitation to open the NRA's annual conference? Or is it because of the 40,000 dollars they're contributing to your campaign?'

'I have a number of viewpoints in common with the NRA and it was natural for me to accept the invitation, for that reason, and because the conference attracts a lot of people to Minneapolis, and the publicity is good for our city.'

Bob turned off the radio and called Kay Myers.

'Yes, Bob?'

'Sorry to be calling so late, but do you feel like a coffee?'

'Why?'

'I don't know. Talk about the Gomez case. If you have the keys, I could take another look around his apartment. Maybe he's been back.'

Kay Myers's sigh sounded like a drip in a well. 'Even if I did have the keys, you're suspended from duty. What are you up to, Bob?'

'That,' said Bob, 'is one helluva good question.'

They hung up.

Bob searched his memory. It was his habit to use a system of associations to store information. Sometimes it worked, sometimes it didn't, like with Dory. An actor who plays the part of an insane captain, plus a man who really is insane. Gregory Dupont. Simple.

24

RECOIL, OCTOBER 2016

IT WAS STARTING TO GET dark as I watched Cody Karlstad walk through the parking lot. In the half-hour I'd been waiting up there on the roof there had been a lot of activity down below, cars coming, cars going. Through the telescopic sights I followed Karlstad until he reached the big blue pickup, unlocked it and climbed in. My pulse rate was low, even though I hadn't taken the beta blockers as I had considered doing yesterday. I'd worked out that the reason I didn't hit Dante properly was because my pulse rate had been too high.

The interior light came on.

I knew that gave me seven seconds. I knew because this was the fourth day I'd been there at the same time, and each time he had carried out exactly the same ritual. He put his briefcase on the floor in front of the passenger seat, slipped the key in the ignition, fastened his seat belt and turned on the ignition.

Cody Karlstad was a white, middle-class part-owner of an agricultural machinery dealership. He had three children and a wife who worked in the local church. Cody Karlstad was a frugal man. Despite the fact that his car was worth 50,000 dollars he parked it every morning in the free parking slot at Southdale Mall. That was seven o'clock, before the mall opened; he had five thousand vacant parking slots to choose from but he always picked the same one, just about in the centre of the desert. After that he headed over to the machine outside the mall to buy a packet of chewing gum. I guessed he did that so he could tell himself and any parking warden who checked that he was a customer at the mall and qualified to park there free. But of course it could also have been just that he liked chewing gum, or had chronic bad breath. Then Cody Karlstad headed over toward the building where he worked. It shared a parking lot with the women's hospital, and he'd have had to pay a monthly rent of 155 dollars to park there. I knew this because the prices were posted on a yellow metal sign outside the main entrance. I had no idea why the sign was made of metal – did they maybe think the price would never go up?

I was lying on the roof of the parking garage now. Between me and Cody Karlstad was a busy road and a lot of parking lot. Altogether the distance was almost exactly four hundred yards, but through the telescopic sights it looked a lot less than that. With the silencer and the roar of traffic below me no one was going to hear the crack if I squeezed the trigger. *When* I squeezed the trigger. When!

So, I had seven seconds.

Seven seconds before the engine turned over, the headlamps lit up and the interior light automatically went out. But for the seven seconds before Cody Karlstad was wrapped in darkness the lighting would be perfect. On the windshield, positioned above the light, was that white three-by-three square I covered with the cross hairs as I slowly pulled the trigger back. Owing to the angle all I could see were the hands fastening the seat belt, not his face. Perhaps that's why I didn't feel nervous. But I wanted him to fasten his seat belt first, I didn't want him slumping forward and leaving his upper body pressing the horn, which would immediately have drawn attention to the scene. Three seconds. Two. He'd fastened the seat belt.

The rifle butt imparted its slight kick to my shoulder.

I saw a black mark in the white square.

A perfect shot.

I lowered the sights.

In the interior, which was still illuminated, I could see Karlstad's body shaking.

It shouldn't have been shaking. I'd done all the calculations; the distance, the angle, the thickness of the glass, the height of the seat, the length of Cody Karlstad's body from the hips upward. Cody ought to have been sitting motionless with a hole in his forehead. But there he was, shaking like he was strapped to an electric chair.

I loaded the rifle. Took aim again. Calmly. Pulled the trigger. The kick against my shoulder was almost pleasurable. Once again, the shot hit the taped square, an inch higher this time.

And Cody Karlstad stopped shaking.

25

NIGHT-VISION, OCTOBER 2016

OLAV HANSON TOOK ANOTHER CAST with the rod. Saw nothing, could just hear from the reel that the line had run out. He was no fisherman, never would be. But he could cast a long way, and that was something. Pity he was alone here with no one else to see – or more properly hear – the line as it sizzled toward the far bank of the river. The line was still travelling when he felt his phone vibrating. It made him jump. The same way he'd been jumping every time the phone rang following his conversation with Die Man yesterday. But right now he was fishing, so to hell with Die Man, every man had a right to one place where he's his own boss. He let the phone ring three more times before he took it out. He read the name on the display: Joe Kjos.

'Yeah?'

'Hi, Olav, where are you?'

'Never mind. What is it?'

'You asked me to tell you if anything new came up about Tomás Gomez.'

'So?'

'Why, can I ask?'

'None of your business. What you got?'

'Something came in just now, a man shot in the parking lot at the Southdale Mall. There's a couple of patrol cars there and from what I'm hearing Kay Myers thinks it could be Tomás Gomez. Rifle shot from a distance.'

Olav Hanson began reeling in as fast as he could. 'Any detectives on the scene yet?'

'No. Myers is on the phone right now, but she's going up there directly after.'

Southdale wasn't too far away, about midway between where he was and city hall. He might make it.

'See if you can delay her a little, Joe.'

'What?'

'You heard me.'

'But . . . why you want me to do that?'

'I want this case.'

'You?'

Olav knew why Joe was asking; Olav wasn't exactly known for taking on more cases than he strictly had to.

'Yeah, me,' said Olav Hanson and hung up.

There were no indications in Gomez's apartment that he had been back. The couch was still pulled halfway out onto the floor. Bob was sitting on it while checking the cheese melting in the oven. He'd found the landlord Gregory Dupont's phone number, picked up a set of keys from him and bought a semi-cooked pizza in a box from a 7-Eleven.

What do you think you're doing?

What was it about the Gomez case that had him sitting here now, risking the little that was left of his career? It wasn't the victim. Was it Gomez himself, the points of similarity? Was it because he knew how Gomez was feeling? That Gomez had actually done something he had imagined doing himself, and even felt close to doing, waging an all-out war, with no thought of the consequences for himself? But if it was true that he identified with Gomez, then why was it so important for Bob to stop him, of all people? Because it would be the same as stopping himself?

The phone rang. He checked the screen and took it.

'You saying yes to coffee after all?'

'No,' said Kay Myers. 'I need to talk with you.'

'Oh?'

'We've had a sort of execution-style killing at Southdale Mall. I think there are clear similarities to the attempt on Dante's life, I want to know if you see it the same way.'

'I thought I was suspended.'

'Of course we can't put you on the case, but there's nothing irregular about consulting with someone who has relevant information and insight into a case.'

'And if I say no?'

'See you at Southdale,' said Kay Myers and hung up.

Bob stepped out into the cool evening air. He looked across the parking lot. Or parking *lots*, for it was divided up into several sectors that surrounded the shoebox-like buildings in the centre.

The asphalt was still wet following a shower of rain. Bob

headed toward the centre of the parking lot where he saw blue lights flashing up into the sky like Morse signals. But the only sound was the even rumble from Highway 62, which could take you all the way from here into the next county. If that was where you wanted to go. If you thought things might be better there.

Olav Hanson was standing by the band of crime scene tape surrounding the Chevy Silverado. He held up his palm when he saw Bob approaching.

'You're suspended, Aaa-ss. Go home.'

'Myers called me in,' said Bob without looking at his colleague. The doors of the Chevy were open with crime scene techs swarming around it. They looked like beekeepers in their all-white suits. The body had already been moved from the scene.

'Myers isn't here yet, so I'm handling this case and I'm telling you we don't need your help, Aaa-ss.'

Bob registered the strips of white tape and the bullet holes high in the windshield as he took in the scene. Parking garage on the other side of the road. From the angles it was obvious that's where the shots came from. Somewhere high up, probably the roof.

'Did you check to see if they have CCTV cameras over there?'

'We're not idiots, but we do things one at a time. Right now we're trying to find people who might have been here.'

'Been *here*? And seen *what*? A bullet going through a windshield? If they didn't get in touch with the police then, what makes you think they'll want to talk to you now?' Bob had promised not to let himself be provoked when he saw Hanson there, but the repetition of that Aaa-ss had started up the rushing sound again. 'You need to do things in the right order, Hanson, don't you get that? You need to check the –'

'Officer!' Hanson waved his hand at one of the uniformed officers. 'Remove this person from my crime scene, would you please?'

Bob turned and walked away. Crossed the road between cars blaring horns.

At the entrance to the large parking facility he saw the first of the CCTV cameras.

The security room was on the ground floor, a strange oblong shape, with a low ceiling, like something left over after the architects had drawn in the other things they needed. Bob showed the ID card to the two men sitting there. One introduced himself as the duty officer. He had skin with deep, large pores that made him look as if he was composed of pixels. He said he knew there had been a murder out on the parking lot and he had no objection to showing Bob footage from the cameras.

'I'd like to see the roof,' said Bob.

'We don't have a camera there,' said the security guard. 'We have IP cameras, so the weather's too rough for them, especially in the winter. But we've got all the floors covered.'

'Can we go to five thirty and play back all recordings from all cameras at high speed? Simultaneously, I mean. We don't have a lot of time.'

'Sure, but that stuff is old school.' The security guard grinned his satisfaction. 'Check this.'

He typed in a few commands on his keyboard.

'We got two cameras for each field,' he said. 'One that's on all the time and an IPCC-9610 camera that's motion-activated. It has night-vision and –'

'Very impressive, but like I said, we don't have much time.' Bob glanced across at the blue lights in the parking lot.

'OK, OK, then we'll use the IPCC camera here.' The guard tapped in a few more commands. 'See? We skip the pauses, it's non-stop action and the camera automatically zooms in and follows anything that's moving. Check this woman here, for example.' He pointed to one of the tiny images in the mosaic that covered the screen.

'Does the elevator go all the way up to the roof?' asked Bob.

'That and the interior staircase stop at the top floor. From there, there's a separate staircase up to the roof.'

'Perfect. Can we limit what we're seeing to the elevator and the stairway door on the top floor?'

'Sure. Check this.' The guard tapped away with an alacrity that made Bob realise he'd made at least one person happy this week.

The camera followed people and cars as they came and went. As soon as Bob was satisfied a recording didn't show what he was looking for he would ask the guard to fast-forward to the next one. After a dozen of these forward jumps the guard suppressed a yawn.

'Sorry, it's been a lo—'

'Stop!' Bob said. 'Switch to normal speed here.'

The guard tapped on the keyboard and Bob looked at the person coming out from the stairway door. Someone wearing a top with the hood pulled up and shades. He was carrying an oblong package swathed in bubble wrap.

'There you are . . .' whispered Bob. He felt his heart beating a little faster.

The person stopped at the foot of the stairs leading to the roof, turned and looked round.

'Freeze it there!'

The guard's reaction was instant.

'You want him close up too?'

'Please,' said Bob.

Despite the fact that the face on the screen was in partial shadow beneath the hood, and the eyes hidden behind the sunglasses, Bob Oz was in no doubt. This was the man in the composite. This was Tomás Gomez.

'Can you mail me that picture?'

'Sure.' The guard clicked on the Share icon. 'Where to?'

'To every damn patrol car in the city,' Bob muttered half to himself before taking over at the keyboard and punching in the mail address to the duty officer at MPD central.

Clicked Send, said thanks, then headed over toward the shopping mall to wait for Myers.

I got off the bus at the Nicollet Mall. There were always people in this shopping street, even on the coldest winter day. I passed restaurants and bars with music coming from the open doors. I walked by two Latino men standing by a kiosk and sharing a cigarette.

'Hola,' I said.

'Hola,' they answered in unison.

I arrived at the beautiful hundred-year-old building that had once been Dayton's department store. The name may have changed but the stock was pretty much the same. I studied the facade. Noted the security cameras above the entrance. I tightened my grip on the bubble wrap – no one seemed to suspect anything anyway. I took a deep breath, like a diver, before moving on. The moment I was inside the doors I could feel it. The sensation of being somewhere else, that I was now part of Minneapolis's eight square miles of indoor universe, with skyway connections. You could literally spend your whole life in there. You could be born in one of the clinics, live in one of the apartments, eat in the restaurants, go to school there, go to work in an office, get away from things in the theatres and bars. You could die in here, and be laid to rest in the church that was in there somewhere. And as I was thinking that, it struck me: that I was already dead. I just hadn't been laid to rest yet.

I crossed one of the town's streets via a skyway and entered another region, another country.

I walked into a fast-food place and took a seat at the counter, ordered a pizza which you could see being baked inside big, red, infernal ovens. I watched the cheese melting, saw the dough rise, the slices of pepperoni sweating. I was hungry, tired. So tired that for a moment I lost concentration, lost perspective, dropped my guard, and there it was again, the doubt: what the hell are you doing? I pulled myself together and, like I always did, gave a clear answer. Sat up straight in my chair. Looked into the security cameras mounted on the wall above the ovens.

'Your colleague was just here and I showed him the same pictures,' the security guard at the parking garage said.

'I see,' said Olav Hanson as he studied the pictures on the screen in front of them. The lighting and the picture quality were poor, and it had been thirty years since the last time. But he was in no doubt about it. The scars on the face. It was Lobo. He was alive. And he was here.

The phone rang. Joe Kjos.

'Yes?'

'The duty officer at MPD just called. Oz sent them a picture of

Tomás Gomez at a parking garage and asked them to run a facial recognition program on every security camera in the city.'

'Shit! Fried Chicken? But the guy's suspended from duty!'

'That's exactly what the duty officer here just found out. So now he's calling us and wondering what to do, who should he report it to.'

'Report what?'

'That Tomás Gomez has been spotted on a camera at a pizza restaurant at Track Plaza.'

'The shopping mall on Nicollet?'

'Yes.'

Olav Hanson signalled his thanks to the security guard at the parking garage and headed quickly for the door and over to the parking lot and his car.

'Joe?'

'Yeah?'

'Give my phone number to the duty officer and tell him to keep me posted with any updates on Gomez's movements. Just me. Got that?'

Olav got into his car and was about to put the Kojak light on the roof when he saw a Ford pulling into the parking lot. It looked like one of MPD's cars and if he wasn't mistaken that was Kay Myers at the wheel.

'Olav . . .' Joe Kjos said in that slow and annoying way he had whenever he didn't jump when Olav said jump. 'I don't want any trouble. I have to pass this on to Myers, she's on her way out there. So the two of you can argue afterward about whose case it is.'

'OK,' said Olav. 'But give me a twenty-minute start.'

Joe hesitated. 'Isn't this something we should be calling in SWAT for?'

'Let me be the judge of that, Joe. Just give the duty officer my number and those twenty minutes. Do we have a deal?'

'But –'

'Listen, Joe. This is a coupon case. I'm calling in a coupon, OK? God knows I've got plenty of them, right?'

He heard Joe swallow. The coupon system was one of MPD's unwritten rules. In short it meant that if you covered for a colleague – and that could be anything from a minor breach of the rules to something serious – then you had a coupon you could call in next time you needed a favour.

'Twenty minutes,' said Joe Kjos and hung up.

Bob was sitting in Caribou Coffee on Southdale Mall. He checked his watch and was beginning to wonder if Kay Myers had received his text message about where he was when he saw her walk in.

'There you are,' said Kay and slid into a seat. 'Sorry, the techs took longer than expected.'

'What are they saying?'

'Fingerprints on the tape on the windshield. Fingerprints and shoeprints at the edge of the parking garage roof. Apart from that this is a case everybody seems to want. Too many cooks, a lot of mess.'

'You mean Hanson?'

'He's been here and told people that since he's the first detective on the scene the case is his until further notice. He's not even on duty this evening.'

'Then why does he want the case?'

Kay shrugged. 'I guess he's bored, and this seems interesting. Evidently you do too.'

'Me?'

'I went to see the security guard at the parking garage and asked him to show me the footage from the roof. He told me I was the third detective with the same request. And when I sent out a BOLO I was told you'd already done that. That's a lot of cooks, don't you think, Bob?'

Bob shrugged. 'Time is of the essence. This isn't some ego trip for me, I just want to increase our chances of catching Gomez before he manages to disappear again. Where is Hanson now?'

'I don't know, he must've gone. But tell me, if this isn't an ego trip, why didn't you give Assault everything you had on Gomez?'

'Didn't I do that?'

'No. Walker got a phone call from a doctor who said you'd been to see him – he was wondering if he needed police protection.'

'Oh, right, the guy who dispenses Gomez his insulin,' said Bob as he raised his cup. 'You know what, I guess it just slipped my mind.' He drank, meeting Kay's eloquent stare over the lip of the cup.

'The question is,' said Kay, 'do you know anything else about Gomez that might help us?'

Bob pursed his lips and shook his head.

'OK, Bob. I asked you for help. What's your thinking so far?'

Bob smiled at her. He and Kay had started in the Homicide Unit at about the same time. Then as now there were those who believed the doors were held open for people like Kay because she was a woman and she was black, that she reflected the MPD's aim of having the same ethnic mix as the city's population. But Bob had always known that she was a better investigator than he was and that if there was any justice in the world then she would go further, a lot further, than him. And yet she always came to him with cases where she was having trouble. She said it was because his head worked in a different way from hers, that sometimes he was able to help her see cases from another and more fruitful angle. Beyond that they had never been especially close colleagues. Maybe because she'd been one of those slightly too serious types who always went home every time Bob and the others went to a bar to celebrate their little triumphs. Maybe because she wasn't the type to open up and talk about something besides work. So it had been a surprise that after Frankie, when everything started falling to pieces, she was the one who'd been there for him. Covered for him when he didn't turn up for duty and told Walker they'd arranged it between them. Driven him home from work when he hadn't managed to sober up completely. But still kept her distance. All she got for it was trouble she didn't need, it was hard to see it any other way. In the end Bob had figured that Kay Myers was quite simply a better human being that he was.

'Let's start with the victim,' said Bob as he put down his cup. 'Who is it?'

'Cody Karlstad, fifty-three years of age, co-owner of AgriWork, selling everything from combine harvesters and tractors to lawnmowers. No police record, a pillar of the community, trains his youngest son's baseball team in his free time. He's got three kids and a wife who does voluntary work at the Mindekirken, which is –'

'The Norwegian Lutheran Memorial Church,' Bob completed the sentence for her.

'Exactly, that's your people. As you can see, though there are similarities in the method –'

'– there are no obvious similarities in the choice of victims.'

'That's putting it mildly. Dante is a parasite, Karlstad a pillar of the community.'

Cody Karlstad, Cody Karlstad. Bob knew the name from somewhere, he just couldn't place it.

'So no suspicion he was connected to gangs or narcotics?'

'None at all,' said Kay.

Bob ran a hand down his tie. 'What about weapons?'

'He had a pistol, a Glock-17, locked in the glove compartment.'

'I mean, is there any connection to gun dealing, directly or indirectly?'

'No. But he's not exactly anti-gun either.'

'I get that when he has a pistol.'

'Yes, but I was thinking of the bumper sticker on his car.'

'Oh?'

'You didn't see it?'

'Hanson chased me off.'

'An NRA sticker. The one with the two boxes where you can tick off as gun owner or victim.'

Bob nodded slowly. He had it now, where he knew the name Cody Karlstad from.

'We need more guns in the hands of the right people,' he said.

'Sorry?'

'That's what Cody Karlstad said in the *Star Tribune* earlier this summer,' said Bob as he tapped something into his phone. 'He's a spokesman for the NRA-ILA, they campaign against stricter gun laws. A classic more-guns-less-crime fan. Look, this is Cody Karlstad.'

Bob held up his phone that showed a picture of two men in suits posing together.

'Mayor Patterson,' said Kay. 'So Cody Karlstad got to meet people in high places.'

'No great mystery for Patterson to pose for a picture when the NRA are donating 40,000 dollars to his campaign.'

'They did? But Patterson's a Democrat – I thought the NRA only supported politicians on the right?'

'The NRA don't care where a politician stands on agricultural policy, all they care about is where they stand on the Second Amendment of the Constitution. They give politicians marks based on how positive they are about guns and, according to the *Star Tribune*, Kevin Patterson gets an A plus there.'

'So you think gun control is the connection?' said Kay. 'That what we've got here is someone fighting guns with guns?'

'It looks that way.'

'Is Gomez a solitary nutcase or a member of some political terrorist group?'

Bob shrugged. 'How about a solitary, non-crazy political terrorist?'

Kay was about to say something but just then her phone rang. She took the call and looked quizzically at Bob as she listened.

'Gomez has been observed on a security camera at Track Plaza,' she said. She put the phone in her pocket and stood up.

26

SKYWAYS I, OCTOBER 2016

OLAV HANSON WAS PANTING. HE'D run all the way from where he'd parked his car at Track Plaza. He tried to ignore the pain in his knee as the escalator slowly moved him up to the second floor. He got to the top and there, a hundred yards away, he saw the pizza place. It was open toward the communal area, like a restaurant at an airport. He had his phone plugged into one ear and as he had driven from Southdale he'd been getting updates all the way from the MPD's video centre telling him Gomez was still at the restaurant. The video centre received images from over three hundred cameras located indoors and outdoors in the downtown area and was a cooperative enterprise involving law enforcement and local businesses. It had either drastically reduced crime or – as some critics claimed – transferred it to other parts of the city. Concerns about secret surveillance had been dealt with by making the project open to all, using a glass wall behind which anyone could come and sit and see the same pictures as the police. In a word, Olav had an audience. It also meant that what had to happen had to happen somewhere it wouldn't be caught on camera. His shirt was wet with sweat, and he could feel the edge of his holster rubbing against his armpit. The plan was simple but sound. An arrest on camera in front of witnesses and everything done by the book, body search, reading his rights, the whole bit. Apart from the fact that he wasn't going to handcuff Gomez. He'd deliberately left his cuffs in the car and would tell Internal Affairs afterward that he'd forgotten them. He'd take Gomez over to the elevators and order everyone out of the first one that arrived. Because there were no cameras in the elevators. He'd checked. He'd shoot Gomez before they reached the lobby, make sure his fingerprints were on the barrel and say Gomez had tried to grab the gun off him.

Olav put his hand on the butt of his pistol inside his jacket as his gaze wandered over the backs of those sitting at the counter in front of the pizza ovens. None were wearing the hoodie he'd seen on the video at the parking garage. Nobody had the raven-black hair he remembered on Lobo. But if Lobo had moved on, why hadn't the video centre passed on the message? He got his answer when he felt his phone vibrate, opened it up, heard Kay Myers's voice and understood his twenty minutes were already up.

Kay's Ford was held up in traffic. Bob – sitting in the passenger seat – had told her that if she'd had a Kojak light they would have been at Track Plaza inside fifteen minutes. It didn't improve her humour.

'Hanson?'

'Yes?' Olav Hanson's voice came over the speaker.

'I've talked to the video centre and told them to send all further information via me from here. Where are you?'

'I've got this, Myers. I expect to be arresting Gomez at any moment. I'll let you know if I need backup.'

'I repeat, where are you?' said Kay.

'Myers, like I told you –'

'This is my case, Hanson, and I'm asking you to provide me with adequate information.'

'I was first on the crime scene, Myers, it's –'

'Bullshit! The instructions are for the duty detective to take the case until notified otherwise. You want to complain about it, call Walker. So for the last time, and before this thing goes any further: where the hell are you and what is happening?'

There was a long silence.

'I'm at the pizza restaurant,' Hanson said eventually. 'Gomez isn't here any more. What does the video centre say about where he is?'

'Just that he's moved away from the pizza restaurant, and they haven't seen him on any of the skyways so he's probably still inside the Track Plaza building. I've called in SWAT, so if you find Gomez, keep him under observation but do not attempt an arrest on your own. Got that?'

'But –'

'No buts. Let me know if you see Gomez and I'll send in SWAT.'

Another silence.

'OK,' said Hanson.

They broke the connection.

'I still don't get what he thinks he's doing,' said Kay.

‘Maybe he sees his chance to get a St Cloud,’ said Bob.

Kay shrugged. Bob was referring to a part-time officer who had shot and killed a man who went berserk with two knives inside a shopping mall in St Cloud. The officer, who ran a shooting range and was armed wherever he went, even on an off-duty visit to a shopping mall, became a local hero and a poster boy for the NRA, who had bestowed on him the dubious title ‘NRA Officer of the Year’.

‘Hanson may be stupid, but he isn’t crazy,’ said Kay. ‘How this ends is up to Gomez.’

The traffic wasn’t moving and further ahead in the jam she saw a police car, a rescue vehicle and two damaged private cars.

‘OK,’ said Bob, ‘maybe Hanson won’t shoot anyone, but I guarantee you that if he sees Gomez, he won’t wait for us or SWAT. If we stay in this queue much longer he’ll have the cuffs on Gomez and be posing for the press photographers long before we get there. So I suggest you swing up onto the sidewalk and drive round.’

‘You men and your pissing contests,’ Kay snorted. ‘What matters is that *someone* arrests him, not who does it.’

For eight seconds they remained there in silence.

Then Myers put her foot down hard, swung the car up onto the sidewalk and sped past the jammed cars with the horn going full blast.

27

SKYWAYS II, OCTOBER 2016

IT WAS A HARRY WINSTON diamond ring. It lay cushioned on black velvet in the jewellery-store window and twinkled more brightly than any of the others. Tomorrow would have been our wedding anniversary. It was expensive. But I had the money. Monica hadn't wanted a ring like that, though, and she didn't get one either, but I knew she would have loved it. And I would have loved it. Loved to have been standing in the kitchen making our breakfast, knowing that right then she was waking up and discovering the box on the pillow. No, it wasn't correct to say our anniversary *would have been* tomorrow, it *was* tomorrow. You can't stop the days from coming. Time just keeps rolling along, no matter how meaninglessly.

The security guard inside the jeweller's stood with his arms folded, swaying back and forth on his toes. There was no music to sway to, the stores at Tracks quit playing canned music after research showed that it distracted people from their shopping. The guard could see me out here. From the scarred Latino face and the moth-eaten hoodie he guessed I couldn't afford their jewels. Maybe he was wondering what was inside the bubble wrap. When you work security I guess you see potential threats everywhere. You don't ask yourself, 'Is that thing there a rifle?' You ask, 'Can I *exclude completely* the possibility that that thing there is a rifle?' Well, anyway, I guess that's a question people in this country must have been asking themselves ever since the birth of the nation: does that person intend to shoot me?

I raised my gaze. I wasn't looking at the ring now but at the reflection in the glass. Behind me, on the other side of the shopping mall where people were hurrying along, a man was standing talking into his phone as he studied the interior of the pizza restaurant I had been sitting in just a few minutes ago. There was something familiar about him. Could that really be Olav Hanson, the Milkman? If he was looking for me then he'd been quick. I took one last look at the ring. Then moved on. Took a right along a short corridor between a store selling bags and one selling toys, to where the bathrooms were on this floor. I entered the men's room. The stall I had intended to use was occupied, but I taped a note to the door before exiting and rejoining the stream. The people coming my way looked past me, like I was invisible. I liked being invisible, being able to move about freely, being a fly on the wall, listening and picking up snippets of information here and there about the progress of the investigation, being close to them in a place where it would never have occurred to them to look. But I didn't want to be invisible all the time. I needed to show the world who I was. And then: what I was.

I looked up into the camera above the skyway I stepped onto. Looked down again. A cop car glided out into the street below me. Then another. Both had blue lights but no sirens. Like something was urgent, but they mustn't be heard just yet, like beasts of prey sneaking up on their victims. And behind them a large green vehicle with SWAT written in white on the side. The cars stopped, men in black carrying automatics and wearing visors jumped out and ran toward the entrance. I turned and hurried back the way I had come.

Kay pulled up outside a sidewalk restaurant in Nicollet Mall where smokers sat shivering under heat lamps with their glasses of beer. As Bob stepped out of the car Kay was already heading up the street and fishing out the ringing phone from her jacket pocket.

'Hey,' shouted a waiter. 'You can't park –'

'MPD,' said Kay, holding up her ID without slackening her pace and putting the phone to her ear. Bob had to jog to keep up. The heels of her shoes beat out an angry rhythm against the sidewalk as she spoke into the phone in short, quick bursts:

'He turned in a skyway? OK. We're a minute away.' She dropped the phone back into her pocket. 'The video centre thinks Gomez is still on the second floor of Track Plaza.'

Kay Myers stepped up her pace.

Olav Hanson made his way further into the centre. There were a lot of people now it was evening and he wasn't able to take in all the faces heading his way. The plan could still work if he could only locate that damn Gomez. But it had to be now. Soon the place would be swarming with police, and once Gomez was under arrest and being held in custody it would be more complicated to get rid of him. Olav's gaze swept forward and back like a lighthouse. Where are you, Gomez? His fingertips were still damp from touching the sweat rings beneath his shoulder holster. He put a finger to his upper lip and breathed in the smell. Adrenaline. Fear.

A little boy in a Timberwolves T-shirt approached, dancing in front of his parents, blissfully ignorant of the future. Ignorant of the fact that one day he would be what? A corrupt police officer with a failed football career behind him, two failed marriages and a failure of a son? A killer? Olav hadn't killed anyone yet, not directly. What would it feel like to shoot someone, to kill them? He didn't know, but the thought of it didn't bother him as much as it probably should have. Maybe because he wasn't doing it for pleasure but to survive. Anyway, the man he intended to kill should have been in a courtroom long ago, and in a state that still had the death penalty. No, shooting this killer wasn't something he would lose any sleep over. Quite the opposite, he would sleep better. He would even *feel* better, once he got it done. Straightened out a couple of things. Got back to being the man he once was. *If* he could get it done.

There!

He had caught a glimpse of a face in the crowd a little further ahead. It was him. He recognised the hoodie and the bubble-wrap package beneath the arm. Olav Hanson veered over to the left of the walkway to intercept, with the result that two tall, laughing teenage boys bumped into him and he lost sight of Lobo.

'Sorry,' the two sang out in chorus.

'Fuck you,' Hanson muttered as he looked round for Lobo. Gone! Shit, how was that possible? Lobo must have seen him, ducked down and run. Had he recognised him as the Milkman and understood he must be looking for him? Olav noticed the sign for the restrooms up on the wall. He saw now that a corridor ran between the stores where he had just now caught sight of him.

Restrooms. No cameras there. No witnesses if the arrest took place in one of the stalls.

Olav Hanson put his hand inside his jacket again. Fought his way down the corridor. The door to the bathroom swung open, a man walked out and Olav caught a glimpse of the backs lined up along the washbasins. He picked up the sound of men in a hurry and thought of running water, slamming doors, movements that attracted attention, that here was the perfect camouflage. He no longer felt the pain in his knee, just a rush, a delicious free fall, a certainty that the moment had come, the seconds were ticking down to the final whistle at what might possibly be a defeat, but that it was his turn to tackle someone out of the life they were dreaming about.

'Hanson!'

The voice came from behind and cut through the steady buzz of noise from Track Plaza. Hanson cursed inwardly. It was Kay Myers's voice.

Bob walked two paces behind Kay and one step ahead of O'Rourke. Two uniforms behind them.

They stopped in front of Olav Hanson, who gave them a look like a man who had just lost a poker pot.

'Have you seen Gomez?' asked Kay.

Olav Hanson gave a regretful shake of the head.

'That's funny,' said Kay. 'Because it looked like you were on your way to the restroom where the video centre says Gomez just went in.'

'Really?' said Hanson, and Bob registered that the older detective was an even worse actor than he was himself. At the same time something seemed to be going on behind that stupid, staring gaze.

Hanson pulled a face. 'Well, I saw Gomez,' he said. 'But I lost him. Did he go into the bathroom?'

'You have trouble with your hearing?' asked Kay and turned to one of the uniforms. 'Keep people away. No one is allowed to enter this bathroom.'

Hanson looked at O'Rourke. 'If you go in there, remember the guy is armed and dangerous. A lot of people might get hurt, so I wouldn't exactly hesitate to . . . you know –' Hanson raised his right hand and crooked his index finger.

O'Rourke nodded and looked questioningly at Kay Myers.

She bit her lower lip.

'Let's wait and we'll get him when he comes out,' she said.

The restroom was big, big as an airport restroom, with eight urinals, most of them occupied. Further in at least a dozen stalls. There were no windows in here. I walked past the men standing and washing or drying their hands at the basins in front of the mirror. Stopped at a stall with a handwritten note taped to the door, OUT OF ORDER. The O in the middle had an eye, a nose and a smiley mouth drawn on it. A large fan whirred in the ceiling above the stall. I tore off the note, pushed open the door, stepped inside, locked it and unwrapped the gun and the leather case from the bubble wrap. Then I started to strip the weapon, breaking it down to its component parts.

28

SKYWAYS III, OCTOBER 2016

BOB HAD TAKEN UP A position some distance from the SWAT team that was waiting in readiness outside the door to the restrooms. Men who emerged at irregular intervals through the swing door jumped at the sight of those black-clad men with automatic weapons pointing in their direction. Kay, Hanson and O'Rourke stood behind them and watched. Behind Bob, curious passers-by stopped to watch, even after being told to move on.

One of the SWAT team pushed a thin wire through the door. Bob knew there was a micro camera on the end of it. Kay approached him.

'What's up?' she asked.

'What?'

'You're shaking your head.'

'Am I?'

'Yes. So what is it?'

'I don't know,' said Bob. He saw Hanson say something to O'Rourke, who turned and looked in Bob's direction. 'It just . . . it feels wrong. As though . . .'

'As though what?' asked Kay. She was standing next to him. Her arms were folded, same as his.

'As though he's playing cat and mouse with us. And he's the cat.'

'Why –' Kay began, but Bob interrupted her.

'Wait a moment.' He ran after a man in a grey Minnesota Twins sweater who had just emerged from the toilet and was being waved on by the SWAT men. Bob caught up with him outside the bag store. 'Excuse me, sir. MPD. Did you see anything in there?'

The man looked at Bob. 'Like what?'

'A Latino carrying something wrapped in bubble wrap?'

'No. What's going on?'

'You'll see it on the news. When you say no, do you mean he might have been there but that you didn't see him?'

The man hesitated. 'He could have been in one of the stalls, I guess.'

'Thank you, sir.'

Bob ran back.

O'Rourke and one of the SWAT team were studying a phone screen that was relaying a feed from the micro camera.

'We have to go in and take him *now*,' said Bob.

O'Rourke glanced at Bob then held up his palm like a Stop sign. As Bob waited for the SWAT chief to finish looking at the screen he saw that the man in the Twins sweater had stopped next to a guy wheeling a cleaner's cart who looked like Super Mario. He was saying something, then pointing to the toilet, then up at the roof. Super Mario nodded like he understood.

'We need you to get out of here.'

Bob turned, realising that O'Rourke had been talking to him.

'I'm sorry?'

'You're under suspension, Oz, only serving police officers are allowed on the scene. Get out of here. Now.'

'Listen, I'm starting to understand Tomás Gomez. He knows what he's doing.'

O'Rourke looked over Bob's shoulder, pointed at Bob and made a signal.

'Listen to me, O'Rourke. Gomez has a plan. He has to be taken *now*!'

O'Rourke licked his lips. 'That will be all thank you, Oz.'

He felt a heavy hand on each shoulder. Turned. Two sturdy uniformed officers were standing behind him.

'Come on, Detective, we've got orders to escort you out of here.'

Bob looked past them, saw Hanson standing a few yards behind with a mocking grin on his lips. Felt that rushing start up. Saw Kay spread her arms in exasperation. Told himself he mustn't lose control. Not now.

'I'm leaving,' said Bob, and tried to push away the hands clutching his shoulders.

They stayed where they were, just as heavy.

'Escort you,' one of the two said curtly. Bob guessed by the looks on their faces that they weren't interested in discussing it. He bunched and then opened both his hands. Breathed regularly and counted.

'Take him now,' Bob managed to say in a low voice to O'Rourke before one of the two uniforms dragged him almost off-balance and he was led from the scene.

'There's no need to hold me,' Bob said as they crossed the skyway to the neighbouring building.

Still they kept a hold of him, one on each arm.

Think before you speak, think before you act. Tell yourself you can control your anger.

They didn't let go of him until they reached the other side, and Bob realised that he'd managed it. He really had surprised himself by proving that he didn't *have* to go berserk every time. It was just a pity there was no one he could share it with.

What looked like people from a TV news team came hurrying in their direction. In the lead was a female reporter holding a microphone, with two men behind her, one carrying a camera with KSTP-TV on it. They disappeared onto the skyway leading to the Track Plaza building.

'We've got orders to arrest you if you try to come back,' one of the officers said. 'Got that?'

'Got it,' said Bob, who was trying to keep track of where the reporter had gone.

The two officers left, and Bob pulled down the sleeves of his cashmere coat and straightened his tie as he looked around. Met a couple of curious stares but did his best to ignore them. Dignity – what the hell does a man need with dignity? This was obviously the floor for places to eat. And drink. Directly in front of him was a flashy sports bar with giant screens all showing the same baseball game. He had a quick think. Then he took out a loop from his coat pocket, took out the ID card, fastened it to the loop and hung it round his neck.

'What'll it be, sir?' said the bartender as Bob approached the counter.

'Switch to KSTP,' he said.

The bartender laughed. '*Fat chance*. Can't you see the Timberwolves are playing?'

'*Fat chance*? Can't you see this card? It means you do what I damn well tell you to do.'

The bartender peered at the ID. Shrugged, pressed a switch behind the counter that at once gave rise to a unison groan from the watching customers. That fell silent the next moment.

'. . . Track Plaza where police are hunting the suspect who shot and killed a man at Southdale Mall earlier this afternoon. There is a heavy police presence at the scene.' While the news anchor talked, pictures showed the police cars in Nicollet Mall and Bob caught a glimpse of Kay and himself heading for the entrance. The view went split-screen, with the studio anchor on one half and the female reporter Bob had just seen on the other.

'What's happening now, Shirley?'

'Right now we're standing on a skyway because everyone has been told to stay away from the place where the suspect may emerge. There are reports that he's armed, but none of the police are willing to talk to us. But I'll do my best to get an interview, Rick.'

'Thanks, Shirley. We'll be back with more on this story after the weather.'

For a couple of seconds a weather chart filled the screen, then the Timberwolves were back. Following a few seconds of shocked silence there were ironic cheers and a couple of customers hurried out of the bar. The bartender put his forearms on the counter and leaned over toward Bob, biceps bulging.

'I'm guessing you ain't about to use your authority to check the weather, Lieutenant.'

'Detective.'

'Whatever.'

'OK,' said Bob. 'Five minutes of basketball. And a double Johnnie Walker.'

Without turning round the bartender reached up to the shelf behind him, took hold of a bottle and poured a drink.

'Pretty smart trick,' said Bob, tossed back the contents and put the empty glass back on the counter. 'How about letting me see it one more time?'

Things were looking bad for the Timberwolves and got even worse when they missed two desperate efforts at three-pointers. Bob recalled what the coach of his soccer team once said, that losing affects your ability to take good, rational decisions. And Bob had been losing for some time now. At least in sport the games come to an end and you get to start the next match at 0–0. He checked the time. Three minutes had passed, but already he could feel the effects of the whisky.

'Tell me what's happening . . .' a voice behind him said.

He turned. It was Shirley, the reporter. She was standing up close to him and smiling invitingly. She took hold of his ID card '. . . Detective Bob Oz.'

'What's happening,' said Bob, and heard how he slurred a consonant slightly as he fastened his gaze on her husky-blue eyes, 'is that I am halfway down a Johnnie Walker and then you and I are going to have another one. Alice has kicked me out, I fuck everything that moves, and I'm suspended for defending myself against Tony. How about you, Divine Blue?'

'Sorry, Rick, strike one,' she said laughing into the microphone which Bob now saw for the first time. 'Back to you.'

She removed an earphone from under the long red hair, the smile was gone, and she wasn't laughing along with the cameraman and sound technician crouched behind her.

'What the fuck,' said Bob. 'Did that go out live?'

'Just local TV,' Shirley said sourly, in a tone that suggested she was aiming for bigger things. 'But this'll be out on YouTube soon enough.'

'Funny,' said Bob. 'What's happening back there?'

'Don't know, they're keeping us away. A black man against MPD, no witnesses. Poor man.'

'He isn't . . .' Bob started to say, but Shirley and her team were already on their way out.

Bob swore, paid and left.

People were crowded onto the skyway and trying to get a view into Track Plaza. Super Mario was among them, with his cleaning cart. Bob approached him.

'Excuse me,' he said, flashing his ID card. 'I saw you talking to a guy who just came out of the restroom. It looked like he was explaining about something inside, what was it?'

Super Mario looked up at Bob. 'The fan has fallen out.'

'The fan?'

'The fan in the ceiling. It's hanging open. He said someone should fix it.'

'You mean the fan in front of the ventilation shaft?'

'Yeah.'

Kay watched as yet another man emerged from the restroom and froze at the sight of the weapons pointing his way.

'He's been in there nearly ten minutes now,' she said to O'Rourke and Hanson.

'Maybe he knows we're here,' said O'Rourke.

'Sir!' Kay stopped the man who was being ushered past them. 'Did you see anyone else in there?'

The man shook his head and was led away.

'Maybe Gomez has noticed that people are going out but no one's coming in,' said Kay.

The other two didn't respond.

'He's getting away!'

The shout came from behind them and all three turned round. They saw Bob Oz trying to get past the two uniformed police officers who were holding him back.

'Get that guy out of here!' O'Rourke yelled.

'Wait,' said Kay.

'The ventilation shaft,' Bob shouted. 'It's open!'

O'Rourke looked at Bob. He looked at Kay. He adjusted his helmet. 'We're going in now.'

The leader signalled to one of the SWAT team, who opened the door slightly and rolled in a stun grenade. Kay could hear the sound of the grenade bouncing across the tiled floor. The door was closed. She put her hands over her ears, heard two dull thuds and then the SWAT team swarmed in. O'Rourke went in right behind them, and a few seconds later he was back in the open doorway. His face told them all they needed to know, but he said it anyway.

'Our bird has flown.'

Bob followed Olav Hanson and Kay Myers into the restroom. He saw at once that next to where the fan was hanging down was a hinged door in the ceiling, above one of the cubicles. It looked like it was possible to squeeze in through the hole. Bob went over to O'Rourke, who was standing outside the open cubicle. The bubble wrap lay spread out on the floor in front of the closet. Already one of the SWAT people was standing on the toilet and feeding the wire with the micro camera in through the opening above.

'No one here,' he said to O'Rourke. 'Just this.'

He picked something up out of the shaft and handed it down to his leader.

'What is this?' asked O'Rourke.

'It's an insulin needle,' Bob said behind him. 'Gomez has diabetes. He's trying to crawl out through there. Isn't anyone going to go in after him?'

'How about you, Oz?' O'Rourke handed him the needle. 'Or would you prefer to send Myers?'

Bob locked eyes with the SWAT boss.

'No?' said O'Rourke. He pulled off his helmet, unfastened the bulletproof vest, handed his rifle and his pistol to one of his men. 'Good thing Bonzo's up for it then.'

'Hanson,' said Kay, 'find out where these ventilation shafts exit and get some of your men over there.'

'OK.'

Bob watched as two of O'Rourke's men helped him up until he grabbed hold of something inside the ventilation shaft and managed to pull himself up into it. Once he was up they handed him his helmet with the headcam and flashlight and his pistol.

'Radio silence?' one of the men asked.

'If he's there then he'll hear me coming a mile off,' said O'Rourke. 'Just listen in and I'll try to give you guys a good show.'

They heard a rumbling in the shaft and then O'Rourke was gone. One of his men held a phone as the others gathered round. Bob went over and looked at the screen. The mere sight of it gave him claustrophobia. In the cone of light cast in front of O'Rourke's camera all that was visible were his hands and the cylindrical walls of the shaft, and now and then the jerking of the light flashed on the pistol he was holding in one hand. The panting and grunting grew heavier, drowning out any sounds that might be made by someone waiting for him. Every so often O'Rourke stopped and then everyone listened out. But all they heard was a regular whirring noise.

'There's a fan up ahead here,' O'Rourke whispered.

Soon those gathered around the phone saw the same thing, a large fan at the end of the shaft where it split left and right at a T-junction.

'He must have got out this way,' said O'Rourke. 'The shafts going the other way get narrower.'

The SWAT leader pushed the fan several times before it swung out and down on its hinges. He put his head out. On the screen Bob saw the deserted yard with trucks and loading bays closed up for the night. Two uniformed officers came running into the yard with walkie-talkies crackling and guns drawn.

'Gomez must be a tough guy,' said O'Rourke, turning his head downward so that his audience could see it was a drop of at least eight yards to the asphalt. 'Either he knows how to fall properly or he's out there somewhere dragging a broken leg behind him.'

I walked quickly through the downtown streets, between the deserted office blocks, past the empty alleyways where it wasn't safe after dark. But I wasn't afraid. Not any more. They were the ones who should have been afraid. My racing pulse told me only that I was alive, I felt things, and for the first time in a long time. This was dangerous, enjoyably dangerous. The only thing that worried me was that I'd made it a little more exciting than necessary. As though something in me wanted to give them the chance to stop me. Is that what I wanted? Of course not. I had given myself a task. Or had I? Was I even really the one who had given me the task? What I did know was that it had to be completed, that I mustn't give in to the temptation of peace, of at last being able to sleep in the same bed as you, my beloved, of holding our children. Nor could I let myself be distracted by moral queasiness and short-sightedness. The sum total of suffering for all innocents would be so much greater if I failed to complete the task than the suffering it would cause to a handful of innocent people. I had to steel myself. Only two days to go now.

A family came walking toward me along the sidewalk. Talking and laughing, they sounded happy, maybe they'd been to the movies, or eaten out at a restaurant. Maybe they thought nothing bad could happen to them because they did everything right; they worked hard, helped out in the community, helped those who carried a heavier burden than themselves.

'Hola,' I called out as I passed them. But got no response this time, just looks of mild surprise, as though they couldn't work out if it was some kind of joke.

I swallowed. Had to keep my concentration up. Couldn't relax. Even a slight mistake could tip the whole thing over. But, afterward, let it all fall down.

29

FEELING MINNESOTA, OCTOBER 2016

KAY ENTERED THE ALMOST EMPTY sports bar, saw the mustard-yellow coat and slipped onto the bar stool next to him.

'Sorry,' she said.

'For what?'

'For letting them run you off like that.'

'Not your fault. SWAT make the rules when they're leading the operation.'

'I could have protested, but it wasn't the time or the place.'

'Agreed. Don't think about it. You made sure they listened to me about the fan.'

'They should have listened to you and gone in immediately.'

Bob took a sip of his whisky and nodded in the direction of the news broadcast on the screen behind the bar. 'Rick there has just explained to the viewers that the MPD managed to lose the murder suspect Tomás Gomez while they had him surrounded in a public restroom.'

Kay groaned. 'Guess I need a drink too.'

Bob signalled to the bartender. 'A Johnnie Walker for the lady.'

The bartender repeated his trick of grabbing the bottle without looking.

'Not bad, eh?' said Bob.

'He must've practised,' said Kay and waited impatiently for the glass in front of her to be filled.

'Apropos,' said Bob. 'I've been thinking about what O'Rourke said about how it almost seems as though Gomez has had some kind of training.'

'What about it?' said Kay.

'Gomez is strong and supple. He got up into that shaft where O'Rourke needed two guys to help him up. And so quietly that no one else noticed anything. Before he dropped down into the yard he must have been hanging by his fingertips, pulled himself up again and used his head to snap the fan back into place. Not something you or I could have managed. And not O'Rourke either, even though he's in good shape.'

'Well, some people are just stronger than others,' said Kay. She emptied her drink, nodded to the bartender and pointed at the glass.

'I think Gomez has planned this whole thing very carefully. He's been working out with precisely this end in mind. And just the same way both murders were carefully planned, this last little game of his was planned too.'

'You think so?'

'Don't you see? That it's just a little bit too much of a coincidence he ends up in a restroom where the ventilation shaft leads out into an empty backyard. That the fan is just high enough up on the wall for it not to be welded in as a precaution against somebody breaking in that way but low enough to make it possible to drop down from, provided you have training in how to fall, like a paratrooper. Maybe he had the foresight to place something on the ground to break his fall, some kind of mat or something.'

'Where are you going with this? That we should be looking for Tomás Gomez among elite soldiers or police officers?'

Bob took the vibrating phone out of his jacket pocket and checked the display.

'More Walker,' he said as he tapped the keypad and took the call. 'Good evening, chief.'

'Oz,' rumbled Superintendent Walker. 'Did you see that item on KSTP?'

'Should I have?'

'It was broadcast live and you were on it, Oz.'

'Well, then of course I haven't seen it.'

'Of course?' snorted the superintendent.

'You said yourself, chief, it went out live and I was too busy being on it.'

'I mean, have you seen it *afterward*? It's all over the internet.'

'Honestly, chief, I did not know it was an interview, she sneaked up on me.'

'What the hell were you even doing at Track Plaza? You're suspended, Oz! And you were drunk, dammit.'

'I had a Johnnie Walker to deal with, chief. I drank it. I drink. I'm suspended, dammit.'

In the ensuing silence Bob listened to the superintendent's

puffing. The next time Walker spoke he had lowered the volume but not the intensity:

'I want you to stay well clear of this case, Oz. Do you hear me?'

'Aye aye, chief. I promise. Starting now. Got to go.' Bob hung up.

'What does he want you to start on?' asked Kay.

'Finding Gomez,' said Bob as he put the glass to his mouth.

Kay looked at him, eyebrows raised.

'We close at ten,' said the bartender. 'The whole centre does.'

'OK,' said Bob. 'Give us another two each and we'll be happy.'

'By the way,' said Kay, 'there was something left inside that bubble wrap.' She pulled a sheet of paper from her pocket and opened it out.

'A target,' said Bob.

'From a rifle range, you think?'

'A four-hundred-yard rifle target.'

'Oh?'

'You can tell from the dimensions. Professionally made too. Krüger.' Bob pointed to the producer's name, printed vertically but discreetly in the bottom corner.

'Wouldn't have thought someone who hated guns as much as you would know so much about shooting,' said Kay.

'There's a lot people don't know about me, Kay. I'm an enigma.' Bob held the two glasses in front of him, one in each hand, and took a sip from each in quick succession, without getting a laugh.

'No,' said Kay. 'You're just One-Night Bob, nothing too mysterious about that.'

The corners of Bob's mouth rose in a smile. 'My cousin called me Rundbrenner Bob.'

She looked uncomprehendingly at him.

'It's a Norwegian expression. It means someone who screws

around. A *rundbrenner* is a big wood-burning stove. One that spreads its warmth around to a lot of people. You get it?'

'But you can't spread warmth, Bob. Because there's nothing burning inside you.'

'No?'

'It's dark and cold in there, isn't that right?'

'*I'm looking Chicago,*' sang Bob as he raised his glass in a salute, '*and feeling Minnesota.*'

'What's that?'

'You're not a grunge fan? So tell me about Chicago.'

'Chicago?' She emptied her glass. 'I spent most of my time in Englewood and that's not the Chicago you want to hear about.'

'Yes I damn well do.'

'No. I saw my mother . . .' She closed her eyes and sighed. 'Forget it.'

'Forget it?'

'It's just the booze talking. Time I was getting home to feed the cat.'

'Come on, Myers, I'm sensing a crack in your armour here.'

Kay looked at the last glass in front of her. It was still full.

'My dad ran off before I was born,' she said. 'Nothing unusual about that in Englewood. Or that he was just another victim of the crack epidemic. What was special was that he would come home and rob my mother when he needed money. Because my mother had two jobs, she actually managed to put some aside for my sister and me to get an education. After the third time he broke in, beat my mother up and stole from us, she bought a gun. All she had to do was go into a store, fill out a few simple forms and she left carrying a weapon. I know you hate guns, but I tell you, when my sister and me were sleeping there in my mother's bed and she had that pistol underneath the pillow, we all felt safer. And that's a safety you middle-class liberals know nothing about because it's just something you take for granted. But for three girls in Englewood the gun was the great equaliser. It meant we didn't have to be helpless victims and let someone terrorise us because he was physically stronger. It didn't stop my mother from crying inside, but that gun changed our daily lives. Not a shot was ever fired from it, but it made us that little bit safer, we slept better, we could go to school and get ourselves an education. And I know the statistics that show what guns can do to a society like Englewood in the long run. But I'm being honest, you don't care a damn about the long run when your life is about surviving one night at a time.'

In silence Bob raised his glass to Kay, but she shook her head, she had to drive and she was pretty sure she was already skirting the limit.

By the time they left the bar, Bob was unsteady on his feet.

'My car's over at Southdale,' he said to Kay as she got into her Ford, 'and I need to clear my head anyway.'

'Bob,' said Kay, 'you're too drunk to drive and you shouldn't be out at this time. Let me drive you home.'

'Thanks, sweetie, but it's OK. Your cat awaits, and they have buses here.'

It began to rain as Bob was waiting for the bus. The young couple also waiting checked on a phone and told the other three at the stop that the police had cancelled all public transport until further notice because an armed suspect was believed to be loose in the area. Bob groaned and started to walk. It was too far to walk all the way home to Phillips, but he ought to be able to make it as far as Dinkytown, and from there he could pick up a bus outside Bernie's Bar.

Maybe take a last drink there.

Maybe.

A drink and someone to talk to.

Liza.

God knows why he kept thinking about a woman with a limp who showed no interest in him and gave him nothing but sarcastic comments. Was this the level he had sunk to? On the other hand, there was something about the way she combined an acute bullshit detector with black humour, and what he suspected was a warm heart. Of course, he could have been mistaken. But he wanted to know. Not that she needed a guy like him, she knew that well enough, she'd told him straight out. Maybe it was this simple, that you start wanting someone you don't really want once you see she doesn't want you. Like two losers underbidding each other until one ends up a winner. Bob laughed and saw a couple of heads turn in his direction and realised he was still drunk. And wet. Soaking wet. The cashmere coat hung on him like some drowned furry animal. He passed a store window where the lights were out for the night and pressed his face to the glass. It looked like a forest at dusk, when all the creatures come out. And far inside he saw light coming from a door that was ajar. Bob hammered on the store door, long and hard, until finally the door back there opened and a man walked to the front of the store and unlocked the door. Mike Lunde took off his glasses and gave Bob an anxious look.

'Detective Oz?'

'Tomás Gomez shot and killed a man just a few hours ago.'

'Oh no.' Mike Lunde's face twisted into a grimace, as though the information caused him physical pain.

'It's on the news,' said Bob.

'I've been working non-stop on the Labrador since I closed the store – it has to be ready by Saturday. Have you caught him?'

'No,' said Bob. 'We think he's on foot, so we're looking for him here in downtown. I'd like to come in, in case he tries to hide out here.'

'I doubt whether you're on the job, Detective Oz.'

'You do?'

'You're drunk.'

Bob opened his mouth, expecting some plausible explanation of his predicament to emerge. But it didn't. He shrugged.

Mike Lunde sighed. 'How about a cup of coffee?'

30

DEATH PENALTY, OCTOBER 2016

'SO NOW HE'S OFFICIALLY A killer,' Mike Lunde said with an unhappy shake of the head.

They were sitting in the smaller of the two workshops as Bob sipped at the strong black coffee which Mike told him he needed.

'Yeah,' said Bob. He'd hung his clothes up to dry and was wearing sweatpants and a sweater borrowed from Mike. 'One attempted murder, now an actual murder. Victim is a family man who as far as we know never hurt a fly. Gomez can count himself lucky we're on this side of the state border.'

'Because of the death sentence, you mean?' Mike stood working his scalpel around the eyes of the Labrador retriever up on his workbench.

'Yeah.' Bob leaned back in his chair. He was already beginning to sober up. And not feeling too bad either. 'Where do you stand on that? Do you think we should be executing people too?'

Mike paused his cutting and peered up into the air. 'It's a difficult one. I'm against capital punishment because I believe that as a society we should be taking a lead in the whole civilisation project, and that means not taking human life. And as I read somewhere, the long view suggests that fewer murders are being committed here. And that applies also to other states that don't have the death penalty, I think?'

'True enough. But?'

'Well, that man they executed four or five years back . . .'

'Donald Moeller.'

'That's right. He raped and killed a nine-year-old girl, didn't he?'

'Yeah. She went to the store to buy sugar. They were going to make lemonade. After he raped her, he cut her throat.'

Bob saw that pained expression cross the taxidermist's face again.

'Sorry, Mike, maybe you have kids yourself.'

'That's OK. Actually that's the point. If it had been my own child, how would I have felt then about capital punishment?'

'Like Tomás Gomez,' said Bob.

Mike gave him a puzzled look.

'Cody Karlstad, the man who was shot this evening, was a passionate supporter of the right to bear arms. The way they see it, they're fighting for a principle of freedom. In their view, that trumps the knowledge that these weapons take more innocent lives than they save. In a court of law that would be called being an accessory to murder.'

'So you believe . . .'

'Yes, I believe Tomás Gomez has introduced the death penalty and appointed himself judge, jury and executioner.'

Mike nodded but said nothing.

Bob walked over to the coffee maker and poured himself another cup, sat down again and watched in silence as Mike worked on. Looking at the dog's eyes he could see that Mike had finally found the pair he had been looking for. And a thought struck him. That he should quit being a cop and study instead to be a taxidermist. Stuff the things he most wanted to hang on to in his life. The things he'd loved.

'Mike?'

'Yeah?'

'You ever had woman trouble?'

'No.'

'Never?'

'No. Or rather yes. The summer I was twenty-two.'

'So you haven't had many?'

'I guess I haven't.'

'So how many?'

'Two.'

'Two?'

'My wife and I started going steady when we were fifteen. When I was twenty-two I fell in love with a Saint Paul girl from Summit Hill. We were both students at MCAD, studying sculpture. I was shy but very definite about it, so I first of all broke with my future wife before I asked the girl out for a date. She said yes, we became a couple, and I spent the next two months learning the difference between infatuation and love. I think she got it too, so there was no big drama when we broke up. And fortunately the woman who was to be my wife was willing to take me back.'

'So that's the only woman trouble you've had in your life?'

'*And* only my second woman.'

They laughed.

'You're the only one your wife's had, I'm guessing?'

'No,' said Mike. 'She had one other. At least that I know of. She was twenty-five, I think. It was a Norwegian writer she met when he visited the Hosmer public library – you know, that little old one in Powderhorn. She fell head over heels for him and says it was because he read to them in Norwegian, that we have this latent yearning toward our own original language.'

'Did she tell you or did you find out?'

'She told me.'

'How did you react?'

'I took Norwegian lessons.'

Bob laughed and Mike raised a hand theatrically and declaimed, *'Vodann-stå-dettil-på-setteren-ida?'*

'Meaning?'

'How are things down on the farm today.'

'And it worked?'

'Oh yes. In fact, I believe we owe our firstborn to that line. But I suspect she thought it meant something completely different.'

They both laughed.

'Anyway, you fought for her, Mike.'

Lunde shrugged. 'Fought and fought. After a while we realised we'd both been lucky and hit the bullseye first time around. That we were made for each other.'

'You're a lucky man.'

'Don't I know it. And you?'

'Me?'

'When a man asks another man if he's ever had woman trouble it's usually because he's having woman trouble himself.'

'What kind of woman trouble are you talking about?'

'Well, I can't possibly know that,' said Mike as he worked at the hair on the dog's tail with a comb and scissors. 'But maybe it's related to that loneliness in your eyes. What's her name?'

Bob lowered his head. Maybe it hadn't been such a good idea to sober up so quickly after all. 'Alice,' he said.

'What happened?'

'Same story as yours. She met someone else.'

'And that left you lonely?'

Bob stood up and walked over to a white hare that looked as if it had frozen in mid-hop. He gently stroked the fur. 'Before I met her, I didn't know what loneliness was. Or maybe I just covered it over with other women. She opened me up like a clam, and I discovered there was another Bob in there, a sensitive, tender guy who could love, cry, ask for help . . . yeah, all that kind of stuff.'

'All that kind of stuff,' Mike echoed with a slight smile, still intent on his work.

Bob put two fingertips against the hare's nose. 'But when she left me, I found out she had nullified the effect of my antidote to loneliness. Women. Casual sex. Alcohol. Work. I try, and for a short while it's OK, but I know it can't last. I'm like that open clam, the sphincter is gone. I stand there gaping, defenceless, and all the time I'm drying out inside and smelling worse as each day goes by.'

Bob was almost surprised to feel that the hare's nose was neither cold nor damp, so likelife was the illusion. Around its round pupils the eyes were brown, shading to black at the edges. But

Bob was looking at the area closest to the pupil, where the brown shading was lighter, like amber. Like Frankie's eyes.

'The only consolation is that after a while you get numb to it,' said Bob. 'You stop caring, self-respect doesn't seem all that fucking important. Nor does the respect of others either. In fact, nothing does. Nothing seems to matter.'

'Apart from work?'

'Not even that.'

'But the way it looks, you work night and day.'

'That's just because I want to be the one who brings Tomás Gomez down, not Olav Hanson or one of those other idiots.'

'Is that why you haven't told any of them about a taxidermist where Tomás Gomez has an order waiting to be picked up?' Mike Lunde didn't look up from his work, but he had that slight smile on his face. It reminded Bob of the way his father looked after he had had that stroke. 'To be honest I've been wondering why you're the only police officer I've spoken to.'

'Well,' sighed Bob, 'now you know.'

'Thank you for being honest, Bob. Are you going to be honest about that other thing too?'

'Other thing?'

'The reason you and Alice broke up.'

'But I already told you. She met someone else.'

'Before that. The reason the two of you fell apart.'

'And what might that be?'

'I don't know. It could be the real reason you're so lonely. But of course, we don't need to talk about it.'

Bob stood there and swallowed. Looked at the eyes on that hare. No, they didn't need to talk about it. It had worked just fine so far, hadn't it? Not talking about it? Just let the wound heal over and knock back a stiff drink when the pain gets too much or the thoughts can't be driven off. Her eyes were brown. Like caramel, said Alice. He preferred amber.

'We lost our daughter,' said Bob. 'Frankie. She was three years old.'

Lunde stopped working. Briefly wiped his hands together and let his arms drop to his sides. The look he gave Bob was open, naked, direct. What Bob saw wasn't a look that asked for something, some further explanation. And Mike Lunde didn't say anything either, it was as though he was someone who understood that no words added to those just spoken could give them meaning. Daughter. Lost. Three years old.

'She found my service pistol in our bedroom drawer,' said Bob. 'She was playing with it. Alice was home and heard the shot. An hour later our daughter died at the hospital.'

Bob chose his words the same way he always did whenever the situation demanded that he explain what had happened. It was a formula he had learned off by heart. After a while he could recite it without too much alteration. Sometimes, like when he gave his statement to the police, he would add details, volunteer facts. Such as that he had kept the pistol and ammunition easily accessible in the drawer of the bedside table because there had recently been two night-time burglaries in the area. But never a word about what it felt like or about Frankie herself. That would be like opening the floodgates. He knew he would lose it. And still, as he stood there reciting the formulaic sentences, he could feel the pressure.

'I'm so terribly sorry to hear that, Bob,' said Mike.

Bob could see he meant it. There was empathy in his eyes, a mute pain like an echo of Bob's own. Bob could only wonder at the arbitrary way empathy was distributed among humans.

'Alice is a psychologist and she persuaded me to see various professionals who specialised in grief management. They all said the same thing; that experience shows that grief like this often leads to divorce; that it was important to give each other space and not apportion any blame. Of course, none of this was new to Alice, she explained the mechanisms involved to me, described in detail what typically happens to a young couple who lose their only child. We knew. And yet still we didn't manage to stop a single thing from happening. The exhaustion. The apathy. The silence. The outbursts of rage one person feels when they think they're being blamed by the other person. Because of the guilt you *feel*. Hatred for the other, because you feel they share the guilt. Alcohol. Rejection. We completely forgot that we loved each other, we dragged ourselves along with this millstone of grief around our necks that was pulling us both down. Just the sight of each other at the breakfast table was a reminder of what had happened. Neither one of us would let the other forget, because forgetting, escape from the pain the other felt, would be a betrayal. Until in the end we just couldn't take it any more.'

'So the reason wasn't that she found someone else?'

'Oh yes. But . . . she threw me out first.'

'Are you sure about that?'

'About what?'

'That she threw you out?'

'Why wouldn't I be sure about that?'

Mike shrugged.

Bob felt the metallic tang of blood in his mouth – he hadn't even noticed that he'd bitten his tongue.

'Maybe she didn't say it in so many words, but she froze me

out. Wouldn't talk to me, wouldn't touch me. So I accepted the consequences. I packed my bag and I left.'

'So you were the one who left?'

'What? No.'

'No?'

'No! She could have phoned and asked me to come back. But she didn't.'

'I see.'

'OK, she did ring. Twice. At the most. Directly afterward. But my life right then was just a chaotic mess and I . . . I needed it to be, I guess. When I began to get things sorted out and started remembering all the good times we'd shared I got in touch with her. But she told me she'd met this guy, Stan. Stan the Man. It was only a matter of a few months, remember. So . . .' Bob had located the wound in his tongue and pressed it hard against the back of his teeth. '. . . in my book, she had the last word.'

'This Stan . . .'

'A guy who works with Alice. Psychologist. I talked to someone I'd got to know a bit there and he reckoned Stan had been interested in her for a long time. I guess he was just waiting for his chance. He claims to be a researcher, but I checked out a couple of articles he published and I wasn't impressed.'

'But do you think they love each other?'

'Love?' Bob spat it out as though it was a dirty word. But the rushing in the head didn't come. Instead he thought about it, discovering as he did so that if he put the wound on his tongue between his teeth and clamped down hard on it, the pain brought tears to his eyes. 'Maybe. I guess so. Yes, they probably do.'

'Then why are you so angry with her? You were the one who left, and I'm guessing you weren't exactly celibate once you were gone.'

'Not exactly, no.'

'So maybe you're not really angry because she found someone else but because she's happy. And since your daughter's death you feel she has no right to be.'

'You think so?'

'It's not really my business, Bob, but you gave the explanation yourself. That the two of you were bound together by this millstone, that neither one could accept that the other could somehow cut themselves free.'

Bob kept thinking. It wasn't that he hadn't had similar thoughts himself, but it was the first time he'd ever heard them spoken aloud.

'You who spend so much time talking to people who've lost something they loved,' said Bob. 'Tell me something, are we all insane?'

Mike Lunde stood up straight and pulled off his gloves. 'Oh but it's not just people who've lost something they love.'

'It isn't?'

'Take a look around,' said Mike as he lifted off his apron. 'Insanity is the norm.'

Bob nodded. 'Amen to that.'

'I'm done here for today. Where do you live?'

'Phillips.'

'I can drive you.'

Bob had protested, but Mike pointed out that Phillips was just down the road, and that anyway it was more or less on his route.

His car was a Chevrolet Caprice station wagon, 1995 model, with the characteristic imitation wood-panelling on the sides.

'I *know* it's ugly,' Mike said. 'But at least not as ugly as the '85 model.'

'The one that looks like they chopped off the rear end of the coupé and welded on a packing case?'

'That's the one!'

They talked a little more about cars and where Mike lived, in Chanhassen, a comfortable suburb on the south-west side of town where folk trimmed their lawns and pushed thermometers into the ground in autumn so they'd know when the temperature fell below forty-four and the grass wouldn't grow any more. And about Prince, the musician who had died a few months earlier.

'You ever meet him?' asked Bob as Mike drove through the night-time stillness of the streets.

'You didn't see much of him, he ran on a different clock from most people in Chanhassen. And Paisley Park where he lived and worked looked like a factory right there next to the freeway, you didn't exactly call in to say hi. I went along to a couple of the free neighbourhood concerts he gave there, but the only time I talked to him was actually at a Vikings game.'

'You *spoke* to Prince?'

'We were both guests of a satisfied customer of mine with a private box at the stadium. Prince was polite, but he didn't say much. I think he was a shy man. But he said he kept pigeons, and he had a cat.'

'What was he like?'

'I don't know, Bob.'

'But did he seem . . . happy?'

Mike considered this. 'He seemed lonely. You a fan?'

Bob nodded. 'Alice and I kissed the first time to "Purple Rain".'

Mike hesitated. 'Not that it's any of my business, Bob . . .'

'Come on.'

He smiled that half-smile again. 'If you really could get Alice back, are you so sure that's what you want?'

'What are you talking about? It's all I ever think about.'

'I get that. But as it says in one of Aesop's fables, be careful what you wish for. Nothing's changed, Bob. That millstone, it's still there.'

'Sure. But it won't always be there.' He looked at Mike. 'Will it?'

Mike shrugged. 'You've seen those animals in my store. They fade a little, but they don't disappear. Just ask Tomás Gomez. Sometimes I wonder whether I'm really doing my customers a favour by stuffing the things they love. My job is to freeze memories, preserve them in solid form. But there's something unhealthy about it. You don't move on. I can see it in my customers, they're frozen themselves, they're stuffed themselves, you know?'

31

THE GREAT EQUALISER, OCTOBER 2016

BOB HAD TAKEN OFF ALL his clothes and was sitting on the couch holding the Radica 20Q. When he had bought it for Frankie, Alice had said she was too young for a game like that, but Frankie had loved it when Daddy had asked her to think of a question, and only helped her a little bit with the answers. He stared at the TV, an old black-and-white movie on a channel that advertised it only showed classics. English aristocrats hunting a solitary fox across a rolling landscape. Bob had noticed there were messages waiting on his phone but couldn't face checking them. A police siren somewhere out there mingled with the sounds of the hunting horns in the film, which seemed to be about a man with a list of people he planned to kill. Bob closed his eyes and the questions came.

Did Tomás Gomez have a list like that?

How many names were on it?

Who could be next?

The siren sounds were getting closer. The fox hunt was in full cry out there. He imagined Tomás Gomez limping away to some place where he could hide out. A man driven by grief, by the loss of his family, by hatred of a society in which fifteen-year-olds can buy weapons and shoot a young girl as she sits in her wheelchair. He thought about what Kay had said about the gun under her mother's pillow. The great equaliser. Freedom. And he thought the same useless thought once again: that if Alice, he and Frankie had moved north of the border, the statistical chances of Frankie being killed were a fraction of the three-figure number of children that die annually in accidental deaths involving guns.

Did it make him angry? Of course it did. It made his head fume just thinking about it. But did he hate, the way Tomás Gomez obviously did?

He didn't know. He knew only that another question had suddenly arisen:

Just how committed was he to actually putting a stop to Tomás Gomez's crusade?

On his TV screen the fox raced across a field and into a woodland copse. What was it thinking? Where was it headed? Did it have a plan?

Bob looked down at the Radica 20Q. It was lifeless, silent, the batteries dead.

Olav Hanson lay in bed staring up at the ceiling.

Listened to his wife who lay snoring beside him. Listened out for the phone as though it might start ringing even though he'd turned it off. He'd done that when it rang for a third time after he got back from Track Plaza. Three different phone numbers, all unknown. Didn't take much to guess they all came from Die Man. He must have seen the news and known that Lobo was still on the loose. Olav hadn't answered the calls. What could he say? That he'd *almost* managed to rub Lobo out? That he'd have another try at the next crossroads? Die Man didn't often give people a second chance, and never a third. In other words, next time he spoke to Die Man it would be best if Lobo was no longer in the land of the living.

Olav was drifting off into sleep when he heard something. The living room was adjacent to the bedroom and the sound seemed to come from there. A slick, oily clicking. He knew instantly what it was. The barrel of a revolver being pushed into place. He knew because he owned a revolver himself, and that sound was unique. Olav reached for the gun under his pillow, slipped out of bed and crept over to the bedroom door.

Listened.

Nothing.

He peered out through the keyhole. He had two options. Push the door carefully and silently open and see what happened. Or kick it open, dive through and deal with whatever happened next. He swallowed. Tried to slow his pulse rate. And went for the first option.

The door glided open and he peered into the room.

No one there.

But he recognised the smell. And in the light of the street lamp outside he saw the smoke spiralling up above the back of the armchair that faced away from him.

'Sean?' he said quietly.

A head appeared from around the front of the chair and looked at him. Bushy hair, big grin, a thick, hand-rolled cigarette between its lips. 'Yes, Father?'

That *father*. His son somehow always managed to make it sound like a joke.

'I didn't hear you come home,' said Olav, hiding the pistol behind his back at the same time as he closed the bedroom door.

'Firstly, this isn't my home. Secondly, I didn't intend for you to hear me because I was planning on stealing this.' Sean waved the revolver. He must have known that Olav kept it in a drawer in his desk. 'What do you think I could get for this down in Phillips, Father?'

'Keep your voice down, Sean, she's asleep. What do you want?'

'What do I want now, or what do I *really* want?'

'Sean . . .'

'What I really want is to get so stoned I just disappear. I *really* want to be the opposite of what you are. And what I *really* want is for you to throw out that bitch in there from what was once *my* home. But what I want *now* . . .' He took a deep, gurgling drag on the cigarette, held the smoke for three long seconds before releasing it. '. . . is to sell you this revolver for a hundred dollars cash. In my hand.'

Olav Hanson had never seen any reason to regret being born, there really wasn't much he could do about it anyway. What did cross his mind now and then was that he could have prevented the guy sitting in that armchair from ever having been born.

My breath turned to frosty smoke as I watched the YouTube clip on my phone. It was under the item about the murder of Cody Karlstad. The female KSTP reporter was entering a bar that – unless I'd misread the map I studied – was directly across the skyway from the restroom I'd used. She was explaining to the anchor that the police wouldn't let them any closer to the ongoing action involving the suspect Tomás Gomez, but that she had just seen someone with an MPD ID card go into this bar. She then turned to a man wearing a striking, almost yellow-ochre coat and asked him what was going on as she lifted his ID card and read '. . . Detective Bob Oz'. Oz was clearly drunk and didn't realise he was being interviewed. He talked about how he'd been dumped and suspended from duty, how he spent his time screwing around and drinking, and ended by saying: 'How about you, Divine Blue?'

I turned off the phone. Watched the fish swimming around the bowl on the bench in front of me. Then I turned my attention to you. You were naked and sitting in a metal chair. You had straps across your chest, round your throat and forehead. Your arms were secured to the armrests and your feet to the legs of the chair. You'd been sitting there for three weeks now and there was a white layer of frost on your skin and your hair. Behind the chest strap I could just make out the tattoo of an Uzi with a heart around it. That was the weapon you used at McDeath. Other bullets had killed Monica and Sam, but it was the bullets from your Uzi that took away Anna in the sixth year of her life. When I lured you in here you still didn't recognise me, it had been so many years ago. And that evening at McDeath was probably less memorable for you than it was for me. I showed you around in here, showed you what you'd come here for, offered you coffee, and not until the dope in the coffee wore off and you woke to find yourself in that chair did I reveal to you who I was. And the plans I had for you. They say psychopaths have a higher threshold of pain and fear than other people. That may well be true, because it wasn't until I pulled on the rubber gloves and the earmuffs and took out the ice-spray and the knife that I saw fear enter your eyes. That's when you wanted to talk about it, explain to me how it was all an accident. That you really wanted to turn yourself in to the police. But that the detective in charge of the case, a tall blond guy they called Milkman, was in Die Man's pocket, and that he took care to make the whole thing look like the work of another gang. These were just the transparent lies of a desperate man, and I pushed the needle into your ear, most likely puncturing the eardrum, and told you I would do the other ear next if you kept on lying. You swore it wasn't lies, that Die Man and Milkman threatened to kill you if you talked to the police. I punctured your other ear too, but you kept repeating it, over and over, as though the confession was your lifebelt. I believed you. A tall, blond guy. That would have to be Detective Olav Hanson, the one who consoled me after he'd taken my statement, who promised he'd get the people who had murdered my family. I asked where Die Man was, and when you told me I asked if you were joking, I knew what kind of place that was, but you said it was true, he loved that kind of stuff, was hooked on it the same way his customers were hooked on crack. I was thinking about that as I started to cut into your underarms. You clenched your teeth and didn't make a sound. It was only after I cut into your throat that you couldn't hold out any longer. But once you started screaming you only stopped for those brief stretches of time when you were unconscious. In the last minutes of your life all you did was sob. The quiet sobbing of someone who knows it's too late, that he's already dead.

You were sitting here in a chair because you owned an Uzi, an automatic killing machine you had purchased quite legally in a state further west of this one, a weapon no one had ever used to defend his family against an intruder, or his girlfriend against a rape attack, or to put a fresh joint of deer on the dining table. Sure, like the gun lobbyists said, it wasn't the weapons that killed but the people holding them. They think it's enough if you just make sure the bad guys can't get hold of them. If the assumption was valid then it had to mean that almost all the bad guys in the world lived in the United States which alone accounts for ninety per cent of all young victims of gun crime among the twenty-two wealthiest countries in the world. What was freedom? To be allowed to own a weapon designed to kill people because the guy standing next to you owned one as well? Or was it not having to own a gun because you could feel reasonably certain the guy next to you didn't own one either? I could see how fear triumphed over common sense, how – given your socio-economic position, your education and your bad genes – you were only the first mechanical element in the creation of a gun that had already been fired by the time it came into your hands. And how when you – subject as you are to the laws of psychology and economy, just as the parts of a weapon are subject to physical laws – pulled that trigger, then that was just one link in an unstoppable chain of reactions. But it starts with you. The centre, the point at which the stone first hits the water. Now the ripples spread across the still, dark water. The one who sells guns. The weapons activist. The forces behind the killer. The authorities. The executive. The ripples get bigger. And bigger.

I emptied the water from the glass. The little fish flipped and splashed about on the bench and puffed itself up. A protective mechanism. Not to frighten by size but to make itself more difficult to swallow.

When I was done I left, turned the key in the padlock, headed out through the large communal studio, out the door and into the forest that surrounded the low, single-storey house. We'd got it cheap, and we used to hang out here and study each other's work. Children had loved it, the woods and all the strange exhibits in here. In the evenings we had partied, the whole gang of us. Talked about the future, how we were going to make it big, how we were going to take over the world. Monica and I had spent the night out here once. I think that must have been the night the boy was conceived. But Monica said she'd never been so afraid, because I told her this was wolf country. And now, I had read, they were here. The wolves were here, the artists had gone, the only one left was me.

A narrow track led down to the main road where the car was parked. It was a walk of about a mile, but I didn't want anyone to see or hear me coming and going. So tonight Monica and I were going to sleep out here, like we did back then.

I crept down inside my sleeping bag on a mattress of pine branches beneath a tree and looked up into the starry sky. Looked for her. Looked for what was written in shimmering letters and symbols, things that couldn't be seen above the city.

32

THE PASSWORD, OCTOBER 2016

BOB'S EYELIDS FLICKERED. IT WAS the light that woke him. It came from a combined alarm clock and lamp he'd given Alice as a birthday present. The soft light came on at the hour the alarm was set for and then gradually grew brighter, like a sunrise. That was the idea. He'd taken it with him after Stan appeared, when Alice told Bob he could take absolutely anything he wanted. Bob probably hoped she would be hurt by the fact that he'd taken her birthday present but instead she seemed relieved, she'd never been someone who needed a gentle wake-up.

The radio turned itself on. Bob dozed as he listened to the newsreader say that the opinion polls were still predicting that within a few weeks' time Hillary Clinton would be elected the country's first female president. Then came an interview with an election expert who warned against the Bradley effect, this being when pollsters call people up on the phone who don't dare to admit they won't be voting for the politically correct option, as happened a while back in the case of the black California gubernatorial candidate Bradley, or now, with a female presidential candidate. By the end of the broadcast they still hadn't mentioned the hunt for Tomás Gomez, concluding instead with a report that the NRA conference had sold out the US Bank Stadium quicker than any Vikings home game.

Bob got up. He was cold and had a throbbing headache from yesterday's drinking but felt revived after a warm shower. He opened the cupboard above the sink, looked at the pink pill tray, took out the tube of toothpaste and closed the cupboard door. He put the coffee on while still brushing his teeth, switched on his laptop and registered that his internet was down. After thinking about it he called Mike Lunde. The taxidermist sounded busy.

'My internet's OK, yes, but this Labrador has to be finished today, so I've closed the store to be alone here and to give it my full concentration. I'm not letting any Tomás Gomez in here today either. How about tomorrow?'

Bob hung up. Though he much preferred the coffee at Moresite, they didn't have Wi-Fi like Starbucks.

After a bus ride to Southdale he bought batteries at the mall and picked up the Volvo, complete with parking ticket, and drove into Dinkytown.

'This isn't a laptop place,' said Liza when he sat down on one of the stools and put the computer on the counter at Bernie's.

'Sorry, but I couldn't find anywhere else that offered a combination of decent coffee and Wi-Fi,' said Bob.

'You've never even tasted our coffee as far as I know,' said Liza. 'And what makes you think we have Wi-Fi?'

'This is right in the middle of student territory – are you trying to tell me you don't have Wi-Fi?'

'Not for customers, no.'

'I can see I'm alone here, so this stays between us. How much do you want for the staff password?'

'So you think I can be bought?'

'Not with money, perhaps, but I think you're open to a bribe for the right price.'

'And what would that be?'

'The truth.'

'The truth?'

Bob took the device from the inside pocket of his coat and put it down in front of her. 'Radica 20Q,' he said before she had time to ask. 'It can read your thoughts.'

'Right. And if I prefer to keep my thoughts to myself?'

'I'm thinking not so much of your thoughts as of your son's. He's going to love this.'

Liza raised an eyebrow. 'What makes you so sure about that?'

'All intelligent children are curious about things that are intelligent.'

She lifted the ball and studied it sceptically. 'Well, I must say, it looks as if it's been used a lot.'

'It was my daughter's.'

'*You've* got a daughter?'

'Had. Frankie. She died. She'd be happy if another child had the pleasure of using her favourite toy. She was like that.'

Liza's mouth opened slightly. For a moment her eyes went blank. And Bob saw how her face, how the way she was standing, the way she held her hands, how everything about her was changed. Of course, he'd seen the effect before on the few occasions when he'd told someone he'd lost his daughter, how the other person always searched for some kind of adequate response. But never like this. It was as though the words had struck a chord inside Liza Hummels, as though they opened the door to a person Bob hadn't yet met. She became, thought Bob – for want of a better word – beautiful. And her voice was thicker when, after a few seconds' silence, she said, very clearly:

'Hillary Clinton for Prison.'

'Sorry?'

'The password. Not my idea. I hope you like your coffee black?'

Bob talked about Frankie and their family of three without the dam bursting. Liza was the one who now and then dried a tear.

'It was Alice's idea to call her Frankie. It means "free man". She wanted every door to be open to her.'

Liza nodded. 'That's the same reason I called my son Johan.'

'Johan?'

'It's what people call a high-income name. It doesn't make the child any more intelligent, but it gives them an edge when they apply for high-income jobs after college.'

'So Johan's going to college?'

She shrugged. 'Why do you think I work twelve-hour shifts?'

'And if he doesn't want to?'

'Then he won't have to. It's about keeping as many doors as possible open for them, isn't it? So what happened after Frankie's death?'

Bob spoke of the depression, his problems with anger, the separation and his current situation as a detective suspended from duty. And finally, halfway down the third cup of coffee, of his strictly unofficial hunt for Tomás Gomez. By this time two more customers had arrived. One sat quietly reading a newspaper in the corner, while the other was apparently drawing the two of them, now and then looking up from his sketchpad.

'So you have absolutely no personal information about him at all?' asked Liza.

'Nope,' said Bob. 'But we know the story of how his family was killed, and we have these images from various security cameras.'

Bob turned the laptop screen so that she could see it. To his relief, not to say surprise, it was obvious no one had thought of blocking his access to MPD's databases.

'How old would you say this guy was?' he asked.

'Hm,' she said. 'Thirty-two maybe? Not over forty anyway.'

'I agree,' said Bob. 'Let's say that at the earliest he had children when he was fifteen or sixteen. I've searched the database with all murders since 1990 both in Minneapolis and in Saint Paul, and in those twenty-six years there have been four instances of two children and a woman being shot in connection with a gang shootout. But Gomez's name isn't mentioned in any of the newspaper reports. Three involved black families, only one Latino. They were killed in the Fourth Precinct, but here it says their name was Perez and they were Spanish.'

'You think this might be them?'

'Could be. As an illegal immigrant it's not surprising he gave a name like Perez and claimed to be Spanish. At least that made sure they wouldn't be transported back over the border and into the hands of the cartel they were running from.'

'Are there really no more details of the killings?'

'Nix. Deaths involving minorities in the Fourth Precinct have always had less media coverage, and this was in 1995, the worst year ever for murders.'

'I was hardly even born then, baby.'

Bob tapped a number on his phone and held it to his ear. 'That was the year they started calling the city Murderopolis.' He signalled that he had someone on the other end of the line. 'Hi, Kari, how are things in the Fraud Unit? Listen, could you check something for me? A multiple homicide from 1995? Perez. I need the report. And the name and address of the father.'

Bob could hear that Kari at the other end wasn't taking notes the way she usually did.

'Kari?'

'I'm sorry but I can't help you, Bob.' Her voice sounded pained.

'What do you mean?'

'Walker's given me orders not to do anything for you as long as you're suspended. I think it's because of that TV thing of you on YouTube. Even the chief of police is furious – they think you've embarrassed the whole police department. I'm sorry, Bob.'

'I understand. Sorry if I've embarrassed you too, Kari.'

'Me?'

'You in particular, Kari. Have a nice day.'

'You too, Bob.'

Bob hung up, tapped in a new number, got an immediate reply.

'Bob . . .'

'Hi, Kay. Listen, I think I've got something.'

'Bob, you listen –'

'Murder case. Perez. 1995. Can you send me the report and –'

'Walker's given everybody orders not to –'

'Fuck Walker. All I need is the –'

'I'm going to hang up now, Bob.'

'Kay!'

The line went dead.

'Can't pull the women any more?' Liza asked.

'It's been going on for a while now,' said Bob. He put his elbows on the counter and rubbed his skull hard. 'Excuse me.'

Bob made his way to the men's room. Though he had the whole trough to himself he still entered the only stall there and locked the door. It was a peculiarity of his; if he didn't feel certain he would be alone when urinating he would end up just standing there, pressing away at his bladder. When he was finished and buttoned up he remained standing and looked down at the slider bolt for a moment before exiting, washing his hands and splashing water on his face. When he got back to his stool at the counter he saw that Liza had poured him another cup of coffee.

'Liza?' he said quietly, so that she automatically took a step closer to him.

'Yes?'

'What we said about holding the doors open – when you enter a stall in a restroom where there are other people, don't you automatically lock the door?'

She looked uncomprehendingly at him.

'And definitely if you're preparing to make your escape through a ventilation shaft,' he said. 'Gomez hadn't locked the door of that stall. Isn't that odd? I mean, you don't want to be caught in the act now, do you?'

'Maybe.'

'You *maybe* lock the door?'

'Maybe you want to be caught in the act. If you're committing a criminal act.'

'Would anyone want that?'

'To be caught in the act? Oh yes.' Liza leaned across the counter and put her chin in her hands. 'I got into the habit of stealing small change from my father's wallet. I felt so ashamed I started stealing larger and larger amounts so that he'd notice.'

'And did he?'

'I don't know. Maybe he punished me by pretending he hadn't found out. Let my own conscience torment me.'

'Did that work?'

'Apparently. I stopped doing it.'

Bob cleared his throat and nodded slowly. 'It's grounds for hope to know that at least we are potentially capable of stopping. Can you get me a whisky?'

'No.'

'No?'

'No, you can have more coffee. What is it you're hoping to stop doing?'

'Nothing.'

'Come on, Bob. Like you said, this is part of my job.'

'What is?'

'Listening. Pretending to understand. What is it you're hoping you can stop doing?'

Bob smiled and looked down into his coffee. Drew a breath. 'Alice. I give her hell. The divorce papers, the division of property, this new guy of hers – all of it. Even though I know it hurts me most, that my self-contempt just grows and grows when I make myself a worse man than I already am. Sometimes I wonder if what I'm doing is asking for pity. It's as though I want her to see that the man I once was is going to pieces in front of her eyes. I'm a prick, and my own conscience torments me over it, but I just can't seem to stop it the way you did. Just the opposite, in fact – I've turned into a fucking stalker.'

'Have you asked yourself why you're stalking her?'

'Actually I don't think it's her I'm stalking, it's more the places where I was once happy. Where I lived with her and Frankie. Where I picked her up from work. I'm stalking the memories. You know, like those people who have their pets stuffed, to recreate something that's gone from their lives.'

'Do people stuff their pet animals?'

'Oh yes. Even a killer like Tomás Gomez wants his cat back. Incredible, isn't it?'

Liza dealt with two customers who had come in and ordered beers.

Bob watched her. The friendly, professional manner; the quick, assured movements. An efficiency he was sure made her feel good, the pleasure of doing a job well. The pleasure. *I'm stalking memories*. Suddenly it lit up for him, as clear as the answer on the Radica 20Q display.

'Where are you going?' asked Liza.

Bob was on his feet and buttoning his coat. 'I think I know how I can find him.'

33

PORN, OCTOBER 2016

I HAD MY FACE TURNED to the sky and my eyes closed against the bright morning sun. It was still warm, but at sunrise there had been a thin layer of ice on the puddles. I inhaled the air, felt my lungs expand, felt that my body was ready. Felt the slight pressure of the hypodermic with its long point in my breast pocket. I opened my eyes again.

US Bank Stadium.

It looked like a ship. No, a submarine. Or a black iceberg. I was standing on Medtronic Plaza, beside the big Viking ship, and looking up at the black zinc facade. Behind it 60,000 seats waited to be filled. The stadium had a glass roof which kept the NFL fans from freezing. There had been mixed reactions to it, both while they were building it and afterward, once it had opened in the summer. Some hated it and said they should never have pulled down the old Metrodome stadium, but it was always like that with places people had good memories of. I had slept well in the woods that night, with my memories. I needed it, needed it to keep me steady.

I saw the WCCO-TV and the KSTP buses, the cables being unfurled and getting ready for live coverage of Mayor Patterson's opening of the NRA convention tomorrow. I had made a circuit of the stadium and the security looked unimpeachable. It was impossible to get into the stadium without proper accreditation, and there were security cameras above every entrance. Especially here in Medtronic Plaza, which was where most of the audience would be queuing the following day.

I closed my eyes again.

Saw the mayor standing there, all eyes on him, all cameras focused on him. The way his facial expression kind of freezes when he gets hit. The chaos. The anarchy. Running footsteps. Sirens. That whole apparatus we trust in, that we believe can protect us, and save us, and the lives of those we love, is set in motion. But mixed in with the certainty that no matter what any of us do now, it's already too late. My despair had finally become theirs too.

Kay Myers sat in Walker's office looking at the superintendent's back as he stood in front of the blind.

'How d'you like this city?' he asked.

Kay thought about it. It hadn't seemed all that different from the place she'd come from. Pretty similar climate, the lakes, same mix of people, same flat landscape. It had taken her a while to notice all the small differences in the social codes, like *Minnesota nice*, a friendly, polite surface obscuring a conflict-averse and passive-aggressive undercurrent. But even though they were a little more closed and a little less direct than where she came from, the people she met were, in general, decent and righteous people. Of course, that didn't include those she encountered in most of the murder cases that came her way – but then she suspected that was true of any city.

'Basically I like it just fine,' she said.

'Good,' said Walker without turning round. 'It may not be as attractive as Chicago, but I see this city as being oriented toward the future. It's a city where people are willing to think new thoughts. A city where someone like you can enjoy a good life and a rewarding career.'

Kay moved uncomfortably in her chair. It wasn't that she had expected the turn the meeting appeared to be taking, but at the same time it wasn't completely unexpected. She'd picked up on the signals, as people say.

'I've learned that I'm being considered for the post of leader of the Investigative Division,' said Walker. He parted two strips of the blind with his fingers. 'That means that someone will have to take over this office. The post will be advertised, and others will have the responsibility of deciding who gets the job. But if I offer an internal recommendation then that will obviously count for something. Count for quite a lot, I guess we could say.'

Seeing no reason to respond Kay remained silent.

'Now of course there's a certain risk attached when a departing head offers a recommendation,' said Walker. 'If in due course it turns out that there's something shall we say *untoward* about the person recommended, then obviously that will reflect badly on the one who offered the recommendation. Right now, for example, I've got the chief of police on my neck following these problems with Detective Oz. What I need to know, Myers, is that you won't be giving us any surprises.'

'I understand,' said Kay.

Walker turned to her. 'You understand?'

'Yes.'

Walker smiled broadly. 'You've come far, Myers. Not bad for a girl from Englewood. But you're not finished yet. You can be an example for other girls from places like Englewood. The way ahead lies open for you. The only thing that can get in the way is if you mess up and fall.'

Kay nodded.

'I won't keep you any longer, Myers. You look like someone who wants to get back out there on the job.'

As Kay walked back to her desk, she wondered which had been more important for Walker to convey, the promise or the warning. On her way she glanced into the office that was being decorated. The painting wasn't finished yet, paint pots still standing there, but the painter obviously had the day off. On a chair she saw something that looked like a furry brown rodent but was probably a mitten. She almost asked at reception if they knew when the painter would be back, but she didn't. Approaching her desk she saw Olav Hanson pulling on his jacket as he hurried out from behind the divider separating their desks.

'Where's the fire?' she asked Joe Kjos, who she could see was playing poker on his computer screen.

'The video centre,' he said. 'Gomez has been seen at the US Bank Stadium.'

Kay grabbed her jacket and ran toward the elevators.

'Hey!' she called as the doors were about to shut. 'Wait for me!'

A hairy arm shot out between the shiny surfaces and the elevator doors slid back open.

She stepped in, nodded her thanks to the man with the hairy arms and fixed her eyes on Olav Hanson, who was standing at the back of the elevator. She moved next to him.

'Why didn't you tell me about Gomez?' she asked quietly.

'I tried, but you weren't at your desk,' he said, his voice equally low.

She nodded slowly and tried to read his flushed face. 'Well, I'm here now, Hanson.'

'Good,' he said.

By the time Kay and Olav Hanson jumped out of the car by the Viking ship outside the US Bank Stadium three police cars had already arrived.

'Well?' said Hanson to the police officer who stood waiting for them.

'He isn't here.'

'Which cameras picked him up?'

'All the external ones round the whole stadium. It looks like he did the circuit twice before he lit out.'

'Twice?' said Kay. 'He's planning something.'

Kay looked at the two TV buses parked outside one of the entrances. She spoke the thought aloud almost before she'd finished thinking it:

'Patterson.'

'What?' Hanson stared at her.

'Patterson is due to open the NRA conference here tomorrow. Gomez is going for the mayor.'

'Are you crazy?'

'I think Gomez is crazy,' she said and pulled out her phone. 'Think about it. There's a pattern here. He starts small and gets bigger. Like ripples in a lake.'

'Who're you calling?'

Before Kay could answer she got a reply.

'Minneapolis City Hall.'

'This is Detective Kay Myers, MPD. Can I speak to the person in charge of security at the mayor's office?'

As she waited, she saw Hanson had just taken an incoming call.

'New sighting of Gomez,' he said to her. 'Not far away.'

I heard the sirens getting closer. The street I was standing on consisted of low, two-storey buildings on both sides. On the sidewalk across from me was a man wearing a fur cap with a cart and a sign that said he was selling *kielbasa starowiejska* – Polish sausages. When I was here earlier checking out the area I had bought one of those U-shaped sausages from him. It came served with *kapusniak*, a kind of sauerkraut, and it was delicious. Behind the cart was the entrance to a movie theatre with a large, vertical sign in red neon, RIALTO. The sirens were closer now. One or two of the cars had turned them off. Maybe they thought they could surprise me. I breathed in the smell of sausages, boiled cabbage, exhaust fumes and testosterone. Then I crossed the street.

Officer Fortune drove and listened to the female voice in his earpiece as it gave him a running appraisal of where the facial recognition program had last located Gomez. He knew she could also switch to an individual security camera to see where Gomez was headed as long as he was in frame.

'Thanks, we're there now,' said Fortune as he came to a screeching halt at the kerb beside a steaming sausage cart and the startled street seller. Fortune turned to the two detectives in the back seat and saw that both had drawn their service pistols.

'The camera has just seen him enter this building here, but we . . . eh, I guess we should wait for SWAT?'

'No,' the detectives replied in unison as they opened the doors and jumped out.

When Betty Jackson, the ticket seller at the Rialto, saw the two people with their guns and MPD badges approaching her booth she got a feeling of déjà vu. She was the only member of staff who had worked at the theatre since way back in the seventies, when the king of Minneapolis pornography, Ferris Alexander, took over the run-down Rialto and started showing blue movies there. The place wasn't licensed to show porn, but the police raided only when the city council specifically demanded it, because so many of their own were regulars there. Ferris Alexander's porn empire finally collapsed, and he ended up doing time on tax evasion charges, but the Rialto managed to survive without him, and in spite of the fact that theatres specialising in pornography all over the country had to close, as home movies and the internet gradually took over the market. The Rialto didn't make much money, but it was enough to keep the wheels turning. And there were no longer any applicable laws the authorities could make use of to close down movie theatres like they could do in the seventies. The most they could do was insist the theatres be located outside certain designated porn-free zones of the city. The Rialto showed mainly Swedish, Danish and German pornography from the sixties and seventies, mostly classics and some underground.

Things you wouldn't find on the net. But nothing extreme, no animals, underage, defecation, no hard S&M. Straightforward fucking. Generally for the same audience of white men aged sixty plus, probably family men who didn't want to watch porn on the internet at home. Or just lonely men who didn't recognise their dream woman among the slick pornography on the internet. Here they could still see Scandinavian girls with pubic hair and no silicone, the way they remembered girls from their own youth. A mixture of the smutty from the days before pornography became a legitimate business, and innocence from a time when a shred of modesty still existed. So this was in every way a respectable theatre showing adult movies, with a geographical location that put it in a grey area, as half the building lay within the city council's porn-free zone and the other half outside it. The part containing the screen was, unfortunately, within. But Betty soon realised it had nothing to do with this. She saw a slight uncertainty in the eyes of the two officers as they realised exactly what kind of establishment they were about to enter.

'Excuse me,' said the black policewoman as Betty tried to recall the last time she'd heard someone from MPD open a sentence so politely, 'did this person just come in here?'

The woman had lowered her pistol. She held up a cell phone in front of the ticket booth.

Betty looked at the picture on the screen. Normally she didn't look at the patrons, they didn't like it. Instead she concentrated on the hands that shoved the money in through the little window. Only if they looked like a child's hands rather than an adult's did she look up and decide whether to turn them away or ask to see some ID. But the person in the photograph had done something that was almost unheard of: he had actually spoken to her. Told her she ought to try the Polish sausages being sold right outside. As though he *wanted* her to look up and see him. And since Betty, in her seventy-eighth year, no longer suspected men of trying to hit on her, she *had* looked up. It was the same man as the one she now saw on the screen the policewoman was holding up in front of her. No doubt about it.

'He's inside,' she said with a nod toward the door leading into the theatre itself. It was a swing door with no handles on either side. Not as a fire precaution but because a swing door can be opened with a foot, or a shoulder, so you didn't have to touch a handle that you might suspect with good reason had just been touched by a hand that had just been touching something you didn't want any contact with at all, not even secondary contact.

'Turn the movie off and put the lights on in there,' said the police officer.

'Without a search warrant I can't . . .' Betty stopped when she saw the look in the woman's eyes. Behind her were now three uniformed policemen, all with weapons drawn. Betty pressed the intercom in front of her, another relic of the seventies, and said with a sigh, as though this were a daily but regrettable occurrence:

'Mel, stop the movie and turn the lights on. The police are here.'

Kay pushed open the door into the auditorium with her foot, continuing to hold the pistol with both hands. In the security cam footage Gomez hadn't looked to be carrying anything, but that didn't mean he wasn't armed. From where she was standing at the rear left of the auditorium she had time to register a pale and hairy couple going hard at it on the screen before switching her attention to the isolated silhouettes of men dotted about across the hundred or so mostly empty seats in front of her.

'Police!' she shouted as loudly as she could. 'Everybody stay where you are!'

At that exact moment the movie began to slow down, the slaps and groans of pleasure sank in pitch and intensity, as though the people involved had suddenly lost interest. But, strangely, there was no reaction from the audience. There were no groans of displeasure, no cries of frustration and anger. But in the dark two seconds between the projector being turned off and the overhead lights going on she spotted movement. A rectangle of light slid into the room to the right of the screen. A door opening. A green EMERGENCY EXIT sign above it. Then closing.

Kay responded immediately. She ran down the stairs, with Hanson right behind her. She crossed between the front row and the screen, past a man still struggling to button up his pants, pushed open the emergency exit and tumbled out into daylight.

She caught a glimpse of a back disappearing round the corner of a house. Took up pursuit. Round the corner, into an alley, round another corner, another glimpse of the same disappearing back. Ran. Ran like she used to in the alleyways around their old house in Englewood. Running from all the other kids. Running to school and back. Running like she did that night when she was eleven years old and her father had broken into the house to steal their money, but she'd been quicker, taken her mother's money from under the bed and jumped out the window, running, her father running after her. Running as fast as she could but still she could feel how, like some lurching zombie, he was gaining on her. And when they came to the dog yard at the back of the Jenkins house he was right behind. She could feel his fingers clutching at the soles of her shoes as she swung up and over the wire-net fence that was luckily only six feet high or she wouldn't have made it, because as strong as her legs were, her arms were thin and weak. But she did make it, and as she landed on the other side the dog, which looked like a cross between a pit bull and an Alsatian, came charging out of its doghouse, salivating and snarling. It leapt at the intruder with teeth bared. Not at her, who so often called in on her way home from school and gave it something from her lunch box, but at the wire fence and the man on the other side, the one threatening her. She saw her father back off to a safe distance. And through the furious barking of the dog she heard a stream of curses she tried to blank out, because even though she knew he was half crazy from the need for a fix and she hated him, the words were like acid, they burnt through her skin and could not be washed away. There they stood, daughter and father, one on each side of the face, with another man's dog between them. She was crying. She heard him change his tune and start to beg for money, and when that didn't work he gave up and started crying. Lights went on in the Jenkins house, and he turned and ran off. The strange thing was that later, when she looked back over her childhood, she couldn't remember a time when she had ever felt closer to her father than she had that night, when they stood there face-to-face, each with their own despair.

Kay had once again lost sight of the running back ahead of her, but she heard a crack. The sound of a man jumping up at a wooden fence. She cleared the corner, saw sure enough there was a wooden fence surrounding a property and caught a glimpse of a pair of hands as they disappeared over on the other side. She adjusted her stride and jumped. Got hold of the top of the fence with the tips of her fingers and tried to pull herself up but lost her grip and fell back down. As she scrambled to her feet she heard another crack a little way off. Another fence. Swearing. Must be a higher fence. Olav Hanson ran up, his face contorted.

'He can't get over the next fence,' said Kay. 'If we can get over this, we've got him! Give me a leg up.'

'Easier if I take him,' said Hanson. He pushed his gun back into the shoulder holster, measured his six foot four up against the fence, gripped the top and tried to jump. He scarcely even left the ground. With a groan of pain he collapsed against the planks.

'Goddamn knee,' he hissed between clenched teeth. He sounded so desperate that for an instant Kay almost felt sorry for him. She caught sight of a frail-looking fruit crate next to the wall of the house, tipped out the plant pots inside it then stood it, long side up, against the fence.

'I've got this!' said Hanson. He pushed Kay aside and stepped up onto the box. It brought him so high Kay realised he could see over the top to the other side. Abruptly the box began to creak and sway.

'Steady it!' Hanson shouted to Kay as he pulled out his pistol.

'OK, but get the hell over!'

'Keep it steady! He's got a gun!'

As Kay bent and put her weight against the crate she heard Hanson fire three shots in quick succession.

'Don't shoot!' came a voice from the other side. 'In the name of God, don't shoot!'

Kay stood back from the crate and gave it a kick. Over it went, Hanson with it.

'What the hell?' he growled as he lay on the ground.

Kay righted the crate and climbed onto it. On the other side was a yard, boxed in on all sides. She gripped the top, swung herself over, and got down on all fours, like a cat. Pulled her gun and shouted 'Police' twice, then walked toward the trembling man who lay hunched up against the wooden fence, directly beneath a piece of Black Wolves graffiti. Both arms were up and protecting his head.

'Police!' Kay repeated, keeping the gun on him. 'Show me your hands! Now!'

The man raised his arms above his head as though in prayer, but his head was still turned in toward his body.

'Let me see your face!' Kay stopped six feet from the man, far enough away that she'd have time to shoot him if he attacked, close enough to be sure she couldn't miss.

The man looked up. Tears rolled down his cheeks. 'Please!' he sobbed. 'Have mercy, and the Lord shall have mercy on you!'

Kay stared. She recognised him immediately, even though she'd only seen the face on the TV screen and in pictures. She cursed quietly, pulled out her phone and called the number she'd been given in the police car. The call was picked up at once:

'Fortune.'

'Myers here. You still in control at the theatre?'

'Yep.'

'OK. Don't let anyone leave, you hear me?'

'You didn't get him?'

'Oh yeah.' She drew a breath. 'But it isn't him.'

'Not Gomez?'

'No, it's . . .' She looked at the face again. White man, fifties, boyish quiff, big glasses, sort of shiny suit. Not that she saw too many TV evangelist shows, but this face was almost as well known as Jim Bakker. 'Someone else. We'll be right back.'

She squatted down in front of the man. 'Will I find a gun if I search you?'

The man shook his head.

'I believe you,' she said. 'But disobeying police orders during a raid in connection with an illegal movie show is an indictable offence, you do know that? Or don't you, pastor?'

The man's Adam's apple shot up and down and he looked terrified. But when he opened his mouth to speak the words poured out of him.

'We are all sinners, sister. But Jesus Christ Our Lord has given us the power and the mercy in our hearts to forgive. I have been put here on earth to do God's work. Like Jesus Christ Our Saviour, I go to sinners in the very places where they sin.' It was the same smarmy, chanting, almost hypnotic voice that disgusted her so much on the TV. 'But we know that not everyone out there will realise and understand this. So I beseech you to let me go and not to mention my name to the er . . . media, so that I may continue my work in the service of God. And I will remember the names of you two good citizens in my prayers and in my conversations with Our Lord this evening. And He will open the doors to paradise for you.'

'Thanks, but I'm not a believer, pastor.'

'N-not? I understand. Then how about a more tangible contribution to the work you're doing? Our Church has means.'

Kay looked at the bullet holes in the wooden fence a few inches above where the pastor was now lying curled up.

'I suggest instead a mutually acceptable agreement,' she said. 'You never mention to anyone about how we fired a couple of shots at a fugitive we had reason to believe was armed, and we say nothing about you being found at a jack-off movie theatre. How does that sound?'

The TV preacher winked at her, and she could see his business calculator had already weighed up the offer.

'Deal,' he said and held up his right hand.

Kay made a face. Guessing the images that instinctively passed through her head, he withdrew it and offered her his left instead. She took it and hauled him up onto his feet.

Kay and Olav Hanson stood in front of the Rialto and watched the preacher drive off in a taxi.

'He wasn't armed,' said Kay.

'No?' said Hanson. 'He pointed something in my direction, but the sun was in my eyes. Anyway, they were just warning shots.'

Kay thought about those holes in the fence. But now wasn't the time to argue about it, they had more important things to do. When Kay returned to the theatre she found Fortune standing in front of the screen. He took his index finger away from his earpiece when he saw her.

'The video centre hasn't come up with any images of Gomez on any cameras after he came in here.'

'OK,' said Kay. She looked out across the rows of seats. Fifteen to twenty men, all seated in such a way as to maximise the distance between them, the same way she'd heard men automatically do at the urinal trough or round the poker table. 'Everyone still sitting in the same seats?'

'Yep,' said Fortune.

The eyes of the men – all of them were men – were fixed on the floor, the walls, or their phones and watches. Only one met her gaze, a big black man in the second row from the back wearing a red bowler hat and smiling, as though he was enjoying himself. Maybe it was stereotyping, but her first thought was pimp. She made her way up to the back row where a thin white man sat. He was wearing a flat cap and looked like a family man. Another stereotype, she thought.

'Excuse me, sir, but did you see anyone come in just before we did? I mean a maximum of five minutes before we did?'

'No,' he said. 'No one.'

'If someone had, you would have seen it, right?' She nodded toward the door leading to the foyer.

'That's correct,' said the man. He seemed more curious than actually anxious, as though he was still a spectator, which of course he was. Kay wondered what it was that caused men to gather – and yet not gather – in this way.

'What's in there?' she asked and pointed to the paper bag on the seat next to him.

'It's my daughter's birthday today.' The man smiled as he held up the bag. Kay recognised the logo of the toy store – a little boy wearing a mushroom as a hat. 'She wants a Marlin's princess dress that makes you invisible to grown-ups.'

Kay looked at the bag. She was back in Englewood. It was her twelfth birthday, and her father was kneeling at the foot of the steps down to the street. His eyes were crazed, he was badly strung-out. He told her he had a present for her and she had to go with him to the place where he was keeping it. He pointed to a car waiting on the other side of the road. She saw the man sitting in the car. And she did what she was best at doing: she ran. Sometimes she wondered if she'd ever stopped running.

'Happy birthday then,' said Kay. Then she cleared her throat and called over to Fortune. 'OK, they can go!'

'Excuse me,' came a voice from one of the seats, 'but actually we paid to see this movie and it isn't finished.'

Kay didn't respond, she just hurried out through the door to the foyer. She stopped directly outside and heard, before the door closed, Fortune's voice:

'Sorry for the interruption, folks. Kill the lights and roll the film!'

Kay stared at the door to the men's room that was next to the entrance to the auditorium. She had no reason to suppose the woman in the ticket booth had been lying, but it would have been impossible from her position to see which of the doors Gomez had gone through.

Hanson appeared beside Kay.

'What are you thinking?' he asked.

'I'm thinking he went in here,' she said, pointing at the door to the men's room. 'Can you check if it's empty?'

Hanson went in, reappeared a couple of seconds later and beckoned to her. She went in. A weak trickle of water dribbled down the urinal and the mirror on the wall was cracked. But the air inside was fresher than she had expected. She looked up and saw why. A window high up at the back was wide open. She groaned.

'Aha,' said Hanson, who was now obviously seeing the open window for the first time.

'What's outside?' she asked.

Hanson stretched up on tiptoes and peered out. 'An alleyway.'

'Shit!' Kay slapped a hand against the wall and made a mental note to wash it first chance she got. 'That's why none of the cameras picked him up. He's using backstreets, he might have got all the way down to the river by now without being seen. He's playing with us. Why is he playing with us, Hanson?'

Her blond-haired colleague looked at her like he was giving the matter some thought. Then he said: 'Maybe he . . . likes to play?'

Kay closed her eyes. She needed someone else. She needed Bob Oz. But when she opened them again it was still Olav Hanson standing there.

They couldn't see me. But I could see, hear and imagine them. How they were all still chasing around like headless chickens after the suddenly so famous Tomás Gomez. I had made it from the movie theatre down to the riverbank, and was now sitting there, my heart pounding in my chest, watching the water flow. Like time, it took everything away with it. That ought to have brought some comfort. Like those old words of wisdom, 'This too shall pass.' But it didn't. Sooner or later, the same atoms in the molecules of water that ran by here yesterday would return, and history would repeat itself, it was just a matter of time. I took the hypodermic out of my breast pocket. Thought about how he jerked when he felt the prick, how he turned and stared at the seat back. Guess he must have thought a spring inside the seat had gone. I pressed the plunger down so what was left of it arced out into the water. For water it was, and unto water shall it return.

34

ORANGE, OCTOBER 2016

THE JOINT TERRORISM TASK FORCE consisted of people from MPD and the FBI. They had a building all to themselves, within walking distance of the city hall. As soon as Kay walked into the reception area with Walker and Hanson, she noticed that the place was superior to their own – and when they entered the well-lit meeting room which already held eight people she noted that the suits and the outfits were better quality too.

Following a quick round of introductions she learned that four of them were MPD, two FBI and two were from the mayor's own security office.

'Thanks for making it here to JTTF at such short notice,' said Ted Springer, who was wearing a pinstriped Wall Street suit instead of the standard undifferentiated FBI black. Kay picked up at once that he was appointing himself head of whatever was about to happen. But Springer also understood that, at this stage of the proceedings, it was Homicide Division that had all the information, and so he handed over to Walker, who in turn handed over to Kay. She didn't have time to feel the nerves she sometimes felt when addressing a group but went straight into an account of the murder and attempted murder Tomás Gomez was believed to have committed, the hunt for him and the suspicion that Gomez was now focusing on the US Bank Stadium and Mayor Kevin Patterson. A couple of seconds' silence followed her account. Then Springer spoke.

'So this Gomez has twice evaded you by the use of restrooms?'

Kay noticed the implied criticism but ignored it.

'Yes,' she said. 'It almost seems like he plans to let us know where he is, get us on his tail, and then disappear.'

'You don't think he just got lucky twice in a row? What motive would Gomez have for this kind of game?'

'I don't know,' said Kay. 'Maybe he just wants to send a message.'

'What kind of message would that be, Myers?'

Kay exchanged looks with Walker before responding. 'That he's a ghost. That if he wants to hit Kevin Patterson at the US Bank Stadium then we can't stop him.'

'You are aware that it's forbidden for members of the public to bear arms at a sports stadium, even when it's not being used for a sports event?'

'Yes,' said Kay.

'And yet you still believe he thinks the US Bank Stadium is a good idea?'

Kay noticed how Springer tugged at the sleeves of his suit despite the fact that it must be, she was guessing, made to measure. 'Yes.'

'And you think he believes he can outsmart the MPD which alone has over a thousand operatives, as well as the FBI?'

'I'm not saying he's right about it, just that that's the way I think he thinks.'

'Well, Miss Myer,' said Springer – Kay suspected he omitted the final 's' on purpose – 'murder is your business, and there are all sorts of sad and banal stories behind every case and the guilty parties are almost invariably inadequate people. But terrorists on the other hand, no matter how crazy they may be, are often rational and intelligent people, and certainly as regards their operational methods. So if that is what Gomez is planning, he knows perfectly well that in threatening the life of the mayor he is going to have every police officer in the city on his trail. Of course, it is not unheard of to get terrorists with deep personality disorders, but in the majority of cases the terrorist does everything he can to ensure the *success* of his mission. Put bluntly, if we've uncovered a plan to kill the mayor at the stadium then Gomez has screwed up already. This tells me that we're dealing with an amateur. Sure, he's still dangerous. But this is someone we have the competence and the professionalism to stop before the situation becomes critical.'

Something in the way he said 'we' gave Kay the feeling that the 'competence and professionalism' didn't necessarily include the Homicide Department.

'I hear what you're saying,' said Kay, noticing that her voice sounded harsher than she intended. 'But if I were the JTTF I would not underestimate Gomez.'

Springer gave a thin smile. 'Yes, but that's true of most things in life. In dealing with terrorism the trick is neither to underestimate nor overestimate. We simply don't have enough resources to follow up on every threat, and that means being sure you make the real threats your priority.'

'Like vegetarians at a potluck dinner?' It just popped out of Kay's mouth and the silence in the already quiet room deepened. A few years back, JTTF had been ridiculed in the press following revelations that they had infiltrated a group of vegetarians who sometimes gathered to share meals with each other. And not much else, as it turned out. Walker sent her a warning glance and she read his message: don't trip up.

Springer turned to Hanson. 'How about you, Detective? Do you share your colleague's view of this man Gomez?'

Hanson gave a start, obviously taken by surprise.

'Hm,' he said. He thought about it, linked his hands behind his head in an exaggerated attempt to look relaxed. 'On this I'm more in line with you guys in the JTTF.' A wide grin spread across his face. 'I mean, we're talking here about a Mexican with no papers who's been living in a rathole up in Jordan. Doesn't exactly sound like a criminal mastermind, does it?'

No one laughed.

'What does the mayor's office say?' Springer asked, turning to the man and the woman sitting further along the table.

'Well,' said the woman, a blonde with blue eyeliner, 'the mayor is very clear that he doesn't intend to cancel his participation. If the threat becomes public, we'll quote him to that effect in a press statement.' She put on a pair of glasses and read from the screen of her computer: '. . . *I would view it as an admission of bankruptcy for the city if one single illegal immigrant should succeed in preventing me from doing my job as the city's democratically elected mayor.*' She looked up. 'So unless anyone here has information that indicates we're dealing with powerful forces here?'

Kay was on the point of responding but stopped when she saw Walker's almost imperceptible shake of the head.

'Right,' said Springer. 'We'll have a threat assessment ready in a few hours, and I suggest that meanwhile we grade this orange, does that sound OK?'

Kay saw the others round the table nodding. Springer looked at her, one eyebrow raised.

'You disagree, Myer?'

'Myers. I don't know what orange means.'

'In this instance it means that the level of security around the mayor and his family is raised immediately and maintained until after the arrangement ends. Same goes for the NRA leaders currently visiting the city. That sound OK to you, Myers?'

It wasn't what he said, nor the exaggerated stress he laid on the final 's' of her name that made her cheeks flush, it was that thin, ironic smile.

'By all means,' she said. 'This is your field of competence, not ours.'

From the corner of her eye she noted the discreet nod of approval from Walker.

'Good,' said Springer. 'Which of you two detectives has seniority status?'

Given that Hanson looked an obvious ten years older than Kay the question was superfluous. But Kay guessed that Springer needed an answer to legitimise the decision he had already taken.

'That would be me,' Hanson said quickly.

'OK, then you report to me – unless there are any objections from the Homicide Department?'

'Fine by me,' Kay said before Walker could answer.

*

I'm stalking the memories. The words were still on repeat in Bob's head as he parked the Volvo in front of a driveway next to Town Taxidermy, jumped out and tried the door. It was locked. He checked the time. Three thirty. There was no note on the door. He knocked on the window, shaped his palms into a diving mask and peered through the glass into the darkened interior. The door to the workshop was open, but there didn't seem to be any light on in there. Bob sat down on the step and pulled out his phone. He was scrolling through the list of previous calls looking for Mike's number when the phone rang. A premonition that it was Mike, telepathically aware of what was happening, turned out to be mistaken and was instantly forgotten, the way we always forget premonitions that don't work out. He sighed. He had deleted the number from his phone but not from his memory.

'Yes, Alice?'

'Hi. Got a moment?'

He took a deep breath. 'Let me see . . . yes.'

'I saw the video on YouTube.'

'What d'you think? Regret dumping me now that I'm a celebrity?'

'Don't joke, Bob.'

'OK.'

'You probably think this isn't the right time, but I feel I have to.'

'Have to what?'

'Urge you to seek professional help.'

'As in . . . a psychologist?'

'Yes.'

'I thought you might say that. For someone with a hammer every problem looks like a nail. Heard that one before?'

'Bob.'

'I've seen three psychologists, including you and that anger management specialist of yours. Look how much that helped.'

'Bob, I see all the signs that you're on your way into a psychosis. Are you taking your antidepressants?'

'I don't like them.'

'Why not?'

'Because of that ugly pink packet they come in. And they make me drowsy. Flat. Boring.'

'And what are you like when you don't take them, Bob?'

'Moody. Angry. Aggressive. Suicidal. And a lot more fun.'

'Take them, please.'

Bob tried to swallow the lump in his throat. That damn concern in her voice. It always hit him in a place where he had no defence against it.

'Bob?'

'I'm here,' he said. 'Aren't you going to ask me for my signature on the house?'

'No,' she said. 'Not today.'

'Maybe you know I still visit there, the house I mean?'

'Yes,' she said.

'But maybe you don't know the reason. I didn't know myself. I thought I did it to spy on you and Stan the Man. But it's because that's where Frankie died. What I mean is . . . it was where she lived.'

Bob listened. Heard the tremor in her deep breathing.

'Just wanted to say that so you know,' he said and hung up.

I was headed toward Town Taxidermy when, turning the corner, I caught sight of him. He was sitting on the step outside the store, talking on the phone. I stopped at once and ducked back around the corner. Peered out. Doubted that he had seen me, he was concentrating so much on the call. Even if he had seen me, he wouldn't have recognised me from such a distance. But my gaze was sharp, and he was easy to recognise in that special coat. A guy walking past the store gave him a second look, maybe someone else who'd seen that video on YouTube and thought he must be that cop in the orange coat, the guy who had made such a fool of himself on live TV.

He sat there talking into the phone, but that wasn't just any old random place he happened to be, he was sitting there waiting for me, I told myself.

So what did I do then?

Phone booth.

I went back the way I had come. There were still a few of the old phone booths left in the smaller towns scattered around, but this one here had to be the last in all Minneapolis. It stood on the outer edge of the sidewalk and had scratched-up concertina doors that clapped together when you opened them, and a phone book for the sister cities. I fed in a few coins and dialled a cell number. The call I was making was to the taxidermist, Mike Lunde.

Bob continued to sit there studying her face on the screen after he had ended the connection. He missed the picture of her that used to come up when she called. How beautiful she was. And how beautiful he had been in the brightness of her aura. As he was on the point of calling Mike's number the phone rang. And this time it really was Mike.

'Hello, Mike, some telepathy going on here.'

'Sorry?'

'I was just about to ring you. Where are you?'

'At home.'

'Not well?'

'Tired, that's all. I finished the Labrador this morning, finally got the eyes right. So I closed up and drove home to get some sleep. What's this about?'

'I think I know where Tomás Gomez is hiding out.'

'Oh?'

'He's circling round the place where his family died. He can't let go, it's the same as with that cat he wants you to stuff. Just like . . .' Bob stopped.

'Yes?' said Mike.

Bob swallowed. 'It's the same as I've been doing with Alice and Frankie. We stalk memories.'

'I understand.'

'You said Gomez and his family had lived in Phillips West. Do you have that address?'

'He said something . . . I can't remember, Bob, I just woke up. But anyway, remember, his family didn't die in that house.'

'No, but that's the place where they were happy. *Happiness* is what we cling to, Mike.'

Bob heard a yawn from the other end.

'I suppose you might be right. Let me make some coffee here and I'll dig around in my memory.'

'OK, I'll call back in half an hour. Talk then. Wait, you were the one who called me. What is it?'

'Just keeping my word.'

It took Bob a moment to understand. 'You mean . . .? Has he . . .?'

'Yes. Tomás has been in touch.'

'How?'

'Just now. He called my cell phone.'

'What did he say?'

'Just said his name.'

'Just his name?'

'Yeah. He hung up almost straight away.'

'Where was he calling from?'

'I don't know, but it sounded like from a payphone. You know, the clink when the coins drop.'

'Do you have the number he called from?'

'Guess it's here in the Calls log. Just a moment . . .'

As Mike read out the number Bob noted it down.

'Can you repeat for me the conversation in as much detail as you can, Mike?'

'Sure,' said Mike. 'But that won't be necessary.'

'Why not?'

'I used that app of yours.'

'You recorded the conversation?'

'Yes,' Mike said with a quiet sigh of resignation.

'Great. Great, Mike! I'm on my way over to you now to hear the recording.'

'OK.'

'What's your address?'

'It's quite a way, Bob. Know what, I'll meet you halfway. There's a McDonald's on 2nd Avenue and East Lake Street. See you there in thirty minutes?'

35

TARGET, OCTOBER 2016

KAY MYERS'S DESK WAS LOCATED almost exactly in the middle of the open office landscape of the Homicide Department. Maybe that's why she sometimes felt herself surrounded on all sides. And longed for her own office. She looked at the paper target they had found in the bubble wrap left behind in the shopping mall. Studied the bullet holes.

She felt Hanson's presence before she heard him.

'We've had over two hundred calls from people who think they saw Gomez.'

'Oh yeah,' she said.

'Springer acts cool, but JTTF have called up half the police in the city for the opening tomorrow.'

Kay read the text on the target.

Hanson coughed. 'Hope you're not pissed that Springer put me in charge at this end?'

'Not at all,' said Kay. 'You have seniority.'

'Good. Because here's a list I want you to check.' He handed her a sheet of paper. 'I want you to check out first the ones I've ticked. Here . . .'

Kay looked at the sheet of paper. Skimmed through it. 'It says here the caller thinks they saw Gomez *three* weeks ago?'

'Yes, but if you read on, you'll see she thinks she saw him again yesterday. If that's true, then she's the only person we know of – apart from the neighbours in Jordan – who's seen Gomez more than once in the same place. If there's anything in it, then it means we have a place we know he visits regularly.'

Kay glanced through the notes. Aged eighty-three, address Cedar Creek. North of the city centre, more or less wilderness country. There was a separate column for the person taking the call to assess the caller's credibility.

'Credibility rating under half, it says here.'

'Yes, he wasn't sure if the old lady was all there.'

Kay looked up at Hanson. 'Even among calls we get that *sound* serious, eighty per cent turn out to be fantasies. And this is from a senile old lady living somewhere out in the sticks, in wolf country?'

'I hear you, Myers, but I think it's worth following up.'

'If I say I don't agree?'

Hanson smiled and lifted his coffee cup as though to make a toast. 'I recall someone telling me to shut up and call Walker because he'd put her in charge of the case. Well, Myers, you can call Springer. OK?'

Hanson turned and walked off whistling. Kay closed her eyes.

Hoped the slight twinges of pain in her lower back weren't going to be the start of something.

'Excuse me.'

Kay opened her eyes and looked up. Her heart gave a little jump. It was the dark-eyed painter. He hadn't taken off his mask, not even the protective white cap and gloves.

'I promised you an invitation,' he said. He put a card down on her desk, turned and walked away. She watched him go. The cheek of it. He must have been warned he couldn't just wander round inside the Homicide Department where there was so much sensitive information lying about. But he'd taken the chance anyway, risked getting a dressing-down just to deliver this card to her. She looked at it. It was the kind of invitation you buy in a store and fill out your own details on. Here it said that the invite was to Minnehaha Park, in front of the waterfalls. Sunday at one o'clock. There was no indication of what would happen there, nor was the card signed. She slipped it into a drawer. If they'd got Gomez by then, well, maybe. If not, then she'd still be sitting here.

She picked up the paper target again. Ran her fingertips over the bullet holes.

Because sometimes the only thing that is going to make you feel better is shooting a machine gun.

Kay was reading the poster behind the counter when the assistant appeared in front of her.

'Hi, I'm Jim, how can I help you today?'

'Kay Myers, MPD.' She showed him her ID and put the target down on the counter. 'Is this from here?'

The man in the TOTAL DEFENSE T-shirt scratched his chest and studied the target.

'This is a Krüger target, so it's from here all right – we're the only people round here who do Krüger targets. I always try to get our customers to take the target they used back home with them.'

'Why is that?'

Jim shrugged. 'When they see the target maybe it inspires them to come back and try to shoot better next time.'

'I see. Does that make it likely that it was you who gave the person concerned this target?'

'We have another shooting instructor – Barbara. But as a rule, yes, it's me.'

'OK. Have you seen this man here before?'

Kay held up the screen of her phone to Jim. It showed a frozen moment from a video of Tomás Gomez outside the Rialto, the porn movie theatre.

Jim studied the image while Kay looked around. When she came in there had been only the Donald Duck figure, now there were three people in line behind her.

'I see hundreds of new faces every day, I can't remember them all,' said Jim, still peering in concentration at the screen. 'But sure, we mostly get whites in here, not too many Latinos, so I ought to remember the face if he was in here recently. But to be honest I have trouble seeing differences in the faces of people of a different ethnicity from me. Hope you don't find that offensive, Detective, I heard it's a simple biological fact of life.'

He looked up at her, and she couldn't work out whether his look was challenging or not. It didn't make much difference to her either way.

'How about the way he walked, and his body language?' asked Kay. She touched the Play arrow on the video, and they watched Tomás Gomez walk across the street. She thought she saw Jim hesitate. But when Gomez had disappeared inside the Rialto he handed the phone back to her.

'Sorry.'

There was a cough in the line behind Kay. She put her card down on the counter.

'Call me on this number if you think of anything.'

'Will do. By the way, where did you find this target?'

'In a restroom. In the bubble wrap his rifle was packed in.'

'Hey, Jim,' someone in the line called out, 'can you get Barbara to come and help out here?'

'I'm done,' said Kay, and with a nod to Jim left the store.

It had started to cloud over on her trip out and now the sky was covered in a sullen, lead-blue sheet.

She got into her car and drove along minor roads toward 35W and the centre of town. She came to a T-junction in front of a small lake and stopped. The sign facing her said the 35W was a left turn, but it also showed that a right would take her to the 65, a road that ran in a straight line northward to Cedar Creek. Kay had decided she would ring the old lady who had called in the tip-off and try to assess its importance that way, but now she was only twenty, at the most thirty minutes' drive from where she lived. Kay hesitated. Had rush-hour traffic started? And then it was as though the heavens made the decision for her as the sky opened in torrential rain. She could no longer see the sign through the water flooding down her windshield. She set the wipers going. Then she made a left turn signal and headed west, toward city hall.

36

McDEATH, OCTOBER 2016

IT WAS POURING DOWN AS Bob swung into the parking lot in front of the McDonald's. He turned off the engine and peered out. Heard the distant rumble from the 35W, the freeway that passed directly above him and blocked out the view in the west. It wasn't exactly an idyllic location and the cloud cover that swallowed up the daylight didn't make it any more inviting. He saw Mike's Chevrolet Caprice station wagon further ahead in the parking lot. He pulled out his phone and tapped in a name. The voice that answered sounded resigned:

'What is it, Bob?'

'Hi, Kari. My suspension's been cancelled.'

'It has? Because of the terrorist threat?'

'Yes,' said Bob, who had no idea what she was talking about. 'What I need right now is to get a trace on a phone call.

A Mike Lunde received a call about half an hour ago, I need to know where that call came from. Can you take down the number?'

Kari hesitated.

'This is urgent,' he said. 'This terrorist threat . . .'

'Go ahead,' she said.

After hanging up Bob buttoned up his coat. Cashmere was showerproof, but if it got soaked through then the coat would stink like a wet dog for days afterward. He sprinted through the rain to the entrance and nodded to the security guard on the inside. Saw a waving Mike Lunde, who occupied one of the booths facing out onto the parking lot.

Bob bought two vanilla shakes to make it all look legit and then slid in opposite Mike, who had placed his cell phone on the table between them.

'Thanks for coming, Mike. Vanilla shake?'

Mike shook his head with a sad smile. 'Lactose intolerant.'

'That's a bastard. Can we get straight to it?'

Mike nodded. 'So, when the recording starts, he's said his name, I recognise the voice and I start recording.'

'Got it.'

Mike tapped the play button. Bob heard heavy breathing. It stopped. Then the sound of Mike's voice:

'Yes, Tomás, what is it?'

More panting. Again it stopped.

'I know it's taken time, Tomás, but I've finally finished the Labrador and now I can start on your cat. I'm delivering the dog at twelve o'clock tomorrow, so if you could come by at two?'

The panting resumed. And stopped. Like a malfunctioning respirator, thought Bob.

'Trust me, Tomás. Come in tomorrow and we'll have a long chat. We'll work this out.'

The panting came back. Gomez had clearly moved the receiver away from his mouth with the intention of hanging up but then changed his mind. Then came a click, and a long dialling tone.

'He hung up,' said Bob.

'I think he heard it,' said Mike.

'Heard what?'

'My betrayal. That I was lying. He won't come.'

Bob put his lips around the red-striped straw. Sucked up the vanilla shake and looked into the other man's worried face.

'You know what I think, Mike?'

'Yes, I believe I do.'

'So then what?'

'You think I acted worse than I had to. That I *wanted* him to realise it was a trap. That I found a way of warning him at the same time as I kept my word to you and fulfilled my responsibilities as a good citizen. On paper, at least.'

'Is that what you did, Mike? Are you so calculating?'

'I don't know, Bob.'

'You don't know?'

Mike blew his nose on a paper serviette. 'Sometimes we're convinced that a particular action is exclusively the product of a reasoning process, don't you agree? But then – could be a long time afterward – we start to doubt. That good testimonial you gave to a student taxidermist, was that justified? Or was it out of pity for someone whose talent you know is little more than mediocre? Or your teenage daughter's boyfriend, the one you more or less implied to her you weren't too crazy about – was it really like you said, because he seemed so gormless? Or was it out of the anxiety any father feels at the prospect of losing his daughter? It's not easy to know the answer when you have contradictory emotions struggling inside you.'

Bob looked out the window. It had already grown darker in the short time they had been sitting there. Light from passing cars was reflected in the raindrops on the parked cars. With a loud slurping noise the last of the vanilla milkshake disappeared up the straw.

'Know what the people round here call this McDonald's?'

'What?' asked Bob, but never heard the answer because his phone rang. He saw it was from Kari.

'Hi, sweetie, what've you got for me?'

'The call to Mike Lunde's cell phone was from a phone booth.'

Bob noted the address on a serviette beneath a paper cup. 'You're an angel, Kari.'

'Such good news that your suspension's been cancelled.'

'Thanks.' Bob ended the call and looked at the address he had written down. Visualised a map of the city centre. 'Looks like Tomás Gomez called from a phone booth a block away from your store.'

Mike raised his eyebrows. It dawned on Bob.

'You know what, Mike? He was on his way to the store. He saw me sitting waiting outside. He must've figured I was a cop and run off.'

'You think so?'

'Yeah. And then he called you just to get confirmation of what he already suspected. That you've been talking to us. Damn.' Bob grabbed up the cardboard cup and crushed it in his hand. Drops of vanilla milkshake dripped down from the straw and onto the back of his hand. 'I'm sorry, Mike.'

'Sorry for what?'

'That I pressured you into doing this, put you in the line of fire. Because you're in danger now. You do get that, right?'

Mike shook his head.

'No?' Bob licked the back of his hand.

'Tomás isn't hunting for people who are hunting him. He understands they're just doing what they have to do. He already knows who his targets are, and I'm not one of them, Bob.'

'If you say so. What makes you so sure about that?'

'McDeath.'

'McDeath?'

'That's what they call this McDonald's here. The crack gangs used to hang out here. This is where Tomás was eating that night, with his family.'

Bob stared at Mike a moment and then looked around the half-full diner. 'So his family was killed *here*?'

'He said they were sitting at the table nearest the door, so it must've been that one over there.' Mike pointed. 'He said he was happy that evening. It was his daughter's birthday, she was the one who insisted they go to McDonald's. He didn't know this was a gang hangout, he'd just driven by a few times and noticed they had a parking lot. It was a perfect evening. There were balloons, the kids sang a song they'd been taught in elementary school, he and his wife Monica sat there dreaming about the future. Where they were going to live, if the kids should go to university, et cetera. About how lucky they were to live in a land that offered so many opportunities for anyone who was prepared to make an effort. A country that gives you a chance no matter whether you're black, brown or white, if you sit in a wheelchair or you don't come from a rich family. You could make it even if your immigration papers weren't yet in order, because as long as you *willed* it hard enough, you knew things would work out. Tomás had what he thought was an unshakeable faith in the future. But as things turned out it only took thirty or forty seconds to shake it to its foundations. He used to say he wished I could have known the person he was back then. That I would have liked him. But that he no longer exists, that person no longer exists. He died here that day, along with his family. The man sitting in front of me was just his ghost.'

Bob looked at a couple sitting at a nearby table. Their daughter couldn't have been much older than Frankie. 'Is that why you picked this place for us to meet, Mike?'

'It's actually on my way home, but maybe. Probably.'

'And what is it supposed to show me, this place?'

'That it could've been you or me. It could have been you sitting here with your family that evening, Bob.'

Bob Oz pushed the crumpled cardboard cup to one side and buttoned up his coat. 'I'll be at your store at one thirty tomorrow, Mike. Maybe the guy will turn up after all.'

'Why should he, when he knows he'd be walking straight into an ambush?'

'I don't know. There's a certain kind of killer we call a moth.'

'A moth?'

'They seem attracted to the investigation into the murder they've committed. They turn up at the scene of the crime, or at the funeral. They make an effort to get close to the detectives involved. Frequent the bars where they hang out, close to the police station. They're like moths that can't help flying toward the flame, even though they know they might get their wings burned off.'

'You think Tomás might be like that?'

'I don't know. I was talking to someone this morning who thinks that sometimes we *want* to get caught. Maybe Tomás knows the game is almost up. Maybe deep down he just wants to get it over with.'

After Bob had got into his car and watched Mike's station wagon head out onto East Lake Street and disappear into the south-west, he pulled out his phone and made a call. Half expected to hear a pip and then the voicemail message telling him to stop calling her. Instead she picked up after just two rings.

'Hi, Bob.'

37

A DESOLATE PLACE, SEPTEMBER 2022

THE PRIEST AT THE MINDEKIRKEN, Jon Erland, greets me in the lobby connecting the church itself to the offices. When I called him before my departure from Norway and told him about the book I was writing he said he hadn't actually known my cousin, only my uncle, and that I should really try some other source. But once he became aware of my theological background, and I had hinted that it was memories of the Mindekirken when I was a child that had inspired me, he agreed to meet me anyway. Jon Erland looks to be in his seventies and speaks with the same Norwegian dialect as I do, not so surprising since the Norwegian Bible Belt is in the south of the country, like it is in the USA. But he uses words that became obsolete back home in Norway many years ago. He is professionally friendly and open – an American openness that seems to have worn off some of that traditional Scandinavian reserve. He shows me round. The Mindekirken is mostly still as I recall it. Large but austere, as Lutheran churches should be. As far as I can see the only thing that's new is the air conditioning. He suggests we talk in his office. On our way there we pass a Norwegian flag and photographs of the Norwegian king and queen, flatteringly young. Along with the gifts from earlier visitors from Norway it gives the church a strangely museum-like atmosphere, at once calming and a little disturbing. In his office Jon Erland tells me that he only met my relatives at church services, which are still held twice a day every Sunday, one in Norwegian at nine o'clock, which usually attracts a congregation of about forty or fifty, and the second in English at eleven o'clock at which a congregation of between fifteen and twenty is about all they can expect. He tells me that my uncle is buried in the family grave at the Lakewood Cemetery, as I already knew.

'What do people say about my cousin, after what happened?' I ask.

'You mean his posthumous reputation, his legacy?'

'I mean, do people regard him as a hero?'

Jon Erland raises an eyebrow, clearly surprised. 'Why? The whole thing ended in the most appalling tragedy. The best thing one could say about your cousin is that he was a poor misguided soul.'

'That's one way of looking at it –' I start to say.

'No!' says Jon Erland. 'It is the truth. And as we all know, there is only one truth.'

I look at him. 'Only one truth,' I echo. And in that same instant, remember why it was I could never have been a priest.

38

THE RAGE OF ABANDONMENT, OCTOBER 2016

IT WAS DARK BUT THE rain had stopped by the time Bob reached the house. He rang the bell. Heard the footsteps inside, recognised them as Alice's, knew which slippers she was wearing, also that she would be wearing the white lamb's wool sweater she always wore when it was cold.

She opened the door. Smiled. And it seemed to him that she was still the same, beautiful Alice, with her hair tied up in a knot and stray honey-blonde locks of hair tapping at the corners of her mouth, though the wrinkles around her eyes were now more pronounced.

'Come in,' she said.

'Thanks,' he said, and tried not to think how odd it was to be invited to enter his own house. 'And thank you for seeing me.'

He removed his coat and hung it on one of the vacant hooks. Tried not to wonder whether she might have removed one of Stan's jackets from the same hook just before he rang the bell.

She led the way into the kitchen. He registered that she was back to her familiar Alice size, the curves had returned, there was a little more flesh on the bones, all of which suggested to him that she was doing well. Immediately following Frankie's death she had lost weight dramatically, and then gained it so swiftly she became a sort of inflated version of herself. And then lost it again. It was as though she had gone through the whole repertoire of eating disorders familiar to her from her patients. Or maybe it was the pills.

They sat in their usual seats on opposite sides of the kitchen table. She laced her fingers around a large teacup. How many times had he seen her do that, warming her hands, with her shoulders slightly hunched? He noticed that the picture of Frankie on the refrigerator was still there. And next to it, one of Frankie, Bob and Alice together.

'Like something to drink?'

'Water,' he said and stood up. Took a glass from the cupboard above the sink, turned on the tap and said, without turning round:

'I'm sorry for having behaved like an idiot. I want to sign those papers as soon as possible, so that you're also the formal owner of the house, you don't just live here.'

'What?' she said, as though the running water had drowned out what he was saying.

Bob turned off the tap, took the glass and sat back down opposite her. 'On one condition.'

She gave him a cautious look. 'And that is?'

'That we lower the price.'

'Lower? Don't you mean raise?'

'No, lower. Even you won't be able to pay off the loan if we stick to the current valuation.'

'But . . .'

'If in due course Stan the Man wants to buy himself in then, of course, you can pay me more.'

Bob looked at the disbelieving face before emptying the glass in a single long swallow. As he put the glass down he could see that she believed him. Her eyes were shining. A slight shiver passed between her shoulders, as though she wanted to put her hand onto his.

'And there's one more thing I want from you,' he said.

'What's that?'

'Explain loneliness to me.'

'Loneliness?'

'In technical terms.'

'Are you lonely?'

'I'm asking you to explain it, not me.'

'OK.' She folded her arms, breathed deeply and calmly and fixed her gaze some place just above his head the way she did when she was concentrating. He waited. Waited the way he had waited outside her flat before those first, comically old-fashioned dates. Outside her workplace after they became a couple. Outside the bathroom after they started living together and she was getting ready to go out to a party. Outside the delivery room when Frankie was born. Waiting for Alice was something he associated with happiness, because he was waiting for something good. But there would be no more waiting. He knew that now. There was nothing left to wait for.

'The language that describes loneliness is limited,' she began slowly, as though testing her way. 'But first you have existential loneliness. The knowledge that you have been thrown into this world, and that you, me and everybody else are all, in the final analysis, alone. And then you have interpersonal loneliness. A lack of belonging, the feeling that you are alone even when with friends. You feel as though you're inside a bubble, the others seem far, far away because you are, emotionally speaking, somewhere else.'

'Talk about loneliness when the most important people in your life are gone,' said Bob. 'Someone you love. And children.'

It was as though he had pressed a button. Her lips twisted and tears at once sprang to her eyes. 'Bob, please don't start again . . .' Her voice was hoarse.

'I'm not starting again,' he said. 'I'm not talking about us, Alice. This is about Tomás Gomez, the killer we're looking for. He lost his family, they were shot. What I'm wondering about is whether loneliness by itself can have driven him to want to avenge their deaths.'

She blinked twice.

'Go ahead,' said Bob.

She swallowed. Fixed her gaze back onto the wall above him. 'That's trauma,' she said. 'Trauma, not loneliness. Trauma arises when you lose someone you thought you would be spending the rest of your life with. When it was more than an expectation, it was a conviction. Something you based your whole life on. Something that was everything.' She lowered her gaze to meet his. 'The trauma is the wound. But the loneliness that comes with it locks you to your trauma. Sometimes there are physical manifestations. Often intolerable pains that follow the spine down toward the stomach.' She put a hand to her own stomach.

'You feel you want to disappear, but the body is frozen up, and you become simply incapable of drawing warmth from those around you.'

'Silent, locked in?'

'Or raging. Everyone reacts differently. But we often share the feeling that something drastic has to be done. Traumatic memory is circular. Meaning that when something happens that reminds us of a previous trauma it can awaken rage, in this case the rage of abandonment. Everything that has happened before happens again. The whole weight of those previous experiences invades the present. The grief that has up to that point been frozen explodes in a vengeful rage. The violence of trauma is often extreme. People stab in a frenzy, they molest the body, not uncommonly there are elements of sadism.'

Bob nodded slowly. 'The rage of abandonment.'

'That's the technical term.'

'Thank you.' He turned the empty glass in his hand. 'Alice, has it ever . . .?' He stopped.

'Yes?' she said.

'Have you ever felt afraid of me?'

Alice tilted her head. 'No. But as a psychologist I know that as a rule people overestimate their ability to predict how those closest to them will react, especially if the person concerned has been traumatised. Maybe that's exactly the mistake I'm making now. Given your sometimes aggressive behaviour, it is definitely not doing things by the book for me to meet you here alone, like this, where all the memories are.'

Bob gave a crooked smile. 'You mean you should be afraid, but you aren't?'

She nodded. 'I'm probably more worried about what you

might do to yourself than to me. Tell me . . .' Now it was her turn to stop.

'Yes?'

'Are things getting better, Bob?'

'Better? Oh, no question.' Bob smiled and knew that if he squeezed the glass any harder it would break. 'I'm over the worst. I accept that life goes on. I remember you saying that the rational mind forgets things it has no use for. That's true. I can feel how I'm thinking less about both you and Frankie with each day that passes. And you'll see, they'll be even better now that I'm getting rid of the house. It'll be as though none of this –' he gestured toward the photos on the refrigerator – 'ever happened. Don't you think?' He was smiling so hard the corners of his mouth ached and through the tears her face grew fluid and indistinct. It felt as though his skin was on fire. 'But then, there's a part of my brain that isn't rational and smart, and that can't forget, even though it knows it should.'

Alice nodded. 'Maybe we don't have to forget, Bob. Maybe it's more about treasuring the good memories and learning to live with the not so good ones. And . . . carrying on.' Her hesitation had been brief, but Alice was like a song Bob knew off by heart. He knew at once that that pause, short as it had been, meant something. And suddenly he understood what it was.

'Carrying on?' he said. And steeled himself as he waited for what he knew must come. Because of course he'd seen it as soon as he arrived, the way she looked just the way she had done back then.

Alice wrapped her fingers around her teacup and looked down into it.

'Yes, I'm . . .' She seemed to ready herself, then looked up and directly into Bob's eyes. 'I'm pregnant.'

Bob nodded and nodded, his head going up and down like that dog on the parcel shelf in the back of his parents' car.

'Congratulations,' he said, his voice thick and hoarse.

'Thanks,' she said quietly.

'No, I really mean it,' he said. 'I'm . . . happy for you.'

'I know you are.'

'You do?'

'Of course,' she said.

They looked at each other. He smiled. She gave a cautious smile in return.

'You've been dreading giving me the news?' he asked.

'A bit,' she said. 'So it's OK?'

'Yes, it's OK.' He thought about it. It really was. More than OK. It felt . . . yes, like a relief. Alice was pregnant again, and in some strange way it felt as though he now had one life less on his conscience. He'd never thought of it like that before, never realised that he might instinctively react like that to news that could only take her even further away from him.

'Girl or a boy?' he asked.

'We're going for an ultrasound on Monday. I guess we'll find out then.'

'Exciting.' Bob was still nodding. If he did it much longer his head would probably fall off. 'Thanks for talking to me, Alice. Thanks for . . . well, everything really. I'll be on my way.'

They said goodbye without touching each other. When she shut the door behind him, and he headed out into the chill autumn night, it was as though his step was lighter. But then it was as though a pendulum swung across his chest, across his heart, and for a moment he stood by his car, doubled over in pain. Then the pendulum swung the other way, and he drove off to Motörhead's idiotically cheerful 'On Parole' with the volume up full, singing along as the tears rolled down his cheeks.

39

FISH, OCTOBER 2016

BETTY JACKSON LOCKED THE DOOR to the ticket booth and was heading for the switches to turn off the lights for the Rialto sign when Mel, the projectionist, came down the steep steps from his projection room. 'There's a guy still sitting in the theatre,' he said, keeping a tight hold of the railing. Mel was only a couple of years younger than her and had recently had a hip replacement.

'I see,' said Betty. 'Didn't you call down and tell him we're closing?'

'Yeah, but I think he's asleep.'

They entered the theatre together.

She registered that it was the black man in the red hat. She would have shouted his name, but she didn't know it, had never spoken to him, even though he sat there almost every day, usually staying for several hours. Sometimes he was the only person in the whole theatre. She'd hear him talking on his phone when he was alone, like it was his office. But this time it looked as though he'd fallen asleep, his chin slumped down in his chest and the brim of the hat shading his face.

Betty walked along the row toward him with the projectionist, who had actually offered to go first, like he was some kind of gentleman, right behind her. The man sat with one hand resting on his thick thigh and she put her hand over his and gave it a gentle shake. The hat fell off. Betty exclaimed loudly and backed away, into the projectionist. The man's eyes were wide open and completely white. Though it wasn't that that made her jump, her own husband also sometimes slept with his eyes open and his head back. Nor was it the open mouth with the tiny inlaid diamonds glinting in the teeth. It was the hand. It had been as cold as marble.

It had been a more than usually busy afternoon at Bernie's Bar and a very good evening. Liza had turned down the volume slightly on Little Feat's 'Dixie Chicken' so she could hear what he was saying, the tipsy and rather forlorn-looking elderly man sitting at the bar. He was saying he had driven to the big city from a town named Funkley, four hours' drive to the north, to attend the NRA gathering the next day.

'Quite a change for a hayseed like me, this,' he said with a cautious smile. 'Funkley's got five inhabitants. Everyone lives alone, got their own home. It gets kind of lonely. Even though I'm the only man among them.'

'Yes, you'd probably be better off living in Minneapolis,' said Liza, signalling to another guest that she would take his order in a moment or two.

'How so?' asked the hayseed, looking at her with genuine curiosity.

'Well,' said Liza as she tried to think up a good answer, 'we . . . er, for one thing we've been voted the healthiest city in the country.'

'Good for you. But you look just as lonesome as us people from Funkley.'

Liza stepped aside to pull a beer for the impatient customer as the swing door to the back room opened and Eddie – who was to take the final two hours alone – came in.

'Anyone would think the place was popular,' he said as he looked out across the bar.

'You can handle it,' said Liza as she took the money for the beer and nodded in the direction of the hayseed. 'Be nice to this guy here.'

'Always nice to everybody, that's me,' said Eddie.

Liza went out to the back, untied her apron and put on her coat. She had to admit that since morning, every time the bar door opened, she had looked up, half hoping to see that ugly mustard-yellow coat coming in. Maybe he'd be back some other day. Or not. It was OK either way. She left by the back door, onto a sidewalk that was still wet with rain.

An orange Volvo stood parked by the kerb.

'You can see that coat doesn't match the car,' she said. 'Or are you colour-blind?'

'A bit,' he said as he opened the passenger-side door. 'Can I offer you a lift?'

She pretended to think it over.

'So?' she said as they set off down the road. 'Have you found what you were looking for?'

'Perhaps,' said Bob.

'Perhaps?'

'Yeah.'

'Well, anyway you, you look . . . lighter.'

'Lighter?'

'As though you've . . . I don't know. Got rid of something.'

He nodded. 'Perhaps.'

'That's a lot of perhapses there.'

He laughed. 'Tell me about your day.'

She did. Talked about the guy from Funkley. About some of the regulars. About Little Feat. And about how Johan had learned a whole raft of new words and was now spouting them like a waterfall. Now and then the man behind the wheel nodded. Sometimes he laughed. At other times just grunted. Sometimes he asked about something and seemed as though he was really interested. It was easy to talk, so easy she had to be careful not to say too much, she thought. But it was all fine, and she hadn't got him wrong in the bar or that last time he drove her home; he understood what she was talking about, understood her simple, practical and unsentimental way of thinking about things. Liza knew she could scare the type of man who preferred soft, cuddly women, sensitive and delicate women they could look after. And it wasn't as if she didn't need someone to lean on when the going got tough, but most of all she needed someone who respected her and who she could respect in return. Sure, she didn't know Bob Oz well enough to know if he was a man like that, all she knew was that she liked . . . well, what was it about him she did like, actually? That behind all the bullshit he was honest, that he didn't try to pretend to be someone or something he wasn't.

If that was down to courage or just laziness she didn't know, but she liked it. She liked being around him. That was the plain truth. And hell, that was enough to be going on with.

As it had done the last time, the journey to her little home seemed over too quickly.

'*Shotgun shack*,' he said as they both peered up at the kitchen window where they saw the profile of Liza's sister Jennifer who, as Liza knew, would be deep in some romantic novel.

'Is it something you look forward to?' he asked.

'Look forward to?'

'Going inside and seeing your kid sleeping there in the bed, safe and warm. That was always the high point of the day for me. It made it all worthwhile, all the grind.'

She looked at him. Hesitated.

'You think often about that?' she asked.

'Every day.'

'Would you . . . want to come in and see him?'

He looked at her in surprise. 'You sincere?'

She nodded.

Liza unlocked the door and they went straight to the kitchen where she introduced Bob and her sister to each other and told her to carry on reading, Bob wouldn't be staying long. Then they made the short trip to the bedroom and opened the door. Light fell across the little bed. Her three-year-old was wearing pale blue pyjamas. He was fast asleep, one little fist clenched with the thumb sticking up like a hitchhiker. The Radica 20Q lay on the duvet next to him. Liza heard Bob's intake of breath, as though he was about to say something, but nothing came.

After a few moments they closed the door again.

'Thanks,' he said as they stood on the steps outside the front door. Liza wanted to give him a hug but she resisted.

Bob looked at Liza standing there in the doorway. He wanted to give her a hug, but resisted.

'Sleep well,' he said, and with a short, clumsy bow he turned and headed back toward his car.

'You know what, Bob Oz?'

He stopped and turned. 'What?'

'You're not a wolf in sheep's clothing. You're a sheep in wolf's clothing.'

He nodded slowly and smiled. 'I'll have to think about that one.'

And that's what he did as he drove away, listening to 'On Parole', a sheep of a pop song in the wolf's clothing of hard rock. Disguise, there was something there. Not something about him but about Tomás Gomez, maybe deep down a decent, hard-working family man who dressed himself up in the clothing and rituals of a gang member, a cold-blooded killer. Even if loneliness had driven him mad and afflicted him with what Alice had called the rage of abandonment, could a person really go through such a complete transformation? And if not, why had no one exposed the sheep in wolf's clothing?

Two hours later, as he sat on the couch in his apartment and opened his third and final beer, the thoughts still swirled around inside his head: who is Tomás Gomez?

Where is Tomás Gomez?

Kay Myers stared at the ceiling above her bed as though the cracks in the paintwork were a map that might reveal where he was hiding. Listened to the couple making love in the next-door apartment, as though their cries might tell her something. All kinds of disparate thoughts swirled around inside her head. Mrs White's bird. Ted Springer's pinstriped suit. Walker's bass voice. The man at the porn theatre with the present for his daughter. The phone call from Bob Oz requesting the file on Perez, a homicide case from 1995. Was there some pattern here? Something she should have spotted, something that would reveal exactly what his next move would be? She checked the time. Twelve hours until the opening at the US Bank Stadium. Why think about that? It wasn't her responsibility any more. Springer and Hanson, from now on Gomez was their problem. She'd called the woman who rang in the tip-off from Cedar Creek but got no reply. Kay decided she would head up there early in the morning so she could cross it off her list. What she should do now was sleep. The couple through the wall had fallen silent now. She envied them their lovemaking. Envied their waking up together. It had been a long time since she'd had anyone else in her bed, man or woman. She felt the mattress dip at the foot of the bed and an instant later the cat came snuggling up next to her as though it had read her thoughts. She closed her eyes and stroked its head. She thought of the painter. How a mask through which all you saw was a pair of eyes left you free to invent the rest any way you wanted. Make your own imaginary person. What was it he wanted to show her on Sunday? She thought briefly about it, then her thoughts moved on. Who was Perez? What – if anything – did Bob know that neither she nor anybody else had seen?

The phone on her bedside table rang. She checked the screen and recognised the number.

'Yes, Fortune?'

'Sorry to call so late, Myers. I'm at the Regency Hospital, I'm standing outside the mortuary.'

Marco Dante, she thought. *He's dead.*

'An ambulance brought in a body from the Rialto a few hours after we were there. They didn't contact us because they didn't see anything suspicious about the death. It isn't the first time an overweight man past fifty dies of a heart attack or whatever while watching a dirty movie. But then they took a preliminary toxso . . . er, toxsilogical . . .'

'Toxicology test,' said Kay.

'Yeah. And they found traces of . . . hang on, I wrote it down here. Tetrodotoxin. It's supposed to be the same kind of poison you get when you eat those Japanese fish that haven't been cooked properly.'

'Fugu.'

'Eh?'

'Japanese pufferfish.'

'Yeah. So I asked did they think the guy had been eating fish while he was at the movies. But even though those things mean certain death, it apparently works slowly, so the guy could have got the poison in him several hours before he noticed anything. And being as how this isn't exactly the kind of fish you cook in your kitchen at home I figured that here is one restaurant that is going to be in deep shit. But now I've checked the guy out and when I saw his record I called you straight off.'

'I get it. So who is he?'

'Wes Villefort. Male, fifty-eight years, black.'

She groaned. 'You gonna give me his height too?'

'I'm saying black because he was the only black person there.'

The pimp, she thought. 'OK. So, the record?'

'Narcotics.'

Kay thought about this. She saw no immediate connection

between narcotics and Dante, Karlstad and Patterson. The death might just be accidental. Or it might not.

'Thanks for telling me,' she said. 'I'll take a look at it in the morning.'

Olav Hanson headed down toward the river with his fishing rod in his hand.

He needed to calm down and think things over before tomorrow. And he and Violet had quarrelled after Sean's visit the previous night. It ended with her leaving to spend the weekend at her parents. She would calm down, so that was OK by him, it meant he could fish the whole night through if he wanted.

The steep track was muddy. It always was, no matter how long it had been since the last rain. The moon dipped in and out behind the clouds, and in the dark it wasn't easy to see where to put your foot without slipping. Having a bad knee on a tricky slope didn't help and several times he had to reach out and hold on to tree trunks for support. A sound. He stopped. Something moving in the trees. Too big for a squirrel. He peered but saw nothing. Either it was the same dog as last time or his ragged nerves playing a trick on him again. He carried on unsteadily down the track. Events over the last few days had cost him, but with a bit of luck it might all be over by tomorrow. If Lobo really did make an attempt on the life of the mayor then, statistically speaking, the most likely outcome was that the problem would solve itself. Olav had learned this during a meeting that afternoon at which Springer said that the majority of so-called lone-wolf terrorists ended up being killed, whether or not they succeeded. Olav couldn't care less about Mayor Patterson; with that statistical fact in mind he just hoped Lobo would turn up at the US Bank Stadium tomorrow armed with a rifle.

As he reached the river's edge Olav saw that another fisherman hadn't gone home yet. That was fine. It meant he wouldn't be standing there alone on a dark night like this.

'Catch anything?' asked Olav as he pulled the cover of his rod off and made ready to cast.

'Not yet,' the man said without taking his eyes off his line. Olav seemed to recognise the voice, but he couldn't immediately put a face to it. There were quite a few regulars among those who fished down here.

'Perch bites better at night,' said Olav. He heard a twig snap behind him and peered up into the trees.

'Oh, I was hoping for something a little bigger.'

'Oh yeah?' said Olav. He heard a single bark from the trees. So it was the dog. Olav could tell his pulse was high now because he could feel it slowing down again. 'Yellow pike, you mean?' said Olav as he stuffed the rod cover into his jacket pocket. He was looking forward to the fishing now. Showing how far he could cast. 'You need luck for that, man.'

'Not yellow pike,' said the other. 'I'm after the Milkman.'

At first Olav Hanson thought he hadn't heard right, that his nerves were playing a trick on him. Then, slowly, the fisherman turned. The peak of his cap shadowed his face, but once he had turned round completely and raised his head, Olav saw who it was.

'Remember me, Hanson?'

Olav swallowed. Wanted to say no. Then changed his mind when he saw the gun. Tried to say yes, but his mouth was so dry all that came out was air.

'Thirty years, Hanson. That's a long time, but you know what? I remember you like it was yesterday.'

'I . . .' Olav stopped right there, because he had no idea what to say. Maybe it was best to say nothing.

'Remember how you gave me your personal word you would catch the people who killed my family?'

'I . . . we . . . we sure tried.'

'Three weeks ago I spoke to the man who killed my daughter. The girl in the wheelchair, remember? He told me how you interfered with the technical evidence, you changed witness statements and made sure the guilty men were never caught. That that's what Die Man paid you for.'

'Who . . . who is Die Man?'

'That doesn't matter. He is no longer with us. I stuck a needle through the seat and into his back at the movie theatre.'

Olav considered whether to try to go for the gun in his shoulder holster. He'd buttoned it in before he started down the steep track in case he slipped, and that would make it more difficult. No, this wouldn't be like it was with the kid with the knife. But Olav had practised drawing the gun from the shoulder holster, and he was quick. A lot quicker than Joe Kjos anyway. Olav looked up at the sky. A dark cloud heading toward the moon. Olav moved his fishing rod into his left hand.

'What are you going to do to me?' Olav asked.

'Ever heard of *rogue taxidermy*?'

'What?'

'I'm going to stuff you. Then display you. Somewhere public, for the enjoyment of the people. You'll be a modern work of art, Hanson.'

The cloud slipped over, obscuring the moon, and in the darkness Olav Hanson went for his gun.

40

GATED COMMUNITY, OCTOBER 2016

THE TIME WAS EIGHT THIRTY and the sun shone from a cloudless sky down onto the Minnesota Landscape Arboretum, more familiarly abbreviated to Arb. Gunnar Person, the senior gardener in the botanical gardens, registered that it looked like they were in for a fine autumn day. He stepped down from the golf cart and crossed the grass in the direction of a stand of trees. He liked an early start, liked being the first man at work. But today it looked like someone had beaten him to it. The park was fenced in, and it had opening hours, but the fence was low and the park covered a huge area. If someone wanted to get in, they got in. Right now the park was hosting a sculpture exhibition, with pieces on display across the whole area. They showed animals that looked like they were made out of folded paper.

Origami, they called it. Only these were made of metal and they were life-sized. If you could say of such literally fabulous creatures that they had a life-size. Like that rearing, winged Pegasus Gunnar was headed for. But as Gunnar got closer, he saw that the figure of a large man had been placed on the horse's back. He was half naked, and Gunnar was thinking it was probably something to do with someone's stag party. The figure was held in place by the wings, with the upper body and shoulders resting against the horse's neck. There was no way it was a comfortable position to sleep in, but the man was probably so drunk he didn't notice.

'Hey there!' Gunnar called in a loud, cheery voice. 'Time to wake up!'

The figure on the horse didn't move. Gunnar felt uneasy. There was something . . . well, something dead about it. The man's head had evidently slipped down over the far side of the origami-like horse's neck and couldn't be seen. Gunnar walked round it. His first thought was that he must have made some mistake, for there was no head there either. Then he saw the red stub of neck sticking up from the collar of the man's shirt. He gasped for breath and started saying the Lord's Prayer as he fumbled for his phone, found it and tapped in the emergency number. While it was ringing he looked around for any sign of the head but saw nothing. He returned his gaze to the sculpture again, in all its grotesque horror an arresting and almost poetic sight. Almost as though the horse was about to lift off and fly the headless man up to heaven.

Superintendent Walker adjusted his sunglasses. He would have preferred to spend this Saturday morning with his family but knew he wouldn't be able to relax. He was standing next to the Viking ship sculpture in front of the US Bank Stadium. People were already making their way inside, even though the mayor wasn't due to officially open the gathering until one o'clock, almost ninety minutes away. While waiting he stared up at something that was hanging from the mast above him. It was about the size of a tennis ball and evidently didn't weigh much, dancing around in the gusting wind, although he couldn't make out what it was.

'Walker!'

It was Springer from the JTTF. He came walking out through the entrance to the stadium with O'Rourke from SWAT. Springer seemed relaxed, but O'Rourke kept his eyes on the line of people, scanning it incessantly.

'How are things looking?' asked Walker.

'We've got snipers in position covering the whole of the stadium,' said Springer. 'Our people are in the TV room monitoring pictures from every security camera. If someone in the stands takes so much as a packet of pastilles from their pocket, we'll see it.'

Springer glanced at O'Rourke, who nodded his agreement before continuing.

'Everyone going in gets searched, more thoroughly than usual. If someone in the line notices what's going on and tries to leave then we've got people watching for that too. Every stadium employee has security clearance and they're getting searched too. In short: if Gomez tries anything he'll be in trouble long before he gets inside the stadium.'

'Good,' said Walker. He shivered inside his coat even though the sun was shining.

'How about Homicide?' said Springer. 'Anything new?'

Walker shook his head. 'He's keeping himself well hidden. Speaking of which, have you considered the possibility he might be in disguise, even wearing some kind of mask?'

'Of course,' said Springer. 'Today we treat everybody as though they could be Tomás Gomez, no matter what they look like.'

Walker's phone rang. It had to be Hanson. He was late; Walker had tried to ring him once already. He read the name that came up on the display. Rooble Isack.

'Isack,' said Walker. 'It's been a while. Listen, I'm a little busy right now, is this something that can wait?'

'Walker,' said Rooble Isack in his rumbling voice, 'I'm thinking you'll agree that what I have to tell you can't wait, sir.'

'Oh?'

'I'm at the hospital, with Marco Dante. The gunrunner we think this Tomás Gomez tried to kill on Tuesday.'

'Yeah yeah, I'm familiar with the case.'

'We're here because in connection with the assault we were able to carry out a search of Dante's garage and we found all sorts of illegal weapons. We've got a good case against him, but Dante's lawyered up and wants a deal in exchange for information about Tomás Gomez.'

'And?'

'The question is, how much is this information worth to us? And to you, because Gomez is also now a murder suspect.'

'Worth a lot,' said Walker. 'A lot. And you're right, it's urgent.'

'That's all I needed to know. I'll get back to you soon.'

'Thanks, Rooble.'

They hung up.

'Where the hell is Hanson?' asked Springer.

'You tell me. Looks like your man might have got caught up in traffic.'

Your man. During that JTTF meeting, when Springer made it clear he preferred Hanson to Kay Myers to represent the Homicide Division, Walker's first impulse had been to intervene and say the decision was his to make. But Myers had got in before him when she said that was fine by her. Of course, he could have made the change after the meeting, but there was something about this whole case that told him not to. A feeling that this Gomez was an obstacle that could trip them up badly. And in that case he would prefer that it was Hanson rather than Myers who took the fall. The decision was as cynical as it was practical. On the other hand, what could go wrong?

Walker didn't know, but again he shivered in the sunlight.

'Say, Springer, can you see what that thing is hanging up there?'

Springer looked up. 'Looks like a small fish,' he said.

'A fish?'

'Yeah, one of those pufferfish, you know.'

Kay got up early, headed down to the Rialto and interviewed the ticket seller and the projectionist, the only two who had been working the previous day. They couldn't add anything much except to say that the victim had been a regular at the movie theatre. And they couldn't – naturally – provide the names and addresses of any of the other patrons. Kay told them two crime technicians were on their way and that the Rialto couldn't open to the public again until they'd been there and done their job. She drove off, heading for the city hall, and wondering whether to contact the TV preacher and find out whether he'd seen or heard anything. She decided to wait until the techs and the pathologists came up with their findings. Instead, back in the Homicide Division's office, she did what she had made up her mind to do as she lay awake during the night. To do Bob Oz a favour. And – probably – fuck things up for herself. She raised a cup of coffee to her lips as she studied the computer screen. It was a list of all murder cases involving more than one victim. Her first search had been for Perez and 1995. She'd located the report and then widened her search. She took a screenshot of the report and the search returns and clicked on the Share icon. Typed in Bob Oz's email address. Hesitated a moment, then clicked the Send button. Heard the swish of the departing email – and possibly her own chances of promotion – as it flew off and away.

She breathed out heavily, as though she'd been holding her breath. The open office was almost completely silent; the only sound Kay heard was Joe Kjos's voice as he sat a few seats away, talking on the phone. Sounded like he was checking a tip-off. And she had one she needed to check too before she could take her weekend break. She looked at her watch. A trip to Cedar Creek and the woman who called in a potential lead shouldn't take more than forty-five minutes on a Saturday morning.

She was on her way out when something struck her and she stopped, turned and made her way back to the new office. Saw to her surprise that the paint job was now finished. The pots and brushes were all gone. She felt a vague sense of disappointment but dismissed it and headed on out the building.

The mayor of Minneapolis, Kevin Patterson, studied himself in the large bedroom mirror. He was reasonably satisfied. If they didn't have the cameras too low in relation to the podium then the first signs of that double chin wouldn't show. His hair was beginning to get thinner and turning grey, and he'd put on a few pounds after moving into the biggest office in the city hall. But generally speaking he was ageing well, wasn't he? Anyway, a lot of people reacted with surprise when he told them he was in his mid-fifties, and surely not all of them could be accused of flattering a mere mayor? OK, so he didn't have the looks of the politicians the people really took to their hearts. Or their charisma. But he knew that if he played his cards right then a place in the House of Representatives was within reach.

'Not the red necktie,' Jill interrupted his thoughts. His wife had just come in and was checking the knot and brushing the dandruff off his jacket. 'How about the blue with the black stripe?'

Kevin Patterson had chosen red because he'd read somewhere that made it a power necktie, it signalled to the subconscious that the wearer was strong and in control, knew what was going on. He knew he'd end up wearing the necktie Jill suggested, but he could do as he always did before letting her get her way and make the journey a little bit more entertaining.

'You mean because otherwise people might think their mayor has joined the Republicans?' he asked. 'Or because red would make me a better target?'

'Kevin!'

He chuckled. 'Now don't get all het up, honey. Count the security guards outside – they're twice the usual number. Think positive. They say the stadium's sold out, and all I'm going to do is tell them exactly what they want to hear. A sitting mayor being cheered – how often does that happen? Even the sun is shining. You know what, Jill? I think this is going to be one helluva fine day.'

She laughed, patted his cheek, loosened the red necktie and dropped it on the bed.

'You're right,' she said as she opened the closet and took out the blue one. 'It will be a fine day. Just think, by the time we all gather this afternoon Quentin will be back home too.'

The door to their bedroom opened. 'Mom, Siri's lying, she says we're going to have two guards with us in the car today!' That was Simon, eight years old and youngest of their four children. The older three were closer in age, and when Simon came along Siri, now fourteen, had some difficulty in giving up her position as the youngest in the family, along with all the privileges that went with it.

'Siri's telling the truth,' said Jill. 'Come on, Simon, let's go and get your jacket and then we'll leave and pick up Quentin.'

'Then where will I sit?'

'In your usual place.'

'Where's Dad going?'

'Dad's going to give a speech,' said Jill.

Kevin mimed a man giving a speech in the mirror, complete with outrageous facial expressions, and Simon laughed. Jill kissed her husband on the cheek and shortly afterward the mayor heard Simon's voice as he and his mother went down the stairs:

'Can Quentin sleep in my room tonight?'

'You and Siri will have to toss a coin for it.'

'No, she cheats!'

Kevin checked that the blue necktie was tied right, sat on the edge of the bed and fastened his shoelaces. Then he crossed to the window and saw Jill, Siri and Simon setting off in the car, a big, solid Chevy Tahoe. In a radio interview on a car show he was asked if he drove a Chevy because he was afraid of losing votes if he drove a foreign car. He answered no, because by happy coincidence he was a patriotic citizen of a country that actually produced the best cars on the market. He didn't give the other reason, which was that he felt his family would be safer in the home-produced heavyweight if it ever happened to collide with a foreign lightweight. The Chevy drove off and Kevin Patterson let his gaze wander to a small wooden cross standing among some trees by the wall that surrounded the property. The wall was superfluous, the chances of an intruder getting close were minimal since their house was part of a *gated community*, an enclosed area with 24/7 patrolling and dogs to guard the roughly two hundred inhabitants living in the seventy dwellings. Initially Kevin Patterson wasn't too happy about the concept of a *gated community*, but with the growing divide between rich and poor the need for protection had grown too. In 1980 there had been around five thousand *gated communities* in the United States and the number had quadrupled by the turn of the century. God knows how many there were now. But in the modern world, human beings needed protection from their neighbours. That was the simple, brutal truth. The way to deal with the problem was as simple; all you had to do was even out the economic disparities. That was the goal the Democratic Party and Kevin Patterson worked toward. It would take a while, that much was obvious, and there were times when Kevin Patterson felt like Sisyphus when he read those depressing reports of how the income gap was widening, and how even middle-class families were experiencing economic difficulties. Over the past thirty years the rich had grown extremely rich while the disposable income of the middle class stagnated as the price of education, health care and housing soared. When young people could no longer afford an education they no longer started out with an equal chance, they no longer had access to the dream promised by their country. But Kevin Patterson believed in a better world, he truly did. The same way he believed in the freedom of the individual. And that was why, on the way to this better world, he believed in the right of the hard-working man and woman to protect their own property and their lives. Contrary to what some in his own party seemed to think, his support for the NRA was not a cynical attempt to increase his vote.

Kevin Patterson headed toward the bedroom door but then stopped in front of the mirror again.

Sure, he knew that as a friend of the NRA his route to Washington DC, where the gun lobby was the third most powerful in the country, would be smoother. But that wasn't the reason.

He dropped his jaw, showing the folds of his double chin.

Not the *only* reason.

His black SUV stood ready and waiting for him in front of the garage when he emerged from his house onto the gravel drive. A security guard in civilian clothing held the back-seat door open for him.

'Anything new from the stadium about Gomez?' asked the mayor.

'No, sir.'

Even before he opened his eyes Bob Oz knew there was a headache waiting for him. The question was just where on the Richter scale it would be. He opened one eye and peered out. Nothing snapped, the world appeared to be fairly stable and safe. He opened the other eye. Not too bad.

He remembered, after he'd finished the last beer from the refrigerator, that he had a small amount of whisky left in the kitchen cupboard. But it can't have been much.

Bob picked up the phone lying on the bedside table and saw that it was almost midday. He also saw that he'd received a text message during the morning.

Goodnight to you too. Liza

He was puzzled. He scrolled down and realised it was a reply to a message he'd sent shortly before 3 a.m.

Gof night. Bov

Below that was another message.

You got mail. Kay

He opened the inbox on his phone. There was mail from Kay Myers, sent an hour ago. With two attachments. He opened the one named *Perez 1995*. It contained photos of a number of closely written pages, and he realised it must be the police report she had refused to let him have the previous day. Because the screen on Bob's phone was small and the headache was impossible to ignore he got up, put coffee on, opened the attachments on his computer and enlarged the images. He had no idea what had caused Myers to change her mind, but that wasn't important. He sipped the scalding hot coffee as he read through the document.

According to the report the killing had taken place in a parking lot, not in Phillips West but in Hawthorne, a neighbourhood that was at least as lawless as the Near North. The victims had been seated in a car and got hit in a drive-by shooting: Candice Perez, a single mother, and her two children, Emilio and Nathan. There was nothing about a father until the final page, where the report noted that the registered father of the children was Chuck Perez, a known drug dealer. But it was difficult to connect this as a motive for the killings because Chuck Perez had been shot and killed, probably in a gang-warfare-related incident, in 1992, three years previously.

Bob scanned the report. There was nothing there about a girl in a wheelchair. In short, this wasn't the case Tomás Gomez had described to Mike Lunde. Bob swore. So where was the story about his family being killed? Was it just something Gomez had invented? Not unlikely. In Bob's experience, criminals were notorious liars. Bob opened the second attachment. This was a list of murder cases involving multiple victims and it went back further than 1990, the cut-off he had chosen for his own search. He clicked them open one after the other. The way it looked, killings with more than one or two victims happened only once or twice a year. He raised his coffee cup, then jerked it, spilling hot coffee into his lap. He scarcely noticed. His gaze was riveted to a case from 1986. Three victims. Again, a mother and two children. The woman's first name was Monica. But it was the surname he was staring at.

41

WHITE, OCTOBER 2016

HE'D CHECKED OUT THE FINAL lead, a tip-off from a long-distance truck driver who claimed to have met a strange man who looked like Tomás Gomez at a truck-stop cafe just the other side of the Iowa border. Joe had talked to the people who worked at the cafe and it turned out that guy was a well-known local character who just liked talking to truck drivers at the cafe.

Now it was time to get over to Arb where there was other work to do. The patrol who rang it in said the corpse had no head and no papers that could identify who it was, but there was a bullet hole in the chest leaving little doubt that it was a matter for the Homicide Division. Joe explained that he had a couple of other things to do first before he could get out there but that a technical team was already on its way.

A phone rang somewhere out in the deserted office landscape.

Joe shrugged on his jacket. He was actually pissed with Olav for not making him part of his stadium team and leaving him with this shit job instead. The phone was still ringing. Usually it got transferred to reception automatically after a certain number of rings, but since this was Saturday there was no one in reception. Joe Kjos had no intention of taking the call, but as he walked past Myers's desk he realised it was her phone that was ringing. She'd only just left, so he picked up anyway.

'MPD.'

'Good morning, my name is Jim Andersen. Kay Myers, is she . . .?'

'She just left. This is Detective Joe Kjos, how can I help you, sir?'

The caller hesitated, and Joe Kjos hoped the guy would say no so that he could get out of there, get this last job done and finally enjoy the weekend.

'I'm an instructor at the Mitro shooting range,' the guy said. 'Your colleague who was here left her card and asked me to call the number if I remembered anything about the Latino she was looking for.'

'OK?'

'I still don't recall any Latino, but then something came to me. She traced us through a target you guys found inside some bubble wrap.'

Joe Kjos checked the time.

'There was a guy in here with a rifle wrapped in bubble wrap. But he wasn't Latino. He was white.'

Joe Kjos sighed but located a pen on Myers's desk and made a note. 'White, sir?'

'White. I remember because he insisted on me working out the height adjustment for a shot from four hundred yards.'

'Was there anything unusual in his behaviour? Did he seem aggressive? Drugged?'

'Absolutely not.'

'Did he give you a name or a phone number?'

'No.'

'Anything else you can tell us about him?'

'Not really.'

Joe Kjos breathed out in relief. 'OK. Let me take your number and we'll be in touch if we have any more questions.'

Bob Oz was pulling on his coat as he ran down the steps and out into the street with his phone pressed hard to his ear.

'Pick up,' he whispered as he headed for the Volvo parked higher up the street. 'Pick up, damn you.'

Searching the net for the murder he had got at least a dozen hits, most with the headline 'McDeath'. He'd scrolled his way through them.

Family celebrating birthday at McDonald's killed in gang shootout.

Mother and two children killed, father only survivor.

Still no arrests in McDeath massacre.

'Kari.'

'There you are! Sorry for calling you on a Saturday, Kari, but I need the address of a Mike Lunde, he lives somewhere in Chanhassen. I'm going to give you a phone number, are you ready?'

'We're in the middle of lunch here, Bob, can this wait?'

'No. Oh fuck!'

'I'm sorry?'

'My apologies. Someone's broken the wing mirror on my car. No, it can't wait. I've got . . . I know who he is.'

'Who who is?'

‘The killer, Kari.’ Bob had fished his keys out with his free hand but then dropped them on the road. ‘I thought he was telling me a story he heard from one of his customers. But it was his own story. Mike Lunde told me everything exactly like it was, in detail. He confessed, Kari! And I didn’t realise.’

42

THE HOUSE OF HORRORS, OCTOBER 2016

'I SAW THIS GOMEZ COME walking along the road there,' the old woman said, pointing.

She and Kay Myers were standing on the upper floor of a fine old timber house that lay on a rise above the otherwise flat landscape of Cedar Creek. From here Kay looked out over dense forest, swamps, meadows and ploughed land. On her drive out Kay had gathered from the signs that this was a protected area for ecological research.

Kay peered in the direction of the narrow, twisting road almost a hundred yards away from the house.

'How can you be sure it was Tomás Gomez, Mrs Holte?'

'Because I've seen him on the TV, of course. That he's a wanted man.'

'Yes, but what I mean is, that's quite a long way away. I don't think even I could see so clearly who someone down there was.'

'Ah, but the older you get, the better your sight gets, I can assure you.'

For a moment the two just looked at each other, then Mrs Holte began laughing, a funny, clucking, little old woman laugh. It made Kay think of a cocoon, shrunken and dried up, with silver-grey hair and dry as an old spider's web. She'd been standing waiting at the door as Kay parked in front of the house and invited her in without even asking what this was about. Once Kay told her, Mrs Holte explained that she hadn't answered the calls because she turned her phone off when she wasn't making a call on it because the only calls she ever got anyway were from telephone sales people.

'I'm just kidding you, honey,' said the woman. Then she suddenly reached for something next to the window behind the drape and pulled out a rifle. Kay froze, and before she had time to act the woman had lifted the weapon to her cheek. 'Like this,' she said.

She closed one eye and with the other peered through the telescopic sights. The barrel was pointed toward the window. Then she lowered the rifle. And laughed that clucking laugh of hers again when she saw the look on Kay's face. 'I just used the telescopic sights. I took this over after my husband died.'

Kay shivered at the thought that she herself and her car had probably been in that viewfinder as she drove up toward the house.

'So you saw a person you believe to have been Tomás Gomez pass here yesterday morning.'

'Yes. He parked in the passing space down there.'

Kay took out her notebook.

'What kind of car was it?'

'Oh, sweetie, I don't know much about cars. But it was a big one. Nice car.'

'Colour?'

'Mostly wood.'

'Wood?'

'Wood-panelling. My husband's car had the same thing. I've seen it here several times.'

'Really?'

'Before yesterday it was three weeks ago. He came walking up the road with another man. The other man was white. Probably one of those crazy artists, I thought to myself.'

'Artists?'

'Yes. They disappeared into the trees along that track you see there. Probably on their way to that nasty house of horrors they've made for themselves in there.' Mrs Holte shuddered. 'Uergh.'

The time was twelve thirty when Kevin Patterson stepped out of the SUV in front of the US Bank Stadium. The square was almost deserted, but loud music and cheering could be heard from inside the stadium. Patterson assumed someone was doing a display of trick-shooting, something involving a gun. Four security men accompanied him to the VIP entrance, passing what remained of the line at the public entrance. Some stared as though not quite sure where they had seen his face before, because he didn't play for the Vikings and he wasn't a TV preacher either, he was just the mayor. But there were some who did recognise the face, and one voice called out: 'Make America great again!'

Patterson smiled and waved back even though he knew the man was a Trump supporter and would vote Republican. And that the guy probably didn't know that the slogan wasn't invented by the Trump campaign team but had a long history and had been used by both parties at various times.

Inside the VIP entrance Patterson was led past the elevators and up to the private boxes and a large, rather provisionally furnished room. A window with a view of the podium and lectern out on the ground was obscured by a thick tarp.

A man wearing a pinstriped suit and with an accreditation ID around his neck approached and introduced himself as Ted Springer from the Joint Terrorism Task Force. He assured the mayor that everything was under control and he would be able to walk out to the lectern at the time arranged.

Patterson walked across to the tarp, pulled it to one side and looked out. It was a fantastic stadium. In his speech at the opening of the stadium he'd said that even an old cornball like him could get tears in his eyes looking around the place. He'd asked his speechwriter to take some of the best lines from that earlier speech and add them to the one he was due to deliver in twenty-five minutes. Suddenly something dazzled Kevin Patterson, a quick, bright flash. The man who had been the mayor's chief of security for the last ten years must have registered it, because he leaned close to Patterson and asked in a low voice, 'Anything wrong, sir?'

'No, no, it's er . . .' Patterson began. 'Have the private boxes been checked? I think I may have seen something up there.'

'They've been temporarily closed, sir. Do you want me to double-check with the security man there?'

'No, no. I'm sure everything is as it should be. There's so much glass around here. Lot of glass, lot of reflections.'

Patterson looked at his watch. Twenty-four minutes.

*

There were four of them in the tiny room and the air stank of sweat, hospitals and some men's perfume that Rooble Isack assumed came from the man in the sickbed.

'Well, Dante,' said Rooble, 'do you want a deal or not?'

Marco Dante looked over at his lawyer, Al Gill. Rooble had heard about Gill. He was the type who would sell his own grandmother if the hourly rate made it worth his while. Until yesterday Rooble and the Aggravated Assault Unit had been concentrating on finding out who shot Marco. Then JTTF entered the fray, asking that no stone be left unturned in the Gomez case, and suddenly search warrants they would normally have had to beg for were being thrown at them. The Aggravated Assault Unit had found enough in Marco's garage to charge him as a front man for the extensive sale of illegal weapons. On conviction he faced a possible four-year sentence.

'We want you to drop the charges relating to the front-man activity,' said Gill, shifting his gaze from Rooble to Rooble's colleague and then back to Rooble again. 'But if you want my client to provide you with information about Tomás Gomez you're going to have to drop illegal possession of weapons and the sale of weapons too.'

'You mean you want us to drop everything?' said Rooble.

'Gomez is a killer,' said Gill. 'He has already made one attempt on the life of my client and is certain to try again if it becomes known that he has provided you with information that could lead to his arrest. As a free man my client will probably be able to deal with this, but given Gomez's gang connections he would be an easy target in jail.'

'Gang connections?' said Rooble. 'Is Gomez a gangbanger?'

'Think of it as a foretaste of the kind of information my

client will be able to provide you with. Do you want the rest, or don't you?'

Rooble sighed. 'OK, all charges are dropped.'

'On whose authority . . .?' Gill said.

'It's already been cleared with Superintendent Walker of the Homicide Unit. Let's hear you, Dante.'

Dante looked at Gill, who gave a short nod.

'Tomás Gomez came in and bought a gun a while ago,' said Dante.

'You know it was him?' asked Rooble.

'He didn't exactly show me his ID, but I've seen pictures from the security camera on the TV news and yeah, it was him all right. He bought an M24 with telescopic sights and the whole shebang.'

'Including this holster?' Rooble Isack asked. He held up a photo.

'Yes.'

'Carry on.'

Dante shrugged. 'There's isn't a lot more to tell. He didn't say much. In fact, he didn't say a single word. Just pointed to what he wanted, paid and left.'

'Had you seen him before?'

'How do I know? The guy was wearing sunglasses, he had a hoodie pulled up.'

There was silence in the room.

Rooble leaned forward to Gill.

'Explain to your client that this isn't worth what we're offering to pay. And tell him I agree with you, Gill: if we drop the deal and have him sent to jail then he'll be a sitting duck for Gomez's gang.'

'Now listen here, Detective Isack –' the lawyer began, but was interrupted by Dante.

'OK, OK. Like I said, I'm not certain who Tomás Gomez is, but he reminds me of a guy who disappeared a long time ago and no one knew what happened to him. A cold-blooded, brutal killing machine. They called him Lobo. I sold an Uzi to him a long, long time ago. Must have been back in the eighties.'

'I remember people talking about a guy called Lobo when I was in Homicide,' said Rooble. 'It was before my time, but I understood that he was either dead or had gone back south of the border again.'

'What you mean is, you never found him, right?' Dante laughed bitterly. 'So, I'm not saying this was Lobo, I'm just saying this Gomez guy looked like him. And he had the same tattoo on the back of his hand. One of those five-pointed stars drawn with just one line.'

Rooble exchanged a look with his colleague and leaned closer. 'Anything else?'

'Yeah, he had the same, like . . . scars on his face. But . . .' Dante seemed to be searching for the right words but couldn't find them.

'But what?' Rooble said impatiently.

'But Lobo had this, like . . . this very expressive face. This guy here, his face was dead. He was like a walking dead man, if you get my meaning. And then his hands . . .'

'You already told us about the tattoo.'

'Yeah yeah, but that wasn't all.'

Kay was walking along the rough track. The trees had taken on the shading of autumn, but still clung on to their leaves. She stopped at a decaying sign which related that the forest around her was a so-called white cedar forest, and that some of the trees were over 250 years old. The place was also home to a unique fauna. Here, she read, one could encounter the red-shouldered hawk, the red-headed woodpecker, coyotes, badgers and deer. Depending on the season one might also see bison, black bears and wolves. Kay shuddered, hoped it wasn't the season for any of them, and continued along the track. Gradually it began to narrow, the trees on both sides grew thicker, and she noticed that the wild sound of birdsong that had accompanied her walk so far had now stopped, the way sound stops when a stranger enters a local bar. Or, she thought, when those living in an area watch in tense excitement as someone walks toward a danger that only they can see.

She pushed aside the branches that dangled across the path and hindered her view, then heard a rustling sound that told her she was approaching a stream. Another sound carried from deep in the forest, like a machine gun. That's the type of association you get from growing up in Englewood, she thought, and concluded it was probably a woodpecker. Suddenly the track ended. Or rather, it divided at a T-junction, with the two forks turning left and right and following the stream in front of her. A mailbox had been lashed with wire to the top of a rusty iron pole driven into the ground. It was difficult to imagine a mailman making his way all the way out here, but at least the box had a name on it in white paint: RT CLUB. Across the nine-foot-wide, murky-green stream she saw planking that had once formed a primitive bridge but was now broken in the middle. Mrs Holte had explained that the house lay a few hundred yards away once you crossed the stream, but the forest was too thick for Kay to see anything. She glanced down at her shoes. Trainers. Made for city walking. New and expensive and dazzling white. She edged her way out along the planks, jumped, making it with her right but not her left foot, which splashed down and sank into the revolting, squelching bed of the stream, before she was able to pull herself up and reach the other side.

The track ahead was now almost invisible, but in a while she saw the outlines of a house through the trees. It was so quiet she could hear her own heart beating, and the thick foliage above her blocked most of the sunlight. She came to a halt where the track ended. In front of her was a meadow of long grass with a red-painted, single-storey wooden building behind it. Though there was no approach road and the building lay in the middle of a forest her first thought was that it looked like some kind of garage or warehouse. The tall grass, the paint that was flaking off the walls and the lack of any well-trodden path leading up to it all suggested that the place had not seen visitors for several years. Kay pulled out her gun and held it before her as she stepped out into the open. Moving quickly to avoid being an easy target, all senses alert, she saw no visible sign of movement, heard no sound. She saw something fastened above the door. It looked almost like the kind of heraldic device families in stately homes have hanging above the entrance. Kay had to approach closer to confirm that it really was what she thought it was.

A squirrel holding a deer-hunting rifle.

The squirrel's fur was torn, probably by some bird of prey. Kay walked to one of the windows. She brushed aside the cobwebs, cupped her hands and tried to peer inside but found herself staring at a wooden shutter that must have been nailed across on the inside. The other windows were covered in the same way. Maybe the idea was to discourage thieves, or to stop people seeing what was inside. Or maybe it was both.

Kay put her back against the wall beside the door, gripped her pistol hard.

'Police! Open the door!'

The total silence that followed did not give Kay the feeling she was alone. Instead she felt as though a thousand ears were listening. She held her breath. No sounds from inside. She studied the lock on the door. It was shiny, new-looking.

Kay hesitated.

She didn't have a search warrant and the lock looked pretty solid. And there was something about the place that gave her the feeling that anyone who went in there alone would regret it. Best to pull back and return later with backup and a warrant.

So then why was she still standing there, staring at the door?

Was it because of how she'd run through the backstreets of Englewood with her father chasing after her, and how she had promised herself that if she got out of there alive she would never be afraid of anything ever again? Because the way to escape from her father, from Englewood and from that whole life that waited for her there was to be braver than she really was? Because breaking free meant breaking the rules?

Kay Myers turned and walked quickly back the way she had come. This time she timed the jump from one broken half of the plank to the other just right. She braced herself and jerked the mailbox and the rusty iron pole up out of the ground, took off the mailbox then headed back toward the house carrying the bar on her shoulder. She noticed the sound of birdsong had returned. Now it sounded hysterical. As if all the tension was too much for them and they were warning of danger.

Kay wedged the sharp end of the pole into the gap between the door and the frame. Leaned her body weight against it. Heard the creak of the woodwork and saw the door move slightly. She could still stop. Because wasn't this exactly what Walker had been talking about when he signalled 'don't trip up'? Don't mess it up for yourself just before you break the tape? Kay hesitated. Then, with a tormented screeching sound, the wood around the lock split and the door flew open.

Kay breathed out. Then she stepped inside. Held the gun in front of her with both hands.

Dust whirled up in a little snowstorm in the sharp sunlight falling through the open doorway and it took a moment for her eyes to adapt to the dark inside.

She stopped breathing.

Blinked as her brain tried to deal with the sight that met her eyes. She mustn't panic now, mustn't let fear take hold. So the first thing she told herself was that they couldn't harm her, they were all dead. That it was only the poses in which they had been arranged that made them look as though they were alive.

It worked. Slowly panic released its hold and she started to breathe again.

Directly in front of her a fox was standing on its hind legs and holding in its forepaws a saw with which it was cutting itself in half. Next to it was a two-headed coyote with the teeth of one head sunk into the throat of the other. Behind them, a massive elk holding a broken toy pedal car in its antlers. Beside it a white unicorn, its side pierced by a swordfish dangling in mid-air.

Behind the stuffed animals hung a banner: THE ROGUE TAXIDERMY CLUB.

Kay looked around. There were small, closed studios lining the walls. Carpentry workshops, she thought, because through doors that were ajar she could see lathes and tools. In one she saw a kind of mannequin in the shape of a hare made out of wire. She counted eight of these booths. Each had a nameplate. Only one was locked, secured by a large padlock. Kay read the nameplate: Emily Lunde, RT Club. The name meant nothing to her. Peering between two planks into the interior she could see the walls of the booth were lined on the inside with some kind of insulation. She located a light switch by the door and the neon tubes in the ceiling blinked a couple of times before coming on and lighting up the whole room. She picked up the metal spike and wedged it into the crack in Emily Lunde's booth door. Pushed hard on it. Instead of the padlock snapping off the soft wood of the plank bent outward. Soon it was so far out she was able to see inside.

She saw light reflected in a pair of yellow eyes.

She saw the man in the chair.

The spike fell from her hands and clattered to the floor.

43

LOBO, OCTOBER 2016

'WELL, SUPERINTENDENT,' SAID TED SPRINGER as he stood next to Walker and picked up a slice of watermelon, 'not hungry today? Not thirsty?'

Springer gestured with his free hand to the table in front of them and the coffee pots and bottles of water, the fruit along with a few simple sandwiches.

'Thanks, I ate before I left,' said Walker. He was watching Mayor Patterson as the mayor stood by the coffee pots talking with someone from the NRA. Someone important, judging by the body language and the facial expressions; two men who could be useful to each other. Walker glanced at his watch. Five minutes before Patterson stepped up onto the podium. The speech would last a maximum of ten minutes. Then it was job done and home to the family. There was still a lot of weekend left.

The phone in his pocket vibrated. It wasn't Hanson this time either.

'Yes, Rooble?' said Walker.

'Dante says that Gomez is Lobo.'

'What?'

'Tomás Gomez is Lobo.' Rooble spoke clearly and calmly, so it wasn't a case of Walker not hearing him, more that he just didn't believe what he had heard.

'*The* Lobo?' said Walker.

'Yes. The Wanted poster was still up on the wall when I started in Homicide. I remember the description referred to a star-shaped tattoo on the back of one hand. Hanson said it was a cartel thing from south of the border.'

Walker closed his eyes. Opened them again. Lobo. He turned to Springer, who was holding the slice of melon up in front of his face so it looked like he was grinning from ear to ear.

'Bad news, Walker?'

'Yes. We need to postpone the speech.'

'Why?' Springer took another mouthful of melon.

'Gomez is almost certainly identical to a man called Lobo, a notorious serial killer.'

'What difference does that make? We already know Gomez is a killer.'

Walker looked at Springer. He realised he had no good answer. That the unease he felt in the pit of his stomach at the news was not an argument. Walker heard Rooble's voice and realised he was still on the line.

'What?' he said, putting the phone to his ear.

'I said, Dante said there was something strange about Gomez's hands.'

'What, exactly?'

'They had stitches along the sides, like seams. That the skin seemed to sort of move when he moved his hands. Like he was wearing gloves.'

44

CAT, OCTOBER 2016

BOB TURNED INTO ERIE AVENUE in Chanhassen. Middle-class villas with plenty of room between them, trees and neatly trimmed lawns on both sides.

He stopped in front of the address Kari had provided.

Two floors. Big but standard family home with a yard in front, lawn with the grass cut short, double garage.

He didn't see the Caprice, but of course it could be in the garage.

His phone vibrated. He was about to reject the call but changed his mind when he saw it came from Kay Myers.

'Kay, thanks for the report. And the list.'

'You're welcome. Now it's your turn to help me.' It could have been just a poor signal, but it sounded like she was freezing.

'Where are you?'

'At a deserted house in a forest with no tracks. Listen, I broke in here without a search warrant. I found something.'

Bob didn't respond. Cops called it an own goal when you found something that could have been used in a court of law, if only you'd followed the rules.

'So what am I going to do?' She sounded desperate. Bob had never heard Kay Myers like this before.

'Get out of there the same way you went in,' he said. 'Cover your tracks and make out like you didn't find anything. Get the search warrant then come back.'

Bob heard her trembling intake of breath. Were her teeth chattering? Or was she starting to cry?

'I broke open the door, but if that's "tripping up" then what's the point of being a cop? Tell me that. I sent you those reports because it's our job to protect people against . . . against monsters like this. I don't need a bigger office, Bob, I just need to stop this . . . this sickness.'

'Easy now, Kay, you hear me? You're stressed out. What's going on there? What have you found?'

Kay drew a breath and then let it out again. Saw it freeze and hang in the air a moment before disappearing.

'A body,' she answered.

'We just lost the signal. Did you say a body?'

'Yes.'

'Whose body?'

'I don't know. I'm guessing one of Tomás Gomez's victims. We got information that he was seen here.'

'OK,' said Bob. 'You're sure this is a murder?' He spoke slowly, calm and quiet, as though he was talking to someone who was hysterical, not a colleague in the Homicide Division just doing her job. Normally she wouldn't have tolerated it, but right now it was something she appreciated.

'No,' she said, feeling her pulse start to slow down. 'But I think so.'

'What do you mean?'

'I can't see how he died.' She looked at the man in the chair and again lost control of her voice.

'But?' said Bob, calm but insistent.

'But he couldn't exactly have done it himself.' Kay felt a sudden urge to laugh. There were no marks on the body of the naked man sitting bound to the chair. But the face had been skinned. The eyes glowed white in the frozen red flesh where the skin had been. Likewise the hands. He looked like he'd pulled on a pair of red rubber gloves that reached halfway up his forearms.

'Kay?' said Bob. 'This line is very bad. Are you . . .'

'I'm still here. If this is Tomás Gomez's work then he really is a sadistic bastard.'

'The dead person – what about the age? The ethnicity?'

'A lot of stuff is missing here, but I think maybe Latino,' said Kay. She felt calmer now. Bob's questions had helped her back into professional mode and now she was just annoyed with herself for briefly losing control like that. 'Age is a guess too but I would think maybe forty or fifty.'

'OK. Can you do something for me: can you take a look at his back?'

'His back?'

'Yeah.'

'I'll try.'

'Try?'

'He's tied to a chair. I just need to loosen the strap round his chest.'

Bob said nothing.

Kay had to tighten the strap before she could loosen it. The frozen corpse creaked as she did so. She stood behind the wooden chair and pushed at the back. The body didn't move. She pushed harder. She felt as though the corpse might snap in two if she used too much force. Then the buttocks and thighs seemed to lift from the seat of the chair and the whole body slid forward a few inches. Enough for her to see.

'He has tattoos.'

'What kind?'

'Gang tattoos. X-11. And Black Wolves.'

'I thought so.'

'What did you think?'

'Call the station and ask them to get out there.'

'I told you, I didn't have a search warrant. What did you think?'

'You had reasonable grounds for suspicion. The smell of the corpse.'

'There's no corpse smell in here.'

'No? He's been dead five days at least, probably a good while longer.'

'He's frozen. He's been refrigerated here in some kind of freezer. Bob, tell me, you thought what? What is it you know?'

'I know it wasn't Tomás Gomez who killed that person in the chair.'

'How?'

'Because the man in the chair *is* Tomás Gomez. Better known as Lobo. I have to do something here now, Kay, I'll call you back later.'

'Bob!'

But Bob Oz had already hung up. Kay's whole body was shivering with cold now, and she knew it would be a while before she could get the heat back in her body. A long while. It wasn't the flayed, frozen body that had caused her to freak out the way she did and drop the iron bar. It was the animal with yellow eyes in his lap. The stuffed cat.

Bob slipped the phone back into his coat pocket and stepped out of the car. It was strangely quiet, no one around. Did he wish right now that he was carrying a gun? The answer to that was straightforward. Yes he did.

Bob approached the house slowly, keeping his eyes on the windows. The silence was broken by the sound of a mower starting up somewhere. A ceramic nameplate hung by the door, clearly the work of a child, probably made in a handiwork class at school. Here, it said, live Sam, Anna, Monica and Mike Lunde. The same four names Bob had found on the net in the reports of the McDeath killings in 1986. Only the father survived. One report had printed a photo of the family, formally posing in smart clothing, obviously professionally taken at a photographer's studio. Bob thought Mike Lunde looked happy in the picture. Happy, young and naive. One hand rested on the shoulder of his daughter Anna, sitting in front of him. Her long fair hair reached all the way down to the wheelchair, and her smile was radiant.

The mower stopped.

Bob pressed the doorbell. Heard it ring inside the house. Pressed again. Heard the ringing inside but no sound of approaching footsteps. He thought about the body Kay had described. Things were starting to fall into place now. Bob rang a third time. Then he walked round the house to the back, cupped his hands against the glass of the porch door and peered inside. Just then the mower started up again.

In the semi-darkness he saw a tidy room with furniture. It was slightly old-fashioned and conservative, as he had halfway expected. There was an open-plan kitchen with a worktop. A large painting of the family hung above the fireplace. It looked as though the painter had used the same photograph as the one in the report on the net. Bob's eyes gradually grew accustomed to the dark and he now saw that what he had at first taken to be an ordinary chair, standing with its back to him on the far side of the room, was actually a wheelchair. There was someone sitting in it. The sun caught the glossy fair hair hanging down over the back of the wheelchair. Bob called out a 'Hello!' but the person in the wheelchair didn't react. Thinking the shout might have been lost in the noise from the mower Bob knocked on the window. Still no reaction. The person sat there, quite motionless. Maybe she was just sleeping. He tried the porch door. It wasn't locked.

Bob pushed the door open. The penetrating, insistent engine noise of the mower entered the room with him. Still the figure in the wheelchair didn't move. Bob walked over to her. Swallowed. Recalled Mike's words. *My job is to freeze memories, preserve them in solid form. But there's something unhealthy about that.*

Hysterical violins sounded through his head as he reached out a hand and placed it on the shoulder of the person in the wheelchair. The figure slowly rotated and then – as in the movie – came the scream. The mouth of the figure, a woman, was open. That was where the scream came from. She pulled out the earbuds she was wearing, jerking so hard that the lead came out of the cell phone in her lap and fell to the floor. Bob heard the low buzzing of classical music.

'Oh my God, you gave me such a fright!' exclaimed the woman. 'Who are you?'

45

PORTRAIT, OCTOBER 2016

'I'M SORRY, I DID RING the bell,' said Bob to the woman in the wheelchair. 'Bob Oz. I'm a friend of Mike's. Is he in?'

'Oh, I see,' she said, panting for breath, one hand flat against her chest. 'Just give me a moment to recover. I'm afraid you've missed Mike, he just left.'

'Did he say where he was going?'

'To work. A customer is coming in to pick up a Labrador he's been working on.'

Bob nodded, studying her. She looked to be in her fifties, and her clothes were conservative and almost old-fashioned, in the same way Mike's were.

'I believe I've seen a picture of you somewhere,' he said. 'Aren't you . . .?'

'Emily Lunde,' she said, offering her hand. 'Mike's sister.'

He shook her hand. 'Of course. You're a taxidermist too, aren't you?'

'That's right.'

'Just visiting?'

She looked up at him in surprise. 'No. I live here.'

'I see. Have you lived here long?'

'Quite a long time yes. Ever since . . .' She nodded at the family portrait above the fireplace.

'Ah yes,' said Bob. 'The tragedy.'

'Yes. A cup of tea or coffee?' She smiled. She seemed like someone who smiled easily. And laughed. 'It'll only take a minute,' she said as he looked at his watch. 'I like company, I admit it, it's easy to get that way out here. You could always ring Mike.'

'I'll do that after the tea,' said Bob.

She gave a contented nod and wheeled over to the kitchen worktop while Bob studied the portrait.

'Multiple sclerosis,' Emily called as she filled the kettle.

'What?'

'You're wondering why Mike's daughter and I are both in wheelchairs. Grandma also had MS.'

'I see. So it runs in the family?'

'To some degree yes. Our family was unlucky.'

Bob looked at the faces in the portrait. He saw no trace of doubt in any of them. They believed the future was bright. That all of them would live long and happy lives.

'So you're the one who stays at home and makes *kjøttkaker* in brown sauce?' He said it in broken Norwegian and Emily laughed again.

'Our mother taught us that, yes. What is it you want to see Mike about?'

Bob thought about what to say. 'Just to pick up something he said I could borrow.'

'What's that?'

'A rifle.'

'Ah. Well, he took that with him. Maybe he misunderstood and thought you were going to meet him at the store?'

'Maybe,' said Bob. He saw no trace of suspicion in her open face. Perhaps that was why he felt a pang of conscience. 'Where does he keep it?'

'The rifle? In his room.'

'Mind if I take a look? I want to make sure he remembered the bullets.'

'Bullets?'

'He forgot last time.'

'Well, I don't know, I'm never in his room, I live down here.' She pointed through the open door to a corridor where Bob saw a staircase. 'Second door on your left.'

'Thank you.'

Bob walked into the corridor and took the stairs in four or five long strides.

Pushed open the door. The room was white, clean and tidy. The bed was made, the drapes parted. There was a TV on the wall. In spite of the items of personal property lying about – a cell phone on the chest of drawers, a hanger with a pair of faded jeans and a hoodie on the closet door – something about the room gave Bob the feeling that it was abandoned, and that the person who lived there wouldn't be coming back. Just like that apartment in Jordan where Tomás Gomez had lived.

An apartment that seemed to know others would arrive there looking for answers.

On the bed, on top of the pillow, lay a brown face mask with holes for the eyes and mouth. In fact it was a complete head covering, including a full head of hair. On the blanket was a pair of thin brown gloves. They lay like the hands of a person lying in the bed would have laid.

Bob picked up the mask and looked at it more closely. Shuddered as he recognised the face with the scar on the cheek. At the back the skin was cut away low on the neck and up to the crown of the head, and there was a lace woven through perforations in the skin to make it easy to take on and off.

He ran his fingertips over the gloves of human skin and across the tattooed five-pointed star. He thought of Tomás Gomez's fingerprints they had found at the crime scenes. On the handle of the restroom. It was all beginning to make sense now. Mike Lunde hadn't escaped up through the ventilation shaft at the shopping mall, he had simply taken off the hoodie, the Gomez mask and the Gomez gloves. Probably put them in a bag which he hid under his jacket. Dismantled the rifle to make room for it too in the bag. With practice, the routine wouldn't have taken more than a couple of minutes. After that he'd pulled down the fan, tossed one of Gomez's insulin syringes into the ventilation shaft and then strolled out of the restroom like a quite ordinary white man out shopping, walking straight past Kay and the SWAT team. It was a trick he could repeat time after time without ever getting caught. Bob' s gaze fell on a paper bag in front of the closet. It was from a well-known toy store, he recognised the logo – a boy wearing a mushroom for a hat. There was a branch right next to the restroom at Track Plaza. He looked inside. Lifted the scrunched-up sheet of gift wrapping. Out fell a pair of sunglasses, the same type as they'd seen Gomez wearing in the video recordings.

Bob looked at the cell phone. It was turned off. A police voice expert would be able to confirm that the recording of the alleged Tomás Gomez who called Mike Lunde was in reality Mike Lunde himself, standing in a phone booth and calling his own cell. That that explained why the breathing seemed to sound as if it was turning itself on and off.

Bob walked into the bathroom. Clean and tidy here too. He opened the door of the cupboard above the sink. The usual bathroom stuff. Several packs of brown contact lenses from different manufacturers. Of course. Have to get the eyes right.

On the bottom shelf Bob saw a familiar-looking tray of pills. Pink. Bob picked it up and read the long and unpronounceable name of the antidepressants. He read the doctor's signature and the date. The tray should have been empty, and when Bob counted the number of pills left he concluded that Mike Lunde must have stopped taking them and that, coincidentally, he must have done so at about the same time as he stopped taking his own pills.

He walked back into the corridor, down the stairs and stopped in the doorway of the living room.

'Find the bullets?' asked Emily as she poured tea.

'No,' said Bob. 'He took them with him. Did he say anywhere else he might be going, apart from the store?'

'No. Where would that be?'

'Yes, where would that be?' Bob looked at the steaming hot tea on the counter in front of him. 'So did he say what he was going to be doing today?'

'Only that he would be unveiling his masterpiece. He's been looking forward to that.'

Bob swallowed. 'You know what, Emily? I see Mike left his cell phone in his room and I really need to get hold of him, so that tea is going to have to wait until another day.'

She looked up at him, smiling and rather surprised. 'Of course, Bob. Any time.'

Bob ran out to his car, the sound of the mower screeching in his ears, his pulse hammering like a speeded-up watch.

46

ENTER, OCTOBER 2016

BRENTON WALKER WAS LOOKING AT Kevin Patterson's back as he stood by the opening of the drape, ready to mount the podium and be greeted by the cheers and the sunshine. He was going to be introduced over the loudspeaker as soon as the next musical offering ended. Patterson raised and lowered his shoulders, he rolled his neck like a boxer getting ready for a fight, fastened a button on his suit jacket, unfastened it, fastened it again. Walker's seething sense of disquiet had started to abate, perhaps because there was now no way back and it was too late to do anything about anything they might have overlooked. That was a lesson Brenton's father had taught him: the need to accept things you cannot change. It was advice his father himself never followed, and that caused his downfall as a local politician.

The band was still playing out there, the crowd singing along.

'Ten seconds please,' said a man wearing a headset. 'Break a leg, Mr Mayor.'

Springer was standing next to Walker. His walkie-talkie crackled into life and a grating voice spoke: 'Foxtrot, I see a male, white, age around fifty, about five foot nine, entering one of the private boxes.'

Walker saw Springer's face turn pale as he picked up the walkie-talkie and spoke quietly into it: 'Do you have a sighting on him, Foxtrot?'

'No, he disappeared into the back of the box, into the darkness.'

'Listen up!' Springer shouted into the room. 'There is someone up in one of the boxes. Does anyone know how this happened or who this person is?'

There was silence all around Walker. All that could be heard was the sound of the band and the crowd singing. And the man in the headset who was talking into his microphone:

'Norma? Be a sweetie and see if you can get the band to do one more number. Something has, er . . . come up back here.'

47

RED LIGHT, OCTOBER 2016

BOB DROVE AS FAST AS he dared – and as fast as the Volvo managed – along the highway to the city centre.

He drove with one hand and held his cell in the other. Yes, he wished he had a pistol. Yes, he wished he had a Kojak light. Yes, he wished he had a better brain and had deciphered the writing on the wall earlier. When she took the call he could hear she was running.

'What's happening, Kay?'

'I'm headed for my car. I've made a few calls and done some checking and it looks like the house in the forest is owned by a group of artists who practise something they call *rogue taxidermy*. I just spoke with one of them and she told me that after they rented new premises in the city the place out at Cedar Creek has hardly been used. I asked about the refrigerated room, and she said a number of the artists used it, including this Emily Lunde, the woman who owns the booth with the body in it.'

'Emily Lunde?'

'Lives out in Chanhassen. I'm sending a patrol car out there now.'

'Don't do that. Not . . . yet anyway. She probably isn't involved.'

'Oh?'

'She's the sister of the man we're looking for. His name is Mike Lunde. Emily Lunde is confined to a wheelchair, she can't have been out in a forest with no tracks through it in years. Mike Lunde is the one who's been using that booth.'

'Who is Mike Lunde?'

'A taxidermist. He's been wearing a Tomás Gomez mask.'

Bob waited and let that sink in, let her brain trace the line from the flayed body and Tomás Gomez on the security videos.

'Jesus,' Kay whispered, as though not daring to say it out loud. 'Are you saying that –'

'Yeah. He's been using Tomás Gomez's face and hands.'

'But . . . where is he now?'

'He's not at home, his sister says he's gone to work. Unfortunately he's left his cell behind so we can't track him that way. And he's taken his rifle with him.'

'God. He's at the stadium. Gomez . . . or, yeah, the guy the cameras picked up there yesterday while he was doing reconnaissance. He's going to shoot someone there.'

'Someone?'

'The most obvious target would be Mayor Patterson. Any minute now he's going to be speaking in front of 60,000 people, and it's going out live on TV.'

It was Bob's turn to join up the dots.

'It *is* Patterson,' he said quietly. 'His masterpiece.'

'What?'

'He told his sister he was going to unveil his masterpiece today. I thought he was referring to this Labrador he's been working on.'

'What?'

'Mike Lunde is going to crown his work with the unveiling of his last masterpiece. And an unveiling needs an audience.'

Bob heard a change in the acoustics around Kay and realised she must now be sitting in her car.

'Give me a description,' she said. 'I need to ring Walker and warn them they're looking for the wrong man.'

Bob gave Kay a quick description of Mike Lunde and the few bits of personal information he had about him. She repeated after him, he confirmed it, then she hung up.

Saturday traffic was light and Bob had already reached the city centre. He stopped at a red light. Hesitated. A left turn would take him to the store, a right to the stadium. Kay hadn't queried why Bob hadn't mentioned this Mike Lunde before. Maybe because there wasn't time. Maybe because she didn't want to know. No matter which way he turned now, he would still have a lot to answer for. But right now he didn't care a damn about that. Right now all that mattered was to make the right choice, chop the tree down from the correct side and let the splinters fall where they would.

The light changed to yellow.

48

A BEER OUTDOORS, OCTOBER 2016

O'ROURKE'S MEN WERE IN POSITION outside the door of the box. On the frosted glass he noted the logo of one of the Vikings' sponsors. Two men stood ready with the little battering ram, three others behind them with weapons trained on the door, the lights on the gun barrels lit.

'Kilo and Lima are ready,' he whispered into a walkie-talkie.

O'Rourke breathed slowly as he waited for a response. Could feel in his pulse that this was the good kind of tension, on the right side of being nervous. It brought a strange feeling of safety to know that he was so alert. They were totally prepared for just about any eventuality. On the other hand they could never know exactly what lay in store for them. But that was what he loved about the job. The combination of the intoxication of control and the thrill of the risk. It was like fucking and being fucked at the same time.

Then Springer's voice was coming through the walkie-talkie.

'Alpha. Do you have to use stun grenades?'

'Have to,' said O'Rourke.

'We're worried that might create panic in the stadium.'

'Tell the band to play louder.'

'Nothing plays louder than a stun grenade, and the flashes of light will be visible all over the stadium. Sixty thousand frightened people. You see what I'm getting at . . .'

O'Rourke saw all right. Not using stun grenades would deprive them of a tactical advantage and increase the risk of loss. On the other hand, nothing SWAT did was free of risk, and if only one man had been observed in there then the risk was acceptable. His decision was easy.

'OK then, we go in without the stun grenades,' said O'Rourke.

Brenton Walker stood in a corner watching Springer talking into his walkie-talkie while the female member of the mayor's own security team explained the situation to Patterson. Walker's phone rang and he saw it was Myers calling. He pressed Reject. Seconds later the phone gave a slight tremor, like a shudder. He read the text message:

Gomez is a white man, 58, real name Mike Lunde.

Walker tapped the Call symbol and Myers answered before he had raised the phone to his ear.

'I found Gomez's body,' she said. 'He's been flayed. Mike Lunde has been using his face as a mask.'

Walker – who liked to think he was capable of calm in moments of crisis – heard his own response, explosive and involuntary: '*What?*'

'Lunde is a taxidermist. He's left his house and he's carrying a rifle, that's about what we know. I'm on my way to the stadium now. JTTF have people working round the clock on this who can locate a photo of Lunde and send it to you.'

'Good, JTTF are here.'

'OK. So the name is Mike Lunde, address 1722 Erie Avenue, Chanhassen.'

He hung up at the same time as he heard Springer speak into his walkie-talkie:

'OK, let's go, Kilo.'

O'Rourke followed directly behind the five who went in front. By the time he was round the corner they had already surrounded the man sitting alone at the table and were pointing their automatics at him. The man's eyes were wide and black with fear, his mouth was open and his hands raised, though no one had given him the order. In front of him on the table was an open beer bottle with a handle that O'Rourke identified as a local brew, an Utepils. In a cupboard with a glass door behind the man he saw several more bottles of the same beer. O'Rourke wasn't sure if it was the bottle or the look on the man's face that told him straight away this was neither a sniper nor a terrorist. But rules are rules, so he nodded to his men and they took up position behind the chair in which the man sat. They lifted him up, laid him on the floor on his stomach and handcuffed him. O'Rourke squatted in front of him.

'Where are the others? Tell me right now or we'll blow your

head off and say you attacked us.' The routine empty threat was delivered without its usual conviction.

'What?' the man stammered. 'I'm on my own. I'm the janitor here. I'll pay for the beer, I promise!'

Walker stood beside Springer and listened to O'Rourke's voice over the walkie-talkie. The band had stopped playing out there, and now there were a few whistles from the crowd as a clearly impatient Patterson kicked his heels at the exit.

'Owen Ruud,' said O'Rourke. 'He's got an ID says he's the stadium janitor. Looks genuine. And he's not Latino, looks more like a squarehead. It's his day off today, he says. Came along just for the mayor's speech and to have a beer.'

'Owen Ruud is on the list!' called one of the JTTF men sitting at the rear of the room with an open laptop in front of him on the table. 'Can someone ask them to take his picture and send it to me so we can be one hundred per cent certain?'

'OK! Ready to go again,' Springer called out to the room. 'Mayor Patterson, when you're ready, sir.'

'Wait!' called Walker. 'I've just received a message from one of my colleagues. It seems that Gomez is a white man and –'

'Mr Mayor!' Springer interrupted. 'If the janitor is the man we've been looking for we have him now and we won't be letting him go. You're quite safe, so go ahead!'

'We can't know if it's the same man!' Walker shouted, aware now that all eyes were on him, including Patterson's.

'We're grateful to the Homicide Unit,' said Springer. 'But we're in charge here and this situation is under control. Mayor, all 60,000 people out there have been thoroughly searched, regardless of ethnicity, religion, sex or sexual orientation. But the final decision must, of course, remain yours.'

The whistling had increased in volume.

'Announce through the loudspeakers that the mayor has been held up in traffic,' said Walker. 'That'll give us time to get a picture of the suspect and check if his face shows up on any of the security cameras.'

'People saw me arriving,' said Patterson and peered out from behind the drape. 'Listen to them. I have to get out there. This is live TV, remember.'

'Mr Mayor, sir –' Walker began.

'Now listen!' Patterson turned and stared directly at Walker. 'Suppose it gets out that I stood here and refused to go on even though the terrorist specialist unit said it was safe to do so, and it gets out that the man I was so afraid of was the stadium janitor. Or let me put it this way, would you want a man like that as your mayor?' He turned to the man wearing the headset. 'Tell them to introduce me.'

The man in the headset said something into the microphone as Patterson turned his back on Walker and started rolling his neck again. Walker told himself he hadn't tripped up, he'd done his bit, said what he had to say, and the mayor had made his decision. Soon he would be going home to eat with his family.

A deep bass voice crackled across the stadium loudspeakers, accompanied by a drum roll that would probably soon give way to the national anthem: 'And now, ladies and gentlemen, direct from city hall . . .'

Or rather, if Walker were to really cover himself completely, there was one small correction that needed to be made.

'The suspect is not the janitor,' Walker said quietly, addressing the mayor's back. 'His name is Mike Lunde. He's a taxidermist.'

'Here is our city's mayor, here is everyone's mayor and good friend to the Second Amendment,' intoned the voice over the loudspeakers.

Walker saw how the layer of skin pressed up against the collar around Patterson's neck tensed. Maybe it was the word 'friend'. Maybe something else. The man with the headset drew the drape aside and they all looked out onto the stadium. As expected the drum roll had segued into the national anthem, which drowned out any whistling there might have been or the absence of applause. Still Patterson stood motionless in front of the opening.

'Something wrong, sir?' asked the headset.

Patterson turned. Not toward the headset, but toward Walker.

'What did you say his name was?'

49

THE MASTERPIECE, OCTOBER 2016

'IT'S LOVELY,' SAID JILL PATTERSON as she stroked the dog. 'Absolutely lovely.'

'Thank you,' said Mike Lunde.

The two of them and the children, Siri and Simon, sat in the store in a little circle around Quentin. Jill kept stroking him, she said the Labrador's coat seemed so glossy and bright. Outside, on the other side of the street, their Chevy stood parked, with their private bodyguard Hector Herrer inside. From where she was sitting she could see that the other one, the extra security man from the JTTF, had taken up a position outside the car and was monitoring the street in both directions. The JTTF man had wanted to come into the store with them, but Jill had explained that Mike said they should always be alone in the store whenever they were looking at Quentin. The JTTF man had said OK, but he asked them not to be too long. Jill hadn't replied. After all, this might be the last time they would ever see this nice taxidermist, whom everyone in the family had become so fond of. Mike had been to their home in Dellwood and listened as she and Kevin and the children talked about Quentin. The Labrador retriever had been their beloved companion until the day he ran out into the road and got run over by the neighbour's Lexus. The children had insisted that Quentin be buried in their own back garden, and they had even had a priest for the burial. But so great was the children's grief that after just one week Jill said to Kevin that they had to do something, the kids wouldn't leave the grave, they spent every evening weeping there. Kevin's first response had been that maybe the grave had become a place for the kids to get rid of all their frustrations, that maybe it wasn't just about Quentin, maybe what was happening was good for them. But Jill said it was grief, and that children shouldn't grieve, that could wait until later. She'd spoken to a friend who knew a friend who'd had the family's pet rabbit stuffed and spoke of it like a resurrection. She was the one who had recommended Town Taxidermy to Jill.

Of course, neither Jill nor the children had been present when the grave was opened. After a mere fourteen days the fur was still pretty much unchanged, and Mike had said it wouldn't be a problem to repair any damage. They agreed to use as much of Quentin as possible, not just the teeth but the whole skull. That way she felt she could tell the children it wasn't just a copy of Quentin, it really *was* Quentin. Mike took the dog's measurements for the mannequin he had to make, and he studied the family's photographs and home videos showing the animal. The better to capture Quentin's character and personality, as he explained.

Siri sat next to her mother and began stroking Quentin too. Because it had turned out just as Jill hoped, it really *was* Quentin. Mike hadn't just captured the dog's personality, he'd caught the way he walked and had frozen their beloved pet in mid-stride. And the look in the eyes! It was Quentin's look exactly. It really was an exercise in pure magic. Simon, their youngest, stood up and ran across to the fox. Felt its teeth. Then ran over to the wolf and tugged at its tail. She hoped he wouldn't break anything, he was a bit of a handful. But Mike took it all calmly enough. Simon came running back and put his arms around Quentin's neck.

'Simon, be careful!' his big sister called.

Simon obediently let go.

'But he doesn't move,' Simon complained as he stood in front of the dog and called out: 'Quentin! Wake up!' He hit the unmoving dog on the snout. 'Quentin!'

Jill laughed what she herself heard was a slightly nervous laugh. 'Simon, sweetie, don't do that. Quentin is a . . . he's a . . . still dog now.'

'But I don't want a dog that stands still! Man!' Simon stood in front of the chair Mike was sitting in. 'I want a *living* Quentin!'

Mike cocked his head to one side. 'You know what, Simon, it's actually completely impossible to get back someone who's dead, no matter how much you loved them. You see, death . . .'

Jill could see that Simon had been about to lose patience and run off again until Mike said that word – death – with such weight. Now the boy stood quite still and stared at Mike.

'Death . . .' said the taxidermist, 'death is a door with a spring lock.'

Simon blinked.

'And the pain,' Mike went on, 'the pain of losing the one you love, or all the ones you love, well, that's enough to drive anyone out of their mind.'

Jill was a little shocked at Mike's choice of words. After all, this was a child he was talking to. On the other hand, he had such a good way with the kids, so maybe he was getting through to him with what he was saying. But no, he had lost Simon's attention, and now Simon was tearing about inside the store again.

'Don't touch that!' she called as Simon approached the rifle leaned up against the wall directly behind Mike. She'd seen it as soon as they entered, and if it had been anywhere else she would certainly have said something. But here, among all these stuffed animals, it seemed natural, just another of the many tools of Mike's trade. They had to have used something to shoot that large deer and that bear, she had reasoned with herself. But now that Simon stood staring in frozen fascination at the gun it gave her a bad feeling. She saw his little child's fists clench and open, could see how he itched to reach out and touch it, dangerous and tempting. What was it about guns that made them so irresistible – and to small boys in particular? It was like the ring in that movie the kids loved, she thought. *The Lord of the Rings*. Jill got hold of Simon and pulled him onto her lap. He pretended to resist, but she knew how much he liked it when she coddled him. Especially with his sister looking on.

'Now we all have to say thank you to Mike for making Quentin look so fine,' said Jill.

'Thank you, Mike,' the children said almost in chorus.

Mike just sat there and smiled. He looked almost sad. Maybe it was because he didn't want to be parted from Quentin. It was almost enough to make you feel sorry for him. Jill leaned forward and said in a quiet, comforting voice: 'I want you to know that this is going to ease a lot of the pain in our family. I'm really looking forward to when my husband gets to see Quentin.'

Mike nodded. 'I hope I can repay all he's done for so many other families in Minneapolis, Mrs Patterson.'

She smiled. 'Thank you, that's true. Kevin *has* done so many good things as mayor.'

'Like opposing anyone who's tried to limit our God-given right to carry weapons,' said Mike.

'Yes, indeed,' said Jill. She felt the smile stiffen slightly on her lips.

'This military sniper's rifle here, for example.' Mike picked up the rifle. 'It was purchased illegally, but it wouldn't have been difficult to buy it legally. Isn't it reassuring to know that we are such a well-armed people that everyone, absolutely everyone, is able to defend themselves against everybody else?' He smiled broadly.

Jill Patterson swallowed. 'Of course. It wouldn't be fair if only a few of us could.'

Mike's eyes had grown more intense, his voice higher. He was speaking more quickly. She could see that Siri had noticed it too, she'd stopped stroking the dog.

'We're able to defend our families,' said Mike. 'Because dying yourself isn't the worst thing. The worst thing is to go on living after the people you love have all been killed. Don't you agree?' He nodded in the direction of Quentin, at the same time doing something with the rifle that made a metallic, oily sound. She assumed he was loading it.

'Since it's your husband who makes all this possible, as I said, I'm going to do for him exactly what politicians like him have done for families such as my own.'

Jill felt Siri take hold of her hand, and Simon stopped wriggling about in her lap. Jill's mouth was dry and when she spoke her voice sounded hoarse and strange:

'What would that be, Mike?'

'What he and people like him did for me,' said Mike Lunde as he looked down at the rifle, 'was to put weapons in the hands of those who took from me everything I loved.' He raised the rifle to his cheek. 'So now it's my turn.'

50

HECTOR, OCTOBER 2016

HECTOR HERRER SAW THAT GERARD, the security man JTTF had sent over yesterday evening, was hearing something through his headset. Hector had suggested he be included in the same loop but Gerard told him this wasn't part of 'JTTF's protocol'. He knew it had to be something important because Gerard, who had so far been leaning against the hood on the passenger side keeping a look-out, straightened up suddenly and went for the gun in his shoulder holster. Hector lowered the window on the passenger side.

'What's up?'

Gerard held one finger to the earbud and lifted the other hand holding the gun – a Glock – to indicate that he was still listening. But Hector saw now that Gerard's attention was drawn toward the store, Town Taxidermy. Hector took out his own gun and loaded it.

'Copy that,' said Gerard and took his finger away from his ear. Without taking his eyes off the store he said: 'Message from the stadium. The store owner, Mike Lunde, is dangerous and potentially armed.'

'Meaning what?' said Hector, not because he hadn't understood, but because he wanted it confirmed.

'Meaning they think the store owner is the assassin. Is that Mike Lunde in there with them?'

'Yeah,' said Hector. He knew that now wasn't the time to start handing out blame but had already worked out his own part in it. Others had been responsible for giving Mike Lunde the security clearance he needed to enter the Patterson home, but it was Hector who had told Gerard it was safe for Jill and the kids to go into the store alone. Of course, he could excuse himself by saying he was only following Jill's expressed wishes. Excuse himself by saying that the view from out here in the street was as good if not better than from inside the store. Excuse himself by saying he had spoken to Lunde and rarely met someone who inspired greater confidence. But Hector had departed from his principle of being always, no matter what the hour, as close to the Patterson family as possible, and for that there could be no excuse. Hector was already out of the car and heard Gerard behind him, running to keep up.

'We're going into the store,' Gerard said into the headset.

Right at that same moment Hector's own security chief spoke into his earbud: 'You get that message, Hector?'

'Yeah, we're on our way in.'

Hector had known Gerard for only a few hours but from the way he moved and readied himself he could see they must have gone through a similar training. So they didn't need to exchange words but automatically split as they crossed the street so that they wouldn't be seen from the store, then made their way separately from different sides toward the store window. Hector risked a quick look inside, but the lighting was dim, and all the stuffed animals in the window blocked his view so he couldn't see much. He and Gerard moved in a crouch past the display window then pressed their backs against the wall on either side of the doorway. A handwritten sign hanging on the door handle said CLOSED. The O was drawn like a smiley. But Hector had noticed that when Mike Lunde opened the door to Jill and the children they had been moving straight toward the back of the store as the door swung closed behind them, so unless it was a spring lock the door should be open.

Gerard pointed to Hector and laid his hand flat on the top of his head and then pointed to himself – a tactical signal meaning *you – cover – me.* Hector shook his head firmly and returned the signal. After a moment's hesitation Gerard nodded.

Hector put his left hand on the door handle, pressed down and pushed carefully.

It wasn't locked.

Hector pointed to the top of the door with his gun then put the barrel against his lips. Gerard understood and nodded, he clearly recalled the jangle of the bell when Mike Lunde had opened up for Jill and the children.

Hector took two deep in-and-out breaths.

Then something happened to Hector that occasionally happened in situations like this. In his mind's eye he saw the silhouette of his father's head against the sun, and heard the deep voice, at once reassuring and challenging: 'I see you.'

Hector pushed the door open wider, careful not to make the

bell ring but just enough to enable him to slip inside. Bodyguards wear dark glasses for a number of reasons, and style is not among them. One is to avoid a situation in which bright sunlight makes the pupils so small that the bodyguard is temporarily blinded on entering a darker room. Hector pulled off his shades and tossed them aside before again raising the pistol in both hands. He had time to see the family sitting in a ring around Quentin, Jill facing him with silver duct tape over her mouth and hands behind her back. He had time to see Siri and Simon in chairs, hands bound by plastic strips to the struts on the chair backs. And he had time to see Mike Lunde, who was sitting beside Jill. And he had time to see the barrel of the rifle Mike Lunde was pointing at him.

Hector even had time to see the flash of light from the mouth of the gun.

And then it was as if he had been hit by a truck, he felt himself tumbling backward, out of the door, felt himself hit something and collapse onto the sidewalk, felt he couldn't move, the light was disappearing. Felt someone take hold of the shoulder straps of the ballistic vest he was wearing under his jacket and pull him over the asphalt as the voice of the JTTF man whose name he could no longer recall spoke above him in a loud, panting voice:

'November. Herrer has been shot by the suspect, repeat Herrer has been shot. Pulling him to safety, bleeding heavily, looks critical. Suspect is in the store with three hostages. I need an ambulance and backup. Now!'

Hector thought he should take off his shades, because it was too dark. He searched the sky for the sun. Looked for the face. Listened for the voice that was supposed to say *I see you*. But it wasn't there. Hector neither heard nor saw anything.

51

MESSAGE, OCTOBER 2016

JILL PATTERSON FELT THE WARM tears running down her cheeks and lost the sensation as they ran onto the tape. They were cold by the time they ran back onto the skin and down over her chin. She wanted to close her eyes, shut out all this, but forced herself to keep them open, forced herself to look at Simon and Siri, who stared at her from above small, taped mouths, as though she, their mother, was the only person in all the world who could save them. And hadn't she really always been the only one?

Mike Lunde's voice beside her was calm, almost like someone talking in his sleep.

'I'm sorry you had to see that man get shot, Mrs Patterson, I would have preferred things to be different. But as your husband preaches, it is the right of every citizen to protect his house and property against intruders. And there is actually a Closed sign on the door.'

Like someone breaking the surface for a breath of air, Jill closed her eyes. Momentarily.

'Siri and Simon . . .' Mike Lunde began, and Jill at once opened her eyes wide again, seeking to catch her children's eyes, as though she thought they would be doomed if they so much as looked at him. But she had lost them, their gazes were already on the taxidermist.

'Don't be afraid,' he continued. 'This will soon be over. I promise, cross my heart and hope to die.'

Jill tried to blink away the tears as Mike Lunde drew his forefinger twice, slowly, across his throat.

Bob was two blocks away now but had to stop when the traffic lights in front of him turned red. He swore. He knew that, at this particular junction, there was always a long wait for the green. A car with zebra stripes pulled up alongside and he heard the sirens at the same time. He lowered his window. The sounds were coming from several cars and they seemed to be getting closer. Bob turned on the radio and tuned in to the local news channel.

'. . . at the opening of the NRA conference at the US Bank Stadium. At this moment in time we have no information as to why Mayor Patterson has cancelled his appearance, but our information is that he was at the stadium. And I'm hearing right now that the mayor and his party have just left the stadium with a police escort and sirens going. We do not know what if anything has happened to the mayor. All we know is . . .'

Bob felt his phone vibrate. He pulled it up. It was Kay.

'Hey, what the hell is going on?'

'Mike Lunde,' said Kay. 'He has the mayor's wife and children with him in the store. He shot one of the bodyguards. I'm on my way there now.'

Bob glanced up at the red light, looked left and then right and saw a trailer approaching. He hoped the Volvo was having one of its better days and caught a glimpse of the staring man in the zebra-striped car as he put his foot down hard on the gas pedal.

Bob turned down the street where Town Taxidermy was located at the same moment as an ambulance entered at the other end, sirens blaring. He leaned out of the window and saw two police cars outside the store. They had stopped in the middle of the road, blue lights flashing. Bob drove the Volvo up onto the sidewalk, jumped out and ran past the crowd of onlookers toward the store and ducked under the crime scene tape. Four police officers and a man in a dark suit were taking cover behind the cars. Two had service rifles aimed in the direction of the store, two had service pistols.

'Get out of here!' yelled one of the officers, a sturdy man, his face flushed as he waved his arms at Bob.

'MPD, Homicide Unit!' Bob yelled back and ducked down behind the police car. He held up his expired ID card, showing it to the guy with the flushed face and the one in the suit, who had to be FBI. 'Detective Bob Oz. What's happening?'

'He's in there with the hostages,' said the officer. 'No sign of life.'

'What are you doing here, Detective?' the FBI guy interrupted.

'I know Mike Lunde. Who are you?'

'Gerard Zimmer, JTTF.'

Bob nodded at the SUV that stood with both front doors open. 'Where's your partner, Zimmer?'

'On his way to the hospital. Or the morgue, hard to say. Bullet caught him above his vest.'

'OK. So what's happening now?'

'We're waiting for SWAT. They're on their way from the stadium. Should be here in about –' Zimmer checked his watch – 'four minutes.'

'Four minutes,' Bob repeated. He stood up and started unbuttoning his cashmere coat.

'What are you doing?' the police officer shouted. 'Get down! Zimmer says the guy in there has an M24!'

'I know,' said Bob. 'And I know four minutes is a long time and that having SWAT here guarantees nothing.' He folded his coat and laid it on the hood of the car.

'Where are you going?' asked Zimmer.

'To talk to Mike.'

'Our orders –'

'– are your orders, they aren't mine,' said Bob.

'So who gave you yours?' Zimmer was standing now and blocking Bob's way.

'You can shoot me if those are your orders, Zimmer.'

Bob walked round Zimmer and crossed the street, coatless. His shirt was wet with sweat, ice-cold on the shady side, warm on the sunny side. Behind him someone shouted. But it was too late now. He just had to hope that they wouldn't shoot him.

He walked to the store doorway and stopped. 'Mike!' he shouted. 'It's Bob. I'm coming in.'

Bob waited. No answer. He pushed open the door.

The bell jangled as he walked in. Four people sat in a circle around something. A dog. The Labrador retriever Mike Lunde had finally managed to get the right eyes for. Mike was holding a rifle pointed at him, but strangely enough Bob felt no fear.

'Bob,' said Mike. 'You're a little early. We said one thirty.'

'Sorry about that. OK if I come in a little closer?'

'Are you carrying?'

'Not since Frankie died.'

Mike lowered the rifle. Bob took two steps toward the rearing black bear, picked up the stool in front of it, placed it in the circle and sat down.

'Turned out well,' he said with a nod to the dog.

'Thank you.'

Bob took in the circle. Met the red, pleading eyes of the two children and the woman. He recognised her, she was the woman who had come in to talk about the eyes with Mike. Bob nodded to them, trying to convey to them that this would turn out OK, they weren't about to die. He doubted he'd succeeded. He looked back at Mike again.

'How are you feeling?'

'How do you think?'

Bob shrugged. 'Like me. Angry. Aggressive. That's the way we get when we don't take our antidepressants. But you're better at hiding it than I am.'

'Maybe.'

Bob folded his hands. 'What is it you want, Mike?'

'Hm. You guessed your way this far, you should be able to work out the answer to that one too.'

Bob nodded. 'Revenge for your family. Finish that masterpiece you talk about all the time, the one you had me believing was the dog. But then all these staged murders, and this mysterious figure that kept disappearing. Tomás Gomez. Actually you told me everything I needed to know to flush you out, but I couldn't put it together. Did you want me to stop you?'

'No,' said Mike. 'But maybe I wanted you to understand me. Afterward, at least. That's what every artist hopes for, right?' He gave a cautious smile.

'The thirst for revenge isn't so hard to understand, Mike.'

'But there's more than that. There's a message.'

Bob saw something moving on the chest of Mike Lunde's white shirt. A red dot. SWAT had arrived.

'But if there's a message, surely you don't have to kill innocent people.'

'Gomez, Dante and Karlstad were not innocent people, Mike. Nor was the Milkman, or Die Man either. And Hector I shot only in the shoulder, I hope.'

'I don't know anything about any Milkman and Die Man, I'm thinking about these people in here.'

'In here?' For a moment Mike seemed not to understand. Then he started to laugh. Looked over at Mrs Patterson and the children as though he expected them to laugh along with him. 'You surely didn't think I would kill women and children that have nothing to do with this. I've explained to them. That the only reason they are here is to show that they *could* have been killed. By a depressed, free citizen with access to weapons, the Second Amendment and the District of Columbia versus Heller.'

Bob leaned over sideways, across SWAT's line of fire. The red dot on Lunde's chest vanished.

'But now that you've made your point, shouldn't you let them go?'

Mike shrugged. 'It was all such a long time ago. Thirty years. Give or take a few minutes.'

'The children are so afraid, Mike. Experiences like this leave their mark. And I'll work just as well as your hostage.'

Mike looked at Bob in silence. Then he bent forward and picked something up from under his chair. It was the scalpel Bob had seen him using in his work.

'Cut them loose.'

Bob took the scalpel from him, stood up and carefully continued to cover the line of fire between the display window and Mike Lunde as he cut the tape binding Mrs Patterson and the children. He indicated to the mother that she could pull the duct tape off their mouths, but either she didn't understand or for some reason didn't want to understand. Bob nodded toward the street, and she took her children by the hand and hurried them to the door.

'Don't forget Quentin,' said Mike.

Both children at once broke away from their mother and ran back to the dog, lifting it, one at each end, and carrying it over to where their mother stood, holding the door open. She gave Bob a look that he interpreted as gratitude before she followed the children out. The store bell jangled merrily as the door slid shut behind them.

'How long have we got?' asked Mike. The rifle was now between his knees with the butt on the floor and his hands around the barrel, which was pointing up toward the ceiling.

'Before they storm in? Fifteen minutes maybe.'

'That's plenty of time. Shall I make some coffee?'

'I think it's best that you sit right where you are. They've got snipers out there just waiting to get a sighting on you.'

'Aha.' Mike's smile was sad and resigned. But not just that. There was something else. Hope, thought Bob. Like at a parting you know is final, at the same time as you sense something new and unknown lies ahead of you. Bob felt a little bit the same way.

'So you want to tell me what happened?' asked Bob. 'Had you been planning this long?'

Mike Lunde shook his head slowly. 'Tomás Gomez just happened to come in here one day. Just like you did. Said his cat was dead and Mrs White had recommended me. It was thirty years since the last time I saw him, he looked very different. But you know, it's in the eyes. I never forgot those eyes. The eyes of the guy who killed my little girl in that parking lot. Who stood over me and was about to kill me too. We got a real good look at each other before he heard the police car coming and ran off. And even so, Gomez didn't recognise me when he came into the store.'

'They called him Lobo, he was a killing machine, you were just another number to him. Did you kill him straight away?'

'No. I had several conversations with him. I went to his home and ate with him.'

'And then?'

'Then I took him to a studio up in Cedar Creek where I kept his stuffed cat. He was pleased with the job I'd done. I gave him coffee. With Rohypnol in it. When he woke up he was tied to a chair.'

'I know, we found him. Why didn't you kill him immediately?'

'Why do you think?'

'I think you had to act out those fantasies of revenge you've been living with these past thirty years. You tortured him.'

'Yes.'

'And did it meet your expectations?'

'No.'

'No?'

'I got sick, I had to throw up.'

'Even though you've spent your whole life cutting up animals?'

'It was the first time I had ever inflicted pain on a living creature. The worst thing was that Tomás regretted it. Talking together here in the store he never said in so many words exactly what he'd done, only that he'd caused untold harm to others, that he didn't deserve to live. His gang life was behind him, he said, he worked casual jobs, but he still had nightmares every night. In that respect it might have been a harder punishment to let him go on living. Lonely, but haunted. But the torture at least gave me the name and address of the person he had bought the Uzi from, Marco Dante. I learned where his boss Die Man hung out. And that the detective I had trusted took bribes to keep any suspicion from leading to Tomás and Die Man and their gang. And I got his face. And the skin of his hands. When he was dead I took his clothes and the keys to his apartment.'

'The rest of his body you freeze-dried.'

'In a manner of speaking, yes.'

'So Tomás Gomez bought the Uzi he killed your daughter with from Dante?'

'That is correct.'

'And after you shot Dante, you left enough clues and witnesses who saw you disguised as Gomez to make sure he would be the suspect.'

'Yes.'

Bob glanced at his watch. 'Tell me about Cody Karlstad.'

52

KENTUCKY FRIED, OCTOBER 2016

'ISN'T THAT THAT GUY WHO was in here?' the customer said, gesturing with his beer glass toward the small, muted TV screen on the wall behind Liza. That was one of the things she'd change if she ever took over the place. Two big TV screens instead of one small one. But only for turning on when something was happening, something that brought people together. Super Bowl, presidential elections. Stuff like that.

She turned around to look.

It was KSTP-TV with a flashing BREAKING NEWS line above the picture.

A female reporter was talking to the camera. Behind her police cars were visible, and a big military-looking vehicle with SWAT in white lettering along the side. Then Liza saw the picture of a face in the upper-right corner of the screen. With the name under it: Bob Oz. MPD. With a trembling hand Liza grabbed the remote and turned up the sound.

'. . . went inside and persuaded the hostage-taker to take him in exchange for the release of Jill Patterson and the two children. Bob Oz is now in there with the hostage-taker, who is believed to be the owner of the store. He is Mike Lunde, a fifty-eight-year-old widower.'

'So, Shirley, you're able to confirm that the officer involved is the same Bob Oz you met briefly two days ago at Track Plaza.'

'That's right, Rick. But in a completely different role here. Before Jill Patterson and the children were taken away from here with the mayor she had time to say how they will be eternally grateful to Detective Oz for his courage, and that they are praying he will survive the ordeal.'

Survive. Liza's hands went to her mouth. She took deep breaths. In. Out. In. Out. Breathe. And then she did something she hadn't done for so long she couldn't even remember when the last time was. She prayed. *God, let him survive. I don't ever have to see him again if that's what you want in return. But dear God, don't let him die.*

Kay Myers ran crouching past the police cars outside the taxidermist's store and didn't straighten up until she was behind the big SWAT vehicle where Walker was standing. A few feet away Springer and O'Rourke seemed to be in the middle of a heated discussion.

'What's going on?' Kay asked, panting to get her breath back.

'Springer wants SWAT to take Lunde out,' said Walker. 'O'Rourke says that'll put Oz's life in danger.'

Kay turned toward the two men.

'No!' she screeched.

They stopped their discussion and turned to look at her.

'No, you mustn't try to take Lunde out.'

'Thanks but we can get along without any interference from you, Myers,' Springer snorted. At least he remembered the 's' in her name this time.

'Shut up and listen,' said Kay. 'Oz and Lunde know each other.'

'Kay, don't . . .' Walker began – but it was too late to stop her and they both knew it.

'Lunde won't kill Oz,' said Kay. 'But you, Springer, you idiot, you just might do that.'

With a half-laugh Springer shook his head. 'According to our information Detective Oz is an unstable, alcoholic police officer who has been suspended for disobeying orders and is responsible for putting himself in this current situation. He has risked the lives of three innocent civilians, he's no hero, he just wants to look like one. That's understandable, given the fucked-up state of his own life. You say he and Lunde are friends, maybe that's why he keeps sabotaging SWAT's snipers by blocking their line of fire.'

Kay noticed the saliva spray from her own mouth and how some of it landed on Springer's pinstriped jacket as she answered: 'But can't you get it through your thick head that Bob Oz is in a position to get Mike Lunde to hand himself over?'

'Superintendent, we don't have time for this,' said Springer. 'Can you talk to this Fury?'

Kay waited to feel Walker's big hand land on her shoulder. But she didn't. When she turned she saw Walker was looking directly at Springer.

'Why?' said Walker. 'Sounds to me like she has a point.'

Springer glanced at O'Rourke as though looking for support.

'I don't know who it was gave Bob Oz his nickname Kentucky Fried,' said O'Rourke. 'All I know is Bob Oz just went in there unarmed and got three hostages released. And I'm not willing to risk the life of a man like that. Not as long as only those two in there are in danger.'

'Let me give you the short version,' said Springer with a deep sigh, as though he were dealing with dull-witted children. 'I've talked to my bosses and they tell me Lunde is someone who has murdered one decent citizen, Cody Karlstad, tried to kill one of Patterson's bodyguards, and in the process traumatised Patterson's family. Like any other terrorist, Lunde's wet dream is to commit these evil deeds and get himself arrested so that every microphone in the media gets pushed into his face so he can broadcast his sick, political message to the nation. Now that is not necessarily something we want. Got that?'

Kay wasn't sure she had heard properly. Didn't they want to take Lunde alive? Who were *we*? And who were *my bosses*? She had a feeling she wouldn't get any answers if she asked Springer. On the other hand, maybe Springer was making all this up because he would prefer a dead body to a live terrorist telling the whole world how he'd tricked Springer. Lunde had given the MPD and the JTTF all the leads they needed, but still Springer's anti-terrorist group hadn't managed to stop him kidnapping the mayor's family.

Kay glanced across at Walker. He looked a little less upset than she did. Was it because he knew something she didn't, something to do with having a top job at city hall, and knowing what it takes to climb even higher? Something about how not to trip up? Or was she just under pressure and seeing daylight ghosts?

'Give Bob five minutes,' she said. 'Or I'm going over there . . .' Kay nodded toward the KSTP-TV bus further down the street. 'And I'll tell them exactly what you just said, Springer.'

Kay wasn't looking at Springer, she was looking at Walker. His head was on one side, and he was smiling at her. Not encouragingly, not happily, but proudly. And regretfully. The way he might smile at someone who's done the right thing, something he perhaps would have done himself back in the day, when he had the guts for it. The way you might smile at someone you'd like to help back up on their feet, but when winter comes, and a place like this gets iced up, then all you can do is look after number one.

53

HUNTING TROPHY, OCTOBER 2016

'I MADE A HUNTING TROPHY for Karlstad a couple of years ago,' said Mike as he folded his hands behind his head. Like someone who's finished a piece of work, thought Bob. 'A buck he wanted above his fireplace. I didn't know then that he was a local big shot in the NRA. I went to his house out in the suburbs to have a look at the fireplace. Wife, three children. Cody Karlstad had everything I didn't have. In his opinion what we needed to reduce crime was more guns, not fewer. He thought the gun was our foremost symbol of liberty, he thought we should be like certain other countries, have an automatic weapon as part of our flag.'

'Did you hate him?'

'No. Actually I quite liked him. He seemed a caring kind of person.'

'But all the same you shot him?'

'As I said before, it's about more than revenge.'

'The message.'

'Yes.'

'Which is?'

'That one day the gun you make is going to be aimed at you.'

'And the dead are to communicate this message?'

'That's what taxidermists do.'

'Do you really think people will listen to your message?'

Mike shrugged. 'The noise level is so high these days you have to shout loudly to be heard. Which is why I hope people will understand my use of such radical methods. But those involved at least died for a good cause. Even that corrupt detective became, in the end, a part of the work of art.'

'Oh?'

'I gather an anonymous artist has exhibited him in Arb Park. Minus his head.'

Bob studied Mike's face, not sure whether he was speaking metaphorically or meant it literally.

'What happened to the head?'

'Ah, I wanted to cleanse it of everything it has ever seen or heard. And done. Cleanse it completely.' Mike turned his innocent blue eyes on Bob.

Bob swallowed. 'So now the head is . . .?'

Mike nodded toward his workshop. 'The leather beetles are busy.'

Bob took a deep breath. Was about to ask the name of the detective but changed his mind.

'The gun. Who is it pointed at now?'

'At me.'

And sure enough, Bob saw that the barrel was pointing at Mike Lunde's own chin. 'Tell me, Mike – was *I* ever a part of the plan?'

'Not the plan. You were a good listener.'

'But I might have stopped you. Ruined everything. You told me all I needed to know. If I'd only gone a little deeper . . .'

'I realised early on that you wanted to keep me to yourself, so that you could get Tomás Gomez on your own. Your hunter's instinct blinded you, and I counted on you not suspecting me until it was too late. Anyway . . .' Lunde put his thumb against the trigger. '. . . we all need someone to confess to.'

'Because?'

'Because we're all lonely.'

Bob stared at Mike Lunde's thumb. 'You told me Tomás Gomez once said that he would have liked you to meet the person he once was. That you would have liked the person he once was. But you were thinking about you and me, right?'

'Maybe. But as I told you, that person died along with his family. So it really wasn't all that strange to walk around wearing the mask of a dead man. Both of us are ghosts. You understand?'

'Yes, I think I do.'

Mike Lunde closed his eyes. 'Bob?'

'Yes?'

'Are you my friend?'

'I think I am.'

'Can you help me this last bit of the way? It's so hard.'

'I . . .'

'Just put your thumb here, on top of mine. Help me squeeze.'

'You don't need to do this, Mike. There are people who can help. Treat your depression. Not just give you pills.'

'Please, Bob.'

'I can't, Mike. I haven't carried a gun, haven't touched one, since . . . since . . .'

'Since your daughter died. I know that. Do it for her, Mike. Give meaning to my death. As a protest against everything meaningless.'

Bob looked into Mike's eyes. The older man smiled gently. It was so quiet and so peaceful here. It was quiet out there too now. Much too quiet. Bob couldn't hear it, he could just sense the running footsteps, the whispered commands. In a few seconds they would be here.

'If I hand myself over now, the whole thing will have been in vain. It would no longer be a genuine work of art. It's all about the eyes, Bob. The eyes have to be right.'

'But . . .'

'You can tell them. Explain about the work. Because you're another one who has lost what you loved most of all. But you can start a new life. It's not too late for you.'

Bob knew exactly how it would go down. A window shattered, a stun grenade that paralysed the senses, then a burst of automatic gunfire before Mike had time to turn his rifle against them.

Bob Oz closed his eyes. Then he whispered her name, the name of his greatest joy. Frankie.

Kay Myers had taken out her pocket mirror. Now she was holding it round the corner of the SWAT vehicle and could see four men wearing black protective clothing, two on each side of the entrance to Town Taxidermy. Beside her she heard O'Rourke almost whispering into his walkie-talkie.

'Ready in five, four –'

There was a single, isolated bang.

She realised it wasn't someone from the SWAT team who had started too early, and that the sound came from inside the store. Bob. Everything – sound, light, time – seemed to freeze.

'Go now!' O'Rourke shouted.

Before his men could react the door opened.

Bob Oz stood in the doorway peering into the sunlight. He was wearing a shirt and holding something that looked like an ID card above his head. Kay slipped the mirror back into her jacket pocket and stepped out from behind the vehicle. Heard the whirring sound of cameras from further down the street – the media had been thronging outside the police tape ever since she arrived on the scene. Bob walked away from the doorway and the black-clad figures swarmed in behind him.

Kay walked toward Bob. It struck her that he looked very tired. And very lonely. Without thinking about it she found herself putting her arms around him.

With her chin resting on his shoulder she saw one of the black-clad men re-emerge and gesture with his hand. Right hand, fingers drawn across the throat: Mike Lunde was dead. The odd thing was that the signal was given not to O'Rourke but to Springer.

'Can you tell them what they need to know?' whispered Bob.

'Me?' said Kay. 'Where are you going?'

'Let's see if I can give you an answer to that some other day.'

Bob Oz carefully extricated himself from her embrace and crossed the street to where Walker stood waiting.

Kay headed to the store doorway. Pushed it open and went in. The SWAT team was obviously now going through the other rooms on the premises, because the body was still in the chair.

The shot had entered under the chin. The top of the head was gone, like a breakfast egg. But the face was intact. And it was a face she recognised. Lunde had not escaped from the Rialto. This was the man she had spoken to inside the theatre, the man who told her he had bought an invisibility dress for his daughter's birthday. He'd looked like a nice man. And sounded so honest. So maybe it was true, maybe he had bought something for his dead daughter. But wedged down in that bag from the toy store he must also have had his own cloak of invisibility: Tomás Gomez's face, his hands and his clothes. And in that same instant it occurred to Kay that he hadn't escaped via the air-conditioning duct at Track Plaza after all, he hadn't risked breaking his leg on any jump. When they later studied the footage from the security cameras, she knew they would see the man in front of her emerge calmly from the restroom and walk straight past them all.

She looked at Mike Lunde again. Because he resembled someone, didn't he? Or no, not exactly resembled. But shared something with somebody. With Bob Oz. And now she saw what it was. Even in death, the taxidermist looked lonely.

54

HERO, OCTOBER 2016

BOB CROSSED THE STREET FROM Town Taxidermy and walked toward the SWAT car where Walker stood. His face and posture gave nothing away, but Bob took the warmth in his voice as recognition.

'Good work, Oz.'

Bob pressed his ID card into Walker's hand and kept walking. Passing the police car he retrieved his mustard-yellow cashmere coat, then ducked under the police tape and slipped away through the spectators. Fortunately, no one seemed to realise he had just played a central role in the drama they had witnessed. Then came a loud, authoritative female voice:

'Bob Oz!'

He looked up and recognised the face of the TV reporter from the sports bar. The same guy holding the camera on his shoulder behind her. A red lamp blinked above the lens and Bob assumed it meant they were on air and live. They backed away in front of him and slowed down, but he didn't stop.

'Can you describe how you felt in the middle of all this drama?' The reporter put the question with exaggerated body language and a bright red, ingratiating smile as she pushed the microphone into his face.

'Yes, I can,' said Bob, and her smile grew even wider. 'But not to you.' He looked straight into the camera. 'Viewers, change the channel to WCCO and you'll hear my whole story. You'll also get better news there. You'll even get better weather.'

As he walked on in the direction of his Volvo Bob registered the crestfallen look on the reporter's face.

A young man with a shoulder bag appeared beside him.

'From the *Star Tribune*. That was some answer you just gave!' He laughed and sounded as though he meant it. 'But are you sure you wouldn't rather talk to a proper newspaper than WCCO?'

'I was kidding,' said Bob. 'I don't want to talk to anyone. OK?'

'I understand,' said the young man. But kept trotting alongside Bob. 'Right now you just want to be left in peace. But once things have quieted down, maybe we can talk then. Here's my card.'

Bob stopped by the Volvo, picked up the parking ticket wedged under the wipers, took the card in order to get rid of the guy and stuffed both into his coat pocket.

'You'll get column inches with us,' said the young man.

'What would I want column inches for?'

The boy shrugged. 'To say what you think about this. About Lunde. About his project.'

'His project?'

'If the rumour that he is actually Tomás Gomez is correct then it looks like all of this was a political attack on the NRA and the gun laws. From today on you're a hero, whether you like it or not, and right now people in this state will be interested to hear your opinions. We've got a presidential election coming up and research shows that the majority of people make up their mind which way to vote the last two days before the election. I don't know where you stand politically on gun control or anything else, and it really doesn't matter to me. But just think about it, Mr Oz – right at this moment in time there's a small window open for you when you do actually have some kind of power.'

Bob unlocked the Volvo. 'You think I can change anything?'

'*Contribute* to change, perhaps.'

Bob looked across the roof of the car at the boy standing on the other side. His cheeks were flushed. He looked as if he cared about things, looked like a decent kid.

'You're an optimist,' said Bob. 'What's your name?'

'Bob.'

'Another one?' He laughed. 'How old are you?'

'Twenty-two.'

'OK. I envy you, Bob.'

'Envy me being twenty-two?'

'That as well.'

The older Bob got into his car and started the engine. As he drove off he looked in the mirror and saw the boy following with his eyes. A naive optimist, twenty-two years old. Had he once been like that himself? Bob hoped so. And he hoped that it was the Bob in the mirror who would use the little bit of power he had, not himself. The city – and the world – needed naive optimists more than it needed resigned realists.

55

CASHMERE, OCTOBER 2016

SUNDAY WAS ANOTHER SUNNY DAY. Kay Myers followed the handwritten directions showing her the route through Minnehaha Park. They invited all adults and children along to something entitled 'Emma the Hare and Freddy the Fox'.

She came directly from 1025 Bar, the place where the cops drank, where those who wanted to had gathered to pay tribute to the memory of Olav Hanson. That not everybody did might have had something to do with the fact that it was a Sunday. It might also have been connected to the fact that on the Saturday the *Star Tribune* had already run a story about the thirty-year-old killings known as 'the McDeath massacre' involving Mike Lunde's family, in which it was implied that the late Olav Hanson had protected the guilty. Walker said a few words that were so vague they could have meant anything at all, and a tearful Joe Kjos started reading something from written notes but had to give up. Bob wasn't there, but it was Bob and not Olav people talked about as they drank at the wake. Walker told Kay he had rescinded Bob's suspension with immediate effect following the hostage drama on Saturday. That meant it was operative from Saturday morning, so they didn't have to explain to the press what a cop under suspension was doing in the middle of the whole drama. And with all the other stuff going on around them at that particular time, the MPD definitely needed a hero.

'I'm telling you this as an example of the sort of trade-offs you're going to have to make when you take over,' Walker was saying. 'Have you got the stomach for it, Myers?'

Kay thought about it before replying that, as regards Bob Oz, that decision was one she would have had no problem taking.

As she walked along the path that twisted through the centrally located park she passed families with children on their way to the waterfalls. They looked happy. And safe. This is what our job is, she thought. It's to keep these people, these citizens of our city, safe. She realised she had thought of Minneapolis as *our* city. Was that maybe for the first time? *To protect with courage, to serve with compassion.* MPD's motto. She had to smile a little at herself. But maybe it was a day for big words and big thoughts.

She had arrived at the wooden deck in front of the paddling pool where many of the families were now gathered. Here must be where it was going to happen, here, where the roar of the waterfall wasn't too overwhelming. A number of children were already gathered in front of a wagon on which a miniature stage had been built.

'You came,' said a voice next to Kay.

She turned. She'd never seen him without his mask but recognised the voice at once. He was black, but much lighter-skinned than she was. Younger than she had thought too.

'Kay,' she said.

'Alex. Maybe you'd like a coffee afterward?'

She looked at him. 'Maybe,' she said.

'Then let the show begin,' he said with a smile.

He disappeared behind the wagon. A blaring fanfare emerged from what sounded like a ghetto blaster that had seen better days, then the drapes parted and a glove puppet that looked like a hare wearing a princess's crown made its entry. The children cried out 'Look, Daddy!' or 'Hey!' or else just cheered in general excitement. Then all went quiet.

'You think maybe I'm just a hare?' the hare said in Alex's rather feeble imitation of a girl's voice.

The kids responded with an excited mixture of yeses and noes.

'The ones who answered right got it wrong,' the girl's voice said. 'And the ones who answered wrong got it right.'

Kay closed her eyes to the sun. It was October, election day soon, but still it warmed. You take the good days you get.

Come Monday the sky remained high and cloudless and the air clear. It stayed that way until dusk, when a couple of lonely clouds appeared. They seemed so high up they must have come from outer space, with the sun tinging them blue and emerald green. From where Bob was standing, phone to his ear and leaning against the Volvo as he looked over the downtown skyline on the far side of the river, the massed buildings looked like a ragged iceberg against a background of orange fire. He'd thought a lot about Mike Lunde over the weekend. Seeing the city buildings in that way, like a work of art, led him to think back over some of the smaller details of the case. The way Mike had said an anonymous artist had apparently exhibited in Arb Park. Referring to it like that, did that mean Mike Lunde himself was Anonymous? Well, that was just one of many questions surrounding the case he knew he would probably never get the answer to. Anyway, now it was time to put it all behind him and move on. Because, really, that was the only way.

Finally the call was answered.

'Hello, Bob.'

'Hi, Alice. Thanks for the messages over the weekend. Sorry about the very brief replies, it's been a busy weekend tying up loose ends in the Lunde case. I've done nothing but sleep and work.'

'I understand, and the most important thing of all is that you're OK. But remember that your body knows how close you were to losing your life. That's a heavy psychological blow, even if you don't feel it right now. The symptoms of post-traumatic stress can come –'

'– later on. Much later.' He finished the sentence for her. 'Thanks, Alice, I remember you saying that. And thanks for what you said about the pills too. It really helped.'

'Good.' He could hear she was smiling.

'But talking about most important things . . .' he said.

'We've been to the hospital, got back home just now.'

'And?'

'It's a girl. They say she looks healthy and well.'

'That is so good to hear,' said Bob. 'So good. So . . .' He swallowed. 'You've made me very happy, Alice.'

Silence for a few moments.

'Thank you,' she said quietly, and he could hear in her voice that she was crying.

'No, thank *you,*' he said. 'Say hello to Stan.'

He slipped the phone back into his coat pocket. Stood waiting. He liked waiting. Liked to see the darkness rise up from the ground, up from the Mississippi, climb up across the facades around him and over the glass walls. The cold came quickly. He'd read somewhere that cashmere is eight times warmer than sheep's wool. Not a particularly precise way of expressing it, and maybe not even true, but that never stopped him advertising it as hard fact whenever anyone asked him about his choice of coat.

Lights came on in the skyscrapers. And in the sign above Bernie's. Fifteen minutes later, Liza stepped out into the street. Stopped, as though surprised.

'Again?' she asked, acting exasperated. 'This is . . . what? The third day in a row? Is this your famous siege technique in operation?'

'Don't flatter yourself. I just happened to be in the neighbourhood,' he said. 'And I needed someone to split the cost of gas with.'

'You don't say?' she said and got in as he held the car door open for her.

'I'll accept payment in the form of a bit of *kveldsmat,*' he said as he got in and started the car.

'*Kveldsmat*? What's that? Some kind of Norwegian thing? Like supper?'

'Yep. You'll get used to it.'

She laughed. 'Now who's flattering themselves? I take it back. You're not a sheep in wolf's clothing, you really are a wolf in sheep's clothing after all.'

'Speaking of sheep's clothing, did I ever tell you this coat is eight times warmer than sheep's wool? That it's made of goat's hair that has been *combed* from the bellies of goats living five miles above sea level? That each goat yields only three and a half ounces of hair per year, so that to make a coat like this takes –'

'A lot of time and a lot of hard work?' She gave him that exasperated look again.

Bob thought about her words. Nodded. 'Exactly. A lot of time and a lot of hard work. If you want a cashmere coat then you have to *will* yourself to get a cashmere coat.'

'I get it. And then, if you can be bothered, and if the coat fits?'

'Then you've got a coat for life, baby.'

'Oh my God, you are so full of bullshit.'

They drove for a while in silence. Then they started laughing. First her, then him. They laughed harder and harder. They didn't stop laughing for a long time.

56

DEPARTURE, SEPTEMBER 2022

THE STORY ENDS THERE. FULL stop. There is no more. Because stories aren't like life, which always has more to offer.

So I don't know what more life has to offer to Kay Myers, only that, six years on from the Mike Lunde case, she is now head of the Homicide Unit and shacked up with a younger colleague.

Nor do I know what life has to offer Brenton Walker. For a while he was a likely candidate as the city's next chief of police until a diagnosis of cancer slowed him down.

Hector Herrer made a full recovery and now works for the governor of Minnesota.

Kevin Patterson wound up in Washington DC, not as a politician but as a well-paid lobbyist for the agricultural sector. He never made it to the House of Representatives, something some commentators attributed to the damage done to his reputation by NRA lobbyists in the wake of his change of stance on the issue of gun control.

But life has nothing more to offer Marco Dante. He was discharged from hospital a week after the dramatic climax of the Mike Lunde case. Two days later he walked to his car outside the Jordan projects. It was the middle of the day and there was no one else around when he unlocked his car. He didn't notice the tiny jerk in the door as he opened it, nor did he see the two strands of fishing twine wound around the door handle on the inside. Attached to the other end of them were the two pins Dante had just jerked loose from two hand grenades, placed beneath the pedals in such a way that when he pushed down on them he would press on the levers. Dante started his car. He pushed down on the accelerator with his foot, felt a resistance and then felt the resistance give way. That was when he knew something was wrong. Looking down at the floor between his legs he saw one of his own hand grenades with its lever lying next to it. A thinner man than Marco Dante might perhaps have made it out in time. But to cut a short story even shorter: life had no more to offer him.

One who didn't think life had much more to offer was Bob Oz. How wrong can you be? I push open the door to Town Taxidermy, and there he is. The red hair is a little thinner than in the pictures from back then, the face more lined. But the cashmere coat is the same, and for an instant it occurs to me that the man sitting motionless on a chair between a bear on its hindlegs and a leaping lynx has turned into the Bob Oz I wrote about in my story; stuffed, frozen in time, arrested in mid-movement. But then – as the bell above the door jingles – he looks over, his eyes light up and a smile spreads across his face.

'Holger!' he says as he gets to his feet.

Over the past two years Bob and I have exchanged hundreds of emails and spent hours of screen time in each other's company. I've offered him a percentage of any royalties from the sales of my book, but he rejected the offer, said the conversations were free therapy for him. Bob has become what I would call a friend. Even though this is the first meeting in person it feels natural to give each other a warm embrace.

He and Liza have moved into a small house in – ironically enough – Chanhassen, just two streets away from where Emily lives. He's left the police and now works as head of security for a tech company. Not just because the pay is twice as good, but because two years ago Liza gave birth to their baby boy, and Bob wanted a more structured life. And Liza has been offered the chance to take over a bankrupt bar in downtown for next to nothing. The brewers are actually going to pay her to get the place back on its feet again. Bob has admitted that there are times when he misses police work, but that his decision to leave remains one of the few he never regrets.

We sit down. We talk a bit about family stuff, and then I say:

'So this is where you and Mike were sitting that last time?'

'Right here.'

We fall silent. I look out into the street as the scene plays itself over in my mind.

'You must have been afraid,' I say.

'Actually no. He was so calm. And it was all so quiet. Like in a . . . like in a church.'

'I see.'

'Have you been out to Lakewood Cemetery?'

I nod. Less than two hours earlier I had been standing in the company of his sister Emily by the grave where Mike and his family lie buried. A full stop carved in stone. Although in fact, for Mike, life had come to a full stop long before that.

'You told me you remember Mike as happy,' says Bob. 'I never got to see that side of your cousin.'

I nod. 'We used to go drinking in Dinkytown. Me, him and Monica, the love of his life. Sometimes Monica brought along a friend who I think they hoped I would fall for. I never met anyone with such faith in the existence of deep and lasting love. I don't mean a naive faith, but a . . . well, an overwhelming conviction that it existed, despite the negative experiences of the majority.'

'I know what you mean,' says Bob with a wry smile.

'What do you think of love?'

'What do I think of love? I think . . .' He scratches himself behind his ear. '. . . that just occasionally, in between all the little loves, a big one comes along. But it doesn't necessarily look all that big on the radar, so you need to have your wits about you. And that sometimes a little love can grow, given the right kind of care and nourishment.'

I give him a long look. 'Was that your line when you were One-Night Bob, picking up all the girls?'

Bob gives a loud laugh. 'One-Night Bob was a pig. But he had integrity, and he never used the word "love". That's something only the new Bob has earned the right to say.'

The door to the workshop opens and a young man wearing a blue apron comes in, pulls off his latex gloves and says hello. His name is Alan, he's the new owner of the store, and from our correspondence I know that when he graduated from his taxidermist studies in Iowa he was one of only three students. But he's optimistic about the future of the business, he thinks the customers are on the way back. We've arranged for him to show me how Mike Lunde made his mask, and he takes us into the workshop, where a deer's head is mounted on a stand. Alan explains that the process wouldn't be very different if a human head were involved. I take notes as he demonstrates how you begin by cutting a Y-shape in the back of the head with a sharp knife.

'You always cut from inside the skin out, so you don't cut off the hair. Then . . .' He holds up an ordinary, flat screwdriver which he says you insert under the skin and then push along, and little by little the skin comes loose from the cranium.

I can see that Bob is thinking about Mike.

Alan explains how he cuts across the earhole, folds the skin up over the head, then moves to the mouth, separating the gums from the skin and folding it back again. He then presses his index finger into the eye socket from the outside, and the thumb from the inside while cutting with the sharp knife, careful not to leave any disfiguring marks visible from the outside.

Bob leaves the room, and I excuse myself and follow him, leaving my notes behind.

We stand in the street outside.

'There are times when I wish I was still a smoker,' says Bob, stamping his feet on the sidewalk. The air is cold and sharp today, like the start of the Minnesota winters I've heard about but never experienced personally.

'What's on your mind?' I ask.

'I'm wondering what it is that makes a person want to kill, when killing and causing suffering to others can no longer bring your loved ones back to you.'

'You wonder because you don't understand?'

'No. I wonder because I'm made that same way too. When Frankie died I wished someone had killed her. Because that way I would have had someone I could take my revenge on.'

'You think that would have eased your pain?'

'Yes. A bit. Why are we made that way? Why fight for what's already been lost?'

'Hm. The teachings of evolution maybe? If we just swallow our losses and allow the powers of evil free rein, the same thing will just happen over and over again. So we fight for a future in which we might, just possibly, get another chance.'

'That's very naive.'

'Naive, or optimistic. At least better than apathy and quiet resignation.'

'So your book is going to be a defence of violent revenge?'

I shake my head. 'I just want to tell a story about how good people can become monsters. For a little while back there, Mike was probably the most famous serial killer in the whole of the United States. Then there was another school shooting, or someone taking revenge on their old workplace, some news item with more victims than there were here, and Mike gets forgotten. And, strangely enough, that can make for a better and more general story.'

'What do you mean?'

On the other side of the street I see an old lady who's just bought something from a cart I noticed particularly because it advertises Ambassador Hot Dogs, which I used to dream about as a boy when counting the months and weeks until my next trip to Minnesota.

She's bought two hot dogs.

'Jack London, as I'm sure you know, was an author as well as a journalist,' I say. 'He said that fiction is truer than fact. And that the best thing you could do with the facts was to make them look like fiction.'

'And that's what you intend to do?'

I shrug, and watch as the old lady bends to a homeless man sitting on the sidewalk with his back to the wall of a building. She gives him one of the hot dogs, straightens up, they exchange a few words, she laughs at something and then walks on.

'I'm going to try, at least,' I say. 'It's probably the only thing that gives any meaning.'

Jo Nesbo is one of the world's bestselling crime writers. When commissioned to write a memoir about life on the road with his band, Di Derre, he instead came up with the plot for his first Harry Hole crime novel, *The Bat*. His books *The Leopard, Phantom, Police, The Son, The Thirst, Knife* and *Killing Moon* have all since topped the *Sunday Times* charts. He's an international number one bestseller and his books are published in more than 50 languages, selling over 60 million copies around the world.

Robert Ferguson has lived in Norway since 1983. His translations include *Norwegian Wood* by Lars Mytting, the four novels in Torkil Damhaug's Oslo Crime Files series, and *Tales of Love and Loss* by Knut Hamsun. He is the author of several biographies, a Viking history and, most recently, *Norway's War: A People's Struggle Against Nazi Tyranny*.